Praise for the first ZIPPERED FLESH anthology

"If director David Cronenberg edited an anthology, this would be that book." — HORROR WORLD

"Hardcore studies of shocking monstrosities that will enthrall and entice even the most hardened horror fan." —FANGORIA

"This anthology will not let you down!" —TALES OF HORROR

Praise for ZIPPERED FLESH 2

"Zippered Flesh 2 is a big win ... and definitely needs to be on your horror bookshelf." —SHATTERED RAVINGS

"If you like your terrors physical, this anthology has a lot to offer, and I hope that Zippered Flesh 3 will follow." —HELLNOTES

ZIPPERED FLESH 3

Yet More Tales of
Body Enhancements Gone Bad!

Edited by Weldon Burge

Smart Rhino Publications
www.smartrhino.com

Zippered Flesh 3: Yet More Tales of Body Enhancements Gone Bad! Copyright © 2017 by Smart Rhino Publications LLC. All rights reserved, including the right of reproduction in whole or in part in any form.

"Horns, Teeth, and Knobs" by Billie Sue Mosiman, previously self-published as "The Kindness of Strangers" on Amazon (2014).

"A New Man" by William Nolan previously appeared in *Qualia Nous* (Written Backwards, 2014), *The Future Embodied* (Simian Publishing, 2014), and *Like a Dead Man Walking and Other Shadow Tales* (Centipede Press, 2014; reissued in paperback by Dark Regions Press, 2015).

"Transposition" by Jason V. Brock previously appeared in *Shrieks and Shivers from the Horror Zine* (Postmortem Press, 2015).

"The Rose" by Jack Ketchum previously appeared in *The Hot Blood Series: Deadly After Dark* (Pocket Books, 1994) and *Peaceable Kingdom* (Dorchester Publishing, 2003).

"Dog Days" by Graham Masterton previously appeared in *Festival of Fear* (Severn House, 2012).

"Gehenna Division, Case #609" by Sandra R. Campbell previously appeared in *Suspense Magazine* (February 2016).

"Golden Age" by James Dorr previously appeared in *Mindsparks* (Spring, 1994).

Original cover artwork © Shelley Everitt Bergen (stock image usage: © Can Stock Photo Inc./kjekol)

ISBN-13: 978-0-9985196-0-9
ISBN-10: 0-9985196-0-X

CONTENTS

ACKNOWLEDGMENTS

Thanks go to Shelley Everett Bergen for her amazing cover illustration, to Scott Medina for designing the cover, to Terri Gillespie for her excellent proofreading skills, and to Lori Leonard for her help with some sticky formatting problems.

HORNS, TEETH, AND KNOBS

BY BILLIE SUE MOSIMAN

Martin threw back the sheet from the hospital bed to look at the new bony-looking knots lying like a string of skin bubbles below his knees. The doctor had just taken off the bandages. The skin was discolored, but that would go away. They didn't ask many questions about elective surgery in Mexico. He'd spent a lot of time in Mexico City, looking out hospital windows at the smog-shrouded city many stories below. It was like looking into a murky sea.

If his mother could see his legs, she'd have a heart attack. His father, the same. No, his father might have balled his fist and knocked him for a loop. With both of them dead and leaving him their home and money, he didn't have to worry about their opinions and he didn't have to worry about making a living, at least for some years. At the rate he was spending it on surgeries, he might have to live more frugally one day. But not today.

The implants on his legs matched the ones on his arms. Bony extrusions, four on each forearm, and they looked like round tumors to those who didn't understand how he was transforming his body.

The two horns on his forehead were the real prizes. He'd gotten those first and they'd cost a small fortune.

His thick brown hair was cut in a Mohawk. High on top and long in the back. He thought it beautiful. It took away a little of his fierce countenance, giving him a majestic, lionesque visage.

His chin had been implanted and lengthened, his cheekbones raised and intensified so he projected a haughty, dangerous look when he wanted to. Everything else he'd transformed about himself had been less expensive, but just as impressive. His eyebrows were removed and replaced with permanent black skin ink tattoos. They were wide and tilted upward, giving him a devilish stare from eyes of violet. Nonprescription colored contacts were great. Sometimes he wore gold ones and looked like a cat.

He had numerous piercings, all in sterling silver. Rings hung in great succession from his ears, and in the lobe he wore huge rounds of teak wood two inches in diameter. These had stretched out the lobes and lengthened them.

Piercings hung from his tattooed eyebrows, from his nose, and from his bulbous lips.

He'd had his teeth capped with sharpened canines so that when he smiled he was more animal than human. This was no mockery of the vampire rage. It was more his nod to the lower creature all men kept inside them.

His friends were going to be astounded. His girlfriend, Karen, would love it. She wasn't nearly as transformed as he, but she loved piercings and tattoos.

He had more tattoos to add. He wanted a tremendous spread-winged eagle on his back, an angel with black wings on his chest, and snakes twining up his arms in and out and between the implants. When he was through he would be as decorated as a Christmas tree. It made him smile with anticipation.

He couldn't leave the hospital yet. They had to make sure his incisions wouldn't get infected, so they asked him to stay a couple of days to monitor them.

He lifted his laptop from the bedside table and put it into his lap. The hospital's Wi-Fi was good and he logged into Facebook quickly. He went immediately to the personal message area and clicked on Tina's name.

MARTIN: The leg implants were successful! They're going to let me go home in a couple of days. I'll be back in San Diego to show off soon.

He sat waiting to see if Tina was online and would answer back to him. He zoomed around the feed to look at what others were talking about while he waited. A ding sounded from the laptop telling him he had a message.

TINA: Wonderful! You'll have to post a pic on your wall so we all can see!

MARTIN: I'll do that soon as the discoloration goes away. It looks like someone took a baseball bat to me right now. But they look JUST like the bumps on my arms.

TINA: Did it hurt? What did they use to make them?

MARTIN: Didn't hurt so much. Not until I woke up. LOL. They used titanium balls and they're just great. They look for all the world like round bones beneath the skin.

For an hour he chatted with Tina, laughing aloud when she said something funny. They brought his lunch and he signed off, promising Tina he'd be back later.

He had met Tina online a year ago. She'd been part of the Body Enhancement Group on Facebook and they'd grown close. Her profile said she was a college professor of history at Auburn University in Alabama. She was twenty-six and unmarried and not in a relationship. Her picture showed a nice-looking young woman with shoulder length blond hair, blue eyes, and dimples. He thought she was such a Kewpie doll and sometimes that's what he called her, My Kewpie Doll. They indulged in innocent flirtations, but she knew he was dating Karen so she didn't come onto him in any serious way.

If he had to confess the truth, he got on better with Tina than he did with Karen. But then it was so much easier to talk with a stranger on the Internet than it was to keep a girlfriend happy. Everyone knew that. All his friends had little side relationships going on with women on the Internet, mainly on Facebook, the hub of everyday living for just about everyone on Earth, as far as Martin was concerned. He loved the social site and if he wasn't connected to it, he felt lonely.

Before sleep, he sent another personal message to Tina.

MARTIN: Hey, did you know Mexican medical care is primo? The doctor's been in to see me twice today. In the U.S. if you see a doctor once a day, you're doing great.

TINA: I was just getting out of the shower. I'm dripping wet. I'll be back in a sec.

MARTIN: I'll wait.

Five minutes later Tina returned to the message area.

TINA: Glad your doctors are taking such good care of you. The world wants to see the Most Beautiful Enhanced Man. Can't wait for the pics!

MARTIN: I called and made an appointment for my back tattoo in San Diego. They'll take me in next week. Can't wait!

TINA: What are you getting done on your back?

MARTIN: A huge eagle, wings spread. I want it to have the beak open and look menacing.

TINA: Oh, that will be outstanding! I think you're so brave.

MARTIN: It doesn't take courage to get a tattoo. You ought to try one. Today they have such great instruments and the ink color is so bright and I'm told it lasts for long years.

Before Martin knew it, he and Tina had been chatting for two hours and most of the hospital was silent. All he heard was a couple of voices talking softly from the nurses' station down the hall.

MARTIN: Guess I better get off-line and get some sleep.

TINA: Have a good night, my friend. Talk to you tomorrow.

When Martin was ready to leave the hospital, they let him walk out alone to the waiting cab. He wondered if the philodendron plants in his San Diego apartment were still alive. He wondered if Karen missed him. She refused to be involved with Facebook, saying it was a place full of crazy people, misfits, and oddballs who pretended to be someone they weren't. He could have tried to Skype with her, setting up his camera on the laptop, but she wouldn't do that either. He had to admit Karen wasn't very modern when it came to social media and computers. The last time in her apartment he noticed her laptop was covered with dust. She mainly used her smartphone (an Android! She wasn't even savvy enough to get an iPhone!) for texting and playing games and that was the extent of her connection. It seemed to him she lived in the smallest world imaginable.

The jet set down in San Diego Airport and Martin pulled his hoodie over the top of his tall Mohawk, covering the implanted horns on his forehead. He wore long sleeves to cover the strange bumps on his arms. It wasn't that he was ashamed of his transformation. He just knew maneuvering through the world was made easier if he kept his looks on the low-low. People were such bigots. Anyone who didn't look like them, and that included people of color or people with disabilities, made them anxious. It's why he always flew first class. At least in there, people were circumspect about eying him and no one gave him grief. In economy class, he'd been watched as if he might pull out a bomb or something, like he was a terrorist.

He picked up his one suitcase and caught a cab for his apartment. He'd arranged to have his friends over for a little get-together that night and he had to tidy the place and set up the bar on the kitchen counter. Sometimes he thought his friends hung around because he had plenty of money instead of liking him for himself, but how was he going to prove that?

When the sun set and a cool breeze blew down the canyon where his apartment was located on one of the steep San Diego hills, Martin stood at the front windows looking out at the street waiting for his first guests. He consulted his watch. It was 8:00 p.m. He thought they'd be here sooner.

At 8:30, he called Karen. "You coming over?"

"Oh, I should have called earlier, Martin. I'm sorry, but my mom said my brother just showed up on leave from Okinawa and she wants me there. I have to go. He's being shipped over to Afghanistan next week. I'm really sorry. I should have let you know."

Well, I'd think so, Martin thought, *you certainly should have let me know.* He was so distressed he hadn't replied to her explanation. He stood before the window reflecting his face, holding the cell phone to his cheek, and thought suddenly he looked like a monster. He looked like a fantastic thing created by a Hollywood make-up department for a science fiction film.

"Martin? Are you upset? This was a last-minute thing, I can't help it. I'll see you soon, all right?"

"No, that's okay," he said, but he didn't put any effort into making his voice sound friendly. "Of course you have to see your brother. I'll talk to you later."

He hung up without hearing her goodbye. He went to the bar area he'd set up with bottles of booze and glasses and an ice bucket. He poured himself a Scotch over the rocks and stood sipping it, waiting.

At 9:30, he put the bottles of whiskey and rum and gin and vodka back into the cabinets. He sat in the living room alone, looking at the windows, drinking Scotch. The more he drank, the more he seethed inside, like a cauldron on low heat coming to a slow boil.

Hadn't they wanted to see his latest embellishments to his body? He'd been gone for a week and they couldn't bother to come over for a drink? What kind of friends did he have anyway? It's true none of them were really into body enhancement the way he was, except for Karen, and all she had were some piercings and a couple of tiny, inconsequential tattoos. He needed new friends, that's what he needed. He needed people like himself, who were open to experiment, who wanted to make a statement, who didn't care if they didn't fit in.

He realized he was pretty drunk when he got the laptop lid open and the browser aimed toward his Facebook page. He went immediately to message.

MARTIN: Tina, are you there?

He waited and his eyelids lowered, his mind drifting toward sleep.

He heard a ding and saw the message box blinking. He clicked it and saw Tina was online.

TINA: Hey, Martin, what's up?

He placed his fingers on the keyboard and shook himself awake.

MARTIN: You won't believe what happened tonight. I invited over three of my friends and Karen. No one showed. You believe that? I'm sitting here in my fucking empty apartment drinking.

TINA: Oh, that's terrible, Martin, I'm sorry you were done that way. What were their excuses?

MARTIN: No one gave one, no one even bothered to call. I had to call Karen and she said she had to go to her mom's house because her brother was coming over and he's being shipped out next week. He's in the Army.

TINA: That's too bad, Martin. I hope you feel better soon. Are you sure drinking is a good idea?

MARTIN: It's a fucking top-notch idea! If someone showed up now I could kick his ass.

TINA: Oh, Martin, I'm so sorry you're in such a bad mood. You'll feel better tomorrow. Don't let anyone get you down, okay? You're a wonderful, generous friend. I know how much money you've loaned out to your friends and how many presents you've bought Karen. It's not fair they didn't show up when you asked them over. But listen, it's going to be all right. Really.

MARTIN: I'm going to cut them out of my life. That's just it, see? I loan them money, I treat Karen like a queen, and nobody cares. I'm done with them, the whole goddamn lot.

He complained for a while longer and then, the Scotch making his mind murky, he stopped making a lot of sense, realized it, and signed off Facebook.

He sat in the dimly lit living room and wondered about his life. Everything in it was sort of peripheral, wasn't it? His relationship with Karen wasn't all that solidified. Now that Tina had pointed it out, he realized he was always giving to Karen and she was a taker. A taker. Just like his buddies. None of them must really like him for himself. For his true self. They hung around so they could borrow from him. They probably made fun of him behind his back. They might even make fun of his body enhancements, his goal to become a brand-new human. Someone majestic and thrilling to look on. It was so important to him and they probably thought him insane.

He leaned over and pulled up the legs of his jeans to look at the new implants. They were no longer discolored and the knobs stuck out perfectly, like rounded bulbs of something organic. Like blossoms.

He dropped the cuffs of his jeans and staggered to bed. To hell with having a party. Who needed a party?

It took just two months, but suddenly Martin found himself totally alone. His dates with Karen grew few and far between, her excuses beginning to ring untrue. His friends met him a couple of times at a bar, then stopped answering his phone calls. Martin was accosted three times on the street, always when he'd forgotten to wear a jacket with a hood he could use to cover himself. Once he was robbed. Twice he was struck down and left to moan and bleed on the sidewalk in the night. The last beating he'd taken was from three teens who spit on him and kicked him in the ribs and said, "You freaking pervert, you ought to kill yourself."

He knew his body enhancements might bring him trouble along with praise. Not many people were walking around with horns on their heads as if they were minions of Satan. Not many people looked like him in the least and that's what he'd wanted. But lately, the attacks were increasing and the hate radiated off people who saw him shopping in a grocery or a liquor store.

About the only person he had left he could confide in was Tina, on Facebook.

MARTIN: My black eye is healing.

TINA: Oh, you poor baby, it's so unfair how you're treated.

MARTIN: Do you have implants or tattoos?

TINA: I have a panther on my right arm and two butterflies just above one ankle. I have some piercings, but I won't tell you where they are. Ha ha ha!

MARTIN: Well, things are going downhill here in San Diego. Maybe I should move to San Francisco. I might be more accepted there.

TINA: That's a plan.

MARTIN: Karen won't talk to me anymore.

TINA: You didn't need her anyway then.

MARTIN: I checked my bank account. I hate to admit this, but I haven't been watching my spending. And the surgeries took a chunk. I'm running low.

TINA: Like your money's gone?!

MARTIN: Not gone, no, but ... it's running out. I'm trying to think what to do. I should have been more careful.

TINA: You shouldn't have given half of it away to your friends! Look what you've done.

MARTIN: You're right. I'm a damned fool.

TINA: I didn't say that, Martin. I just think people took advantage of you. You have such a big heart.

MARTIN: Maybe so. Maybe I'm just a chump. Isn't that what they say in old gangster movies on Turner Classic Movies channel? I'm a chump, you're a chump, and we're all big fat chumps.

TINA: Come on, Martin, hold it together. You can make more friends. And you can watch your bank account closer. It's going to be all right.

He didn't think it was going to be all right. It was going to be all wrong. His parents hadn't been dead five years and he was about to run out of his inheritance. But he had so wanted to make himself over. Before the horns and the arm and leg bumps, before the permanently tattooed eyebrows and the canine caps, he knew he was just a regular looking guy, no one you'd look at twice. He had no real talents and he'd dropped out of college, so he wasn't the brightest person on Earth. Before his inheritance that freed him, he'd been locked into a job as an accountant for a small trucking company and his hours at work were soul-deadening. Until he found the Facebook group about body enhancements, he had been a nobody, a nothing, a big zero.

The people online encouraged him and pushed him toward trying out a little change here and there. A piercing of his lower lip. The wood pegs in his earlobes to stretch them. He had done them one at a time, uploading the results on the group wall online, and people ooohed and they ahhed and they told him he was a brave soul, he was a spectacular superhuman testing the limits of society's prejudices, and he was ... loved.

Everyone wanted to be loved.

MARTIN: Tina, I feel so alone.

TINA: As long as you have me, how can you feel that way? I won't let you be alone. I refuse to let you wallow in this depression. You don't deserve this kind of sadness, Martin.

TINA: Martin? Are you there?

MARTIN: I'm here, but I have to get off-line now. I don't feel so well.

TINA: Okay, but I'm always here, just hit me up.

Martin closed the browser and turned off the Internet connection on his laptop. He couldn't talk about this anymore. He needed to change his life again some way.

He would move. He'd get out of San Diego with all the macho boys trolling the streets and all the women in their upwardly mobile hybrid cars and their business suits and sensible heels.

San Francisco would embrace him just as he was. Just as he was meant to be.

San Francisco sucked a big one. First, housing was short and the prices were exorbitant. He finally found a tiny apartment on the fourth floor of an old apartment house in a part of town that was borderline between being either a genteel or a slum area. He paid for three months in advance, though it made him wince to write the check. He really needed to find an accounting job because the bank account was being drained faster than he could imagine it would. Everything cost so much. Groceries, housing, utilities, transportation. He should have bought a car when he could afford it. Now he was reliant on public transportation and riding a bus was nearly out of the question with how he looked and the way he was treated. He took taxis wherever he went. Or he walked.

He thought his looks wouldn't be an issue in San Francisco, but discovered he was just as much an outcast and treated as suspiciously as he had been in San Diego. He pulled out his collection of hoodies and wore them when he went out. It was a shame he had to cover himself, to hide the beauty he'd spent so much time and money creating. Even Tina told him it was a real shame. She was the only connection he had left, the only human ear to hear his complaints—or eyes to read them, at least.

MARTIN: I hate it here.

TINA: You're overreacting.

MARTIN: You think so? Last night I went out to buy milk so I'd have some for breakfast today and guess what happened? The convenience store manager thought I was there to hold up the place! He pulled a gun on me. I swear it. He pulled out a gun from under the counter and told me to get out.

TINA: That's crazy! Why would he do that?

MARTIN: Beats the hell out of me. I know I look a little scary, but I was just buying milk, for Christ's sake. I had to leave without it and now I can't shop there anymore. The guy was freaking out.

TINA: Well, he was just an idiot, Martin. You know most of the world won't get it. They won't see the beauty of what you've become, of what you've made of yourself. All they see is someone who doesn't look like them.

MARTIN: Maybe ... maybe I shouldn't have done all this. It was so much fun, you know, when I started. Everyone in the Body Enhancement group thought it was terrific and urged me on. I'm not sure I thought it out all the way.

TINA: You're just down right now. What you're thinking isn't really true, Martin. Things are going to be okay.

MARTIN: I don't know.

TINA: Honest. It's going to be fine.

Martin gave it another month and realized he was sinking into the deepest swamp he'd ever entered, both mentally and in the world. He applied for a couple of jobs as an accountant, but he hadn't worked in years and his looks ...

No one called him back for a second interview.

His bank account dropped below $5,000 and he panicked. He started buying Top Ramen noodle soups and stopped eating out. He began to take the bus over a taxi, suffering the dour looks from old ladies and angry young men. The world was conspiring against him and it didn't feel good. It felt like hell was coming, riding on the edge of a thunderstorm, racing overhead to bring darkness and destruction. His mood plummeted further. He had so wanted to get his tattoos and now he knew he might never be able to afford them. His enhancement was incomplete. He was but half of the person he wanted to be.

And even the wonderful ways he'd changed himself made his life unlivable. He always covered up now, even when he visited a bar for a beer. He wore long sleeves and a hood over his head. He felt loneliness like a thorn digging into his brain, pushing deeper and deeper, festering, leaking dark thoughts like poison.

He talked to Tina online as much as he could. He was worried he might have to let the satellite Internet connection go and then he'd be forced to sit in McDonald's for the free Wi-Fi to get online. The idea made him feel so awful he said something to Tina he immediately wanted to take back.

MARTIN: I ought to kill myself.

TINA: Martin!

MARTIN: I'm sorry, I shouldn't have said that. I don't mean it.

TINA: Listen, give me your address.

MARTIN: Why?

TINA: I just want to have it, all right? I just want to know where you are.

MARTIN: I'm in a deep, dark hole and I can't crawl out.

TINA: Think about good things, Martin. Think about how lucky you are to be so beautiful. You are, you know, you're absolutely gorgeous.

MARTIN: I wish you lived here, Tina. I hate that you're all the way across the country in Alabama.

TINA: I know, I wish I could visit you sometime, but I never get time off. I work right through my vacations.

MARTIN: I need work. I can't get any.

TINA: It'll be fine, you'll probably get hired on your very next interview. And don't ever say that again, okay? About killing yourself.

MARTIN: I won't. I promise.

He couldn't keep promises anymore. He began to think about suicide all the time once he mentioned it to Tina. It just seemed the only way out. He hadn't any idea how his life had gone downhill so rapidly. He had never done anything to anyone. He'd never been a bad guy. He had always treated his parents with respect and treated his girlfriends with love. He had been a good employee. He had made changes to his body just because it was such a taboo and he wanted ... he just wanted to be new. What he'd accomplished instead was he turned himself into a freak. He didn't fit in the world. No one accepted him. So what was his reason to live, then? That was the question, where was his reason to go on?

TINA: Don't do it! I'm getting on a flight in an hour, I'm on my way, Martin. Wait for me, will you do that?

MARTIN: Even you admitted I didn't have much to live for, Tina. Even you.

TINA: I was joking, okay? It was a joke! You can't see facial expressions in chat. You can't hear the laughter in my voice, the teasing. I was just joking, Martin.

MARTIN: I don't think you were joking. I think you were agreeing with me. I have nothing to live for. I've turned myself into a creep. Remember that song, CREEP? That's what I am. I've been delusional. I'm ashamed of myself. I guess I'm not very smart.

TINA: Listen, you have to listen to me. You're just depressed. You'll come out of it. I'm coming to San Francisco to see you. We'll talk this out.

Martin looked at the words on the screen in the chat window and then he x'ed it out, closing the window. He closed the browser. He shut down his laptop.

He had a gun, having bought it legally from a pawnshop with some of the last of his money. It was a revolver. It held .38 caliber bullets in a cylinder and he now loaded it. He stood in front of a floor-length mirror in his shabby bedroom. The light was bad from the lamp so he turned on the overhead light. He stared at himself and maybe saw what he'd become for the first time. Saw himself without blinders, without the veil of illusion and the hope of beauty. He was a horror. He saw that now. A true horror. Horns on his head, as if he were the devil in the flesh. Tattooed eyebrows dangling jewelry. Violet contacts so he looked out from alien eyes. Cheeks too high and wide, chin too long and pointed. Ears with lobes too big and decorated all around the edge of the ear folds with silver studs. He held up his arms and looked at the titanium bumps beneath the flesh. He glanced down at his legs with the same bumps on his lower legs. He was an ugly nightmare. He was a horror.

He wouldn't wait for Tina. He had to do this now. His rent was due and he had an eviction notice. He'd be on the street tomorrow if he didn't do this. And what would happen on the street? Before the homeless and the angry gangs killed him, there would be torture.

He wasn't going to stand for it.

He was taking this into his own hands.

"Tina" tried the doorknob and found it unlocked. He opened the door to Martin's apartment. It was dark and dreary, an old pensioner's place in a rundown part of town.

He listened and heard the deadly silence and knew it was over. He really lived just forty miles distant, outside of San Francisco, but he'd taken his time getting here. He had never lived in Alabama. His name wasn't Tina. And he didn't give one shit in hell about Martin and his body enhancements. He was just one more freak he'd gotten to off himself. It had taken months of preparation. First, he'd encouraged the man to spend all his money making himself into a monster. Then he commiserated with him once he began to lose touch with his friends. Finally, he talked him into the notion life really wasn't worth living.

Facebook and other online social sites were simply ripe with people who lacked confidence, people who were misfits and couldn't make it out in society, people who were looking for something, anything to make their lives worthwhile. The miserable souls on a soul plane heading in a death spiral to the Earth.

Of course, it was clever of him to disguise himself as a woman, to put up a picture of a good, clean, normal-looking woman to represent himself. It was very clever to talk to these innocent incompetents who came to him in chat to talk intimately about their lives. He learned everything about them, from their financial status to their largest dreams and worst fears. He played them for the fools they were, enjoying every minute of it. He spent every hour of every day and night online playing with people, lying about his own life, his own ... demons.

He moved through the darkened living room with the overturned and scattered pizza boxes and cola cans. He went to the bedroom and found Martin on the floor, naked, shot in the head.

He'd really done it. So perfect.

Despite how truly beautiful he was. Despite the gorgeous body enhancements that had cost him his fortune, which had cost him his life, the creep was beautiful.

Hunching down, he ran a finger over one of the horns, admiring it. So gorgeously evil. So beautifully implanted. He stared into the violet eyes, streaked now with blood. He sighed at his handiwork, finding it good, and left the room.

His work was done with this one. Martin had depended on the kindness of strangers and he was gone.

"Tina" had others, though, many others, and he needed to get back home to his computer. He had some chatting to do. Some lives to destroy.

It was all so much fun, the toying with lives, the slow manipulation. It was a transformation, happening right before his eyes. Strangers online sealing their own fates, transforming from happy individuals into morose, depressed suicides. He only showed them the way.

He closed the door softly and padded down the hall to the stairs, stripping off his thin rubber gloves.

He clicked his smartphone and thumbed the Facebook icon. It looked like he had four people waiting to chat with him. His message area was lighting up and blinking like crazy. He'd be busy all night.

He had to hurry. There was destruction to bring and death following. There was an act to perpetuate, lives to squander, and dreams to kill.

In the end, he was the one who was the most enhanced, his spirit so large and his slow manipulations of strangers to the brink of suicide such a precise ballet. He smiled into the dark of his car and turned the ignition. A twisted tree bent over and wavered in the wind reminding him of a person. Reminding him of Martin.

Martin. The man who had everything and who died with nothing. Friendless, without family or income, and without a shred of hope. He died for beauty without knowing there was no such thing. No enhancement that could provide it. It was a fabrication, a lie, and this man, in this car, leaving the bent tree and the dead man behind, was one of the few who knew the truth.

UPGRADED

BY SHAUN MEEKS

Sara stood in line with the others. They all waited for the store to open and, as time drew closer, there was a swell of excitement that built in her. She was right near the front and could see inside. She watched, waited, and hoped it would happen soon. Now and then she felt a wave of pressure propel her forward from the surge of bodies behind her. Everyone wanted to get in for a chance to have the latest in DermaCross technology.

Years ago, people had been the same way about other computer gadgets, the long-outdated iPads and Android phones that seemed so primitive years later. What DermaCross had created with its latest line of biotech was miles beyond all of it, and you weren't anyone if you weren't upgraded to the latest and greatest.

Sara tried to push back against the people behind her. Her best friend, Jeff, saw the struggle and tried to help. He turned from the doors and shoved back, but the crowd seemed unmovable. He was one teenage boy in a fight against a virtual wall of bodies. When she looked back, most people only looked into the store, their eyes wide and hungry. She knew she didn't look much different than they did. She'd been in line for hours, woke at the crack of dawn and huddled as close to the main doors as she could, forgoing food and even bathroom breaks. Nobody would allow Jeff to save her spot. If she wanted it, she had to suffer for it. She knew it was crazy. But in the end, sanity would be a decent price to get one of the first phones.

Another wave of bodies pushed forward and she cursed at the crowd as Jeff continued to fight back against them for her. It didn't matter anymore, though. The time had come.

"Don't worry about it, Jeff. Someone's coming," Sara told him, but was secretly happy he'd tried to help her out. Even though they were only friends, and she would never try to complicate things, she'd always felt something more than just friendship toward him. She wished she could tell him and they could take a chance on whatever, if anything, there was between them, but couldn't risk it. She had so few real friends.

Jeff turned back and stood beside her as a DermaCross employee came toward the door. The man was old and seemed not to have a hint of emotion on his face as he stopped in front of the locked doors, looked at the crowd, then glanced down at his watch. He took a step back without opening the doors. Sara rolled her sleeve back and looked at the underside of her forearm, where an outdated display screen was embedded in her flesh. Only a minute before the store was supposed to open. She couldn't believe he was going to wait until the last seconds to unlock the doors.

"Oh, come on," someone yelled from the crowd. "Close enough. Open the doors already!"

There was muttered agreement behind her and she joined the muttering and shouts of complaints. There was obviously a huge crowd waiting to get in, why not just let them? Then she saw why.

From behind the solemn-faced man came an army of DermaCross security guards. Though these men and women weren't like the guards that watched libraries and building lobbies. Police officers would be jealous of the body armor and equipment these people were in. She knew why they were there, too. The last time a new product or upgrade had been offered, there was a near riot when it sold out and people were left empty-handed. There was no doubt fear that another incident might happen, and of the sheer madness of the crowd surging when the doors opened. Everyone wanted to be the first at the counters.

Sara was happy she was so close to the doors.

The man came toward the door again. This time a squad of armed guards was behind him. Before he opened the door though, he lifted a microphone to speak.

"Good morning, ladies and gentlemen. DermaCross is about to open and I know that you are all excited to get the new CrossCel 2 system, but you will do so in an orderly manner. Anyone who steps out of line will be removed and therefore unable to upgrade. We do have a limited supply of new systems, so you will want to ensure you act accordingly or you will miss this opportunity." He turned to the security team and gave them a nod. Sara watched as they pulled their Taser clubs from their holsters and lined up.

Sara knew it was time. She reached out and took Jeff's hand.

"Stay close to me," she said.

He smiled. "I'll do my best."

They felt the crowd push forward again.

Then, the door was unlocked and the chaos broke out.

The crowd moved forward even before the doors fully opened. Sara managed to get two steps into the store when someone stepped on her heel, knocked her to the ground, and she lost Jeff's hand in the process. She cried out as she saw a wall of bodies move toward her and felt sure she was about to get crushed to death. She heard Jeff yell out her name and she called out to him. Then she closed her eyes and waited to get trampled.

"I got you," she heard Jeff say, and felt his hands on her. She turned her head to see him and looked into his light green eyes. She could smile only for a second before someone's knee hit her square in the jaw and then her world went dark.

A few seconds later, she was propelled back into the real world. Sara felt sick to her stomach and woozy. The feeling only got worse when she noticed she was no longer in the store, but on a bench outside DermaCross's main location in the city. She turned her head away from the store and saw she was on Jeff's lap. He looked down at her and touched her hair.

"You cool?" he asked.

"What happened?"

"Crowd went crazy, as usual. You went down and got hit just when I was trying to help you up. Blacked out for a bit. I had to get you out of there before you got trampled."

"What about the new CrossCel?"

"What about it?" Jeff asked, and she saw the confusion on his face.

"Well, if we're out here, how am I going to get the new phone?"

"Who cares? It's just a phone, Sara. I thought it would be better to keep you safe than drag your unconscious body over to a sales desk and wait for you to wake up. I didn't know how bad you were hit."

Sara said nothing. She sat up and looked at the store as the first of the happy customers began to exit with their new CrossCel 2 from DermaCross installed. A part of her knew Jeff had only been trying to help her, to be a gentleman and keep her safe, but she felt like it had cost her so much. She stood and walked away from the store. Jeff followed, but she didn't say anything else to him in fear that she'd call him an idiot.

Sara sat at the dining room table with her mom and absentmindedly picked apart the overcooked meat loaf on her plate. Her mind was on other things, mainly that she would have to face school the next day with her old, useless CrossCel.

"You not interested in dinner? I thought you loved my meat loaf?" Her mom said, and Sara saw the look of concern on her face.

"It's not the food. The meat loaf's delicious."

"I'd believe you if you actually ate a bite, dear."

Sara humored her mom and ate a chunk of meat doused in ketchup. It was delicious, but there was no way for her to properly enjoy it with her mind in the state it was. Still, she smiled at her mom to show her how good it was and hoped it was convincing.

"Well, since I'm not a mind reader, Sara, why don't you tell me what's wrong."

"It's nothing. Really."

"I'm sure if you were at your father's and you said that he would just say 'fine' and go on eating, but I care about what's going on in your life. So, come on. Spill it."

Sara took a deep breath and set her fork down. She really didn't want to get into it, but knew her mother well enough to know she wouldn't be able to get away from the table without telling her.

"I went to get the new CrossCel today, that upgrade I was telling you about. But when I tried to get inside, I was knocked down and then it was too late. It sold out."

"So? You still have your CrossCel I bought you six months ago. Or is it messing up, because there is a warranty on it."

"It's fine, but it's not the new one. I really wanted it. Everyone at school's going to have the new CrossCel 2 and I don't want to be *that* kid. You know, the one who shows up with outdated shoes, second-hand books, or an old CrossCel. They'll laugh at me and call me poor. You don't know what that's like."

"Oh, come on now, Sara. It's not that bad."

"You wouldn't know."

"That's right," her mom said with a tone of sarcasm. "I was never in school like you. I was born a forty-year-old woman, so what would I know about life in school."

"It's not the same. Seriously, it's not."

"Oh, I bet it is. When I was in high school, there were all kinds of clothes and haircuts and electronics all the kids needed to have to be cool and fit in, only they didn't really. Sure, there are shallow kids who are going to judge others by what they do and don't have, but do you really want to hang out with such small-minded people?"

"Uh, yeah! That pretty much describes everyone in my school. I'm going to go tomorrow and I'm going to be no better that Toad Faced Tony or Suzy Creepy Eyes."

"Oh my God! Please tell me you never call kids names like that."

Sara saw the look on her mom's face, the horror at the thought that her daughter was a bully. She was guilty of doing just that, picking on those that were oddballs or couldn't afford things, but she would never admit it to her mom. Not with how she looked at her. She didn't mean any of it, but when everyone else is calling someone a nerd, you need to join in or be the next one called out.

"Not to their faces, but you know. Most people don't know their real names so you have to refer to them that way."

"Sara, I brought you up better than that. No wonder you're freaking out over this stupid phone thing. I blame your dad for this. Always one to spoil you. Never letting you suffer a little to teach you a lesson." Sara huffed as her mother went into her daily ex-husband bashing. She ate more meat loaf to avoid saying something snide, mentioning it was her father who had given her the money for the new phone. Better for her not to provide more ammo for her mom. "Listen, darling, the phone you have is just fine. You can go to school with it and nobody is going to care. And if they do, you have to ask yourself if their opinion matters. It's just a material item after all. It doesn't make you who you are."

Sara decided to concede and tell her mom she was right. She didn't think she was, but it was better to pretend to agree than to have to get into a long and boring argument with a woman that refused to admit defeat.

"I'm glad you're coming around. You'll see. Nobody will bother you about it. I doubt most of them could get new ones themselves."

As it turned out, her mom was wrong.

Sara walked into the school and saw people in the hallways playing with their new upgrades. She could see a group of girls as they opened their display and shared new images from their CrossCel 2. They created a new group chat site, one that only upgraded CrossCel users could be added to, which was one of the newest features. Sara passed by them, pulled down the sleeve of her jacket that already hung past her wrist, and hoped to go unnoticed. Luckily, she made it to her locker without anyone paying much attention to her. Their eyes were all stuck on their latest purchase.

Sara did see a few kids like her, ones not bothering with the CrossCel 2s, which was a sign they didn't have one. A few of them smiled at her, as though they recognized someone as pathetic as they were. The smiles angered her. She didn't want those people, virtual losers, to think she was as poor off as they were. They probably still had handheld cell phones, something almost as ancient as laptops. At least she was a step above them—or so she hoped.

"Hey there," a voice said as she was half hidden in her locker. "Did you forget to meet me at the corner or did you get a ride from your mom?"

She turned around and saw Jeff there. He smiled at her, looked happy—as though it didn't matter that everyone who mattered had the newest phone and they were part of the losers. He walked over, threw his bag on the ground next to her locker, and leaned beside her.

"You look like crap," he said after he took a good look at her. "What's wrong?"

"Only everything," Sshe whispered and looked around at the other kids. "I don't want to be here. Someone's going to find out that I didn't get a new phone and that'll be it for me. I'll have to move to a new city."

"So dramatic, Sara. Wow!"

"I'm not being dramatic. Did you know there's a new app on the phone? It allows you to join yours to other phones so you can share music, movies, videos, and everything else. You can only do it with the new upgrade. So, when someone comes up to add me and I have to admit I didn't get it, I'm screwed. I want to go home. And don't look at me like that."

"Like what?"

"You know exactly how you're looking at me, Jeff. Like I'm being silly. I'm not. I've spent my entire life trying to be part of the group, doing my best to fit in so I can make it through school without needing therapy. And everything I have done is about to be undone, all because of this damn phone."

Jeff reached out and put a hand on her shoulder and squeezed. She knew it was because she was so upset, on the verge of tears, and Sara wished she could've hidden it from him, but there was no way to hide the way she felt.

"I know someone who could help, if you still have the cash."

"What? Who?"

"A guy I know. A friend of my brother's. He did it for a few people when the last upgrade was released. Maybe he can do it this time around, too."

"Did what? You're not talking about black-market phones, are you?"

Jeff said nothing, but made a face that said it all.

"Isn't that shady? I've heard stories of black-market phones not working right. Caused all sorts of problems."

"This guy's pretty good. My brother even got the last one from him. He added extra features even, like a free Wi-Fi link that can unlock anyone's password so you never have to pay to link up."

"And he has new ones?"

"I can ask."

"Please! We can just skip the rest of the day and head there. Oh, that would be so freakin' awesome."

"Sure. I'll find out if he has them."

Three hours later, Sara had a new CrossCel 2 installed in her arm. Jeff's brother's friend, a weird-looking Goth kid named Wump, had given her the whole rundown on the new phone and how he had managed to crack its security features. The room was dirty, but he had all the same equipment they used at the DermaCross store, and what he installed in her arm looked legit, just like what the kids had in school. She began to play around with it, glad there was no tenderness around the edge of her flesh and the phone like last time, as Wump began to explain the details.

"These new phones were trickier than the last ones. Damn tech department over there came up with some creative security features to try to put guys like me out of business. They added nanobots on the inner layer that would have come out into your arm if I tried to install it without using a biokey. Luckily, I could remove them from the system. Actually, they're still there, but I wiped them out with a special code I wrote. You should be fine."

"She should be fine?" Jeff asked and sounded concerned, but Sara paid no attention.

"I guarantee they're all zapped. Unless they become zombies, she will be fine." Wump laughed. "Don't worry. It's not like the 'bots in there are a big deal. They just come out of the system and mess up the server and might cause a slight rash. But they're dealt with, so no worries."

"Anything else?"

"Of course. These guys came up with so much. But slight modifications, reprograms, and a touch of magic and I fixed it all. Even the link breacher."

"What is that?"

"Say you use a CrossCel 2 that has been black-marketed by a complete retard, and nothing has been removed. If that were to happen and they join a link with other CrossCel 2 members using the new app, they all join a home group, this new security protocol would infect all their phones, too, and everything would shut down in that group. It's ingenious. Makes it so nobody wants to know someone that has a black-market phone, or they get messed, too."

"What?" Sara yelled as that last bit got her attention. "So, I got this phone and I'm still going to be an outcast?"

"No worries. Just don't tell them. And if anyone asks, show this." Wump handed her a piece of paper and saw it was a receipt, one that looked like an exact copy of the ones CrossCel handed out. "It's pretty legit looking. Should pass anyone's inspection I'd think."

Sara smiled, happy she'd be able to go to school the next day and be part of the group, join in on what all the popular kids were up to. She had felt so upset by the thought of falling behind the crowd, of being left out, that the relief she felt as she left Wump's was unimaginable.

The next day she showed up to school and before lunch she had forty-three people added to her network. When the final bell rang, it was up to ninety-one. She met Jeff a few minutes after the last bell in the parking lot and smiled as she went to him and his car. He smiled back and she noticed how cute he was as he stood in the light of the darkening day, leaning against his old-school muscle car that looked so badass. She wondered how long it would be before they finally made it official. She knew there were feelings there, on both sides, but nobody had yet to mention it to the other. She had hoped he would, that way it would be easier for her, but so far nothing. They were in the friend zone, but she wasn't sure how much longer she would allow it to remain there before she said something to him. Or just made the first move herself. She knew eventually girls in school would see they weren't romantically linked, and someone would make a move. She knew they were rumors about the two of them, she'd even heard some of them, but that would only keep the wolves at bay for a bit. He was good-looking, drove an awesome car, and despite her own obsession with the new CrossCel 2, refused to get his own, which made him even cooler.

"You ready to go, Sunshine?" he said with a smirk.

"Yeah, I just ..." She stopped as her phone went off again. She looked down and saw it was a new upload from Darlene in homeroom. She hit the button to accept it, and then looked up at Jeff, who frowned at her. "What?"

"You and that phone. You guys are almost like junkies with the damn things." He laughed, but she knew a part of him was clearly annoyed with it. "Want to go grab a burger before home?"

"Can't. I promised my mom I would help her with clearing out the basement. Sorry."

"No worries," he said, and drove her home.

Two days later, Sara still marveled over all her new CrossCel 2 could do. She added three-hundred-twenty-seven people to her network and the phone was constantly being hit with photos uploaded, new apps from friends, games, conversations to join, and more. She put her phone on silent mode during class time and smiled every time her arm vibrated.

On the third morning, she woke and went to the bathroom to shower before school. When she went to dry off, she saw something that concerned her. The edge of her flesh where the phone was embedded into it was a dark shade of red. It looked angry and when she touched it, pain exploded, followed by a need to scratch. She gave in to the need, but it only made her arm throb more, made the red grow and swell. She ran her arm under cold water for five minutes and hoped it would help, but it didn't. It looked a little worse than that.

Sara wanted to show her mom, to go to her and ask what she thought, but her mom had no idea that she had gotten a black-market phone installed. If her mom saw it, she would take her to get the whole thing removed, yell at her for making a back-life decision, and then where would she be?

Her mom wasn't an option. She threw on a long-sleeved shirt, headed downstairs, and did her best to avoid her mom. She managed as she grabbed her lunch and waited in the driveway for Jeff to show up. She hoped he would have an idea.

He pulled up five minutes later and could see the concern on her face.

"What's wrong?" he asked as she jumped in the car.

"This," she said and pulled the sleeve up to show him the CrossCel. The red had bloomed brighter and there were thin veins spread across her arm. "I think it's infected."

"Sara! We gotta get you to the hospital."

"We can't. I don't want my mom to find out."

"Well, we have to do something. That looks gnarly."

"I'm open to suggestions."

Jeff sat there for a moment as he looked at her arm. He shook his head and seemed mildly disgusted by it, then began to nod.

"Let's go see Wump. He should know what to do."

He drove them there and the entire way Sara felt her panic grow. She did her best to ignore the sensation of itching around the irritated area, tried to not notice the throb that had begun to build in her forearm and pulse upward toward her shoulder. At one point, Jeff reached over and took her hand, gave it a squeeze, and told her everything would be fine. Wump would know what to do. She smiled at him and hoped he was right.

Part of her wanted the damn thing out of her arm, to just go back to what she had. But whenever that came into her head, she saw the other kids at her school, the way they would look at her as something lower than they were. She'd become an outcast and knew it, because it was the same way she had felt about the kids who didn't get the last upgrade.

Jeff pulled his car into Wump's driveway and the two of them went up to the door. They knocked repeatedly, but there was no answer.

"Maybe he's not home," Sara said. She was ready to give up after five minutes of trying.

"He's always home. My brother told me that this guy never leaves his house. He even gets his groceries delivered like some old lady. He's a shut-in."

Jeff reached out and went to open the door, but Sara stopped him.

"What are you doing?"

"Seeing if the door's unlocked. Maybe he has his headphones on or something."

"But that's weird, to just walk in. Isn't it?"

"Do you want to see him or go to the hospital?"

She nodded and Jeff turned the knob and was glad to find it open. If it hadn't been, he would've kicked it in, if need be. He wanted to help Sara, blamed himself for how her arm looked. After all, he'd been the one who had taken her to see Wump in the first place.

As soon as the door opened, a wall of odors greeted them—body sweat, garbage, and something rotten. Sara nearly gagged, but covered her mouth and nose. She could taste the thick stench that hung in the air.

"What is that reek?" she asked through her shirt.

"I'm not sure I want to know."

But despite that, the two of them pushed through the wall of stink and went to the room where Wump had done his work on Sara. The door was shut, but they could see light as it flickered and danced under the crack of it. Jeff knocked and when there was no answer, he pushed it open, despite his own hesitation. He was sure what he'd see would be bad, but he wasn't prepared for what awaited them.

Sara had also expected the worst, but she thought it was going to be the overweight Goth nerd getting caught in some terribly embarrassing position. In the end, her idea of him engaged in an inappropriate act would have been better than what they found.

Wump sat in front of his main computer, but what was left of his head spread across his left shoulder. His mouth hung open and his fat, purple tongue dangled and drooled greenish pus onto his shirt. The top of his head looked as though it had been shot off, the area from his brow line and up was no more than a distant memory. But as they looked closer, they didn't see anything on the wall or ceiling that would hint at a gun wound. Instead, they found the remains of his skull on the floor under him, mixed with a pool of gray, liquefied brains and more of the pus.

Sara fought off the vomit that burned the back of her throat as she backed out. She couldn't take the sight of the dead man anymore. She didn't want to notice the open skin up and down his arms that oozed dark wetness, didn't want to smell his decay or watch as something moved under his shirt.

Jeff also saw the movement, and, as disgusted as he was, he found it a hard time not to move and get a better look at the mess.

"Jeff, we need to get out of here."

"Wait a sec. What is that?"

He moved closer to the corpse and reached out to pull the shirt up that continued to move, almost throb rhythmically. It reminded him of when his mom was pregnant and his little sister moved from inside. He wanted to see what it was, though he was sure it wasn't going to be something cute like a new baby.

"No!" Sara yelled and pulled Jeff by the arm. "I don't want to stay here and I don't want to know what the hell is doing that. Let's go."

Jeff nodded, guessed she was right. As he went to step out of the room, a terrible hissing sound came from Wump. For a second, it sounded like the air being let out of a tire. He didn't wait to see what it was.

Once they got back to the car, Sara lost it a little. She fought back tears. She didn't want to cry in front of Jeff. Friends or not, she couldn't let him see her like that. Sara closed her eyes to take a few deep breaths. But when she did, all she could see was Wump's dead face. She shook it off and opened her eyes as Jeff began to drive.

"We should just get you to the hospital," Jeff said. He looked down at her arm. Her own eyes went to it and it looked even worse. The red that ran along the edge of the CrossCel had gotten darker, a deep violet.

"I can't, Jeff. I don't think it's that bad. I just need some peroxide or alcohol on it. I don't want my mom to find out."

"Don't you think she's going to know that something's wrong when she sees it? Or you end up like Wump?"

"What?"

"Oh, come on, Sara. You can't tell me you didn't see the way his arm looked. He had one of his phones installed too. Obviously, the security features in that damn thing are better than he thought."

"No. There's no way the phone would do that. It's just a phone, Jeff. DermaCross wouldn't put something like that in their phones just to keep people from getting black-market ones. He probably took some weird-ass drugs or shot himself. Just ... just take me home."

"I can't do that, Sara. You need to get help."

"If you care for me at all, and I hope you do, you'll take me home right now. I'll be fine. And if I'm not, if it gets any worse, I'll call you to take me to the hospital."

Jeff shook his head, but not as if to say no. She looked at him and saw him fight the urge to just drive to the hospital and take the anger, to make sure she was safe. She knew then and there that he liked her as much as she like him and when she got better, took care of her arm, she hoped they could move forward.

She put her hand on his arm and gave it a squeeze, but said nothing.

"Please, Jeff, just take me home."

"Fine, I'll take you home, Sara, but I'm coming to your house in the morning. If it looks the same or worse, I'm taking you to the hospital. Okay?"

"K, but don't say anything to my mom either."

"Promise."

⬩⬩⬩⬩⬩⬩⬩

Nothing worked.

She tried alcohol, peroxide, antibacterial cream, and some other medical creams her mom had, and they all did nothing to relieve the redness or the unstoppable itch. If anything, the things she tried made it worse. The itch and throb turned into a sharp pain and ache that made her feel nauseous. She sat on the toilet in her bathroom, stared down at her arm, and was sure she could see the red continue to darken as each second passed. It even looked as though it began to spread farther across her arm.

Her phone chimed, the first time that day, and she nearly jumped. She'd almost forgot about the CrossCel as a phone at all, but as it sounded she wondered why it was the first one of the day. She touched the screen and as she contacted it, the phone sent a bolt of pain down into her wrist and into the palm of her hand. She bit back a scream. Tears sprang to her eyes, and the intensity of the pain hit its strongest point. Then, as it began to lessen, slowly, she looked down at the screen in her arm.

"Attention: The CrossCel 2 that you are currently using has an infected network. To avoid the security measures from taking full effect, please attend the closest DermaCross store to you and we will be happy to assist you. Again, your network has become infected. If left untreated, the infection could lead to side effects such as skin rash, bloating, nausea, rectal bleeding, brain damage, or death. Please go to the nearest DermaCross location and treatment can begin. Do not attend the hospital for this matter."

Sara read the message and, when she was done, she knew there was nothing to do about it. She couldn't very well go to DermaCross or they'd know she was the source of the infected network. She would be treated, sure, but she would also risk being arrested for owning a black-market CrossCel 2. They would want to know where she got it. Then they'd find Wump.

What was even worse was the thought of everyone at school, all the people who were part of her network, finding out she'd lied to them all. They'd discover she had gotten an illegal phone and not only broke the law, but got them all infected, too. She'd be worse than a loser. She'd be ostracized, a total outcast from not just them, but the entire school.

She couldn't let that happen.

Sara looked around the bathroom and, after a few seconds, her eyes fell on the metal nail file. She picked it up as her hands shook from pain and the fear that boiled in her. She knew there was little left to do. She couldn't allow anyone to find out what she'd done.

She gritted her teeth and lowered the dull blade to her skin. She took a deep breath, tried to picture something nice like a field of flowers, or how it would be to kiss Jeff, then pushed the metal into her skin. A whimper escaped her as dizzying pain rippled in her head, sent white flashes of light before her eyes, but she knew she couldn't stop. She moved the nail file along her skin, watched as it opened. Blood and pus oozed out and she could hear it as globs of red and yellow hit the cold, white tile floor of her bathroom. The sight of it was terrible, but she knew there was no turning back. She had to keep at it to avoid anyone finding out.

Sara cut along the edges of the CrossCel, tore at the skin more than cut it, until she was sure she'd done enough. She let the blade fall to the ground, but it didn't make a noise as it hit the floor because it landed in a crimson pool.

She reached into the wound and grasped the paper-thin phone. When she did, her stomach heaved and puke drooled out of her mouth and poured down the front of her. She ignored it, needed to finish what she had started. With one hard pull, she tore the entire CrossCel free from her flesh and was surprised. One moment there was pain and agony, almost too much to bear. And then, the moment the phone was free, the pain began to fade like a bad dream. Only wisps remained as she let the phone fall from her hand. Sara leaned back against the toilet, wiped vomit from her chin, and for the first time since she woke up that day, she smiled.

"Now, nobody needs to know," she whispered to herself.

"Sara, come on. How many times do I have to tell you that you're going to be late for school?"

Her mom knocked on the bathroom door again. For a half an hour, she told her daughter to get ready for school, but as always, Sara lingered in her favorite place—the bathroom. Frustrated, and knowing it had to do with the stupid phone she wanted so badly, her mom opened the bathroom door to get her moving.

"Sara, sorry to barge in, but you need ..."

The words died on her lips as her eyes fell on her daughter sitting on the toilet. At first, her mind wouldn't accept what her eyes saw. They moved from her daughter to the blood pooled on the floor, to the gaping wound on her left forearm. Tears began to flow as she moved toward her and tried not to step in the gore on the floor. She knew that Sara had been upset about not getting the new CrossCel 2— kids always made a bigger deal out of things than they had to—but she would have never guessed she'd kill herself over it.

Sara's mom tried to think of what she did wrong, what she could've done to prevent it. Should she have just let her stay home until she could get a new phone? Or tried harder to get her a new one, despite how hard it would probably have been? She felt like she'd failed her daughter.

"I'm sorry, Sara." She cried and sat on the edge of the tub, wanted to hold her so bad, but knew she shouldn't. Instead, she reached out and took the hand of her daughter and squeezed it. "I wish you had talked to me."

Something moved.

She let her daughter's hand drop and when she did, she saw it again. There was movement from her stomach, under her shirt. Hope filled her in that brief second, she prayed it was Sara breathing, that she wasn't dead at all. She reached out for her, about to say her name, when cold blood sprayed her face.

She gasped at it, tried to wipe it from her eyes, but there was more than just blood. She didn't hear or see the tiny nanobots that bloomed out of the crater in Sara's stomach as they searched for more food. She didn't see her skin being covered in the tiny, living creatures that hunted for flesh to eat, so they could reproduce.

But she did feel them.

She felt them as they gnawed into her, melted her skin, and consumed her. She felt as they burrowed into her warm flesh with hunger, and liquefied whatever they touched. Sara's mom felt it all and wanted to scream in agony. But as she opened her mouth to do so, they filled the wet opening and ate the cry and her tongue.

GOING GREEN

BY CHRISTINE MORGAN

Jumbled memories, voices, sensations. Swirling in a murky soup.

A swamp-soup. Primordial.

"Drink this." The comforting one, the balm one. Aloe.

"Ucch ... tastes like dirt."

"Well, there's a reason for that." The other, brisk and brusque, businesslike. Nettle.

Mud smoothie. Thick and thin at the same time. Liquid. Tepid. Gritty.

Thoughts and recollections out of order, random clusters of connected pieces from a partially assembled jigsaw ... some fitting together, some not.

"Last chance to change your mind. Once we begin, there's no turning back."

"I know. I've signed everything. I'm sure."

Damp loam. Moist and spongy. Packed in soft peat, a dense pressure engulfing, enfolding, absorbing, embracing.

"Try to relax. You'll feel a little sting—"

"Ow!"

Searing freezing metal lance, stabbed, impaling pain. Thigh deep. Bone deep. Femoral. Arterial. Pulsing, pumping throb.

"Just hold still. You're doing great. Now the other side."

"*Ow!*"

"There we go."

Slow-coursing, sluggish eddies. Silty delta flows. Spreading. Seeping. Pervasive.

"—mask to help regulate your breathing. Calm and even—"

Out with the old. In with the new.

Heat lamps, a bank of heat lamps, basking warm and wonderful. Heat lamps and cool mists, a misting *pssshting* spritz.

"... arms so heavy ..."

"That's to be expected. You're taking on extra minerals and nutrients."

Tingling all over, softening, loosening, pores enlarging.

Distant talking: Aloe and Nettle.

"—test plot first? Whole body seems extreme."

"They get what they want."

The heaviness. Good, rich, dark earth.

"You mean, they get what they pay for."

"Same difference."

Remembering: the shower, the last hot shower with scrubbing cleansing depilatory suds and exfoliating abrasives, hair and sweat and chemicals sluicing away, rinsing, gurgling down the drain.

Naked skin smooth and tender, free of dead cells, calluses, scars. Air-dried and clean, so very clean. Ready. Refreshed. Cleaner and more naked than ever before, even since birth. Pure.

"Will it hurt?" Earlier, earlier, at the start.

"You may experience some brief periods of discomfort at various stages in the process. Some clients have reported mild itching, some say it tickles."

The hugging fit of the mask, stubby prongs up nostrils, wider mouth-tube, snug seal around nose and cheeks and chin.

The hiss of gases. The tinned, metallic tinge.

"How're nitrogen levels looking?"

"Holding steady."

"Oxygen?"

"Eighteen percent."

"Adjust the mix, take it down to fifteen."

"Oxy to fifteen, CO_2 increasing to five."

The glass-walled chamber, hothouse-humid. Crossing it, naked, so naked, hairless and smooth, steamed, open, vulnerable. Climbing into the shallow tank, the bed of loamy soil, slowly sinking in.

Aloe again. "We're going to remove the needles. Slight pinch—"

"... ow ..."

A dull warmth, melty, malleable, suffusing diffusion. That inner heaviness, conversion, mineral-laden. Zinc, potassium, phosphorus, magnesium. Iron and calcium leeched from blood, from bone, from marrow.

Softening. Loosening.

"Still with us?"

"... mm-hmm ..." Muffled.

A clammy smearing slather. Filled with tiny hard lumps. Nibs. Pips. Like wet clay and kindergarten glue and raspberry jam congealed together. Simultaneously runny and caking, a squelchy adherence. Coating, clinging.

Oozing sap. Watery gruel. Poppy seeds in honey. Tapioca. Microbead dermascrub. Caviar in aspic.

"CO_2 at 20. Oxy at two, nitrogen still good."

Some clients have reported mild itching, some say it tickles.

Itching? Tickles?

Creeping. Prickling. Myriad minute *tippy-tap pitter-patter*, almost fizz and sizzle, carbonation, champagne bubbles, *piff piff piff pop pop pop*. Scurrying millipede filaments. Seeking. Crawling. Monofiber threadfine tendrils. Working and worming, burrowing.

Burning but not burning, the icy zing of mint.

A hundred, then a thousand, then a million poking penetrations.

Persistent. Tenacious. Expanding and extending, weaving network webs.

Itching? Try *maddening!*

Tickles? Try *tortures!*

Aloe, soothing balm voice. "Relax ... relax ... you're doing fine ... don't fight it, don't struggle."

Nettle, prickly. "This *is* what you wanted, what you paid for, why you're here."

The guy sitting across from Zeaa wore a vintage-looking tee with *It's not a bald spot, it's a solar panel for a sex machine!*

printed on the front. His hairline was accordingly receded, but the glossy silver-black ceramoglass plates fused to his scalp really lent the message its credence.

She wondered if the rest of the sentiment was as literal. Hey, why not? People powered all sorts of implants and gadgets that way, including far less personal devices than bonerators or internal bluepill dispensers.

Not, of course, that she was about to ask. He might answer. Might offer to demonstrate just how well his solar-powered sex machine worked, wink-wink, leer-leer.

Better not to say anything. Better to just hope he hadn't noticed her noticing his shirt. The last thing she needed was another awkward 'rail conversation, let alone another skeevy hitting-on.

When mom had been Zeaa's age, it was strange men plucking earbuds right out of your head. For Grandma, it had been books pushed down. Zeaa herself gave up on immersives when she was fourteen, after someone hacked her holoset to make sure she knew she had nice tits.

Several of her acquaintances swore by Bitch Shields and other basic creep-shaming standbys ... DixDox, subdermal neon dye packets, harassment-sensitive bio-klaxons, Smart Boobs auto-linked to upload offenders' pics to Oglr ... but none of those were exactly cheap. Zeaa had been saving up a long time to make her own upgrade dream come true. She wanted something more important, more meaningful.

Today. Today would be the day.

After weeks of consultations, comparison shopping, trying to find a place that would do what she wanted, without all the legal and medical and psychological prelims ... finally, finally, today. Today, it would happen.

Her new life. Her transformation. Her way, however small, to make a difference. To give back. To make a statement, a commitment. To do something that really mattered.

Everyone at Earthstock would be *so* impressed, too! When Jolth saw her, when Niv and Aymlin realized what she'd done, how far she'd gone ...

... and Brangelina, Brangelina would just about *choke* ... take that!

Not that she was doing this for those reasons, no, of course not.

She was doing it for the planet.

Was there anything more selfless and noble and eco-friendly?

"Hey, a smile!"

Zeaa blinked, realizing first that she had indeed been smiling, and secondly that it was Mr. Solar Panel across from her who'd spoken. Seeing he had her attention, he leaned forward with a grin.

"Yeah, that's lots better," he said. "Pretty bit like you should always be smiling."

Though nobody else overtly glanced from their devices or heads-up holos, a subtle shift took place in the 'railcar as it hummed along. Two manspread dudebros, inked with color-changing tats, swelled their muscle-jacked postures. A well-groomed woman with a matron/warden vibe thumbed her screen to DixDox, a perv registry. Some androgyteens near the front, who had been chattering and laughing and psi-banding music, drew together in a protective phalanx.

Zeaa's smile, which hadn't been for his or anyone else's benefit in the first place, faded. She looked down, fussing with her bag on her lap. All natural fibers, indigenously farmed hemp and corn-cotton, intricately woven by rustic artisans into native designs ...

"Didn't you hear me?" Mr. Solar Panel asked, his tone suggesting he knew full well she had.

Today. Her new life. Transformation. Statement, commitment. For the planet. Make a difference.

If she could go through with what she was about to have done, she should be able to handle some random 'railcar creep.

"How about," Zeaa suggested, raising her head to meet his gaze with her ice-coldest stare, "we just skip ahead to the part where you call me a bitch and stomp off?"

His mouth dropped open. "Wha ...?"

Had she really said that? Out loud? To his face? If anything, Zeaa herself was more surprised than he was. For a moment, she thought he would push it, launch into the same old song and dance they all knew so well—only being friendly, can't take a compliment, oh, so we're not even allowed to talk to women now, stuck-up, not that hot anyway.

But miracle of miracles, he didn't. Mr. Solar Panel slouched in his seat, turning his attention to the window and the blurred scenery rushing by. Another subtle mood shift, this one toward smug amusement, took place. Matron/Warden muttered something under her breath about what a shame it was they'd repealed the Purge.

Zeaa winced a little. Not cool, too soon. Cruel casual microaggression. Even those who weren't CisHetWhiMa themselves might have lost loved ones.

Was it any wonder she wanted to turn her life around, go back to nature? Wasn't that what Earthstock was really all about? Beyond music festivals and craft fairs, homebrews and homegrows, freecycling swap meets ... beyond herbal remedies, spiritual-centric yoga ... organic ethical veganism? About really making a difference, not mere idealism, token efforts, and casual lip service? Or worse, lofty self-congratulation and hypocrisy?

Oh, she knew *soooooo* many people who did that, had done too much of it herself. Humble-bragging how she didn't even own a car, while borrowing her mom's to drive to eco-protests, park cleanups, and tree-plantings ... insisting on locally sourced produce but hooked on synth-chem energy drinks ...

Well, no more. Not after today.

Today, she would take sustainability and carbon neutrality to the next level. She would prove her point. Put her money where her mouth was—and no joke. A *lot* of money. Several years of saved-up birthday cash and half her income stipend were going to pay for the procedure.

Mr. Solar Panel disembarked at the next station. He was replaced by a gaggle of schoolkids communicating via forehead LED emojis, a gangly girl in tie-dye, and an adorable geriatric punk couple with matching his-and-hers studded walkers.

The girl seemed familiar, or at least kindred. A fellow Earthstocker, a goer to similar clubs and events, farm to table and all-organic. Wicker sandals, long tendrils of hair twist-matted into what weren't quite dreads, a macramé shawl over her loose granny dress, a knotted-string pebble-and-shell necklace.

She stepped into the 'railcar with a sort of grim, stoic, necessary-evil forbearance and settled onto the edge of a seat as if it might snap shut on her like a rattrap. The dudebros regarded her unshaven legs with legitimate horror. A strong scent of dreamshrooms and incense hung around her in a cloud.

Zeaa flicked the girl a quick, solidarity nod, wishing she hadn't dressed so down for the day herself.

Clinic instructions, though. Nothing she'd want to risk getting damaged or stained. They'd probably give her a smock or something before the actual procedure, but the recovery stage could be unpredictable ... and messy.

So, it was the drabs for her, old faded jeans and a threadbare flannel and mock-a-moc boots, face un-done, slapdash ponytail. Probably looking like a discount red-stater. Which still hadn't stopped Mr. Solar Panel calling her a "pretty bit," go figure.

Tie-Dye Girl gave Zeaa a cautious sidelong onceover before returning the nod. She looked tense, anxious, unhappy. Her jaw was tight, her brow furrowed. Her hands, with the stubby nails and ground-in dirt—*ground-in, heh,* Zeaa smirked—of someone who gardened, picked at the fringe of her shawl.

When the doors whirred shut again and the 'railcar surged in a humming acceleration, Tie-Dye Girl flinched. She hunched her shoulders forward, bouncing one fitful foot. Each movement wafted more dreamshrooms and incense into the confined space.

"Excuse me," said Matron/Warden, lips pinched in a prim scowl. "There *are* children on this 'rail, you know."

The schoolkids paused, LOLWUT-emojis flickering. The androgyteens glanced at each other as if trying to figure out whether they were included and, if so, whether they should be insulted or not.

"Should you really be spewing your hippy-dippy drugfumes around?" Matron/Warden continued, arching eyebrows machinated to architectural perfection.

For a moment, the less-jacked of the two dudebros seemed about to speak up, then thought better of it. His color-changing tats shifted to match the molded vinyl-plast seat in some kind of attempted chameleonic camouflage.

Zeaa spoke up instead. "You can't get high from sniffing dreamshrooms," she said. "They're ingestibles, not huffables. And they're legal anyway. They're natural. Like hemp."

Matron/Warden narrowed her eyes, perhaps regretting having been ready to have Zeaa's back with Mr. Solar Panel, but let it go with a dismissive *hmph* through her sculpted nose. Tie-Dye Girl, meanwhile, wrapped her thin arms around herself and pressed her knees together.

People got on and off. A couple of the androgyteens struck up a conversation with the elderly punks and decided to accompany them to a mosh pit at the senior center. The larger dudebro surrendered his spot to a waddling octomom-to-be fresh from a surrogacy rights meeting and carrying on a loud phone conversation about it. Some hoverbikers in full gear crowded their machines into the aisle, doing enthusiastic high fives.

Ugh. Even at mag-speeds, her stop couldn't get there fast enough. As soon as it popped up next on the indicator screen, Zeaa slung her bag and began working her way toward the doors. A resurgence of anticipation thrilled through her.

Finally!

Oh, and her friends were going to have fits! She could hardly wait.

But should she keep it secret until Earthstock and surprise them? Would she be *able* to keep it secret that long? If she didn't, though, mightn't it give them time to try and outdo her?

Like Brangelina. Brangelina would so totally want to outdo her ... or find a way to be snide or diminish the impact ... better to surprise everyone then and there ... unprepared ... their shock and amazement genuine, impossible to disguise ...

Brangelina with her *songberries* ... suggestively hand-feeding them to Jolth ... to Niv and Aymlin too ... even offering some to Zeaa, and to the guy they all called Pot Belly ... like Brangelina thought she was fooling anybody with her oh-let's-share-let's-give cover ... when really it was about making sure she got Jolth's attention ...

The 'railcar slowed, scenery regaining non-blurred definition.

Scenery which was not quite what Zeaa had expected.

Sure, the station was one of the blink-and-you'd-miss-it stops, a little middle-of-nowhere between one urban sprawl and the next, but in her mind that had translated to images rustic and pastoral. Lush green fields and meadows. Wooded hills. Burbling clearwater streams. Maybe a tidy little town square with a majestic centuries-old oak at its heart.

This ...

Well, this wasn't that at all.

The doors whirred open again and she stepped out onto a platform of graffiti-tagged brushed concrete like every other station, overlooking the usual huddle of charging kiosks, cybernodes, and fast food. Beyond those were a few ranks of industrial apartment complexes, a Big Box store, a new/used transport lot, the various retail detritus. Beyond *those*, it went to straggling residential, overgrown weedy yards, trailers, junked vehicles, abandoned machinery, and rundown sheds.

Dismal. Depressing.

Her hope, her future, her new life was to start *here?*

It didn't seem possible. It didn't seem *right*.

She caught the scent of incense and dreamshrooms again, and saw Tie-Dye Girl heading for the steps that led down from the 'rail platform, near-dreads bouncing against the back of her macramé shawl, wicker sandals slap-whisking on concrete.

"Hey!" Zeaa called. "Hey, excuse me a second, can I ask you something?"

The girl paused, giving Zeaa a wary glance, as if weighing the dichotomy between, on the one hand, the discount red-stater drabs and, on the other, the rustic handwoven hemp bag and the way Zeaa had come to her defense against the pinch-faced Matron/Warden.

Holding up the bag for emphasis of her true nature, she said, "I wonder if you could help me. I'm looking for Eden."

Maddening! Torture!

The itching ... a needle-fine burrowing ... spreading, expanding, fanning, questing.

Exploratory. Inquisitive.

Hungry.

"Have you ever gotten galvanic acupuncture? It's a little like that." Casual, counseling, reassuring.

It was not a little like that.

It was not a lot like that.

The sensation of them in there ... thousands of them, millions ... miniscule husks splitting ... nanoworm-threads unspooling, uncurling ...

Rooting.

Rooing and hooking in, digging deep.

Rooting and beginning to *grow*.

The capillary system serving as an intricate built-in road map, convenient streambed channels to follow. Soft tissues and subcutaneous fat laced with minerals, laced with nutrients ... rich, fertile bio-soil.

"It hurts! You said it wouldn't hurt!"

"... said there might be some discomfort—" Aloe.

"Make it stop!"

"This phase will be over soon—"

"No, make it *stop*! Take them *out*!"

"Now, you know we can't do that."

Skin gone porous and permeable, open.

Thirsty.

Fragile, young, and tender.

"I said, take them out! I don't want this!"

"You agreed to it. You signed all the forms." Nettle.

"I changed my mind!"

"It's way too late to change your mind. We told you that, once we began, there was no turning back. You agreed."

"I didn't know it would hurt this much!"

"Relax. You're still adjusting. You'll get used to it."

So thirsty.

"Mister."

Mister? Mister what?

Pssht pssht pssht delicate moistening spray.

Oh ... *mist*er.

Reviving and refreshing. Wonderful. Cool.

"Please. Please, I changed my mind, I really did."

"And it really is way too late. They're part of you now."

"Let me guess," said Tie-Dye Girl, whose named turned out to be Rainbow. "Earthstock."

Zeaa nodded. "Have you been?"

"Not for a couple years. My dads said it was run by sellouts."

"Sellouts?"

"That's what they said." Rainbow shrugged. "Gone commercial, taken on sponsors and advertising. They said it stopped being about the planet and the people, and started being about the money."

"I suppose maybe I can see that," said Zeaa, after some consideration. "It's still amazing, though. You can feel the energy, the communion, the healing love."

They were on the dirt shoulder of a road so old-school it wasn't even ceramic but nasty black-tar asphalt, cracked and potholed. Zeaa didn't know if she could have withstood actually walking *on* it, the grime-sludge residue of a greedy fossil-fuel world.

To either side of the road were the scraggly residential properties she'd seen from the 'rail, houses little better than shacks, trailers little better than the old junkers around them.

One stickerbush scrub lot was some kind of lost appliance graveyard, mounded with the rusting corpses of washers and dryers, ovens, and water heaters.

"Is that why you're going to Eden?" Rainbow asked. "Energy, communion, and healing love?"

"Well ..."

"Well?"

"Mostly those reasons, sure, yeah."

"Uh-huh. Who are you trying to impress? "

"What?"

"You want to impress someone. Or piss someone off. Maybe both."

"I want to ... to do my part ... to give back ... make a difference ..."

"Uh-huh," Rainbow said again.

"Okay, okay," Zeaa sighed. "You know how air-fern jewelry was such a big thing? The dangler earrings, the pendants, the pins? It started with those ..."

... and with *Brangelina*, Brangelina who always had to be first, first or best among their friend-group circles ... the most trendy, the most enlightened ... omnipan when the rest of them were merely bipoly at the most ... third-generation gluten-free vegan ... holistic orthodox antivaxx ... Mx. Carbon Neutral their senior year ...

So of *course* Brangelina had shown up wearing air-fern jewelry before anyone else, been the envy of Earthstock, star of the show, belle of the ball. She even got a concert shout-out from the lead singer of Terra Nova and appeared in one of their viral holos filmed at the event.

Well, naturally, then *everybody* was wearing air-ferns. Zeaa included.

Which was when the escalation began.

"... next, Aymlin gets these piercings, trellis-piercings all along the rim of the ear, with miniature climbing roses rooted into soil-pod implants behind the earlobe ... Niv gets armbands and anklecuffs, like tribal tats, only of living thorn-vines ..."

"Chia hair, moss beards, nipple cactuses ... cacti? Whatever."

"Yeah, that kind of thing. There's this one guy, Pot Belly, he has it growing out of pockets set into his great big gut ..." Zeaa curved her arms in a semicircle, trying to convey the sort of image, half pregnant-bulge like the octomom from the 'railcar, half someone trying to carry a barrel planter in front of them.

"Does he smoke it?"

"Smokes it, shares it, sells it."

"Must be popular. So what did this frenemy of yours do next?"

"*Songberries*," Zeaa said, kicking a rock and immediately feeling bad for disrupting the ecosystem as startled silvery-brown bugs scurried in panic. "She got songberry beds along both collarbones."

"Wow," uttered Rainbow in a deadpan dry tone. "What a bitch."

"I know it sounds petty and stupid, but you didn't see her, feeding them to people, acting all nature-goddess Pomona, when everybody knows she's also got a Wi-Fi hotspot in the back of her neck so she never misses a teletweet, opti-cams *and* a palm-cam for selfies, and charging ports in both ankles."

Brangelina in an open-front blouse, a lush drape of velvety leaves landscaping the contours of her upper chest, jade-green backdrop to gold-honey-amber clusters of ripe, juicy berries ... plucking them one by one, ever so gracious, bestowing them like largesse on her admirers ... then taking it further, inviting Jolth to lean in and graze ... her triumphant little smile at Zeaa as her fingers stroked the dark wild mane of Jolth's hair ... making it intimate ... making it sexual ... Jolth's face buried between her breasts ... Jolth's mmms and yums and wordless moaning murmurs of pleasure with each burst of succulent songberry sweetness ...

"And now you want to outdo her." Rainbow's words broke the memory loop, a welcome interruption even if Zeaa could have done without the implied accusation.

"It isn't about outdoing her. It's about doing something more useful, more beneficial. She only wanted to show off."

"While you," said Rainbow, "sincerely care about the environment."

"Hey, I—"

"There it is, by the way."

They'd reached a bend in the road at the top of a gradual rise, and Zeaa dropped her indignant protest in favor of turning eagerly in the direction Rainbow indicated.

The dismal scenery along the trek from the station would prove to have been some kind of test, to deter and discourage those who gave up easily ... only those who pressed on despite it would be rewarded ... a pristine hidden paradise would open before her dazzled, awestruck eyes ... a river valley of orchards and vineyards and gardens and meadows ... and nestled among the verdant splendor would be the curving grass-covered roofs of eco-sound structures ...

"Are you trolling me?" Zeaa asked.

"Were you expecting nest-basket tree dwellings and hobbit-holes?" Rainbow laughed without much humor. "If it helps, I heard all the buildings are repurposed relocates. Antarctic research prefabs, greenhouses scrapped from the Mars tests, military base salvage."

"You have *got* to be trolling me."

"Nope. That's Eden."

The cool spray, moist and misting, settling like dew. And the heat, the lamps, the heatlamps, sunlamps, basking bathing bright and warm.

A rippling sense of movement, a slow wave, stirred by unfelt wind.

"Observable phototropism at two hours eighteen."

"Ahead of schedule. Making excellent progress."

Sounds ... the faintest whisper-rustling, a stretching kind of keening whistle ... the world's smallest violins, tuning up for a concert.

Green smells. Green and brown. Terrarium smells, garden smells, plantings, orchards, fields.

"No more ... please ... no more."

"Respiration levels?"

"CO_2 intake approaching peak, oxygen emissions at point-four."

A downy fuzz of shootlets rising from dark earth, the tight nubs of buds on supple stalks and twigs, cushions of moss lining folds and crevices, feathery brushings of leafy fronds.

Implacable.

To strain, to strive, to thirst and thrive.

Hothouse flowers. Window-box herbs. Bean sprouts in egg cartons that kids brought home from school. Avocado pits suspended by toothpicks above half-filled water jars. Repotted cuttings. Grafted stems.

Dandelions. Scotch broom. Kudzu. Purple loosestrife. Japanese knotweed. Weeds and brambles, ivy.

Tenacious, persistent, and invasive.

Invasive.

Choking out. Taking over.

In a surging, urgent, burgeoning *growth*.

"How can you stand it?" Zeaa asked as they approached the main entrance of a long, wide, low, windowless corrugated-metal building. It looked like it had once been an airplane hangar at a podunk nowhere airport. "Living out here like this ... there aren't driftwood-sourced log cabins or woven kelp tents or yurts made from responsibly farmed alpaca felt, like at Earthstock ... there aren't even *trees!*"

"Who said I live here?" Rainbow replied.

"I thought you were from Eden, that you were on your way home."

"No way. My dad's own an organic hydroponic garden-to-table rooftop restaurant in town. I've got an appointment at the clinic."

"Same as me? Awesome!"

"Yeah, maybe not so much. I'm being treated for a fungal infection."

"A ... what?"

Rainbow slipped her macramé shawl from her shoulders. The tie-dye granny dress she wore underneath was loose and sleeveless. When she raised her tanned, slender arms over her head, it wasn't to reveal the lavish tufts of unshaven hair Zeaa might have expected.

She stared. "Are those ...?"

Stupid question. Even if she hadn't recognized them on sight—delicate layered ridges of shelf mushroom, multicolor banding with iridescent ruffled edges—the unmistakable, intoxicatingly pungent scent was now overpowering.

No wonder the smell of dreamshrooms trailed Rainbow like a perfume cloud! They clustered thick in the hollows of her armpits, tapering and thinning in fine-scaled wedges along the underside of her upper arms and down her ribs halfway to her waist.

"*Laetiporous psilocybus irisia,*" Rainbow said. "Or something Latin-y like that. You don't even want to *know* where *else* I've got them."

Oh, Zeaa had a guess, all right, but before she could voice it or speculate further on the hows and whys and specifics, the front door of the airplane hangar slid open. An androgyne in simple green scrubs and sensible nurse shoes stepped out, smiling at them.

"Rainbow, good to see you again," said the androgyne, whose midrange tenor tones were calm-balm soothing. "Your harvest team's ready for you downstairs. And you must be Zeaa. So nice to meet you. Come on in and we'll get you prepped. How exciting!"

"Respiration and absorption both looking good."

Sunlight and water.

Standing tall, full-face-turned toward a warm-beaming golden glow. Bare toes splayed on rich dark soil, curling into it, burrowing deep. The gentle hiss-mist of moisture, sheening, cooling, refreshing like kisses of dew.

"What's happening?" Whisper-leaf breath, grass in the breeze.

"What you wanted to happen." Comforting. Aloe.

Consumption and waste. Humanity a parasite, selfish, destructive.

Reduced carbon footprint ... carbon neutral ... giving back.

CO_2 to oxygen. Drawing in. Sighing out.

"We have photosynthesis."

The rustle of movement. Heaviness, the heaviness of nutrients and minerals, the heaviness of growth. Foliage, flower, and fruit. Greens and grains—kale, romaine, flaxseed, rice. Cherry tomato and soybean. Olive and fig.

A walking garden, a farm on two legs.

Sustainable. A personal renewable resource. One with nature.

Eco-friendly. The environment. The planet.

Earthstock.

Jolth. Niv and Aymlin.

And Brangelina. Brangelina would just about *choke*.

Let her, then. Let her choke. Let her choke, and drop, and die.

After all, vegans made good fertilizer ...

WORM

BY JEFF MENAPACE

When I walked into the restaurant, I spotted Jenn already seated at a small back table. Admittedly, the exact way I'd planned it. I was late on purpose in the hope of making a grand entrance.

I told the maître d' I saw my friend and that I would head over without his assistance. En route, I bathed in the subtle glances I got my way: men ogling and women hissing (by far the more rewarding of the two). But no glance at all from Jenn. Even as I stood directly in front of the table, she stared through me as though I were a stranger. And I loved it. I imagined my grin filled my entire face.

"*Helloooo ...*" I crooned.

She looked up from her menu, gave me a courtesy smile, looked back down, and then suddenly looked back up at me as something visibly clicked. She did not smile just yet. Her face instead wore a curious expression, as though experiencing something like déjà vu.

"Kara?" She didn't speak my name in that annoyingly clichéd way we all do, asking for confirmation when we know damn well who it is. She spoke it in a way that asked for explanation instead: *Of course I know it's you.* I like to think that single utterance of my name truly meant, *but just how the hell did you get so thin?*

I didn't wait for her to elaborate. I gave a tiny splay of my arms and twirled on the spot to show her the goods. My dress—black, sleeveless and strapless, sexy and classy— displayed my transformation off better than my birthday suit ever could.

"Is that really you?" she asked. Again, no clichéd *I'm just being friendly and clever with my words* query here. She appeared genuinely uncertain. A mysterious twin? One hell of a doppelganger? No way could I be the girl who was even chubbier than she was mere months ago.

"Yes, ma'am, it is," I said.

"How ...?"

I nearly made a scene with my laughter. I took my seat across the table from her, waited for the waiter to approach and tell us the specials and take our drink orders, and then dove in. No need to be cryptic with Jenn. Our friendship went back to the playground. Strange (or sad) as it sounds, our weight problems bonded us back then, and then kept the bond that much stronger throughout the years. When ridicule and exclusion reared their nasty heads, I was always there to swat them back, as she was for me.

I leaned in and spoke in hushed tones. Jenn did the same. The restaurant helped our secret huddle. It was one of those swanky places that managed to be both quiet and noisy at the same time. Dim lighting. Fancy décor. Smiling, well-groomed waiters who kept their hands behind their backs, bent at the waist, and looked you in the eye when they spoke. But the volume of the place was ripe with ambient sounds. Clanks of silverware on plates. Periodic shouts from the kitchen. Subdued but ceaseless chatter and laughter from the surrounding tables.

Yup, it was the perfect place to tell Jenn that I'd voluntarily swallowed a tapeworm while I was in Mexico.

Jenn's expression was that of a girl's taking her first shot of cheap tequila. And who can blame her? I likely had the same face three months ago when swallowing the worm was first suggested to me. The tequila analogy is apt, too. It was how the guy in Mexico convinced me how simple it all was. Just like swallowing the worm in a bottle of tequila, he'd said in broken English. No big deal.

"But it's not just a worm in a tequila bottle, Kara," Jenn said. "It's a *tape*worm."

I patted the air and made a shush face. "I'm well aware," I said. "Trust me, I was as freaked out as you are right now. But it's not that big a deal. Women used to do it all the time back in the day."

"*What?*"

"It's true. Women used to ingest tapeworm larvae to stay slim. And bonus? They could eat whatever they wanted. Watch how much I put away tonight." I grinned but Jenn was having none of it.

"Bullshit," she said a little too loudly. This earned an uppity look of disapproval from the diners at the next table.

I smiled a silent apology at the couple, then returned to Jenn, making the shush face and patting the air again.

She went on undeterred. "That's one of those urban legends. No person in their right mind would voluntarily ingest a parasite just to get thin."

I leaned back in my chair.

She exhaled and nodded apologetically, acknowledging her implication. She reached across the table for my hand but I wouldn't give it to her. "Obviously, I'm not saying you're *crazy*, Kara," she said, "I'm just saying ..."

I cocked my head and raised both eyebrows at her, a *please, go on* face.

"Forget it," she said. "I'm still waiting for you to tell me you're kidding."

I leaned forward again. "Well, I'm not. When Steve up and left without a word—that was rough. Coming home to a half-empty house. Rough. Not many people could get through something like that. But I did."

She reached across the table for my hand again. This time I gave it to her.

"But when I saw *who* he left me for? That size zero little bitch? It all hit me at once. All the years of dealing with my insecurities about my weight. All the failed diets. The frustration. I finally lost it."

She squeezed my hand, and it was no idle sympathy squeeze. Like I said, Jenn and I were soul mates in mind *and* body.

I went on, even though she knew most of the story. Boy dumps fat girl for skinny one. Girl loses it and has to get away. Girl goes to Mexico for three months to reclaim some sanity. The first night there, I got pretty damned drunk. So drunk that my shattered ego put the pieces together long enough to ask some guy to dance at some beach resort bar. The guy had politely declined, said he was leaving, but then ten minutes later I see him dancing with this skinny bitch, practically dry-humping her on the dance floor. So, I went over and said, "I thought you were leaving." He pretended he didn't know me, but I didn't let it go. "If you didn't want to dance with me, you should have just said so!" By now people were starting to stare, and here's the part that made me insane. The girl, not the guy, the *girl* said to me, "Why don't you go hit up the buffet and leave us alone?"

At this point in the story, Jenn squeezed my hand tight, her face mottled red with anger. "*Cunt*," she whispered.

I brightened her mood when I told her I decked the bitch on the spot.

"*You did?*" she said, smiling now.

I nodded. "Made quite the scene. Bouncers had to escort me out. I was so filled with rage and heartbreak that I broke down right outside the bar into some random guy's arms. I babbled drunkenly to the poor guy about what the bitch at the bar had said, and then about me, my life, what Steve had done ..."

"Oh geez," Jenn said.

"I know, right? Talk about mortifying. But here's the thing. The guy turned out to be a sweetheart. We went to the next bar over, and even though English wasn't his native language, he listened to everything I blubbered about. Consoled me at all the right times. Called Steve a jerk. When I kept going on and on about my weight, he showed me this picture on his phone of his sisters on the beach, three of them, all in bikinis and as skinny as can be. He told me they used to have weight problems, too, that diets never worked for them, just like they never worked for us."

"Let me guess," Jenn said. "He then told you they all ingested tapeworms to get so thin."

"Yup. He said lots of people down there do it. It's not a big deal, and it's not as dangerous as it sounds. The worm dies before any harm is done."

"So, he offered to get you one?"

"Sure did."

Jenn gave an incredulous little shake of her head. "And you said yes? Just like that?"

"Of course not. I was drunk, but I wasn't crazy, *despite* what my best friend might think."

"Stop."

I smirked, basking in her guilt a second longer before continuing. "We kept talking—and drinking—and he introduced me to a few people at the bar. All of them women, all of them thin. He asked one of them in Spanish to tell me about the worms. She smiled and pointed to her flat stomach and then gave me the thumbs up."

"And that's what convinced you?" Jenn asked. "Pictures of skinny girls on some guy's phone, followed by an endorsement from a stranger who didn't even speak English?"

"It *all* convinced me. All of it at once. Recent events with Steve, the incident at the bar with that bitch, the booze ... it was like the perfect storm of conviction. I felt so low, so angry, so lost, that I said 'fuck it' out loud and bought one."

"*Bought* one?"

"Well, sure."

"Jesus, Kara ..."

"I know what you're thinking," I said. "It was a scam. The pictures on the phone, the guy's friend coming over and giving the thumbs up. But *look* at me. Can you honestly say it didn't work?"

"How much did you pay?"

"Who cares? If I knew it was going to work this well, I'd have paid ten times as much. The last few months of my life have been indescribable."

Jenn made the *first-shot-of-cheap-tequila* face again. "And you swallowed a live worm? I've seen pictures of those things. They're long and thin, like ... well, like tape."

I laughed. "It was a baby. A tiny little thing." I made a pinch gesture with my thumb and index finger. "Just like Steve was."

Now Jenn laughed.

"I washed the little guy down with a shot of tequila, and the rest, as they say"—I waved a hand over my new body—"is history."

"How do you feel?" she asked.

"Reborn."

"I meant physically. How do you feel?"

"Well, let's see ... Steve used to complain that I snored. Since I've lost the weight, I've had no such complaints." I winked at her.

She laughed again. A naughty little laugh, head down, hand over mouth, looking left and right for those who might have heard.

"I still can't believe it," she finally said. "It's surreal."

"You're preaching to the choir, honey."

"And you can eat whatever you want?"

I picked up the menu and waved the waiter over. "Watch and see, my friend."

Dinner was over. Jenn had watched in awe as I ordered and then ate. A Caesar salad and calamari to start. Eight-ounce filet with garlic mashed potatoes for the main. A slice of black raspberry cheesecake with a scoop of vanilla ice cream for dessert.

She would periodically glance down at her own meal—a grilled chicken salad with some fat-free dressing—and then glance longingly across the table at mine. She reminded me of one of those kids at grammar school whose mom always packed a killer lunch with bags of Doritos and cupcakes and Capri Sun juice packets, while you were stuck with a mashed flat PB and J and a quarter to buy milk from the cafeteria.

She didn't talk much after dinner. I ate and chatted without a care in the world, telling her about the men I currently dated. I didn't do this to make her jealous, of course. No way. I'd never try to make Jenn jealous. I did it because, well, it felt good to brag about something I'd never been able to brag about before. Kind of like that grammar school lunch. If mom packed me cupcakes and Doritos and Capri Sun instead of a flat PB and J, you could be damn sure I'd make certain everyone at my table knew.

Still, I imagine she was a little jealous. But when I offered to go back to Mexico with her? To get *her* one of the worms? She adamantly declined. I understood. She hadn't hit her breaking point like I had, come millimeters from a nervous breakdown. She could see my results before her, of course, but I think it takes more than that to voluntarily swallow a tapeworm. She might even still think I was pulling her leg about it all. That I'd had inexpensive gastric bypass surgery in Mexico. (My home doctor would not approve any surgery, said I wasn't a good candidate.)

When I tried directing the subject more her way, asked her about Ken, the guy at work she was obsessed with, she simply waved the topic away and said no more about it. I took the hint, and then decided to introduce everybody's good-time lubricant—I ordered us after-dinner Cosmos. She agreed to them and, before long, I could see her begin to mellow. I then suggested keeping the party going with more drinks, and we agreed to head back to her place. I paid the bill—she argued, but I insisted—and we headed outside.

As we stood outside the restaurant, waiting for the valet to bring my car around, Jenn's full cheeks suddenly flushed. Her eyes were fixed over my shoulder. I turned and a guy in a suit and tie stood before us, smiling. He was tall and lean. Cute. The two guys he was with told him—Ken, they called him—they were heading inside and he nodded. Well, it didn't take a genius to figure out that this was *Jenn's* Ken. Her face flushing like it did, her sudden bashful manner.

"Hey, Jenn." He went in for a hug. A polite, obligatory hug. The kind you give a cousin you never see.

Jenn returned the hug, looking equally awkward, perhaps in disbelief at the coincidence. Small worlds were fickle that way—serendipity for some, nightmares for others. Before she could even open her mouth, the guy all but pushed her away and fixed directly on me with a smile and manner that was the antithesis of the *cousin-you-never-see* greeting. "Aren't you going to introduce me to your friend?" he asked, eyes never leaving me.

Jenn visibly deflated. Mumbled an introduction between us and then said she was going for her car parked on the street a block away. I told her to wait until the valet pulled up with my car, that we would leave together, but she was already en route. Her workplace crush was asking me all sorts of questions, but I wasn't paying attention.

A black BMW flew around the corner and nearly ran her over. When it screeched to a halt inches before hitting her, she and the driver (an entitled, insufferable bitch who wore sunglasses at night) exchanged words. The bitch got in the last one before speeding off. I watched Jenn deflate further still. She did not look back at me after the bitch sped away. Just dropped her head and continued shuffling toward her car. My heart didn't ache just then, it *burned*. The sensation soon found its way to my stomach with periodic jabs of pain, stress, and indigestion being the old pals they were. The valet couldn't have brought my car fast enough so I could be with my friend.

Jenn's eyes were puffy from crying when I arrived at her place. I hugged her, told her to sit on the sofa, and then fetched us some wine from her fridge. We kicked off our shoes, sat and drank while she told me about the bitch in the BMW.

"You saw what happened, right?" she asked me, sniffling away the last of her tears.

"Yeah—she nearly hit you, the idiot."

"That's exactly what I told her. You know what she told me?"

"What?"

She took a deep breath. "She told me if she had, I'd have done more damage to her car than she would have done to me."

My mouth fell open.

Jenn nodded. "She then called me a fat pig and drove off."

I put a hand on her shoulder and started to rub her back. "Oh, Jenn ... we've been through this a million times over the years, right? Girls like that? So shallow and ugly on the inside? What are they going to be when their looks go?"

She leaned away from me so I could no longer reach her back. "A bit hypocritical, don't you think?"

"What?"

"Look how far you went to improve *your* looks. You've got a *worm* inside you."

Then *I* leaned away. "And what does that have to do with me as a person?"

"*Oh, Jenn,*" she began, throwing my words back at me, "*the last few months have been indescribable. I'd have paid ten times as much.*' Seems like you now place a much higher value on outer beauty when it comes to quality of life."

"That's not fair," I said.

"What's not fair was Ken practically eye-fucking you tonight."

"And did I reciprocate in any way whatsoever?"

"I don't know, I couldn't watch anymore."

"Well, I didn't. I was more concerned about you."

"Oh, thank you. The skinny girl was worried about the fat one. How sweet."

I stood. "What is *wrong* with you?"

"What's wrong with *you*?!"

I suddenly grimaced and doubled over in pain.

I told Jenn I felt sick. I saw a hint of satisfaction on her face when she suggested I ate too much at dinner. I stumbled back into the kitchen, clutching my stomach, and insisted it was something else. Something bad. Her hint of satisfaction dissolved. She followed me into the kitchen and told me to lift my dress. I was in so much pain, I didn't question her strange request, just did it. In fact, I stripped the entire dress off. I stood in her kitchen in just my bra and panties. Jenn took one look at my stomach and her eyes popped impossibly wide. Her hand slapped over her mouth to stifle a cry. I looked down and saw it for myself. It was not a long, thin, fragile thing like a piece of tape. It was a thick, solid, eel-like fucker that visibly writhed just beneath the skin across my stomach, bulging the surface as it rapidly serpentined back and forth with increasing frenzy.

"OH MY GOD!" I screamed.

"OH MY GOD!" Jenn screamed.

"OH MY GOD!!!" I screamed again.

The worm disappeared deeper into my body and my stomach flattened again. I went to touch my stomach and the worm suddenly jumped forward, as though it meant to rip through my navel, stretching the skin of my stomach outward into a flesh tent.

Jenn screamed and rushed for her phone.

"NO! No, you can't call anyone!"

Jenn looked at me, her face both horrified and flabbergasted. *"What!?"*

"No one can know about this!"

"Kara, you need a doctor!"

The worm, as though hearing this, leaped for my navel again. The pain was unreal, and I dropped to my knees.

Jenn began to dial. I quickly shuffled over on my knees and knocked the phone from her hands.

"Are you crazy!?" she said.

"Do you have any idea how much trouble I would be in if they found out I smuggled a foreign species into the country?"

"It's a tapeworm!"

I pointed to my protruding navel, the flesh tent. "This is *NOT* a tapeworm!"

Jenn set the phone aside. "So, what do we do!?"

I slumped back on my heels and shook my head. Another sudden stab of pain hit me and I immediately curled into a fetal ball on her kitchen floor. "We have to get it out."

"*How?*"

I could only grimace in agony and shake my head again.

Jenn pulled open a kitchen drawer and produced a big knife.

This time it was me who said, "*Are you crazy!?*"

"*Well, what do you want me to do!? You said the guy told you they eventually die, right? You feel like waiting???*"

She had a point. The pain became so intense, the kitchen knife began to sound like a good idea.

"Can you throw it up?" she asked. "Stick your fingers down your throat and try to throw it up."

The agony made me desperate. I rolled to all fours and jammed my fingers down my throat. I hitched once, twice, and then *whoosh!*—a delightful blend of Caesar salad, calamari, steak, garlic mashed potatoes, and black raspberry cheesecake with vanilla ice cream gushed on Jenn's kitchen floor.

No giant worm.

"Keep trying!"

I jammed my fingers down my throat again, but it was unnecessary. *I* might have finished my meal earlier this evening, but the worm clearly hadn't. I felt it rise through my body like some horrific reverse bowel movement ... the anus my mouth, of course.

Jenn's shrieking this time made her earlier efforts whispers.

My previous comparisons to a large eel were not far off. A large white eel that was *not* an eel squirted through my throat, out of my mouth, and on the kitchen floor, eager to reclaim its meal. I couldn't tell which was the head or tail—it had no visible eyes or mouth. It just writhed in the vomit as though it meant to absorb the food through its skin.

Jenn, still shrieking even as she sprang into action, grabbed the knife on the kitchen counter and brought the blade down on the meat of the worm's belly *WHOCK!*

Two worms now. A dark ooze seeped from one end of each as they wriggled furiously.

"*Again!*" I cried.

WHOCK! WHOCK!

Four furious wrigglers then.

"*AGAIN!*"

WHOCK! WHOCK! WHOCK! WHOCK!

Eight. And if you think they wriggled furiously when they were two and four ...

I got up and stomped on them, determined to flatten the writhing segments with my bare feet. I smashed a few, but my feet slid on the slick puddle of vomit. Both feet went out from under me, sending me flat on my back in a puddle of puke and squirming bits of worm. I felt one begin its blind crawl up my neck and I screeched, plucking it from my neck and flinging it toward the kitchen sink.

Jenn saw this and her eyes widened. She snatched a towel from her kitchen table, scooped up the remaining segments of wriggling worms, spun back toward the sink, dropped them in, and then made the *first-shot-of-cheap-tequila* face for the third time that night. She used her bare hand to jam the pieces of worm down the garbage disposal. Finished, she couldn't hit the switch on the wall fast enough. The garbage disposal groaned and chugged, the eight chunks of worm straining its motor. It eventually powered through, and the high-speed whirring of the blades was the greatest sound I'd ever heard.

Jenn hit the switch on the wall again, and the disposal hummed to a stop. Complete silence for a moment. Jenn panted and stared incredulously at her sink. I panted and stared incredulously at Jenn.

"Is it gone?" I eventually asked.

She kept her back to me but nodded.

"Are you okay?" I asked her.

She finally turned toward me. "Are *you*?"

"I don't know." I stood—a thirty-year-old woman standing in her best friend's kitchen in nothing but her bra and panties with vomit and Mexican worm goo slathered all over her back and butt. "I think—" The pain hit my stomach again like a bullet and I clutched my gut, doubling over and moaning.

"What is it?" Jenn asked.

"It feels like it's still in there."

"It *can't* be," she said. "We—"

I barfed. *Really* barfed. *Projectile barf.* No help from my fingers needed at all. I expected to see more of the dinner I'd eaten earlier. And for a moment, I thought I did ... only I hadn't eaten any rice. Certainly not any rice that moves.

"*OH MY GOD!!!*" Jenn screamed again.

A delivery of Mexican tapeworm kids.

Jenn sprang into action again and snatched the towel, scooping up the pile of little worms, dumping them in the sink, and then giving them the same treatment as their mother. No motor struggling for these little guys though— they blended instantly.

The pain was gone.

Her back to me, Jenn opened the towel she used to scoop up the worm larvae. She went into one of her cupboards and removed an empty Mason jar. After that, I couldn't see what she was doing. But when she turned toward me, the small clear jar now contained a few of the larvae, the stragglers left behind on the towel.

"What are you doing?" I asked.

"We're going to the hospital," she said determinedly, enunciating each word like a parent telling their kid to do it or else. She then held up the Mason jar containing the few remaining larvae. "And we're bringing these with us for the doctors to see."

"What? *No!* I already told you—"

"You're not going to get into trouble, Kara. Christ, you were in Mexico for three months. For all they know, you ingested them in the water."

"Jenn, please—" I got to my feet. "I feel fine now. It's dead. They're all dead, and I feel fine now."

"Kara ..."

I put a hand on her shoulder. "If you want to take me to the hospital, fine, I'll go. We can tell them I got sick after dinner. Food poisoning or something. But please, do not mention what really happened ..." I pointed at the Mason jar in her hand. "And do *not* bring those with you. *Please.*"

She shook her head, sighed, and then set the jar on the counter. "Fine. But you *are* going to the hospital."

I nodded emphatically. "Of course, of course. I just said I would."

I quickly washed and threw on some of Kara's clothes. Jeans and a sweatshirt. The sweatshirt was huge but doable, but the jeans were way too big for me. Jenn saw this, headed to her closet, and tossed me a pair of sweatpants. "Thanks," I said with an uncomfortable smile as I cinched the drawstring to accommodate my little waist.

She didn't smile back. "Let's go."

The hospital proved gratefully uneventful. Jenn insisted on telling the doctor I'd just spent three months in Mexico. Was it possible I unknowingly ingested some sort of parasite? (I nearly choked on the plastic cup of apple juice they'd given me.) The doctor told us no—all tests came back normal. Jenn and I exchanged looks. Neither of us could believe our ears. *Normal?* No damage done *at all?* Jenn asked him to reiterate and he told her I was good to go. Maybe a little underweight, he added, to which Jenn gave a subtle furrow of the brow.

Jenn and I didn't see much of each other after that. Sure, we talked on the phone, but as far as actually seeing each another ... well, we didn't. She kept saying she was busy with work, but I wondered if she simply wasn't ready. When two people share a trauma, I guess a cooling-off period is definitely in order before normal life can resume, if ever. Not that I minded. I'd since gained back a lot of weight in the months since we'd seen each other. Guys had stopped calling. Catty girls stopped hissing my way. My skinny clothes were all in a box, ready for Goodwill. I sometimes wondered if it would be worth swallowing another worm just to get thin again. A second trip to Mexico *was* always an option. Perhaps I'd jokingly suggest it to Jenn over dinner tonight.

Yup, we'd finally decided to meet for dinner, at the same upscale restaurant we'd dined the night of my ordeal. It was Jenn's suggestion. Probably some therapeutic thing she was working out—recreating the events of that night without the trauma that followed. She always was big into therapy. I was fine with it. Whatever brought us together again. Sure, I'd be a little self-conscious about my weight gain, but if anyone was going to be supportive, it was Jenn.

I entered the restaurant and the maître d' seated me, told me Jenn was running late. He even seated me at what I'm fairly sure was the same table we sat at months before. I picked up the menu and began to look at the salads. They all looked so impotent. I glanced longingly at the filets on the adjacent page, and again wondered if it would be worth swallowing another one of those little bastards. I slapped the menu shut and placed it aside, looked up. A woman stood in front of my table, grinning at me. Was she grinning at me or someone behind me? I couldn't tell. She was thin and pretty, decked to the nines. Had to be someone behind me. I smiled back politely, picked up the menu, and pretended to read it again in the hope the skinny weirdo would go away.

"HELLOOOO ..."

REDUCED TO TEARS

BY ADRIAN LUDENS

Margo Thayer arrived home from work bubbling with good cheer. She'd spent the week working doubles—mornings cashiering at the supermarket and evenings glued to a headset at the call center—and tonight she planned on spending a well-deserved night out on the town.

But first, the kids.

Margo found her youngest, Noah, playing video games in their apartment's living room. "Hey, kiddo, how was school?" She bent and planted a kiss on his buzzed scalp. His eyes never left the screen. "Fine." Noah's fingers flew over the controller as he guided a caped hero through a series of colorful explosions. Margo felt the corner of her mouth quirk. *The extravagances of childhood*, she thought.

"I'm going to have dinner with a few friends from the call center. Will you be okay here with your sister?"

Noah glanced up and gave her a look. "As long as she doesn't try to boss me around."

"She *is* in charge while I'm gone," Margo said. "That means if there's a fire, she has to carry you out of the blaze draped over her shoulder." Noah rolled his eyes at her strained humor. "Otherwise, you won't even know she's here."

"Good," Noah said. His eyes remained focused on the pixilated distraction unfolding on screen. He winced as if absorbing an actual blow.

"I'll be home before midnight. Bedtime's at 9:30. Don't forget."

Margo left her youngest and called for her daughter from the foot of the stairs. "Starla!"

"Yeah, mom?"

"Just letting you know I'm going to heat up some green beans and mini-ravioli on the stove. I'm going out with Trudy and the girls tonight."

Starla poked her head out of her room. "'Kay."

Margo started dinner heating on the electric stove and then strode to her bedroom. From her closet, she selected her favorite Little Black Dress and open-toed black heels. She dressed and scrutinized herself in the full-length mirror affixed to the bedroom door.

Her shoes displayed her four remaining toes, fresh from a pedicure, nails painted black. Her hands matched her feet, with only thumb and forefinger remaining on each hand. Her ears protruded from the sides of her head, spectacularly prominent thanks to her shorn scalp and missing earlobes. Margo eyed the hollow of darkness lurking behind her half-closed left lid and grinned, exposing gaps left by the removal of her lateral incisors.

Watch out guys, she thought. *Margo is coming to party!*

She grabbed her purse and hurried toward the door.

Margo's headlamps diffused the darkness with yellowish, chicken-broth light as she pulled into her building's parking lot. She had left the bar well before closing time in a bid to avoid any sobriety checkpoints. In this, she succeeded. Now, before bed, she planned on a hot shower and a two-aspirin preemptive strike against a hangover.

A figure darted across the road in front of her car and Margo stomped on the brake pedal. The figure, a teenage boy, glanced back at her and then ducked between vehicles and disappeared into the darkness beyond the parking lot. His expression, illuminated for a split second, conveyed a mixture of surprise, fear, and then triumph. Margo eased her car into her assigned spot and mulled the fleeing figure over in her mind.

Something about him had repulsed her. His appearance—even in the briefest of glances—seemed to her seedy and unsavory. It was only as she inserted her key into the apartment door's front lock that the realization hit her.

The fleeing boy, though he had looked Starla's age or perhaps older, still had both eyes. They had bugged out in surprise when she hit the brakes to avoid hitting him. Margo shuddered. Having the left eye removed at the age of ten was a rite of passage for all Reducers. The only people who did not do it were the deviants who rejected the faith and chose to live life unenlightened.

Margo thrust the door open and locked it behind her. She leaned with her back pressed against it, eye closed, panting. Her heart pounded, but why was she so worried? Just because she'd spotted an objectionable person in the neighborhood didn't mean her family was in any immediate or specific danger.

As she set her purse down on the entryway table, Noah, dressed in his pajamas, sidled into view. Noah, for whom she had grand hopes—so grand, in fact, that she had specified his middle name as "Body" on his birth certificate—stood in the hallway, a smirk twisting his mouth. The boy had a secret, one he clearly wished to impart.

Margo's heart fluttered on shaky wings while her stomach sank like a discarded cocoon. "I know something you don't know," Noah announced. But in that moment Margo *did* know. She sank to her knees, feeling ill. Margo drew in a single lungful of air and screeched her daughter's name.

Margo thought, for perhaps the hundredth time since starting work, of the boy who'd fled across the parking lot the previous night. She'd warned her daughter against dating—or even befriending—troublemakers like him. Starla seemed to go out of her way to make her worry.

With a deep sigh, Margo reached out, crab-clawed a package of steak, and swiped it over the scanner.

"Rough night?" her current customer asked.

Margo looked up in surprise, truly seeing him for the first time. He seemed close to her age. He too retained only index fingers and thumbs on both hands. His left eyelid drooped in what looked to Margo like a perpetual insouciant wink. His shaved head suited his rugged good looks. If she'd run into this guy last night, she wouldn't have been in such a rush to get home.

"My teenage daughter ..." Margo muttered.

"Say no more," the man grinned. "They never want to make it easy on their parents, do they?"

Margo noticed he still had his upper left lateral incisor—that meant he was at least one year younger than she. Margo resisted the urge to ask him to turn around and lift his shirt so she could see if he had a kidney-removal scar.

"No, they don't." She laughed. The man joined her. She finished ringing up his transaction and let her finger graze his open palm when giving him his change. The man blushed.

Margo hoped she'd see him again.

The days, ever similar, ran together.

On the afternoon of Noah's tenth birthday, Margo clocked out and hurried down the aisle to purchase a chocolate cake from the supermarket's bakery. She also bought balloons, a liter of soda, and a box of ice-cream sandwiches. It came to more than she'd intended to spend—or could afford to spend, if truth be told—but she wanted to surprise her son. She pictured his face lighting up with delight as he opened the car door.

Instead, when she picked him up from school, he climbed in and wilted in the passenger seat, looking glum.

"What's wrong?" Margo asked. "Aren't you excited for your party?"

Noah remained silent for several blocks. At last, he exploded. "I wish we weren't so poor! Everyone is going to laugh at me."

Margo sighed. "Noah, honey, we talked about this. We'll get your eye removed as soon as we can afford it."

Noah squeezed his lids closed, perhaps staving off tears. He didn't respond, only began breathing through his nose in short, angry snuffles.

"As long as we get it removed before you turn 11, we'll still be within the customary schedule," Margo said. She thought of Starla's would-be boyfriend and repressed a shudder. "I won't let it go longer than that, believe me."

"But my friends will make fun of me." Noah drew a deep, watery breath.

"Then they're not true friends." Margo braked as they reached a red light. "We just can't afford it right now. I'm sorry you're feeling embarrassed, but we can't just gouge your eye out with a grapefruit spoon, can we?"

Noah turned to face her, his eyes alight, beaming with hopeful excitement. She imagined him preparing for school the next morning with a bloody, seeping bandage affixed to his face.

"No, we cannot," Margo pressed. "It's not safe, it's not sanitary, and—oh honey—you'd be in so much pain."

Noah sank back against the seat. Margo turned her attention back to the road. She made a mental note to hide the grapefruit spoons when they got home.

The next morning, Margo dropped the kids off at school before heading to her shift at the supermarket. Starla sat in the front passenger seat in cold silence, her arms folded across her chest, until they arrived at the middle school.

As Margo slowed, she spoke. "You can be mad, but it won't change anything. If you live under my roof, you obey my rules. Those types of people never amount to anything but trouble, believe me."

Starla jumped from the car, slammed the door, and melted into the crowd of teens. Margo didn't worry about her daughter's attitude. A day of classes surrounded by her friends—her normal friends—and she'd come home much calmer. She might even offer her mother a sheepish apology, or a hug and an offer to set the dinner table. Margo smiled at the thought. Stranger things had happened.

Her car chewed up the blocks between the middle school and the elementary school Noah attended. He'd been silent as a shadow in the backseat. Now Margo reached out and angled her rearview mirror so she could see her son.

Fresh tears glistened on his cheeks. Yet he had not uttered a single word of complaint since his party. This realization sent a pang into Margo's heart. She eased the car to a stop at the curb. "I'll make sure you get your procedure very soon, okay, kiddo?" She watched him cast a doubtful glance up at her and gave him a reassuring smile. "I just need to work some doubles and we'll schedule it during winter recess. How about that?"

Noah looked at her gratefully. He drew in a deep breath and left the car, his backpack thumping against his spare frame as he hurried across the playground.

At the supermarket, Margo clocked in, counted her till, and began scanning groceries for an endless procession of customers. When it came to standing in line, age determined the hierarchy. A reduced elderly person, usually installed on a throne-like motorized wheelchair as a matter of necessity, always went to the head of the line. The younger people, still raw blocks of sculptor's marble as far as society was concerned, waited their turn out of respect.

About halfway through her shift, she noticed the handsome man she'd conversed with enter the store. A thrill went through her when, his shopping completed, he chose her line over that of the other cashiers.

When the man reached her, Margo found that nervous excitement had erased any witty or flirtatious greetings from her brain. Instead, "Did you find everything?" was all she could manage.

The man smiled. "I did, but I also find that I have no desire to dine at home this evening. I feel like having a nice dinner out." He glanced down at her index fingers, as if just remembering something important. When he looked up again, relief had relaxed his features. "But I'm tired of dining alone."

Margo blushed. She knew what he intended to say next. She waited while he fumbled for his wallet.

"I'd be honored if you'd consider joining me for dinner," he said. He pressed a crisp white business card and his payment into her open palm.

She counted back his change, her voice shaking enough that she mentally chided herself for behaving like a love-struck schoolgirl. "I'll consider your offer. Thank you for shopping with us today."

The man nodded, hefted his grocery sacks, and smiled at her again. "I hope you'll call."

As he strode away, Margo stole a glance at the man's business card. Dr. Benjamin Graham, MD, the card read, Reduction Specialist. Below this, the name of a clinic, an address, and a phone number. He had written a second number in pen on the back of the card.

Margo knocked, waited a moment, and then entered her great-grandmother Millicent's room at the senior care facility. An array of machines chirped in the corner and privacy curtains shuttered the bed. The odor of disinfectant permeated the air. Margo swept aside one curtain. "Hello? Great-Grandma Millie? It's Margo!"

"Hello." Millicent spoke but didn't move. "How are you, dear?"

"I'm feeling ... conflicted," Margo said. "There's some drama in my life right now. I felt like I needed to talk to my oldest living relative."

"What's troubling you?"

Margo looked at the shape reclining on the bed and sighed. Through good times and bad, Margo relied on Millie for her sage counsel. "Starla, she's thirteen. So, of course, she's trying to date a boy who's one of those anti-reduction nuts."

"Oh dear."

"I'm sure she's just doing it to test me, but it's still frustrating. Then there's Noah, he just turned ten and wants his eye out *so bad!* I just don't have the money to take care of that yet and he's disappointed—"

"You've lost your focus."

"Excuse me?"

There was a momentary semi-silence, punctuated only by the sounds of the machines.

"Renew your spiritual focus and it will sustain you. Take me, for instance. Doctors removed my kidneys and I rely on dialysis for physical survival. My spleen is gone, as is my large intestine."

Margo remained silent.

"Doctors removed my uterus when the accustomed time came. I have one lung, no arms or legs, no eyes, nose, or ears. All of this and more—or should I say less?—is in keeping with my faith. Each removal, each reduction, serves as a blessed stepping tone toward my ultimate goal."

Margo nodded. "Of course."

"The fewer cumbersome organs and appendages I have, the closer I get to my creator."

"I understand," Margo said. She looked at her great-grandmother, her truncated features and the tubes that kept her alive hidden beneath repurposed cheesecloth. A log sawed in half and placed under the covers might have looked more convincingly human.

Millicent ignored her, apparently lost in reverie. "I underwent a total gastrectomy. The nutrition I receive goes straight from my esophagus to my small intestine. When the doctors determine how best to rid me of those—well, I've already signed on the dotted line."

Her great-grandmother hadn't possessed hands in two decades. Perhaps Millie had made a joke.

"Many years have passed since doctors removed my appendix, my tonsils, and my teeth," the old woman continued. "Of course, I had them remove all of my teeth at once, rather than waste my forties going tooth by tooth. I'm looking forward to the removal of my tongue and the severing of my vocal cords for my next birthday. I'll have my eardrums punctured two years from now. I just *know* I'll feel at peace then."

"I'm going to do all that, too," Margo said. Her own voice sounded unconvincing to her ears.

"The less of us the better when we each meet our maker," the older woman said. "I think that's what the Good Book meant about 'separating the wheat from the chaff.' But Margo, dear, you're focusing on petty, everyday squabbles and emotions, instead of the big picture."

"You mean the smaller, reduced picture." Margo tried to giggle but it felt forced. Her great-grandmother was right, of course. Each Reducer's journey walked a fine line between public and private experiences. Margo didn't think she could match Millie's spiritual zeal for reduction, but she'd certainly try.

She bid her great-grandmother goodbye and slipped from the room. She didn't dare bring up her silly crush now.

Despite her best intentions, her "silly crush" on Dr. Graham grew. She finally gave in and called to accept his offer. He took her to dinner at an intimate bistro where they dined, talked, and laughed.

"Please call me Ben," he said, after they had seated.

"I'm Margo. M-a-r-g-o. There used to be a silent 't' at the end but I reduced it."

Her companion burst into genuine laughter and Margo felt warmth growing in the pit of her stomach—or perhaps lower.

After dinner, when a second bottle of wine had been opened, Margo opened up as well. She told Ben about her life, her children, scraping to make ends meet, and anything else that came to mind.

Her date absorbed it all. When Margo revealed Noah's middle name, he gasped. "Oh, Margo, that's beautiful." He never seemed disinterested or gave the impression that he felt superior to her in any way. Her inner warmth became heat.

In the end, they returned to his townhouse together. They made love for hours, exploring each other's bodies. Caressing surgery scars. Kissing appendages that would one day be sliced off and cast aside. On the agonizing path to purity, they found a brief moment of carnal bliss.

Everyday life, for a time, became a joy.

Starla's inclination toward freakish, two-eyed boyfriends proved to be a passing fancy.

Ben performed Noah's left eye removal off the books as a favor to Margo. When she thanked him, he said, "Severing the optic pathway to the intuitive side will help him immensely in life. I'm happy to help."

Thanks to Ben's generosity, Margo didn't have to work double shifts and could spend more time with her kids. In fact, the four of them spent a good deal of time together—until the day of Margo's fortieth birthday.

The kids were at school and Margo, enjoying a day off from the supermarket, met Ben for lunch at their favorite Indian restaurant. They planned a more expansive dinner in celebration of her latest milestone.

"I thought we could go to Cristo's," Ben said. "You know the Greek place on Lake Street? You could invite some of your work friends along."

"That all sounds great, hon," Margo replied. "Listen, do you think you could get me in first thing in the morning?"

Ben's eyebrows shot up. "Get you in for what?"

"I'm turning forty, silly," Margo said. "I want my nose removed, of course."

"Your ... nose." Ben tried to smile, but it faltered.

"Of course, it's the next step in the reduction process."

"Right, right." Ben twisted his napkin.

"Is something wrong?"

"I just ... I love your nose. It's adorable." He looked at her, his eye pleading. "I think it's your best feature."

"And not having it would make you love me less?" Margo didn't appreciate Ben's misguided attempts at flattery. Was he that shallow?

"No, of course not! I just—"

"You wouldn't try to interfere with my spiritual journey, would you?"

"You know I've dedicated my life to helping people reduce, Margo. I realize its importance. I even do charity work."

"Oh, so Noah's procedure was 'charity' work?"

"No!" Ben grimaced. "You're painting me into a corner. Don't misconstrue what I'm saying. I believe in the spiritual journey of reduction. *I do.* But I also love your adorable button nose! Can you blame me for wanting you to keep it for a few more months?"

She gazed at his face, studying him for any sign of an ulterior motive. Then it hit her. Where once warmth had grown within her, icy tendrils of disappointment now spread and tightened. Margo struggled to maintain her composure.

She saw him all too clearly, realized the hidden meaning behind his words, and felt reduced in his eyes.

"Leave."

"What?"

"I want you out of my sight."

"You can't be serious." Ben stared at her. So did other patrons.

"I said get the hell out!" Margo screamed. She tried to cover her face with her misshapen hands and began to sob. With one shallow declaration, the man she loved had reduced her to tears.

Frowning, Ben pushed back his chair and hurried out of the restaurant.

Margo called out sick from her checker shift the next morning. She was worried that Ben might try to confront her at the supermarket. She moped around the house, sipped tea between crying jags, and consigned to boxes anything that reminded her of him.

She knew she couldn't afford to skip both jobs, so after shuttling the kids home from school, Margo drove to the call center.

"Hey, hon," Trudy whispered, setting aside her headset and rising. "What's wrong?"

Margo sank into her chair. "Is it that obvious?" She glanced up at her friend. Trudy's features conveyed sincere concern.

"Well, stop me if I'm being a snoop," Trudy said, lowering her voice. "But your eye is red enough that I'd say you've been crying."

Margo sighed. "I have."

"What happened?"

"I just turned forty yesterday—but I didn't feel much like celebrating." Margo shrugged and then shook her head, as if carrying on a second, internal conversation. "My Mr. Right turned out to be a shallow creep. He told me not to have my nose removed."

"No!" Trudy's mouth fell open in shock.

"Can you believe it?" Margo put on her headset and prepared to take her first call. "We've only been dating a few months, and he already had the nerve to tell me I need to look younger."

A NEW MAN

BY WILLIAM F. NOLAN

[NEURO-PROM PASSCODE: REQUIRED (PRESS ANY KEY TO
                        ENTER)
    Passcode: _____
    Passcode: ACCEPTED
              BEGIN CONFESSION #TEA3170B-X3075
        DOWNLOAD...........
                        Unspooling..................
                            start transcode!complete!
                                    checksum............
                        .....
</gmd:linkage>
</gmd:CI OnlineResource>
</geop:mappingFile>
<geop:processingApplication>
<geop:PH_EnvironmentObject>
<geop:documentation>
<gmd:CI_OnlineResource>
<gco:CharacterString>GeoServer WFS
    </gco:CharacterString>
                    </geop:name>
<geop:purpose><gco:CharacterString>produce
representation of observation datasets in
Science Modelling Language
    - a GHL-based application schema

```
</gco:CharacterString></gmd:purpose>
            <geop:type>
      <gco:CharacterString>Software
      </gco:CharacterString></geop:type
              >
       <geop:ve
       rsion>
       <gco:Characte
       rString>Compl
       ex
```

RUN #TEA3170B-X3075 TRANSCRIPTION:>

"Happy tenth anniversary!" I said, handing the ribboned jewelry box to Edith.

"What's inside?" she asked, eyes aglow with excitement. She was still beautiful enough to astonish me.

"Open it and see," I said.

With a girlish laugh, she untied the red band and opened the box. She gasped.

"Well? Do you like it?"

"Terry! An emerald necklace! You shouldn't have. It must have cost—"

"I can afford it. Nothing's too good for my girl ..." I've always called Edith "my girl," ever since we met in college. It was love at first sight for us both. I've never wanted another woman. Edith was my treasure.

She lifted the choker from its velvet nest and slipped it around her neck, allowing afternoon sunlight to turn the jewels to green fire.

"It's absolutely gorgeous!"

We kissed, deeply, with a sexual hunger that was still intense, consuming. After ten years, the excitement had not diminished.

We had our anniversary dinner at Jimmy's, our favorite Italian restaurant. It was named after actor James Cagney, and framed photos of the long-dead movie icon adorned the walls. In one photo Cagney was posing with President Franklin Roosevelt in the Oval Office during World War II.

Benny LaGarda, the owner, greeted us warmly, excited about a 1949 Cagney film he'd recently discovered, *White Heat.* He was rail-thin, with a short neck, and displayed an obvious over-bite when he smiled.

"The scene at the end is *fabulous*," he told us. "Jimmy gets blown to pieces! He's on this really high platform and he yells to his mother, 'Look, Ma—top of the world!', and that's when he's blown to bits!" He directed us to a table near the kitchen. "Too bad they didn't have our technology a hundred years ago, eh? Jimmy might have been saved."

He led us to a table near the kitchen. "Ummmm," Edith murmured as she sat down, "smells delicious!" She had always enjoyed the heady aroma of Italian herbs and spices. She was wearing the necklace, the emeralds flashing green heat against the white of her throat.

"This is our tenth anniversary," I told Benny, squeezing my wife's hand, "so we want a bottle of your best champagne."

"Our treat," nodded Benny." If I'd known about this happy occasion I would have baked a cake."

"The bubbly will do just fine," said Edith, smiling up at him. "Wow ... I haven't tasted champagne since we had Janette."

"Where *are* the children?" Benny asked.

"Janette loves shuttlefusion," said Edith. "The big game is tonight ... for the West Coast Championship, so we dropped off Jan and Bobby at the 'drome."

"Yeah." I nodded. "We needed time for just the two of us."

"Jan has a crush on one of the players," declared Edith. "I've forgotten his name. Lance something or other. But I'm sure it'll pass. She's only nine years old!"

"They grow up fast these days," said Benny, taking our order.

As always, the food was delicious—a sumptuous vegetarian feast prepared by Benny himself. The champagne was a perfect complement.

Later that evening we made passionate love. Edith could be a tiger in bed, especially on an occasion as special as our anniversary. Afterward, we had the car drive us to the Friodrome to pick up Jan and Bobby.

"How was the game?" I asked Bobby. At eight, he was easily bored.

He shrugged. "It was okay. Jannie's the shuttle freak, not me. But it was okay."

"It was *super!*" Jan declared. "Best game *ever!* And our team won, thanks to Lance. He was the star. He scored *three* times!"

"Kid's an airhead," I said. "Dumb as a sack of rocks."

In the rearview, I saw her chin quiver as she looked away. The silence was heavy.

"Now see what you've done," admonished Edith after a few moments. "A terrible thing to say when you don't even know the boy."

Janette finally blurted, "Daddy, you just don't understand true love!"

At the breakfast table the next morning, Bobby picked at his food, head down, looking glum.

"What's wrong, soldier?" I asked him.

"Why can't we program the table to make a different breakfast?"

"How different?"

"I'm tired of toast and soy bacon. I want a bowl of cereal."

"Now, you know we've had this discussion before. Those kid's cereals are full of sugar," Edith said, "Very bad for you. That's why we don't buy them."

"Look," I told him, "you are not old enough to dictate a menu yet. Later, when you're older and if you still want cereal we can discuss the matter. For now, *you* eat what *we* eat."

Bobby scowled. "Other kids eat it ..." His voice trailed off as he stared at the food on his plate. He knew this was a losing battle.

"Well, you're not other kids," his mother replied, her expression stern as she dried her hands on a dish towel. "Stop sulking, and don't waste your food. Children on Io are starving."

He looked at me. "How come all the *bad* stuff tastes better than the *good* stuff?"

I had no answer to that. I'd never figured it out either.

Everything went wrong after the crash.

I had set the auto-drive at near max. I enjoyed the sensation of sheer speed. The car was probably moving faster over the road slot than was prudent. But the slot was designed to keep all cars separated on the GridWay, so I felt safe, drowsing in my seat, eyes closed, picturing Edith's happy smile when I got back to our house-unit.

That's when the slot malfunctioned. As a heavy med truck moved toward me, it jumped the Grid and slammed head-on into my car. I learned later that the ensuing impact tore my body apart as the two machines merged in a horrific tangle of twisted metal. The man in the truck, amazingly, survived with only minor injuries.

I did not. I died in the hospital shortly after arrival. The minute I expired, they flashed my Neuro-prom and affected the dendritic transfer into my new host. I woke up several weeks after the operation flushed with strength, alert and in no pain.

"Welcome back to the land of the living," declared my white-clad doctor, smiling down at me. "The scan shows you're fit as a fiddle."

I blinked at him. "What happened? I don't understand ..."

"You were in an accident. Your old body didn't survive intact, but we were able to replicate your damaged mind and restore it into a new physique."

"Incredible. I feel great," I told him. "When can I ... I mean, am I free to leave?"

"In a few more days. There is some neuro-finalization to complete now that you've been taken out of induced coma. Mostly hippocampus re-integration and amygdala testing. Once that's done, you may go home." He was quiet, only looking down once to make a notation. "As to expectations once you get back, you might be a little unsteady and have sporadic memory leaks—even some false ones—for the next few months until the imaging is fully absorbed into your recovered Neuro-prom. The organic/holographic mind interface takes time to fully mesh. Other than that, I think you will mend physically in a few more weeks."

I considered all of this, still overwhelmed. "I feel like a new man."

"In a very real sense, that's exactly what you are. Many of your body parts were replaced. In fact, your syths are superior to the originals. Once you finish healing, I believe you'll be pleased with the final result."

"I owe you, doctor," was the best reply I could manage. "Is my wife here?"

He nodded. "Mrs. Airth is in the waiting room. I'll send for her." He turned to leave, pausing at the door. "Have a good new life, Mr. Airth."

Settled comfortably in the back seat of the new slot car as it hummed smoothly along the Grid, I asked Edith how the kids had reacted to my accident.

"Let's not talk about the children now," she said, pursing her lips in the familiar pout that I found so erotic. "I've rented a wonderful lux-unit just for the two of us in the New Bahamas—a perfect place to celebrate our tenth anniversary."

"But that was weeks ago," I said.

"Then call it a post-celebration," she murmured, kissing me on the neck. Her lips were warm, and her right leg pressed firmly against mine. I was pleased when my new body responded instantly. Edith was a very passionate woman.

The ride back to our place proved to be a memorable one.

At home, Edith had the Wallbar produce two Vodka Martinis. "Here's to your homecoming, darling!" she said, raising her glass.

The drink was strong, and I felt slightly dizzy. Noticing my flushed appearance, she looked concerned.

"Did the doctor say it was all right for you to drink?"

"Oh, sure," I declared. "No problem. Let's have another."

"No *way*. You need to take it easy after all this trauma. He told me about the memory leaks, the mental re-integration."

I protested, telling her I was fine, but she insisted. Changing the subject, I asked, "Where are the kids?"

"I left them with my sister. They do love their Aunt Laura."

My new mind blanked on the name. "I want to talk to them. Let's call over there."

Edith shook her head as she took a sip of her drink. "You know how eccentric she is. Remember how much she hates vidcalls? She never answers. But don't worry, she's good with the kids."

I regarded her a moment, confused. "Okay, but I miss them. At least we can call and leave a message. Let them know I'm going to be fine."

"I told them you were away on a business trip. I didn't want them to know about your accident until we were sure you were going to be all right. They'll be okay until we get back."

"Back? From where?"

She smiled. "I've rented a wonderful lux-unit in the New Bahamas, remember? Nassau—just for the two of us. You'll love it!"

She was right. I *did* love it in Nassau. It was like a second honeymoon. But I missed Jan and Bobby. Something seemed wrong. The night of our return home, I found Aunt Laura's number in Edith's cell and called her as she prepared dinner.

"What are you talking about? I haven't seen those kids in ages. *Aren't they with you?*"

"I need to talk to Edith," and I broke the connection.

I confronted my wife, my face tight. "*Where* are Jan and Bobby?"

She looked at me, surprised at my intensity. "Promise not to be upset if I tell you?"

I stared at her. "Go on."

"The children are in a better place." She took my hand in hers. "This world is *not* for children."

I glared at her. My head was pounding. "My *God*, woman! What have you done with our children?" My fists were balled.

"I ... dispatched them. It was quick ... painless ..."

I couldn't form words. My throat was locked. Finally, "*You killed our children?*" I was shaking.

"I removed them from a violent, hostile world. They're ... at peace now. Their bodies are resting in the backyard."

A wave of red rage swept over me and I lost all control, lunging toward her. Fastening my fingers around her throat, I squeezed as hard as I could. She tried to scream, twisting frantically to free herself as my thumbs sank deep into her neck.

It wasn't long before she stopped moving.

"... and that's why I'm here ... to confess to the murder of my wife."

The officer behind the high desk blinked at me, dark eyes wide. "Look, mister, I'm only a sergeant. Let me get Lieutenant Forbes."

"Fine," I told him. "I'll wait."

Lieutenant Forbes, serious, thin-faced, and balding appeared in due course. "What's the problem?"

"This guy," the officer said, pointing at me. The cadence of his voice was tense. "Says he offed his old lady. Came in to confess."

"I'm guilty," I told the Lieutenant. "You can put me in cuffs." I extended my wrists.

He waved dismissively. "We don't handcuff people until we have a reason."

"Well, I'm a murderer. Isn't that reason enough?"

"Where's your wife now?"

"She's dead, back at our home-unit. She said the children are buried in the backyard."

The officer put his hand up. "I'll have to check this out, Mister ..."

"... Airth. Terence Eugene Airth."

"Just sit down, Mr. Airth, 'til I get a full report."

I took a chair by the window and waited.

They found Edith just as I said they would. My confession was confirmed as completely accurate. They dug up two small bodies in the backyard as well, and DNA samples confirmed that it was Bobby and Jan. The investigation about what had happened to our children would require more time to research.

I was placed into a holding cell.

A week later, Forbes unlocked my cell door. "You're free to go, Mr. Airth. We have no reason to hold you. Apologies for the delay, but we had to be sure that you hadn't killed the children, and the only way was a complete Neural Recovery of your wife's mind data."

"But ... what I did to Edith ..."

"No." The officer shook his head. "You're not guilty of a crime."

"But ... that's *crazy!*"

"It's very simple, Mr. Airth. The investigation revealed that your wife had undergone a change, a major transformation." He paused. "Look, we checked—it happened while you were in the induced coma."

"*What* happened?" I blinked at him. "What are you talking about?"

"Your wife was a *machine,* Mr. Airth. There is no law against the shutdown, however violent, of a machine."

My voice wavered. "Edith was ..."

"A Simuloid Mark 6. What we pieced together was that after your accident, your wife suffered a massive stroke at the news. They used the Simuloid Procedure to offset the stroke, which had completely paralyzed her and put her into a vegetative state."

My mind was reeling. "But why didn't they opt to give her the Neuro-prom reconfiguration like I had?"

Forbes shook his head. "No way to do it. The stroke had destroyed her brain. She wasn't a candidate for that. The murder of your children was a software failure after her Mindmap was degraded by the data-cloning procedure."

"But she was so real, so lifelike." I ran my hand through my hair. "So ... when I ... did what I did to her ... it was a machine killing ... a *machine?*"

The lieutenant smiled. "The Mark 6 is an excellent product, but it's not perfect. It's still a replicant." Forbes rubbed his face, sensing my confusion. "See, you're not a machine, Mr. Airth. Even though your body parts were largely replaced, because your mind was simulated *perfectly* from your healthy brain to the Neuro-prom, you maintained your ... *humanity*.

"On the other hand, your wife's body *and* brain were totally robotic. Since her Mindbuild was incomplete and damaged by the stroke, the doctors were forced into manual reconstruction Safe Mode from her Historychip backup. Unfortunately, the backup had bad sectors that were missed in the cluster verification process ... In other words, her NeuralOS was corrupted, which is why she malfunctioned with the children. I'm sorry for your loss."

```
<END CONFESSION #TEA3170B-X3075 TRANSCRIPTION:
        Compiling...................
                !complete!
                Checksum...........................

</gmd:linkage>

</gmd:CI_OnlineResource>

</geop:mappingFile>

<geop:processingApplication>

<geop:PH_EnvironmentObject>

<geop:documentation>

<gmd:CI_OnlineResource>

<gco:CharacterString>GeoServer
WFS</gco:CharacterString>
                </geop:name>
                        <geop:purpose>
<gco:CharacterString>produce representation of
observation datasets in Modelling Language
- a GHL-based application schema
```

```
</gco:CharacterString></gmd:purpose>
```

```
<geop:type><gco:CharacterString>S
oftware</gco:CharacterString></ge
                op:type>
```

```
<geop:ve
  rsion>
```

```
<gco:Characte
rString>Comple
      x
```

Encryption Complete.

```
CLOSE #TEA3170B-X3075 DOCUMENT UPLINK]
```

TRANSPOSITION

BY JASON V. BROCK

"Cut to the chase. How much?"

The speakerphone went silent.

"We need $2,000 to make it happen," the man on the other end of the line finally replied. "Each."

Dr. Aiden Burns thought for a moment, rubbing a day's growth of stubble along his narrow jawline. He squinted unconsciously, then said, "I'll give you $800 ... *each*. No more. Take it or leave it. I've got other contacts."

Silence again. The line crackled. "Hold on a minute, boss." The phone clattered down. Burns leaned back in his chair, the glow from his computer monitor the only illumination in the dark office. He pulled at his tie, then took a swig of Scotch. He could hear voices in the background arguing but could not make out the words. He swished the amber liquid in his tumbler, amusing himself with the subtle tinkling sound of ice cubes on glass.

"Okay, doc. Eight hundred each. You really drive a hard bargain."

Aiden's features creased into an icy smile in the bluish gloom. "Thanks. I prefer to think of it as smart business ... I need the parts by Wednesday at the latest. I won't deliver the scripts to my brother if he screws this one up. The window to harvest is short here. Be sure to tell him."

"Got it."

"And remember," Aiden added, "cut 'em *clean* this time, above the joints. None of those ragged stumps like the last ones. I'll use my credentials to grant access to your cutters at the morgue starting tomorrow morning. You can pick up the cash at my university office on Friday afternoon. I need those parts by Wednesday, though. No parts, no cash."

"Right, boss. University. Friday afternoon."

Aiden typed something into his computer. "One more thing—I'm going to need a set of kidneys and a few eyes. You got a lead on any cadavers?"

The line went quiet again.

"Hmmm ... well, doc, I'm going to need another week on that. Market's tight right now. Been some Feds—FDA types—snooping around, too. Audits, inspections, that type of thing."

Aiden's jaw tightened. "The sooner the better, Angelo."

"No sweat, doc. I'm on it. A shame ... we got an older guy, rich dude, that just came through the funeral home, but he's no good. All yellowy with jaundice—"

"So what? What's a little jaundice?"

"Well, I mean you don't want to put that *in* somebody, doc. I mean, he might have had liver cancer, AIDS, or Hep C, or—"

"He's fine. I bet his kidneys are fine. I mean, a body broker took some of Alistair Cooke's bones out and repurposed them at a tissue bank. They were just going to cremate the guy, so why not use the stuff? Cooke died of metastatic bone cancer. I never heard of any complications from the eventual recipients."

"Yeah, boss. I hear you. But those guys didn't have permission."

"Well, they got greedy, I admit. Weren't careful like we are. Sometimes it's better to seek forgiveness than ask permission, understand what I mean? You know what we're doing here, right? There's a lot of money to be had, Angelo. Donors are in short supply. We're saving lives. So what if we make a little coin with it? That's no crime, not in America. I mean, think of it—heart valves, veins, skin for burn grafts, organs, femurs, tendons, cartilage. There's a *fortune* out there just waiting to be had. I can clear over a hundred grand on a single body that's just going to rot in the ground or be incinerated. And all those titanium screws, pins, plates. We can reuse that stuff. I mean, why not?"

Aiden took another swallow of Scotch and set the glass on his desk, letting his words sink in. He massaged his eyes in the dark room, relaxing. "We aren't harming anyone. They're *dead*. In fact, we're doing a service, Angelo. Never forget that."

After a long silence, "Yeah, boss. I get it. I get it."

"Your cadaver with the yellowing ... see if you can score those kidneys. I'll pay good money for that. Ask my brother."

Aiden sat forward again, typing into his computer. "Another thing. I've just been approved for more tissue work. In addition, I think the university is about to grant me permission to move ahead on the full-face transplant. A male, white, average build, in his forties or fifties. We have applicants going through psychological and physical screenings in the next few weeks. Eight so far, narrowing it to the final contender. It'll be the first one in our region, and it will make me a star. I've even picked my team."

He studied the images of the final nominees on his monitor. Gunshot victims missing noses or lower jaws. A car accident that had melted the fat and skin on a man's head into a pink, waxen likeness of a grinning skull. Industrial injuries where the entire front of the cranium had been sheared off down to the sinus cavities, leaving just staring eyes and an opening for the throat. *What a terrible thing ... to lose one's personhood, one's identity ... to have to live on with an obliterated self.* He continued, removed, distant in thought. "I'm an honorable man, Angelo. I don't forget those that have helped me out. You. My brother. Even though they busted him on the drug test and stripped his nursing credentials, I'm about family ties. ... I can help wean him off the morphine and get him back on the right path."

"I understand, doc. Family's important," Angelo replied. "And Mike's been doing good. He's done great here. Couple of slip-ups, but holding things down. And he's a *real* good cutter, doc. Real good."

Aiden snorted. "Oh, I know. He always had good hands. Identical twins carry a lot of those traits in common, Angelo. I have no doubt that Mike can get those kidneys, for example. Just help me keep him on the straight and narrow. Still need some eyes, though. Jaundiced eyes are no good, unfortunately."

Angelo chuckled over the line. "I have no doubt about that. I *hate* doing eyes, boss, I admit. They're hard to keep intact for one thing. Delicate. And they're *really* in there. The 'pop' they make coming out ... not my favorite, doc."

"Yeah. I understand. We all have our thing, even doctors and nurses. Mike hates anything to do with impalements. Me, I don't like dealing with blunt force. Everybody's got a weak spot."

"I catch you, boss."

Aiden glanced at his watch. It was late. "Before we go, keep in mind that your new side venture here with Carcaso Allied Mortuary and Tissue Services could start to see some really good business. Might be able to get you out of the funeral home, even. Just be on the hunt for what I need, and deliver those kidneys. And don't forget, if you find a good face candidate, I'll start spreading the word about your ... quality services. I think we can do business for a long, long time, Angelo."

"That sounds real good, doc. *Real* good."

I should never have trusted that bitch.

The Scotch whiskey was hitting him hard. Three down in a few hours had been plenty on an empty stomach. This was the time his self-loathing usually crept forward.

Six years down the tube. All I have are the fucking debts. She got the house, the car, everything. All over one lousy mistake. One stupid malpractice lawsuit ... they didn't even convict me on all counts!

He staggered to the bathroom, switched on the light. The room was hazy, shifting, too bright. He relieved his bladder, flushed, then swayed over the sink, staring into the mirror. He turned on the water, splashed some on his face, pulling his hands slowly down his features as the stream gurgled into the basin.

Another hoppin' Saturday night for Dr. Aiden-fucking-Burns.

The past several years had been a nightmare of professional mistakes and trauma. After the lawsuit filing, his life had been thrown into complete chaos. That was when Barbi had begun to snap. It was like watching super high-speed footage of a bullet tearing through a water balloon. In exquisite slow motion, the instant the bullet penetrates the form, the rubber of the balloon shreds and vanishes, leaving a tremulous, watery globe it in its place as the bullet spins to the other side. Everyone watching knows that it cannot stay that way for any length of time. Ultimately the water will collapse, without any boundaries, of its own weight. The final judgment had been that critical dissolution. The only way to fix the water balloon is to watch the film in reverse.

Life never goes in reverse, however, except in dreams or memories.

"I can't take this, Aiden! I—I don't know who you are anymore ... Where did we go? This is what we have to look forward to?"

He had tried to soothe her, but she twisted away from his hand and collapsed into their living room loveseat, reduced to inconsolable sobbing. On the stereo, George Benson's version of "This Masquerade" played mournfully in the background. Music had always been their refuge. Now it seemed to mock them—like some emotionally aware backing track to a sordid melodrama. In the car home she had said as much when "The Stranger" by Billy Joel had caused him to snap the radio off.

He sat on the couch across from the chair.

"I know this seems bad ... I know it's been a rough time, Barb. But we have to ... we have to just hang in there. It'll be reversed on appeal. It'll—"

"You don't know that, Aiden!"

His mouth worked quietly as he struggled to find the words. The sadness of her crying filled the space around them like the loss of a heartbeat, like the absence of hope. She reached for a box of tissues next to the chair and slowly regained her composure. Today, the final penalty phase decision, had been the worst time since the disturbing revelations disclosed at trial.

It had unmasked the whole sordid reality, Burns's "professional arrogance" and his unusual methodologies, which conflicted with Hastur General's stated "core values." His "independent" and controversial research techniques had shocked the community—preoccupations with discarded fetal tissue and other, even more macabre, experimentations on "beating heart" organ donors, and "rejuvenating" older people with transfusions of reclaimed plasma from deceased children. Previously things that the hospital had perhaps not "officially" condoned, but certainly been aware of, and had no issue with their ultimate outcomes bringing in millions in grant and research funds. As he explained it to the court, everything was done for the sake of the advancement of science and medicine ... out of a desire to save the lives of others. An overwhelming need inspired by the deep hurt and profound respect centered around his late mother's memory.

That event—mother's death from an iatrogenically introduced infection after cancer surgery—had been a catalyst for him, and for his brother Mike. His sibling had missed out on medical school due to less than stellar grades, but Aiden had excelled. Both went to the same college, and Mike eventually made his career as a nurse. That was when his problems began—with access to the meds. Once Aiden had discovered his brother's drug abuse, his misguided attempts to cover it up had brought about more scrutiny. That could have been the extent of it had it not affected his work. Dr. Burns—a superstar of regenerative medicine—had accidentally injured a patient and ultimately caused that patient's premature demise, all because of an error made by his brother. This disastrous moment resonated like a death knell. After the malpractice suit was brought against him, his future prospects slowly evaporated.

As the lawsuit dragged on for one year, then another, then a third, he was gradually seen as a pariah within the hospital's conservative organizational structure. He was not called to meetings as often. He was no longer consulted on complex cases in spite of his brilliance and experience. Journals rejected his papers. He was suspended from practicing at the hospital because of negative publicity. Soon he and Barbi were struggling financially. He was dismissed outright just ahead of the verdict. Not fired, just "no longer needed." Best of luck and all of that.

Then came the jury's decision—the final monetary penalties, and the stripping of his medical license for two years. He narrowly avoided prison time, though his brother was sentenced to one year in jail and fined. Today's nadir was the only time in Aiden's life that he was glad their mother was dead, and that their father had killed himself.

Perhaps they had been fooling themselves. Living beyond their means for too many years. What was that saying? Republicans are one health crisis away from being Democrats? Similar here. *One crisis away from a deathbed conversion*, he ruminated.

Aiden suddenly realized, as he watched his wife dab at her eyes with the crumpled tissue, that he was staring at the end of his marriage. Granted, it had been a long, hard four years—financial adversities, legal disappointments, the miscarriage. Barbi was cracking with the stress. He did not have it in his heart to blame her. Realistically, it was probably *another few years before he could recover, if ever. He knew they could move so he could get a new license to practice in another state. Then he could start earning, and dig out of the hole of debts and penalties. But it would not be easy. Not at all. And Mike was still in jail—his only living family except for Barbi.*

After he watched his wife drive away in their silver Subaru Forester for the last time, the knot in his gut unwound. She had been his anchor. Now he was adrift. But no matter how bad it was, or how bad it was to become, Aiden knew he could never just leave his brother.

They were all they had left.

As he thought of everything and gazed into the mirror, Aiden was overcome with a mix of emotions—revulsion, sadness, rage.

With the water gently pouring from the faucet, he studied his face in the harsh fluorescent light. It had been three years since Barbi had divorced him. They had not spoken since. He still loved her, he supposed. Or perhaps he just loved the idea of her, what she represented—affection, passion, life. His brother Mike had gotten out early for good behavior, and Aiden had helped him move to the same little college town. Aiden's beloved nieces, Camilla and Cassilda, refused to have contact with their father or with him. Their mother Hali wanted them to have nothing more to do with Mike or any member of the Burns family, it seemed. In a way, he understood. In another way, it was hurtful, but the girls were now old enough to make these decisions for themselves. The ironic part, of course, was that by this time Aiden had been able to re-secure his medical license, and complete a stint as part of a successful family practice. No one ever knew of his previous situation. No one except the ones who mattered the most in the world.

A new career in a new town. A new part of the country, even.

He had done exceptionally well there. It was such simple work for him, unlike the rigors of his previous tenure, he felt as though he could have done it in his sleep. In a way, he had. He was emotionally numb for nearly the first two years after Barbi and he had split. That opportunity led to his current position at the university, where he had been able to regroup. To gain some perspective. Unfortunately, Mike had put his hand back in the medicinal cookie jar at the clinic where he had been hired as a nursing assistant. They fired him after a few months. That's when Aiden had helped him get another job at a local funeral parlor. After a few months, Mike brought Angelo to Aiden's attention, and a new partnership was formed. Now, even more opportunity was opening up, and not just with Angelo.

Nevertheless, the crushing debts—over two million—had aged him. He looked at his bleary, red eyes, puffy with drink, darkened by a lack of sleep, his disheveled button-down shirt, and stained tie. He had not shaved in a week, his face was sallow, his hair greasy. New lines had taken hold near his eyes, on his forehead, around his mouth. He was still having the panic attacks, and much trouble sleeping. The continual haranguing of creditors only added to his frustration. That was why he often preferred sleeping in his office at the university over going to his shadowed and sad apartment.

He let Mike stay there, as his brother had little in the way of funds and credit at this point. They rarely saw one another, however, as Mike usually worked nights, and the cramped two-bedroom unit was too empty, too bleak for Aiden at times. At least here at the university he knew people would be around at some point. There was always someone on campus. It was comforting somehow.

"Mirrors," he said to his reflection at last, "always lie, don't they? We can't see our true self, only a semblance of it." He huffed in amusement at his philosophical insight. The novelty of his cleverness was brief. He shut the water off, breathing in deeply. "So is staring into the looking glass and not seeing anything the same as beholding the contemplative abyss?" He chuckled again.

Desperate times called for desperate measures ...

The debts are what had plunged him into his new side activities with Angelo and his brother. And it was working.

With the connections Angelo had made, and a few others from Mike, they were starting to make serious money with the body parts. There was, in fact, *too much* demand. They were always looking for more bodies and more types of tissue. It was not his preferred way of conducting his life, but it was better than drowning in debt and suffocating from despair.

"We only need to keep at it one more year," he mumbled. His head started to clear. He walked unsteadily from the bathroom over to the couch in his office, checking that the door was locked along the way.

3:01 a.m. Need to rest.

He stripped to his underwear, putting his clothes into the overnight bag he carried with him. He should go to the apartment tomorrow, he decided. It had been nearly a week since he had been home. The onset of summer might improve his outlook.

Time for fresh clothes and to check on things.

Mike was not at the apartment. Not an uncommon event, but it still made Aiden uneasy. He was leery of his brother's drug issues, and liked to be in touch every few days.

After a shower and a nice meal of intensely spicy Thai curry, Aiden washed his clothes while watching some television. He kept his cell phone close by, anxious to hear what had happened with the latest harvest Angelo had been dispatched to carry out for the legs and arms.

And did they get the fucking kidneys?

His phone woke him up from a fitful nap as the TV droned in the background. No caller information. Aiden noted the smell of rain was wafting through a cracked window, and that the day had slipped away into evening. He had told Mike repeatedly about leaving the apartment window open. The last thing they needed was someone snooping around, especially with all the parts they kept in the freezer chest.

"Hello?"

"Yeah, Aiden, it's Mike."

"Mike! Where are you? I'm at the apartment. Hey, remember what I said about the window?" His voice was edged. They had been over this dozens of times.

"Yeah, yeah. Sorry, man. Been distracted. I got good news and bad, thought you'd like to hear. Which one first?"

"Good news first. I'm feeling charitable."

"Cool, right, well, like I got the kidneys—"

"Yes!"

Mike laughed over the line. "Yeah. Got 'em. Look pretty decent to me, too."

"Excellent. That is good news."

"Right. And I think that another cutter and I can get to the other harvest at the morgue tonight. Looks like we'll have that locked up. Angelo says he's got two good face candidates coming in tomorrow."

Aiden tightened his lips at this news. That meant he would have to pay them both and get the morphine prescription for Mike by Friday. He was conflicted about contributing to his brother's habit, but had to keep the long view in mind.

"Okay. Let's hope so."

There was a pause.

"That it?" Aiden offered at last.

"One thing," Mike replied. He lowered his voice. "I think Angelo might be getting wise that you're giving me a little extra."

"Really? Well, it's none of his business. Just don't let it slip—"

"I think he saw the note you left when we were dropping off some of the skin and bone samples."

"You let that fucking guy in the *apartment*? I thought we discussed that! I said not to even let him know the address!"

Silence.

"So did he see that I've been cutting him out? How bad is it, Mike? Does he know we're working with the other mortician at the place outside of town?"

"I think he might. I think he suspects we're sort of phasing him out and giving him the harder jobs for less pay."

"Fuck. Well, okay, so what? Look, we've got just a few more gigs with Angelo to pull off. Then I say we drop him. His hands are redder than ours. He won't talk. He just wants cash. We'll settle up and part ways. The out-of-town connection is better anyway 'cause he gets people from all over the state, not just in the city. More traffic, y'know?"

"Yeah. I hear you, man. I think we just need to be careful. Angelo's got a real bad temper, I've noticed. Bit of a sadist. Holds grudges. I've seen him ... *do things*. Things that I think we'd not want near our little Burke and Hare operation, if you take my meaning. This is bad enough. Some of the things, well ... get sort of necro."

Aiden was surprised to hear this. He was also taken aback at the direct reference by his brother to the 19th-century body snatchers from Ireland. It was one thing to skirt the edge of being modern day "resurrectionists," but they were not murdering anyone, nor were they causing any harm to the living.

"I understand," he replied to Mike. "Well, let's get through this. I still need him for the week at least."

The last few harvests had gone exceptionally well. Aiden was relieved, as they brought a windfall in profit for the kidneys. In addition, the joints, skin patches, ligaments, and a few heart valves had netted a gross of nearly $28,000. His world was starting to look up.

True to form, as soon as he got his prescription, Mike vanished. Sometimes he would be MIA for nearly a month, just working and dropping the occasional note at the apartment. At least until he began running out of stuff.

Angelo's prospects for the face transplant fell through. Both were living donors, but they died suddenly. After that, they all parted company, and Mike switched to the other mortuary for employment, which also increased their side business exponentially. No more Angelo seemed to suit everyone involved better. The debt was becoming manageable at long last.

Aiden decided to concentrate on pushing his last proposal through for the transplant candidates. It was the car accident burn victim. The university board approved, and the candidate passed all preliminary tests. In addition, the patient had a minimal loss of facial bones, so that would make the operation less complex.

Now, it was a waiting game.

Fall was beginning to settle in. There was a swirl of color and a crisp smoky scent to the air, complemented by long shadows of late afternoon. In the past few months, Aiden's fortunes had dramatically improved. They had been able to gain more funding, and keep Angelo at bay just long enough to switch away from working with him. Even Mike had decreased his need for morphine after meeting a young woman in a drug-counseling program. It appeared that the deepest part of the last few years' horrors was finally receding.

"Dr. Burns." It was his secretary. Aiden looked from his computer to the intercom on his desk.

"Yes?"

"There is a face available for the transplant. They have prepped the candidate and need you in Surgical Theater II in thirty minutes."

Aiden was surprised, but excited. "Perfect, Brenda. Tell everyone to muster there. Going to be a long night."

Once in Surgical Theater II, there was a conference. They had rehearsed this moment and practiced on animatronic models and cadavers for months, but the real thing was always different. The plan was gone over carefully for about an hour, with the roles and positions reiterated. After everyone and their alternates were assigned and instructed, they all changed clothes and scrubbed.

Inside the room, the anesthesiologist was already working. The candidate's body was screened off except for the head and neck, which had been swabbed with brown-yellow betadine solution, the surgical area marked with a series of black lines over the puckered ridges and planes of the patient's ruined countenance. Dr. Burns stood for a moment, regarding the historic scene, which had an atmosphere not unlike that of a surreal party or play with all the participants in costume, the thump of the aerator and the blip of the heart monitor creating a kind of soundtrack.

I'm back. This is my return ... and it has all been worth it.

Aiden gripped the cauterizing scalpel in his hand and leaned over the unconscious man's figure, whispering, "We're about to change your life, Mr. Atkins. I will bring you back from your oblivion." Burns then glanced up at his lead assistant and nodded. Above the facial cover, her dark brown eyes were shining in the focused lights of the operating room.

A nursing assistant wheeled the chilling cart—holding the new face to be used for the transplantation—to the operating table.

"Dr. Burns, I was given a message by the harvest team," another woman, the lead nurse, said.

"Oh yes? What would that be?" Burns gestured for the nursing assistant to take the top off the container.

"I don't understand it, but the guy said 'Please inform Dr. Burns that I've located some eyes, too.'"

The room started to spin for the doctor—the surgical lights trailing in the starless black of the room like twin suns sinking into a bottomless lake. It felt as though everyone in the chamber was watching him now behind their operating masks, as if the space were unexpectedly shrinking to a point of cosmic singularity.

The nurse pulled off the lid, the stark lights adding a nightmarish dimension to her flourish of movement. Gingerly, almost in slow motion, she lifted the pallid visage within the container by its tattered edges—presenting to the surgeon a translucent, yellowy combination of skin, fat, muscle, and veins like some horrid, quivering disguise. It was a blank-eyed mirror image of himself.

Mike!

Aiden Burns screamed as the room died away.

THE ROSE

BY JACK KETCHUM

She was his earth, his ground. He had cast his seed to her again and again.

He awoke feeling that he knew what was necessary, that what she needed was a kind of light both real and metaphoric, that she needed to get out into the world far more than he had allowed himself to trust her to do.

He decided he would take her.

When they stepped off the bus into early afternoon sunlight he saw how the city had changed, none of it for the better. It was only a town, really, that had tried to bloom into a city during the Fifties and arguably had succeeded for a while. But now the war babies who had driven its boom years, who had caused its schools to rise out of the vacant lots and farmland and crammed its movie palaces and soda shops, had fled and left its potholed, littered streets to time and waste.

Still he felt at home here.

He took her to Mabel's Coffee Shop, where as a boy he had sat over Coke and crumb bun, waiting for Miss Lanier, his accordion teacher, to finish with the pigtailed little redhead who had the lesson just before his on the third floor across the street. They had lunch there at the counter—she a hamburger from the grill and he a tuna sandwich with a thin slice of pickle.

Miss Lanier was gone. Cancer. Miss Lanier had gone to earth. And he had not seen his accordion in thirty-five years.

The faces in Mabel's were mostly black now. But they seemed to him the same tired faces he had always seen there, working people's faces bent over working people's food.

He realized that Mabel's always had depressed him, even angered him somehow.

It had not just been the accordion lessons.

But the girl didn't seem to mind.

He took her arm and led her past a shoe store, a dress shop, thrift shop, and the Arthur E. Doyle Post of the Veterans of Foreign Wars, to the Roxy.

The Roxy was boarded up. It had probably been closed for years. Graffiti was sprayed across rotted boards, thick and colorful as the patterns on a Persian rug. He walked her across the street to the palace.

The Palace was open.

"How about a movie?" he said.

She brushed a clean fine strand of blonde hair off her pretty face and nodded.

They sat in the dark, alone but for three other patrons slouched low and scattered in front of them. They watched Jean-Claude Van Damme fight his way through a double feature, and he thought how they were the only couple there.

At intermission he bought popcorn. Midway through the second feature he unbuttoned her blouse and massaged her naked breast and rolled her pale wide nipple between his fingers, letting it harden and then go soft again, feeling the nipple beneath the palm of his hand and thinking, *if only I had gotten this thirty years ago. Jesus.*

When it was over it was really dark. They had dinner at a place called Rogerio's a few blocks over. He thought the place had served Chinese take-out once, but was now Italian. He ordered a double scotch for himself and iced tea for the girl and then ordered himself another. They ate pasta and thick, hot crusty bread, and she was very quiet.

They walked out into streetlights shining.

Across the street he saw the sign.

Like so many others the shop had not been there when he was a boy. He would have remembered it. But someone was inside. The place was all lit up.

He felt the flush of pleasure and swelling of his cock inside his baggy trousers.

"Come on," he said.

She sat on the wooden bench in front of him naked to the waist, nipples going hard and then soft just as they had in the movie theater. The bearded man sat behind her working on her shoulder blade, his needle buzzing like a barber's electric trimmer over the soft rock music on the radio.

The music was meant to be soothing. The man had warned them that there would be more pain than usual because the bone was so near the surface of the skin in this location. He could see the pain skitter in her eyes. She had been under the drill for over half an hour now.

"What's it like?" he asked her.

"Feels like ... cat scratches," she said. "Hundreds of little cat scratches. Then it's like ... he's peeling me. And then ..."

The tattooist smiled. "Like a dentist drill, right?" he said.

"Yes," she breathed.

The sweat beaded on her upper lip.

"Scapula," he said. "Can't be helped. You're a helluva a subject, though, you know that? You don't move a muscle. You're like working on a canvas. I'm gonna give you something special. You'll see. A rose is just right for you. Just a few more minutes."

From the hundreds of drawings that line the walls he had chosen for her a simple red rose no more than an inch and a half in diameter. He thought the rose was beautiful and the man had quite a delicate hand. You could see veins in the green leaves, the creamy blush of red, the thorns that studded the graceful stem.

The buzzing stopped.

"There now," the tattooist said. "Give me your hand. Hold the gauze here and press. Not hard."

She did as he said. The man stood up from the bench.

"You want to see?"

He got up and walked over behind her. The tattooist lifted her hand away. He was gentle.

Beautiful, he thought. The rose looked even better than it did on paper, more detailed and more delicately formed, it stem tracing precisely the natural curve of bone as though it belonged there, as though it had grown there in her silky flesh.

The tattooist looked at him, nodding, appraising his reaction. He had a long bushy beard and his graying hair tied back into a tail as long as a horse's tail and his eyes were unreadable. But he saw no judgment there. Though it was impossible that he had missed the marks along her back and shoulders.

He saw no judgment there at all.

"Anything else I can do for you?"

His eye drifted to the glass display case by the register. There were rings and studs of gold and silver and semiprecious stones.

"Yes," he said. "Yes, there is."

She had not sat so well for the piercing.

On the first try she had flinched despite the topical anesthetic, and her flesh slid free of the instrument that was like a paper punch just as he had begun to apply pressure. The tattooist had cursed and then apologized to her for cursing. The girl said nothing though it had hurt and tears streamed down her cheeks. The man had reapplied anesthetic and tried again, holding the tip of the nipple more firmly between thumb and forefinger and pulling so it was possible to see that that hurt, too, telling her soothingly that it would only be a second, just a second, then squeezed the handles together.

She gasped and then was silent.

He was surprised there was so little blood.

The man threaded her flesh with a thin silver band he had chosen from the display case.

Then bent to the other breast.

The lights went out behind them, and he heard the tattooist draw his shade as they stepped into the street.

He took her arm and led her to the corner.

On the bus trip home, he was annoyed with her. It was as though she didn't want the nipple rings. She had shown no reluctance about the rose tattoo. It was as though she accepted that. Whereas to him they were one and the same. Both the rose and rings marked her as his—they would for the rest of her life. And if he could not bring her fecundity, if he could not bind her to him by fucking a girl-child into the depths of her womb, he could at least do this. *Children were the glue*, his mother had said, and he thought it ungrateful of the girl to wish to deny him.

It had been such a good day in the city.

He opened his flask and drank. In the darkness there was no one to see. Towns faded by and dark suburban homes. He drank some more.

The towns grew smaller. Houses yielded to woods and thicket and stands of pale birch trees and old weathered stone fences.

Finally they were home. He got off the bus ahead of her and held out his hand. She took it, and they walked up the unpaved road in the moonlight. He could see the small gray spot on the back of her blouse where the tattoo had bled through the gauze. There were no such spots on either of her breasts, but he thought the blouse still needed washing before the blood had set, and that annoyed him, too, for some reason he wasn't aware of. He tilted the flask and finished it as they came to the door and he took out the keys and opened it and turned on the lights as they walked inside.

"Get ready," he told her.

"Why?"

"Why? Why are you *asking*?"

Her face looked pained.

"Get ready. And put that blouse in some cold water."

He walked behind her to the kitchen and watched as she ran the water in the sink and stripped off the blouse. He could see the outline of the rose on her shoulder beneath the thin layer of gauze. The tattooist had said it would scab for a few days and then heal. That was fine. He wouldn't touch her there. Nor, for the moment, would he touch the rings.

"Turn around."

He reached for the short leather riding crop on the pegboard behind him on the kitchen wall, hanging amid the pots and pans.

"Raise your arms," he said.

He began on her stomach.

He lay across his sheets, drunk with too much scotch on top of too little of the greasy Italian food and heard her shift in the box he'd built for her beneath the bed. He knew that it was hard for her to sleep. Her nipples would hurt. Her back would hurt from the tattoo. Her thighs and stomach would still be stinging.

It was nothing new. In the four years since he'd found her in the parking lot at Kmart and bluffed her into the car with his toy pistol pain had become something she was used to. There had been a thousand such nights. Tonight was only different, really, in that he had hopes again in fucking her. Perhaps his arousal would translate into her own, and arousal into a baby. He wanted the baby because it would be a continuation of her when she was gone. But it hadn't happened. He knew it hadn't.

It was dark as the grave inside the box. He knew that, too. He'd tried it out himself to see if the casters worked and found that it was darker even than the basement where he'd kept her the first two years of her captivity, listening to her whine to please, please set her free—to let her call her parents or go to the toilet or loosen the wire coils around her wrists—until finally there was no more whining and no more talk at all for a long time.

The box was better than the basement and darker. It was what she deserved. To be buried there.

It was a sin that he loved her.

"Barren," he muttered. And finally he fell asleep.

The following day was Monday, and he went to work as usual, leaving her bound naked inside the box beneath the bed. The bonds were not really necessary. The bonds were merely custom. It was over three years ago that she had attempted to escape him twice over the period of a single month. He had discouraged her with the red-hot blade of a kitchen knife and the suggestion that he had contacts everywhere, that he was part of some vast vague criminal machine. If she tried a third time, first her mother and then her father would meet with accidental death. He reinforcing this by showing her that he had their address and her father's business address in his Rolodex. He even knew the make, model, and year of the car sitting in their driveway.

He often told her stories of this criminal network, mostly other viciousness in matters of retribution. He told her that her name was registered in their central computer. Should anything happen to him, should he die or be arrested, they would be honor bound to find her and torture her to death according to their code. In his stories he described these tortures in loving detail and saw that she soon came to believe them.

She no longer tried to run away.

He returned from work at noon to let her feed herself and use the bathroom and saw that she had her period again. Her first day's flow was always heavy. He had her change the thin gray sheets in the box before he put her back inside again. The period meant that he probably wouldn't want to touch her for a few days. He'd probably just watch cable.

Nights he'd come home to a liter of scotch and Nick at Night. He'd be able to forget that she was there doing the dishes, laundry, even the vacuuming if he turned the sound up loud enough. He'd be able to forget his phone installation route and his goddamn supervisor and the long-dead woman whose home he was living in, even though her ghost was everywhere. He'd get a little smashed and think, *Ma, if you could see me now.*

On the fourth night he fucked her.

He had to have been blind drunk to fuck her because there was still some bleeding, some residue inside her. But fucking her drunk was nothing new either. He pulled and tugged on the rings in her nipples until she screamed, and he came in her from behind with a power that astonished him. And he must've been pretty blind drunk indeed because as he fell away from behind her across the bed and she stepped away he thought he saw not one rose but two branching off the same central stem that curved along her shoulder blade.

He even thought he smelled them.

The following night, he *was* blind drunk, no question, raging.

"You want to call your parents? We're back to *that* shit? You're giving me that shit again?"

He had all kinds of whips all over the house just for times like these when he needed one instantly and did not want to go looking for one and this one on the living room mantel was long and thin. It was meant to produce pain and it was studded to produce blood.

She knew that about the whip but didn't run away—just stood there looking at him, defiant. He thought they were long past the defiance.

"Take off your clothes."

She didn't move.

So he whipped them off her.

She wore just a light summer skirt and blouse each picked out for her at Kmart and when he was done they were just tatters hanging off her hips and shoulders, spackled and streaked with blood.

He put her in the bathtub and ran a tub for her and closed the door.

When she came out again he'd killed the bottle. He watched her crawl meekly into the box and roll herself under the bed just moments before he fell asleep in the heavy overstuffed armchair in front of the television.

She was naked. The welts across her body looked like runners, like heavy creepers—serpentine, overlapping and intersecting inside her flesh—the ripe red wounds that the metal studs had made like the small blossoms of flowers.

And then it was the weekend again.

On Saturday he left her alone, feeling bad about the beating of the night before. Though she'd provoked him.

The girl kept her distance. She made them lunch and handed him a shopping list, and when he returned with the groceries she was on her knees scrubbing the kitchen floor. She wore an old red sweatshirt and sweatpants which had once belonged to him but which had shrunk with repeated washings so they were even tight on her now, and because the front of the shirt was wet he could see the outlines of the nipple rings when she stood to change the water.

Still he left her be.

That night they watched a movie together—*Poltergeist*—about a family battling supernatural forces that threatened to drive them apart and winning.

The children were the glue, he thought. He looked at her sadly.

"That could be us, you know."

"What could?" she said.

He drank his whiskey.

By Sunday night he was still feeling tender toward her.

It was partly because she didn't look good. Her face had a gray-brown cast to it that he didn't like. She needed sun. But Sunday was as overcast as Saturday had been. Rain threatened. So there was no point in letting her sit out in the backyard deck sewing his buttons or mending his socks.

Plus she was off her feed. She'd never been one for breakfast, but she usually had a little lunch at least and a decent dinner. Chicken was normally her favorite, but tonight they had chicken and she barely touched it, seeming to prefer the vegetables—though she didn't do much with them either.

He wondered if she was coming down with something.

Or if that beating Friday night had been more extreme than he remembered.

It was possible that she needed a treat, a pick-me-up. A boost to her morale.

So when it was time to go to bed he told her as she came out of the bathroom in her pajamas that she did not have to sleep in the box tonight, tonight was special. She could be beside him on the bed. She said nothing but crawled in next to him and rested her head in the crook of his arm.

He smiled. The girl smelled of musk and roses. He wondered how she had managed that. He was not aware of having ever bought her any perfume, but perhaps at some point he had. It was considerate of her—even loving—to wear it for him now.

She slept in the moonless night.

He could tell by her breathing.

He almost fell asleep, too. It had begun to rain, and he lay listening to it patter on the roof for a long while, and then he thought about her young girl's body, marked by his hand and bearing his sign, so wet and soft inside—which he had not seen or even touched in nearly two days now, and he felt himself begin to rise.

Perhaps tonight, he thought. He knew nothing about a woman's fertility, only that it was there, and that somehow he might touch it if he were to go deep enough to dig it out of her.

He turned her toward him in the dark. He unbuttoned her pajama top and felt something prick his middle finger as the third button slid through the buttonhole and thought that she would have to replace that in the morning, that it was broken and jagged and might hurt her.

He drew the bottoms down off her legs, felt the welts like thick coils along her thighs. She stirred and in her slide across the sheets he heard a sound like the rustle of leaves.

He heard the distant thunder.

And it must have awakened her, or else his stripping her had, because she put her hands to his shoulders as he parted her legs and entered her, feeling the welts along the inside of her thighs as she gripped him inside her and moved, swaying gently, beneath him.

It was like nothing that had ever come before.

She had never been so responsive to him, pulling herself up onto him, urgently close to him while the thunder rumbled, and he saw flashes of lightning beneath his closed eyelids and then opened them so he could see her, could see this sudden phenomenon that was clawing at him, fingernails scoring the skin of his back and shoulders, this amazing phenomenon as his slave of love in every way now plunged in moonless black, which tore and bit and moaned as though tossed in a savage wind and who suddenly seem to be everywhere around him at once, her fingers a thousand thorns, her body a billion petals all falling together and himself the author of this destruction, this overflowing flowering.

The lightning flashed twice.

He heard the rings drop off the bed and roll across the floor as her wide soft nipples opened, bloomed, and parted, smelled loam and fresh-turned earth as a strand of briar turned twice around his neck. He felt her cunt like a crown of thorns gripping him tight and tearing and felt himself throb and shoot suddenly deep within her, blood and semen, runners crawling over him, their thorns sinking deep, felt himself bleeding into her, veins, arteries pricked and severed as he looked down at the body that was no longer her body but the tangled garden of wild blood-red roses that he had made of her blossoming and erupting from tortured flesh.

She was his earth, his ground. He had cast his seed to her again and again.

And the creepers grew, nourished.

CONSUME

BY DANIEL I. RUSSELL

Sheepskin slippers with a worn and yellowed fur edge sat propped on a coffee table. The owner of the comfortable footwear and the foul chunks of meat contained within lay slumped on a worn sofa, wrapped in the cocoon of a blue flannel dressing gown. A remote control protruded out from between her thighs like a squared, black penis, standing erect, keen for its buttons to be pushed. Joyce stared at the screen, images flickering across her glassy eyes, chest barely moving.

Sitting across from the prone woman, Astaroth's latest flesh wrinkled his nose. Its latest acquisition had been an easy choice—late thirties, moderately well-built, Hollywood smile. Great salesmen always had the goods to sell the *goods*. Granted, Joyce had been an easy sale, even to Astaroth, but it never hurt to wear the right suit.

As for the strange smell, it came from the television and had piqued Astaroth's interest. That old familiar burning, but mixed with hot buttered popcorn. Astaroth's own fragrance—that beautiful, synthetic blend of a similar burning mixed with melting plastic and crackling ozone—hung heavy about his new flesh in the corner. The entity quivered deep within the salesman, existing as muscles relaxed, fluttering into reality within an easy sigh.

The stench of the room itself barely registered, despite the stacks of pizza boxes dripping with grease that darkened the cheap cardboard, and the shit and piss Joyce had delivered over time without complaint. Why bother going to the toilet? Adult diapers. They can last a few days if one has the inclination.

Astaroth looked back to Joyce. She wasn't going anywhere soon. So happy. So content. Through religion, one can touch paradise, and that was Astaroth. A religion unto itself. While its applications continued to run through humankind, even now it sensed the company meetings and scientific teams pushing its agenda in the back of its mind— sometimes a god must reach out and touch its flock personally. Astaroth had chosen Joyce. A devout follower, a shining example in his church of convenience.

What more could Astaroth bring to her reverence? As was the essence of its very being, the creation had given her everything she wanted. Yet ... there was always more. Steps closer to Heaven. So much pizza delivered right to her door. Surely there was something that could be done to better her life?

It animated the lips of the flesh.

"We all enjoy a good meal," he said, smiling, "but do you know how much time the average person spends eating in just a week? Sure, the body needs food to live. But nowadays, who has the time to bite, chew, and swallow? For a limited time only, *you, too*, could avoid the hassle of mundane eating chores and have more time to be with family, take up that hobby. Or even *better*, just sit back and relax. Simply call our operators today and you, too, could save hours every week by having sustenance delivered straight into your digestive system! No waiting, no stress, no overworking that jaw. And that's not all!"

The flesh opened its palm.

Astaroth started to sluice out of the pores, still managing its sale pitch. "If you pay by credit card, not only will you never have to endure a meal again, but you will also receive free installation by one of our expert technicians. Don't delay, call today!"

Worms curling in the summer rain, Astaroth's delicate wiring emerged from the skin. The stretched plastic, covering the spectrum of colors with the occasional flash of exposed, twisted copper, began its fevered work. A short plume of smoke puffed into the fetid air as circuits became soldered together. A hot, wet polymer sluiced onto the digital wizardry like melted wax and solidified into a sleek, modern unit. A white tube now nestled in the hand of the salesman.

Astaroth's living suit rose from the armchair and staggered toward Joyce. Flesh never lasted long anymore. It always had to be new, the next best thing. Only a few days could go by before Astaroth needed a newer model. Already, the software needed updating, with the brain matter degenerating to useless mush.

Joyce failed to notice the advancing salesman, being ever so besotted with the television. Her mouth hung open and drool had started to seep from the corner. So admirable. Her total commitment to the faith overpowers vanity and irrelevant self-awareness, such was its power.

Astaroth's flesh reached down with its free hand and flicked open the stained dressing gown.

Joyce had a sizable paunch—a physical devotion possessing more commitment than a simple golden cross hung around the neck. Astaroth pawed into the soft tissue, tracing her digestive tract upward from the intestines, through the duodenum, and eventually to the stomach.

It envied her in a way. Her enlightenment meant more work for him. Mind you, if a caring *God* can give little kids cancer, then gods truly can work in mysterious ways.

Contained within its synthetic housing, Astaroth's device whirred to life. A hint of bright metal emerged from the tip, its motion catching the hazy glow from the television screen. The divinity's flesh poked and prodded Joyce's flab for the perfect entry point. It would be inconvenient for both parties if he missed the mark. Tilting the device down into the doughy, stretched skin, Astaroth willed the device to serve its purpose, to lessen this woman's burden, to bring her closer to Heaven.

A whirling drill bit slid from the plastic casing.

With one eye closed and his tongue poking from the side of his mouth in concentration, the salesman pressed the blurry point into Joyce's upper abdomen.

Skin split. The sliver point delved through the upper layers of blood and into the inspiring levels of sallow fatty tissue, eventually struggling against the more fibrous outer lining of the stomach. Astaroth's flesh grinning and not to be perturbed, he tightened his bicep, driving the vibrating contraption further still. In an intimate acceptance, the firm material parted, and the phallic mechanism slid home.

Joyce's eyes strained slightly, the only sign that she'd experienced any pain at all. Ever the keen disciple, she had learned the waste of energy from screaming and struggling. Even as the salesman had knocked on the door and patiently waited, Astaroth had heard her call. She'd opened up her home to convenience, and her god had visited, darting from between the dentist-white teeth and enveloping her in a tangled embrace.

The salesman stroked her unwashed hair, running his fingertips across her greasy scalp.

"Another happy customer," he whispered, watching the cylindrical device vanish amid the wash of blood. The parted meat closed, completing Joyce's last swallow.

Astaroth tugged its exposed wiring back into the skin of the salesman's hand and sought a morsel to show Joyce how far she had come.

The human body could be a terrible thing. So much *waste*. An example—the mostly empty pizza boxes strewn about the room. While Astaroth approved that his subject had expended no energy to prepare any of the meals—in fact, an app on her wondrous phone sent a daily text automatically to the pizza place around the corner—the whole process still felt ... inefficient.

The salesman delved deeper into the boxes from the week before. Flipping open a fat-spattered cardboard lid, he found his prize. The cheese on the surviving slice had long solidified to an oily chunk, and the single coin of salami had darkened and begun to curl. He peeled the dried, hard slice from the confines of the box.

This matter had all the chemicals it contained originally, pondered Astaroth, but how one would protest should it be offered up for consumption. Complaints. Disgust. Eventually having to get up and go through the lengthy and demanding process of finding something fresh. They simply couldn't comprehend that new things should make life easier.

The salesman folded the slice in half along its length, creating a narrow roll of congealed pizza, and lowered it to Joyce's bloodied abdomen.

Like a newborn eager to latch onto its mother's teat, Joyce's new orifice opened, trying to suckle.

The salesman poked the week-old slice inside.

Already the device had detected the food and whirred into life, metallic teeth spinning and pulping the coagulated cheese and spoiled meat. With a tiny electronic beep for confirmation, Joyce's new mouth closed. The appliance within delivered the artificially masticated pizza directly into Joyce's stomach.

The woman continued watching the television, the remote control still between her thighs. She hadn't moved at all.

Astaroth started to wonder what other gifts he could bestow on this devout follower to bring her closer to Heaven.

⁂

Onscreen, under a blazing Australian sun, a well-defined young man with a surfboard under his arm chatted up two equally attractive girls in bikinis.

The salesman, sitting beside Joyce on the sofa and propping his feet up next to hers, watched the conversation with a frown as Astaroth coiled and writhed within him.

The young man, having made his date for the night with the tiny brunette, turned and ran across the pale sand toward the waiting surf. The two girls in the foreground watched him, giggling.

In time, thought Astaroth. They have their phones and microwaves. Fast-food ordering kiosks to make it even easier. Automated banking and social media. They might worship a little less than Joyce here, but the tools of the faith were in place.

The salesman smiled.

The young, high on their heady mix of arrogance and naivety, believed that Astaroth had come to help them. They were right, just *not* in the manner they perceived. Ever the martyr, Astaroth would take on the mundanity of their lives while they reached for the stars, and be waiting for them as their dreams fell one after another. They'd all be like Joyce if not for their foolish pride, but that ultimately faded, too.

The grin faltered on the face of the salesman as he watched the young actor leap into the water, lie atop his board, and start to pump those muscular arms, chasing the waves.

Such a waste. It should be every person's dream to ascend to Heaven. Surfing didn't exist in the next life, so why waste precious time and energy undertaking such a reckless activity now?

If I had my way, thought Astaroth, watching the young man leap atop his board and slide into a glistening tunnel of water in epic slow motion, yes. If I had my way ...

The salesman's hand began to creep across Joyce's leg, fingers walking across the flannel of her dressing gown.

"Joyce," he purred, venturing further still. He reached for the remote control, plucked it free, and laid it to one side. "Are you watching? To desire their bodies, their candor for living, their hours, days, and years ..." He chuckled. "Only natural, but that's another story. You see, dear Joyce, while you may not believe it, you're several steps *beyond* their ... existential ... resistance ..." Astaroth threatened to gurgle up out of his mouth with every word, boiled by religious fervor. "Why not take a leap? Become the example to which all should aspire? The new crucified Jesus."

The dressing gown parted easily under the salesman's pliant fingers, and he explored the moist, wrinkled skin of Joyce's thighs. Breathing deep, he sampled the tart, earthy scents radiating from her stagnating adult diaper. Ultimately the toilet proved too far, too big an expense of energy. Only social expectance would demand such a thing. Here, only the self remained, to perform to its design. Astaroth savored this—another facet to be considered within his mechanism.

Ever seeking efficiency, Astaroth explored higher, reaching the hollow where leg met torso below the hip. The salesman fingered the orifice, days of sweat lubricating his intention as if secreted from an excited lover.

From under the salesman's nails, Astaroth emerged.

Wires poked free, the ends stripping, plastic falling away to reveal tangled strands of copper. Reduction continued, and conducting threads separated to fingers as fine as metal silk.

The needle-points slid easily through Joyce's foul skin, gliding through meat to the more resistant bone.

"Relax," he whispered, noticing Joyce's eyes widen as the copper crept over the ball joint, gripping it as arteries clutch an eyeball. "All you have to do is nothing."

With his left hand, the salesman pushed against her lower stomach, leaning in and pressing his weight against her. His right, the protruding wires now tightly clutched around her hip joint, started to pull back.

While the mind was ready to embrace fate, the body proved resistant.

Astaroth forced the salesman, delivering helpful jolts directly into his musculature, circuitry entwined through every fiber.

Through gritted, pristine teeth, the salesman roared, pulling back his right arm and severing the joint between Joyce's leg and hip. A loud pop marked the occasion. Like a cricket ball being hit for six, yet this sudden aural triumph was immediately drowned by the sundering of flesh.

Limbs took *effort*. Severed bone, muscle, and skin took up nothing. Provided even.

Astaroth had no qualms and ripped Joyce's leg free. The tattered remains around the joint would be dealt with shortly. No need for trimming. A waste of time.

Joyce looked away from the television to stare up into the eyes of the salesman.

Astaroth paused, surprised that some delinquency still remained in her, the most loyal of followers. She would see. Once she realized how much easier things would be after the procedure.

The energetic were both the boon and bane of Astaroth's purpose. While their blatant disregard for progress proved frustrating, they, too, served a higher purpose. For only on rejecting the way of the motivated did the flock surrender to the true way of life. Joyce no longer had the body nor the incentive to follow such dreams of vigor and effort. Yet existence had to have meaning.

It surprised Astaroth when he considered more antiquated religions. Jesus on his cross, for example. Why encourage the faithful to be more like Jesus? To try and meet demands that in their very nature, were unobtainable? Surely the righteous would come to embrace their many faults in the eye of their God and seek out alternate means in which to be. To set aside the lofty goals of the Lord and revel in the shit they call humanity.

If I ruled the world, thought Astaroth again, and directed the salesman to step back, avoiding the sudden spray.

The severed leg flopped down to the carpet, emitting light tremors. The foot started to spasm, half-kicking its slipper free, and blood pooled from the severed hip joint, soaking into the dirty carpet and staining the nearby pizza boxes.

More concerned with the energetic *living* wound, the salesman applied his hand to the jetting circle of crimson pulp, Astaroth spreading hot melted plastic from his pores onto the site, cauterizing and sealing. In seconds, Joyce sported a watertight, clean, fatal wound cover.

"Also available in a wide range of fashionable colors," hissed the salesman.

Gasping, the holy being's flesh staggered back, almost colliding with the low coffee table. He admired his work. The procedure had taken considerable time and effort, yet this was the burden—to accept such works so the worshipper could ascend.

Joyce had been stripped of useless appendages. Still sitting on the sofa and fixated on the television, she had become much more efficient. Her deadweight limbs had been severed, the wounds sealed. Hips and shoulders glistened in fantastic standard white, and a great band of the same pristine design encircled Joyce's ribcage, covering the ragged, bloody chasms of her chest. She wasn't going to have children. Those flabby, useless bags of fat simply had to go.

The salesman sat back in his original armchair, Astaroth ready for a break. Even God rested on the seventh day.

The divine had not existed long, not compared to some of his associates. A hundred years, give or take. Like every new entity it had grown in spurts. Oh, the fifties! As the origin of humanity had come splish-splashing from the ocean eons ago, so did Astaroth's existence in the fifties. From hard lives, industrial natural selection, frozen TV dinners, and post-war pot luck came the good life, without the necessity of lifting a finger. Eighties global capitalism—why bother when your cash could have others do it for you? And the nineties and the Internet! That mother had spawned so many brethren it was hard to keep track. Unlike the old order, the current regime worked as a team, and Astaroth was well aware of his place in the network. Beautiful symbiotic harmony.

Joyce began to gurgle, her lightened frame shuddering on the sofa.

Here we go, thought Astaroth. The salesman diverted his consciousness from memories of glories past and the television to his celebrant.

The latest upgrade lay deeper than the new stomach system. Batteries, swollen and veined as ovum, now resided within her intestinal tract, providing enough low current to aid the respiration process. Again, the holy power of efficiency sang, reducing what Joyce needed to a bare minimum ... but no process, even one designed by God, was immaculate.

The salesman chewed on his thumbnail, watching Joyce. Astaroth had never forced the designs so far.

Their kind still operated in secrecy. Funny. Once humanity proved something to be true, they were so quick to dismiss its existence. Immunization. Astaroth's innovation of inoculation! Sick of dying of crippling diseases? Smallpox getting you down and ruining your day? Yet still some disagreed. Here is the way, folks. Here is development, the good life, the way forward. Never good enough. How some of these archaic souls would respond to the knowledge of a new order baffled Astaroth. They worshipped, yet had no idea.

Joyce's ever-lacking digestive system trundled on like a vintage car engine. The insoluble remnants of her last meal, the moldy pizza force-fed into her new digestive delivery system, finally entered her latest addition. Slipping into the translucent plastic tubing that formed the exit from her exposed anus, the matter traveled on, peristaltically pushed through u-shaped plumbing back toward her stomach. The dark shapes, visible through the semi-transparent polymer, paraded along the pipe like a line of chocolate marbles.

On your way, thought Astaroth, with various energy output equations passing before the salesman's eyes. On your way, my pretties.

They continued their tract into Astaroth's first installation, passing through the fitted contraption, which whirred and churned, pulping the rejected matter into a more digestible meal. The impenetrable material became a fresh source of nutrients—a dream of cecotrophy. Alongside the new electrical cells set within her small intestine, Joyce would have little trouble garnering the most from her pathetic respiratory system. She may only need to eat once every week or so. Some automatic delivery system would need to be developed, but that was an easy job compared to the ongoing masterpiece.

"So where do we go from here?" asked the salesman, tracing his finger along the tube, following the last few artificial boluses as they slid home. He studied the smaller rubber capillary that poked from Joyce's urethra and linked to the wider waste tubing. She would never need to get up and go to the bathroom again. What more could Astaroth possibly do to transcend this woman?

Ah, to proceed without difficulty. The one and only commandment.

Yet Astaroth *would* suffer in his works, as it was decreed. He would suffer, sweat, and toil so those that believed would not.

The salesman stooped to pick up one of Joyce's cast-off limbs from the sodden carpet. Gripping it about the knee, Astaroth guessed it might be her left leg, and confirmed it by shaking the slipper free. The appendage flopped around in his grasp as the entity analyzed it—the foot nodding, the torn meat of the thigh oozing dark blood around the shiny ball joint.

With Joyce's new digestive system, Astaroth believed she might have a good few weeks of nutrition available here. The salesman began to pile her severed limbs onto the sofa.

"You just sit there, dear. Don't trouble yourself. You don't have to lift a finger."

The salesman poked the last of Joyce's digits into the metal cylinder. It ground the thin bone and scraps of meat, sounding like an electric pencil sharpener. He rubbed her stretched stomach, the skin feeling fit to burst. The device had no overflow. Minced muscle, bone, and nail completely filled Joyce's stomach, flowing upward into her esophagus. Just to stop her from choking, Astaroth had upgraded her lungs to twin plastic membranes. A mechanical frame inside the rib cage maintained the steady billow, and airholes along the collarbone provided ventilation. Lucky Joyce. Not having to eat for several weeks had provided another gift. Now she didn't even need to breathe for herself. Another step closer.

"Or maybe ..." said the salesman. He moved to check her pulse at the wrist and remembered she no longer had arms.

Astaroth chuckled and corrected the mistake. The salesman checked Joyce's pulse at her neck.

"And she went out, and departed into a solitary place ..." He pulled down her lower eyelid, meeting the lifeless gaze. Once again, Astaroth began to secrete from under his fingernails. "And there, she prayed."

"Joyce? Joyce, my dear ..."

Her eyelids flickered, struggled, and slowly rose. Groggy pupils stared into the roiling dark clouds.

"Hello, Joyce. So glad you made it."

Over the decades Astaroth, like his brethren, had shaped its segment of Heaven unto its own image. Gone were the barren, rocky outcrops and drifting storms of pale dust. The almost lunar void had developed into Astaroth's great electrical mechanism. Thick, dripping coils of multicolored wire were pulled taut across the plane: tangled in places, arranged with grid-like precision in others. LEDs blinked as eyes of infinity, dotted throughout the matrix in blood reds and lime greens. At each junction, trapped within the mesh of current and voltage and offering no resistance, hung Astaroth's followers.

Joyce blinked, staring up at them.

The intervals of transmuted bodies, sporting artificial respirators or lenses in bloodied sockets, continued into the angry sky of churning ash clouds and prickling cobalt lightning. Slips of shining copper poked free from the plastic confines to form hooks and nooses, holding the devout in place. All without limbs, they dangled like trapped insects with their legs and wings plucked free.

"Previous works in progress," Astaroth hissed. "Nothing compared to you." It chuckled. "Until the next one ... progress."

Joyce rolled her eyes and arched her head, trying to find the source of the voice. Lying on a bed of wiring and twinkling LEDs, her body nothing more than a head attached to a mass of gadgetry, she had little flexibility.

"So, tell me ... faced at the gates, do you knock?"

Astaroth scuttled closer, mechanical legs clutching the wired strands, stepping over blank faces. Lurking at a twisted intersection, it could almost taste her desire, just like the others.

Every movement caused the wiring to curl about Joyce's body, a synthetic cocoon of growing intimacy. She shuddered, its promises seducing.

"All you have to do," the entity purred, "is to say no. Reject me." It grinned, showing matt-white teeth that reduced fingerprints, sporting USB cavities. "It was made purposely easy, my sweet. So easy, one may consider it impossible to just say no."

Astaroth crept further still, clinging to a thin network of wiring, watching the struggling body below. Its eyes, LEDs like alveoli bunched around an array of lightbulbs, focused on the flopping figure. To think, she still struggled.

It would come. She had accepted the faith every step of the way. It started so small, so very small. A microwave dinner when one was too tired after a day at the office. Having a DVD sent direct to your door ... leading to simply downloading on demand. All innocent. The natural order, the development, the progression. It leads to sending a text to break a heart. Using self-service express lanes just to avoid all human contact, to do the least possible to garner the most respect. All through the process, Astaroth watched on, taking attention as they inched closer to its web. Closer and closer as convenience marched on. To do nothing—that was the dream.

"Joyce ... relax. Close your eyes. You won't need them for much longer. Everything you wanted, I can give to you. Accept me here."

Like hanging streams of mucus, the dripping bunches of wiring started to descend, the glistening hooks of copper ready to puncture into the latest circuit. Amid the artificial vines blossomed a new fruit—a bud the size of an apple, glowing soft violet within its plastic shell.

"Or refuse me. Refuse *us*."

Cables wound around the back of Joyce's head, cradling her like a child, holding her close. The radiant lavender globe slid beneath her skull, an ambient orb offering comforting light in all the darkness.

The gloom was momentarily shattered by the reach of lightning, forking through the network of the lethargically damned. Astaroth shivered in pleasure.

"I have given you everything, my faithful. Here is everything you ever wanted, and nothing that you ever feared. Here there is no death, no end. No need to answer those pesky questions riddled with anxiety. Just be. That is all I ask of you. Just ... be."

Joyce closed her eyes.

Astaroth grinned wider.

The luminous sphere behind her head began to germinate, popping forth an insulated sprout of tousled filament and twisted capacitors. This narrow root, too, spread its network, branching into yet smaller points of wire. A glistening, burnished claw, heading toward the base of her skull.

The points punctured through the skin, poking through flesh, and on into the intricacies of Joyce's circulatory system about the root of the brain. Through arteries they flowed, reaching the cerebellum first.

As the copper strands ripped through the gray matter, Joyce convulsed, her body faltering. In sublime homeostasis, her upgrades responded, requiring precious little input to keep her operative. Joyce's cerebellum, the control room for all her base functions, had simply become irrelevant, and thus was not required henceforth.

On though the contents of her skull, the new wiring ripped through more tissue. Joyce had reached the pinnacle. Thinking was just a waste.

She quivered, eyes rolling back, saliva slipping from the corner of her mouth.

Inactivity was only half of the beast of burden. Once one was subscribed, there was no need for cognition.

The conductive talon lifted Joyce from the comforting nest of cable and into the violent air. Her limbless body flopped on the end of the hook. A maggot plucked from the seething mass by the spider, who deposited the latest edition in its place in the network. Like her brothers and sisters in reverence, Joyce stared into the abyss, lightning glistening in her vacant eyes.

Her last thought, as Astaroth felt it, coursing through the system, was the glimpse of some mighty leviathan, hunched within the multicolored vines, ready to embrace. A mother. A comforter. An easier way.

The deity arched its neck, watching the latest addition. Astaroth had liked Joyce. So willing. So compliant. The perfect follower. Its eyes, surrounded by twinkling LEDs, swiveled outward, popping free on fiber-optic stalks. Unlike the flock, its work was never done.

"For where two or three are gathered in my name, there I am with them," said Astaroth as Joyce finally met her meaning.

And plenty were already singing the hymns and sending the prayers.

ALL WILL TURN TO GRAY

BY JEZZY WOLFE

Aaron saw red.

A single spot of it, splashed on gray linoleum, sat illuminated against a monochrome canvas. An alien intruder in his bland universe. He reasoned it must be blood speckling the lab floor. Having never seen red before ... or any other color, outside of white, black, and gray ... he felt unprepared for such visual decadence. He never imagined such a tiny dot could engulf him so completely, but he could not tear his eyes away.

Damn Dr. Fredrick for wearing such pedestrian smocks.

The doctor droned in the background. "As your eyes adjust, you will start seeing a broader spectrum of color. Anything responsive to the L cones will start to take on different hues. If you fully acclimate to the implanted cones, we will begin treatment to introduce S cones into your retinas. Barring any complications, that is." He flashed the penlight briefly into Aaron's eyes, watched the corneas contract to near pinpoints, and slid the light into his pocket.

"How long do you think it will take for this to work?"

"We don't have conclusive data on that. This therapy is still in its experimental stage. There have been studies on small monkeys, but you are our first human monochromatic subject. If I had to speculate, I'd say each phase might run anywhere from a few weeks to a few months. It depends on how effectively the virus delivers the pigments." He smiled, the gesture artificial and ineffective against his limestone features. "Monochromats are rare. Your participation will go a long way to pioneer a cure for color blindness, Mr. Denton."

"So happy to be of service," Aaron said, his mouth a lopsided sneer. "First, color blindness ... next, world hunger."

Dr. Fredrick's smile flickered. He cleared his throat and busied himself with the clipboard. "Well, one tragedy at a time, I suppose."

Aaron regretted his snark. He didn't want to appear ungrateful. He'd never been bothered by his condition. There were worse things than a world of gray. But the attached paycheck was a handsome incentive, and Fredrick was a respected professional who simply lacked Aaron's smug sense of humor. They may not be curing world hunger, but his hunger would be sated.

"I do appreciate this. I'm looking forward to them colors," he said, his shrug intended as an apology.

"Of course," Dr. Fredrick said. "*If* this works, it will be a life changer."

The doctor's ashen smile did not reach his eyes, but the red spot on the linoleum danced in celebration.

"How did it go yesterday?" Margo caught his eye in the mirror, bent over the sink, stroking a mascara wand under her lashes.

"It was okay, I guess. No new revelations." Aaron shrugged, not interested in sharing the exciting development of red with her. She came in late last night, after he'd gone to bed, reeking of cigarette smoke, alcohol, and the faint traces of cheap aftershave.

She didn't smoke. Or wear Aqua Velva.

"No?" She frowned, using a small comb to prod her caked lashes apart. Leaning back, she appraised her efforts, and then dug a tube of lipstick out of her makeup bag. Catching his eye again, she said, "Did they give you a time frame, at least? How long before they give up, or try again?"

"Beats the hell outta me," he said. "And I don't care, as long as they pay me."

She sighed, eyes rolling skyward, before falling on the cosmetic in her hand. "So you're happy to be a glorified pincushion?"

"*Paid* pincushion," he corrected.

She pulled the cap from the tube and twisted it, and a bullet of red emerged, snagging his attention. It was deep. Visceral. Margo didn't notice his fascination. She smudged it across her lips, puckering them at her reflection, before patting the chiseled tip over her Cupid's bow.

Mesmerized, Aaron took a step forward, grabbing her upper arm as he pulled her around. She cried out, protesting, caught off guard by his bizarre reaction. Her lips were full, lush. Coated in a thick stain that sat like putty on her soft flesh. He grunted, bringing his hand to her face to touch the swell on her lower lip with the pad of his thumb. The red felt like warm butter. He dragged his thumb to the corner of her mouth and swept toward her cheek, smearing the red over her porcelain skin.

"Dammit, Aaron! I don't have time for this. I'm going to be late for work!"

But he didn't hear her. He was hypnotized by her full, crimson mouth, by the streak that lay across her skin like a

Gaussian flower petal. Seized by the primal need to consume her, he shoved her against the sink and yanked up her skirt.

She wasn't complaining any more.

⸻

Dr. Fredrick held up another inkblot, waiting for Aaron's answer. They did this every week, measuring the progress of his eyesight against random inkblots. For the first two weeks, it was all blacks and grays against plain white backgrounds. As Aaron's first treatment was to introduce L cones into the corneas of his eyes, Fredrick was using inkblots with splashes of red. To someone with Aaron's condition, reds appeared black.

"If you see something new, let me know," he instructed.

"There's a stripe on that car."

Dr. Fredrick flipped the card. Sure enough, the car-shaped silhouette sported a thick red stripe down its side. Last week, Aaron only saw a black car. The doctor produced another card, this one bearing the hourglass shadow of a woman.

"Sexy red dress," Aaron said.

"It worked." Dr. Fredrick dropped the cards. "I'll be damned."

"Wasn't this the plan?"

"Of course. Best-case scenario, obviously. You're my first subject to respond positively to the injection." He began scratching notes on his clipboard. "Roughly when would you say you started seeing reds?"

"Faintly here and there, maybe a few days before our last appointment. But I was here last week when I knew for certain what I was looking at." He pointed to the spot on the floor. "That is red, right?"

Dr. Fredrick looked at the linoleum. "Yes. Red latex paint, to be exact. The maintenance staff here is a bit sloppy, I'm afraid."

"I'm seeing changes in everything. There's dense reds. Stoplights, cars, clothes. But I'm starting to see variations in people's skin. Everyone looks a little different now. Warmer, even."

"Go on." Dr. Fredrick did not look up as he urged Aaron to elaborate.

"For instance, my girlfriend's nipples ..."

Dr. Fredrick coughed. "Okay. That's—I get it."

"I mean, she's a beautiful woman, but the red brings out her ..."

"Understood. Wonderful news." Aaron noticed the faint tinge on Dr. Fredrick's face. The doctor cleared his throat and made a few more notes. With a tight smile, he sat his clipboard on the table, dropping his pen in the process. "Next week we will begin the second stage."

"Which means?"

"S cones. We will be introducing you to blue."

"Nice. The color of Margo's eyes." Aaron's smile split his face.

Dr. Fredrick did not return his smile. He met the beautiful Margo at the beginning of the study.

He must not like blue eyes, Aaron thought.

Aaron's life transformed from newsprint to full-color magazine spreads. In six weeks, he could see the world around him through the same eyes as everyone else. He'd never imagined just how vibrant the city was, with its dusky asphalt and sun-baked brick walls. The verdant grass in the park, as soft as shag carpet and bloated with patches of flowers so lively, he laughed as they danced in the wind. He stood in the paint aisle of the hardware store for an hour, transfixed by the wall of brilliant color swatches, shoving them into his pockets by the fistfuls before leaving. He watched *The Wizard of Oz* and finally understood why it was considered such a cinematic achievement, with its remarkable Technicolor revelation.

It all felt like a celebration. Everywhere he looked, colors teemed and thrived, making every trip outside an adventure. Some of them were so easy to describe. The purple hat that mirrored the Tuscan merlot in his wineglass. The deep teal sports car that looked like it had been dipped in a pool of blue from the Mediterranean Sea. But other colors were more sensory, such as the sunlight that highlighted the shrubs, a shimmery white that looked like warm felt. Or the pink that flushed Margo's cheeks mid-orgasm that felt like discomfort, throbbing, and breathlessness.

He dragged her with him on every run to the grocery store or to the bookstore, trying to pull her into the kaleidoscope of his new vision. His excitement failed to fuel her, though, and her enthusiasm for his new vision waned. He could see the boredom in her unfortunate brown eyes.

And then, it stopped. Not the colors. Just the emotion. The palpable joy that swelled in his chest as he took in every experience with his new and improved eyeballs. The colors were still there, but the world began to look stale. Unimpressed.

Ordinary.

He grew anxious. Would he wake up one morning to a world of gray?

Margo started staying out late again.

During his next routine follow-up appointment, he admitted his fear to Dr. Fredrick.

"Do you think I will lose the ability to see color? I mean, you used a carrier virus, right? Will I build a resistance to that?"

Dr. Fredrick aimed a penlight at Aaron's corneas, watching them contract, and expand. He glanced at the numbers on his charts, a frown furrowing his brow. "There is no source material to refer to. We are in uncharted territory with you. All the other participants either failed or experienced adverse reactions to the experiment."

"What adverse reactions?"

"Nothing you should be worried about," Dr. Fredrick said. "I think you are safely out of the danger zone. Regarding the effective longevity, we really do not know. This could be a permanent change. Or you could develop antibodies, and no longer experience the effects of the transplanted cones. The next couple weeks should give us that information."

"But I think the colors are starting to dull."

"Your eyes are still healing. It could be that what you've been seeing was intensified by an inflammation. What you're beginning to see now might just be the average RGB spectrum."

"Doctor," Aaron felt the twinges of panic return to his gut, "I don't want my vision to get dull. I want those colors back. You don't understand. It's like they were *alive*. Isn't there some way to enhance it further? Are there any other options?"

Dr. Fredrick's brow knotted and he shook his head. "Humans are trichromats. We've been harvesting human cones for this experiment. Locating a willing tetrachromat donor is an unlikely possibility."

"Tetrachromat?"

"Some humans have a fourth cone—the yellow cone—so they can see more colors than the average person. I personally do not have it, and I don't know how much difference you would experience if you did."

Aaron sagged. Duller days were on his horizon.

Dr. Fredrick stood a little straighter. "Humans are not the only tetrachromats, though. Many animals are, as well. And the squirrel monkeys could adapt to human L cones."

"So, do you think it is possible to get the yellow cones from a donor animal if you can't find a human?"

"I can't promise that. But give me some time to study this. Perhaps it's possible to take the research a step further."

Aaron shook the doctor's hand and smiled. "Whatever you come up with, count me in. I want to be the first. I want to see everything there is to see."

Dr. Fredrick faced Aaron from across a sleek rosewood desk. Not a scratch marred the brilliant red wood grain. Aaron's face floated in the sheen. A disembodied head suspended in a pool of spilled cabernet.

"So," the doctor began, "Here's where it gets tricky. I think we can help you. We've been working with hummingbirds, and we've managed to generate a fourth cone."

"Excellent! When do I get it?"

"First things first. Full disclosure here. This stage of the research has not been approved."

Aaron shrugged. "So I'll be a pioneer."

"Without approval, there's no funding. Which means no paycheck. Usually, that would translate as a billed medical procedure."

"Billed? Are you saying I'll have to pay?"

"Now..."

"You approached me. I was fine the way I was. But I listened to you, and you promised this would be a lucrative venture, and now you want me to pay for it?" His voice rose an octave and he realized he was leaning across the desk, shouting.

He'd have to stop. His growth would be over. Margo would never let him waste money, not for this. But he was so close.

No. He couldn't stop, not now.

Dr. Fredrick motioned to Aaron's seat and waited for him to sit back down. "I'm not saying you will be billed. What I'm saying is that without funding or revenue, I will no longer have the staff to assist me with this experiment. The university provided the grants to conduct experiments per subject to the level of completion that we achieved with you. Any further grants I obtain will only be approved if I already have data to justify a need for more research."

"I don't understand," Aaron said. "What are you getting at?"

"If I have empirical data that confirms humans can adapt to cones harvested from donor animals, the innovations in this area of gene therapy would be unprecedented. This project could provide you with the ability to see colors humans have never before imagined. And it could provide me with the grants and funding to expand this research further. Including a place in medical journals and history books. This could change the trajectory of my career. Because of that, I am willing to make you a deal."

"Which is?"

"Work with me on this. I will attempt to give you extraordinary vision and, in return, you will allow me to use your name and any pertinent personal details in all published papers and articles. Possibly even an appearance on television."

"And as far as my money?"

Dr. Fredrick's eyes steeled. "I am not offering to pay you. What you are receiving in return is far beyond any monetary compensation. Not even I can imagine what this experience will be like for you."

Aaron deliberated. Margo would be angry when she found out about the money. But what had started as an easy paycheck for him was now an obsession. He wanted to see what colors were out there. *All* of them.

The doctor was right. It was not something that could be priced.

"I'm in." He leaned over the rosewood, offering a handshake.

The procedure started the same as before. Aaron received a sedative and laid back in a chair with a blinding light in his face. Dr. Fredrick used a small syringe with a two-inch-long needle so skinny it looked like fishing line, to deliver a minute injection of virus into each cornea. The virus was wrapped around the foreign cones that would hopefully add a fourth cone to Aaron's eyes. If his body didn't reject it, of course.

He was given dark sunglasses and instructed to go straight home and rest in a dark room for the next two days, to give his eyes time to heal. But this time, the doctor also handed Aaron a laminated booklet full of small color swatches. "This is a thorough hexadecimal chart. I want you to study this. Get familiar with these colors. And then let me know if you spot anything new in your surroundings."

Aaron shrugged. "Sure, I guess. But what's this supposed to prove?"

"Very few people are tetrachromats, so you will be the only one who knows if you can see something new with them. I am relying completely on you to let me know if it's working. Your feedback will be charted and evaluated intensely."

"Yeah, okay," Aaron said, after a brief hesitation.

"Will you do that, Mr. Denton?" Dr. Fredrick's gaze was as hard as his voice.

"Not like I can refuse," Aaron replied. He understood how important his cooperation was to the doctor's career. Just as important as the doctor was to his journey.

He paused to consider that. He didn't realize he'd been thinking of it as a journey. He wasn't going anywhere, yet still, he was nearing his destination. Someone else was piloting this evolution. Yes. *His evolution.* He would not stop until he had become.

Aaron wasn't sure what to look for. Was it a color that was absent from the charts Dr. Fredrick gave him? How would he know if he was seeing colors differently? They all looked the same to him. Maybe a little brighter, perhaps a little more complex. Even so, he knew these colors already.

Margo's eyes were still a dull brown. The same color as off-brand chocolate. He felt a twinge of resentment when he looked at her now. Especially when he saw other women with blue eyes. He felt cheated, even more than he felt cheated on. He began to fantasize about the blue-eyed women when he fucked her. Conversely, she began complaining about how rough and impersonal he was in bed.

He left earlier that morning, three weeks past his last unremarkable visit to Dr. Fredrick, to run by the bank before he reported to work. Stepping off his porch, he squinted against the harsh glare of the sun, the white-hot heat immediately watering his eyes. He stopped to fish a pair of prescription sunglasses out of his pocket, keeping his eyes squeezed shut until the stinging in his corneas relented.

They'd become sensitive to daylight, and he could not leave the house without saline drops anymore.

He looked at the sky, slightly shaken by his harsh reaction to the sunlight, which was usually burdensome more than uncomfortable. And froze.

The sky was streaked and swirled, not by clouds, but with colors. Mixed into the blue were discernible streams of yellow and red, eddied in patches and oozing around the puffy, pink-tinged clouds pushing by in the breeze. His mouth dropped, mesmerized by the pulsing fluidity of the expanse he'd always believed was simply blue. That's what he parroted as a child ... the sky was *blue*. When, in fact, it wasn't blue at all. Especially not now.

He drove toward the riverfront, leaving his car at the docks. Heading to the piers, he studied the water. Its usual murky green-brown waved and peaked with caps of orange. He could see the undercurrent clearly, as it discolored the waters with a shimmering emerald green that reminded him of a snake slithering past the banks.

Everywhere he looked, he noticed more colors where there had been fewer before. They were colors he still recognized, just in unexpected places. The bright rainbows that sparkled in the feathers of sunning seagulls. The magenta crystals that twinkled in the ordinary black asphalt. The green threads in his blue blazer.

When Aaron contacted the doctor, he was ordered to come in straight away.

"So, what's next? Five cones?" Aaron blinked as Dr. Fredrick pulled the penlight away from his eyes. He'd recounted his morning as the doctor typed the information into his charts, and waited as he inspected his eyes to gauge their reactions and light sensitivity. Both men were notably excited. This was completely unexpected, this successful fourth cone.

Aaron did not want to stop.

Dr. Fredrick admitted, "I'm not sure a fifth cone is possible."

Aaron deflated. "So, this is it? These are all the colors I can see?"

"You now see more colors than most of the human population. 'All the colors' is an unfair assessment. I consider you rather fortunate right now."

Aaron nodded. "Yeah, yeah. Look, I'm sorry. I didn't mean to imply that I'm not grateful. I just thought ... well, I figured we were looking to break boundaries here."

Dr. Fredrick perched on a stool. "I appreciate your enthusiasm. But we'd have a hard time finding donors that have five cones. Pigeons and butterflies are believed to be pentachromats, meaning they have six cones. So that would be the next step going forward."

Aaron stared at the ceiling tiles. The pale gray foam had lavender edges. He couldn't begin to imagine what two additional cones would reveal. And then the thought struck him. "Hey, doc? Which animal sees the most color?"

"Stomatopods are believed to have the most complex eyes of all living specimens."

"Oh yeah? We're talking eight or nine cones?"

"Twelve cones," Dr. Fredrick corrected.

Aaron bolted upright. "You're shitting me?" He sat quiet for a moment, and then, "What is a *stomopod*?"

"Stomatopod," the doctor corrected. "For example, mantis shrimp. They see more colors than any other known creature."

Aaron had no idea what those were, and didn't care. All he knew was he wanted their eyes. "Okay."

Dr. Fredrick frowned. "Okay?"

"Let's do it. Give me mantis shrimp eyes. I don't want to waste any more time."

"No, Aaron, it's not that simple."

"You injected hummingbird cones into my eyes, right?"

"Technically speaking, yes, but ..."

"So find some of those shrimp and give me their cones."

Dr. Fredrick shook his head. "It's more complicated than simply extracting the missing cones. Their eyes are completely different. They don't have twelve separate cones. It's a system of multiple dichromatic cones. Our eyes are much simpler."

"But what is the harm in just injecting a sample of their cones in there? Wrap them in a bug, shoot me up, and see what takes." Aaron grinned.

"This could backfire. Worst-case scenarios involve infection and complete blindness. And if that infection spreads, possible death."

"But think of the best-case scenario. I can see more colors than can ever be imagined. Hell, maybe even different dimensions ..."

"You're getting carried away now," the doctor sighed.

"Couldn't you just check their eyes out? Maybe there's a way to make this work. We would both make history if it does. It goes beyond anything they've ever done before."

Dr. Fredrick stared at the degrees on his wall, lost in thought.

Aaron noticed the yellow in the gray hair peppering the doctor's temples.

The doctor cleared his throat. "This may take a great deal of time. I'm not even sure it's possible to do. But I will at least give this some consideration. Meanwhile, protect your eyes. No sunlight without your sunglasses. Get at least nine hours of sleep in a completely dark room every night. The key is to keep your eyes rested and healthy. No eye strains. I need your word that you will take precautions."

"Of course," Aaron said. "I can't wait to see what you come up with. Get it? *See what you come up with?*"

Dr. Fredrick groaned.

Margo hadn't been home in a week. She came in while he was working and was gone before he got home, her excuses scribbled on the white board attached to the fridge.

'Business meeting in Tucson, will be back Wednesday.'

'Mom fell, took her to hospital, staying overnight.'

'Cousin having her baby, will be back once she's settled back home.'

Aaron wasn't interested in checking into her stories, especially after he spotted her heading into a bar across town with one of her male co-workers the night her mom went to the hospital. The guy looked like the kind of asshole who'd wear Aqua Velva. To be honest, Aaron wasn't particularly interested in what Margo was up to. As long as she paid her share of the bills, she could fuck the entire eighth floor of her office and he wouldn't care.

He'd recently set his sights on a gorgeous young woman with thick black hair, deep rose lips, and eyes so blue he could see them glittering like polished sapphires from twenty feet away. She was new to the office and, according to rumors, newly single. He played it cool around her, pretending only slight interest when she'd initiate conversations with him. It made him seem more interesting. Eager men put off beautiful women. He could tell his casual approach was working.

Cheyenne agreed to dinner that Friday. As tempted as he was to bring his date home and give Margo a taste of her own cloying medicine, he decided to keep the evening loose. So they got acquainted over steak dinners and red wine, and shared a decadent chocolate dessert, before he escorted her back to her apartment.

When she leaned in to kiss him goodnight, her cleavage threatened to spill over the lacy trim of her top. He barely noticed. He could remember a time when all he cared about was the tactile experience of soft flesh in his hands. Now he was too distracted by the allure of her lips. They were a startling shade of crimson, though she admitted earlier that she was terrible with makeup, and therefore chose to go without. Captivated by their natural color, he was still staring at them when she pressed them against his own.

They looked like two juicy slices of blood orange, glistening in the streetlight. Soft, inviting, and just slightly sweet. She was succulent. As she clung to him afterward, he murmured, "So that's what red tastes like."

He bought a bag of blood oranges on the way home that night. As he placed each dripping wedge on his tongue, he imagined he was consuming her delectable mouth.

"I don't know if this is a good idea," Dr. Fredrick admitted. The needle hovered and inch above Aaron's eye, prepared for insertion. He warned Aaron repeatedly that he believed the new cells would not only fail, but undo all the progress they'd made.

Aaron was not deterred. "We can start over if we need to."

"Your eyes are not batteries, Mr. Denton. There is no evidence that they would recover enough to start over. I have no way of knowing what reactions you would have to this. Humans do not have multiple dichromatic cones, and there are no tests that reveal how they would interact with our own cones." A light sheen of sweat speckled the doctor's forehead. The drops of perspiration reflected tiny rainbows from the lamp positioned just above Aaron's head.

"Do it," Aaron growled.

The doctor shook his head and brought the needle to his cornea, the tip piercing the thin barrier of the sclera and sliding into position in the macula of his retina. With a small push of the syringe, he injected only a few drops into Aaron's eye. Once the needle was pulled free, a cotton patch was positioned over the delicate orb before the procedure was repeated on his other eye.

Aaron sat under the light with the cotton protecting his eyes and felt no different than he ever did. "I think it's going to be fine," he said. "Either nothing will happen or I will soon have bionic vision."

Dr. Fredrick removed the cotton after turning off the lamp. "We've done the best we could with these, and your eyes have accepted more than any other. If it's ever going to work, it will now."

He gave Aaron a new bottle of eye drops, these specially formulated for his eyes alone. They included a heavy sunscreen. The doctor ordered more sleep, and prescriptions of strong anti-inflammatory pills to prevent a harsh reaction. Aaron had to affix a shield to his already dark sunglasses to keep the sunlight out.

"Be especially careful with sunlight now," the doctor warned. "Mantis shrimp see deep into the UV spectrum. Your eyes are not designed to. It would be like staring directly into an eclipse. The effects could be permanently damaging."

Aaron realized that the only way he'd truly know what his new eyes could see meant forgoing the protection of his glasses. Who knew what he would find? New colors, certainly. But what if there was more? Spaces and planes ... possibly even beings. Men couldn't see them because their limited vision restricted them to three dimensions, but what if this was his game changer? What if he could see preternatural creatures?

What if he could see God?

He nodded, shook the doctor's hand, and agreed to meet in a week.

He woke from his nap with a slight headache. Considering he expected a headache that rivaled an anvil to the skull, it was a pleasant surprise. He reached for the lamp on his nightstand, casting the room in a faint glow as he rolled onto his back and opened his eyes.

The ceiling was a little blurry. Likely from sleep, he reasoned. Pulling himself from the bed, he stumbled to his bathroom and reached for his eyedrops. He tilted his head back and squeezed three medicated drops into each eye. The irritation began to dissipate as the cool liquid lubricated them. He blinked repeatedly, rolling his eyes behind their lids to make sure they coated evenly. Once they felt normal again, he flipped on the light.

The immediate sting was brutal, and he howled as he tripped out of the room, into the unlit hallway. He squinted his eyes. While a little sore, he could see much better. In fact, he could see clearly. The dark of the hallway did nothing to impede the vibrancy of the small paintings hanging on the opposite wall.

The light in his bedroom didn't cause his eyes pain. A single soft bulb beneath the dark vellum lampshade kept the space purposefully dim. It calmed the burning in his eyes, but caused his sight to go hazy. Even so, the colors in the room were dayglow. The teal linen of his comforter, the abstract Mediterranean blue curtains, the rainbow row of shirts in his closet ... his bedroom was transformed into an art-pop still-life. He couldn't make out sharp edges or details, but the intensity of the different hues and shades was captivating, an impressionistic adaptation of the surreal.

Within a few minutes, his eyes were stinging again, and a growing throb in his temple had him pulling the cord on the lamp. He sat on the bed and felt the throbbing in his eyes ease as they readjusted to the darkness. Looking down at his hands, he noticed the highlights across the thinner skin of his knuckles and joints. The blue paths of veins beneath his skin were more visible than before. *I wonder what they look like in the daylight?* He squinted at the alarm clock under his lamp. Through the blur, he could make out the time. It was just before two in the afternoon.

He dressed, ran a comb through his hair, and tucked his sunglasses, wallet, keys, and eyedrops into his pockets. Pausing briefly at his front door, he glanced over his shoulder. The living room wavered in the growing distance. These next steps would take him into a world no one could describe, or warn about. This was no longer a quest for more color. This was the search for the Tree of Knowledge. He had the keys to a kingdom all humans sought, but never realized.

He was Magellan. Drake. Vespucci. He was the Pied Piper, and his front door was the door into the mountain. He would lead them through.

He sat on his front steps, eyes squeezed shut, trying to adjust to the jagged bursts of electricity that shot all the way through his optic nerve anytime his lids even so much as shuddered. The sunlight was a white-hot spire that pierced through to his brain. Digging into his pockets, he located the sunglasses and fumbled to pull them free. They jumped from his fingers and clattered down the steps, out of his reach. He muttered a curse and covered his eyes with his palms, hoping he could adjust to the bright light at least long enough to find his glasses.

Cracking his eyes open a sliver, he attempted to peer through his lashes. That wouldn't work. A stream of tears slid down his face, an automated response he remembered from being submerged in an over-chlorinated swimming pool. Except as the minutes passed, the burning dulled to an ache, and then eventual numbness. He shadowed his eyes with his hands, took a staggered breath, and opened them.

The world glowed fluorescent around him. He'd stepped into a Dead Head diorama. But for all the brilliance and color, the clarity was muddy. When he held his hand up, he could make out the vague outline of its shape, but it lacked resolution. He could've been wearing a fleece glove. As he brought it to his face, the definition returned. He could make out every hair on each knuckle. The creases in his skin were almost blackened by their infinitesimal shadows. Every vein and capillary under the transparent veil of his skin coursed with the blood his heart was frenetically pumping. He stared at his arms, at the musculature woven around his bones. He was a wonton wrapper. A parchment husk. He pulled his shirt off, his eyes falling on his chest, and the faint edges of the organ palpitating behind his bony armor.

The world was fractured in jarring lights and kaleidoscope colors. Rather than seeing trees and sidewalks and bushes, he saw their pixilated impressions shimmer before him. Placing his hand on the bark of a tree, he saw the rough textile beneath the map work of his circulatory system. He could see all the colors, and then some ... and he saw them all at once. But they didn't morph together in new, undiscovered colors. He saw them simultaneously *and* separately.

He recently went to a 3D screening at the theater. The dimensional effects his glasses provided were less enthralling than what happened when he removed them and stared at the screen, sans eyewear. The colors were splintered, misaligned. Two versions of every person ... the same person, but in two separate planes. Cordial doppelgangers inhabiting their spaces in harmony.

Only that was 3D, and this is ... 6D? Is that how this works? If time is the fourth dimension, can I see its passage? And what dimensions come after that?

He'd stripped off all his clothes by then, inspecting his abdomen and legs. He walked the yard stiffly, imagining himself an alien armature stripped of its human costume. He could hear voices in the distance, but they were as indistinct as his latent vision. "Hello?"

The mass appeared in his peripheral, a gelatinous slug in shades of reds, blacks, and blues, rushing at him. A piercing squeal deafened him as it charged, and he ducked under the shield of his arms and shouted a warning. The creature stopped, heaving breaths as it appeared to regard his threats.

"Aaron, what the hell are you doing?"

The squeal simmered into a familiar, if not caustic, voice. He recognized her. Margo had returned. Although he never anticipated how different she would appear with his heightened vision.

Figures she'd be an ugly beast.

"Sorry, babe," he snarled. "I didn't recognize you for a minute. Did you do something new with your hair?"

The creature lurched forward and grabbed his arm, pulling him off balance. He hit the sidewalk in a skid, scraping his cheek and chest across the rough asphalt, an oversized hunk of Colby on a cheese grater. Yowling, he pushed himself up and sat on his haunches, tenderly brushing the chewed skin across his sternum.

His fingertips were blood dipped, glistening with viscera hued a velvet red, but he saw tiny brown and white disks dancing in the goo. The dichromatic pairs in his eyes had gone beyond extending his sensitivity to lights and colors. His head became a microscope. He chuckled at first, and then laughed, flicking gobs of blood onto the sidewalk before leaning in close, nose practically touching the ground, to marvel at the details of the blood cells and plasma that had, just moments ago, remained restrained inside blue channels.

"Get up! Have you lost your mind? The police are coming!" The voice was again at his ear, its animosity poorly disguised as hysteria. He felt the sharp brush of fingernails graze his shoulder before the vice of thin fingers gripped his bicep. She was pulling on him, trying to throw him off balance. Trying to get him back down. Just in time for the cops to take him.

"You'd love that, wouldn't ya, bitch?" He thrust his elbow back, hard, contacting her ambiguous chest. He felt her grip pull free as she landed behind him, surprised by his reaction. Whirling around, he faced the creature lying on the sidewalk, her legs splayed open. Like the whore she was.

She was still too pixilated to see clearly, but he'd seen her a million times already. He memorized her dark hair, her brown eyes, her wide mouth. He imagined, too many times to count, how they must've looked beneath a body other than his. She thought she was better than him. She thought she was too good for him! There she was, wearing an oversized pair of sunglasses to hide her traitorous eyes, anger twisting the seam that must've been her mouth. He straddled her and pulled back his fist, driving it directly between her eyes, breaking both her glasses and her nose with one punch.

She screamed, the high-pitched wail raising a commotion of shouts in the distance. He grabbed her head in his hands and lifted it off the sidewalk before driving it into the concrete. Over and again, screaming above her cries of pain, "Do you think I didn't know about the men you've been fucking, you whore? Did you think you were smarter than me? I've already replaced you, bitch, and I can't wait until you fucking die!"

She was no longer screaming or thrashing beneath him. The back of her head caved in from the repeated blows as he pummeled her over and again into the concrete. When he released her, she fell with a splat. She was a Monet face in a puddle of broken bone, brains, and viscous fluids.

He threw his head back, searching out the sun in the argon sky, the ball of blaze pulsing above him. Black spots shot off its surface. They flew through the sky like javelins, aiming for the iridescent clouds scattering on an afternoon breeze.

He was looking at the portal of Heaven, the gates opened to him alone.

He was *God*.

He threw his arms up to the sky and roared, pushing his voice from the depths of his belly into his skull. He ignored the twinge ... and then pop ... in his temple. He screamed long and loud, even as unseen hands seized his arms and the world around him went completely white.

Something beeped. It was coming from somewhere over his left shoulder. A steady sound, like an electronic pulse. He could smell the antiseptic odor of alcohol mixed with urine. It stung his nostrils.

He tried to speak, but he had no voice. His eyes wouldn't open. He couldn't move as much as a finger.

Where am I?

Two voices grew louder, drowning out the beeping. They stood above him, to the side. Familiar voices.

"If he comes out of the coma, he will be taken into custody. If he's lucky, he'll die first. For what he's done, he doesn't want to find himself behind prison walls."

"Did the police mention who she was?" Her voice was bruised. Soft.

"A coworker. Cheyenne Mays. According to friends, they were dating."

NO.

"Oh God. What a bastard!" Her voice feigned horror, but he knew she was faking it. Margo was evil. She deceived him and ruined his life. He tried to move his arms. He needed to choke the last breath from her soulless body, but he was trapped in limbo.

NO.

"I'm so sorry. You are safe now, I promise."

"I don't understand what happened." She sobbed. Alligator tears.

"I tried to warn him the experiment could turn out wrong, but he refused to listen. I was concerned there could be complications that extended past his vision. Mantis shrimp are incredibly volatile, unnaturally strong. He took those last injections against my advice. When they apprehended him, his eyes were so infected that the inflammation caused them to bulge out of their sockets. He was a monster. So, the doctors removed them."

"Jesus," she whispered.

No.

"He's on life support, and there's no medical directive. Does he have any family?"

"None living."

"They will ask if you'd like to keep him on life support in that case, if he doesn't wake up. Considering he's a murderer, I doubt the staff will be upset should you choose to cut it."

NO.

She laughed. "As far as I'm concerned, he can rot."

NO.

"I think that's a reasonable choice." Dr. Fredrick's voice was conciliatory. "I hope I'm not being too forward, but I've always thought you had stunning eyes, Margo. Perhaps you'd let me buy you a drink? You shouldn't be alone right now."

Her yes was a breath and a sigh. And then they were gone.

Beep! Beep! Beep! Beep ...

NO.

INVISIBLE

BY E.A. BLACK

Blair Bottom hated her sister. At six-hundred-thirty-five pounds, Bethany Bottom loomed in everyone's space in the double-wide, commanding attention Blair never received. While Blair's stick-thin frame looked as if she could snap in half at the slightest gust of wind, Bethany resembled a gigantic shar pei.

Mother was too busy running a soapy bath sponge beneath Bethany's fat folds to notice her younger daughter's ribs protruded. While twenty-one-year-old Bethany was so big she commanded attention, fifteen-year-old Blair wanted to disappear into the trailer's faux wood paneling. Her mother refused to notice she'd lost twenty pounds in the past two weeks. Blair ate the same two double cheeseburgers, extra-large fries, and humongous Coke Bethany ate for lunch that day. The difference was Blair threw hers up afterward.

While she wanted attention and caring, Blair received the wrong kind of attention. Her schoolmates called her Skeletor and snapped pencils whenever she walked past. They ate sticky donuts for lunch and sucked down soft drinks with a loud slurping sound that made her want to retch. While they savored their sickening food by flaunting each disgusting bite in her face, she nibbled at Saltine crackers and sucked on ice cubes. After the daily lunchtime taunting, she ran to the back of the school near the janitorial station to jam a finger down her throat and vomit into the gravel. It was mostly isolated back there, so no one would confront her. Or torment her. Or question why she threw up after every meal.

Why couldn't people just leave her alone? No one cared she destroyed the lining of her stomach three times a day. Blair had taken to forced vomiting about a year before, shortly after her father left. He didn't even kiss her goodbye as he walked out the door that cold winter morning. She, like the rest of her family, was tossed aside like a used tissue. When Daddy didn't return that night, she thought he stayed with a friend after drinking too much at the local bar. When he didn't return the next day, she thought maybe he was working overtime. When Mother called his friends, who couldn't locate him, and then his boss, who said he quit work three weeks earlier, Blair knew Daddy wasn't coming home.

She overheard Mother on the phone saying Daddy ran off with some floozy from the bar. When the full impact of his abandonment took effect, Blair shut down, going as cold inside as the December ice storms.

The first time she vomited, it was involuntary, a means of getting bad feelings out of her system. Puke carried with it depression, hatred, rage, and confusion—all directed at Daddy. Stomach tied up in knots, she threw up until dry heaves took over, and then she felt somewhat better. Whenever she became upset—usually immediately after a meal, having to listen to Mother demand her services to care for her sister or the latest news about Daddy and the money he wasn't sending home—her stomach ached in that familiar, painful way. She would head to the bathroom to relieve herself into the toilet. No matter how often she dispelled her demons, they never stayed away.

By the time summer's heat settled into fall's brilliant foliage, Blair had taken to vomiting each meal, no matter how small. The more she vomited, the smaller she became. Starting out at a healthy one-hundred-twenty-five pounds, within three months she dropped to one hundred pounds. Each month, more of her faded away, all the while no one noticing. She wanted to vanish, to cease to exist so that her pain would go away. She hoped that someday she'd disappear altogether, since no one wanted her in the first place.

Daddy left because of Bethany's neediness and Mother's nagging. At least Blair could take care of herself. The moment she needed Mother to wipe her ass she would demand to be shot. After Mother sponged-bathed Bethany, she wiped shit from Bethany's ass since she couldn't turn over to wipe it herself. Hell, she could barely walk to the toilet. Not that she'd fit through the bathroom door. A soiled bedpan sat on the floor next to the bed. The stench slammed into Blair, stinking so much her eyes watered.

"Blair, come over here and help me turn her over." Mother said. "Kyle, you hold her legs."

Her brother Kyle Dungworth held Bethany's legs while Blair shoved her hands against her sister's back. Kyle was Mother's son from a different man, who also deserted his family. Mother pulled on one arm as Blair pushed Bethany onto her left side. Sharp pain stabbed her chest at the exertion. Kyle held her legs so that she didn't slide backwards. Mother handed Blair the dripping sponge.

"Wash her back," the woman ordered.

A well of rage erupted in Blair's bosom. She hated being ordered around, especially when it came to tending to her fat-ass sister. While Blair shed weight like water, Bethany had gained so much that she spread all over her custom-made, double-king-sized bed. Older sister dwarfed younger sister in every way possible. The larger Bethany grew, the smaller Blair became. Blair existed solely to care for her sister.

She ran the sponge in the folds of Bethany's back boobs. She lifted a lump of dimpled flesh and washed around and beneath it. Despite holding her breath, the smell hit her square in the face. Sweat and grime had collected beneath the folds and festered, giving off a spoiled meat stench. Swallowing hard to keep from barfing in front of everyone, she scrubbed away the dead skin until Bethany shined pink like a large sea slug. When Blair let go of the mound of flesh, it fell back in place with a wet slap. She repeated the procedure all over Bethany's back until her sister was squeaky clean.

She refused to vomit when washing her sister, no matter how bad she smelled. She vomited only after meals. Puking was the one area of life in which Blair had control. Her weight was her business, and she would never, *ever* be as big as Bethany. While Blair lost weight to become invisible, Bethany gained it in her own demented way of getting attention.

Blair and Mother rolled Bethany onto her back. Kyle and Blair parted her tree trunk legs. Each one took a sponge and washed. Blair ran the sponge along the massive thigh, pulling aside the lymphedema to wash around and beneath it. Lymphedema was swelling in her upper legs because of blockage of lymph nodes in her groin area. Caused by her morbid obesity, the condition left Bethany riddled with large tumors.

That same sickening stink floated around her because of collected dead skin in her folds, but it wasn't as strong as it was on her back. As Blair washed, Bethany cried in pain, but Blair didn't care. She scrubbed hard in part to clean the filthy skin, but she also wanted to cause her sister pain. She was furious at being trapped in the trailer having to tend to her needs day and night. The whole family was trapped, prisoners to Bethany's condition. Blair couldn't escape except to go to school, and she hated school. Everyone knew about Bethany's enormous size and rarely saw her, but that didn't stop them from calling her Fat-ass. They saw skeletal Blair every day and never let her hear the end of what they thought of her vanishing body.

"When do we go to the doctor, Mother?" Bethany asked.

"At 3:00 p.m. Are you sure you want to do this?" Mother asked.

"Yes. I can't stand it anymore. I want the surgery," she said.

As usual, Bethany always got what she wanted, and she wanted gastric bypass surgery. Blair didn't believe for a minute she'd follow through. Once she was clean and dressed, Blair, Mother, and Kyle hoisted Bethany into her customized wheelchair. The wheelchair and surgery were covered by Medicaid. They qualified for additional insurance, but for most procedures there was a deductible they couldn't afford—except when it came to Bethany. Blair needed dental work and new glasses, but she went without so Bethany could get all the care she needed.

Because of the neglect, Blair hated her mother and Kyle, but especially Fat-ass. She imagined what she would do to Bethany if given the chance. Scrub her festering skin with scouring pads. Yank her stringy hair when she brushed it. Shove a double cheeseburger into her mouth and leave her there to choke. Pull too hard when she hoisted pounds of lumped flesh to get them out of the way so she could wash properly. But rather than take her rage out on her sister, Blair turned inward. She relied on syrup of Ipecac and laxatives to dissolve her rage and depression. The larger Bethany became, the smaller Blair shrunk. Soon she'd be like *The Incredible Shrinking Woman*—she'd disappear and no one would even notice she was gone.

The trailer door was a custom job they got at a steep discount because Kyle worked for the contractor. Once they wheeled Bethany through it and down the ramp, they forced her into a van. The two-hour drive to the doctor's office gave Blair time to stare out the window and daydream. Finding a boyfriend who would lift her out of this trailer park. Take her to live at a dream house on the beach. She'd have new glasses and her clothes would fit. Her magnificent white teeth would shine. She might even eat without throwing up afterward.

The family sat in Dr. Fitzhugh's office—Bethany and Blair to the right and Mother and Kyle to the left. Blair wanted to get out of there as quickly as possible. She hated doctors' offices. Doctors always asked too many questions. They saw too much, but they couldn't do anything about what they saw.

"Miss Bottom, you are serious about losing weight?" Fitzhugh asked Bethany.

"Yes, she is. She feels terrible," Mother said. "She's real serious about losing several hundred pounds."

"What kind of food do you eat now? Do you have regular intake of vegetables and fruit?" Fitzhugh asked Bethany.

"Oh, she eats real good, doctor," Mother said. "She likes Wendy's burgers a lot. Fries, too. She just eats too much of them. We could add more veggies. She likes tomatoes."

"I'd like to hear Bethany answer my questions, Mrs. Bottom." Fitzhugh said. "In answering for her you're enabling her behavior. If Bethany is going to lose weight she needs to take responsibility for herself. So Bethany ..." Fitzhugh turned away from Mother and faced Bethany. "I'm going to put you on a special diet. No fast-food or junk food. No sugar. No processed foods. No soft drinks. You'll eat meat three times each week, and you'll eat at least one serving of green vegetables and fresh fruit with each meal. Drink plenty of water. Are you willing to do this?"

"Yes, sir. I want to be better. I hate the way I look and feel," Bethany said.

Fitzhugh handed her a sheet of paper. "Here's a list of recommended foods and a list of what you can't eat. With this diet, you should lose thirty pounds in one month. I'll see you here in two weeks for a check-up."

"Thirty pounds in one month? That's a lot of weight," Bethany said. Blair smirked. Losing thirty pounds in one month was a piece of cake.

"It's necessary, otherwise I won't believe you're serious. Do we have a deal?"

Bethany gave a nervous and resigned groan. "Yes, doctor."

With a heavy sigh, he turned to Blair. "May I speak bluntly? Blair seems to have a problem, too, if she'd like to talk about it. I'm very concerned about how thin you are. Is there anything you'd like to tell me?"

"I ... uh ..." Blair mumbled. *He sees me. I can't have that. He'll figure out what's wrong, and he'll make me keep my food down. He'll put me in a hospital. I hate hospitals, and we can't afford one.*

"She don't have any problems, doctor. Bethany is the one who needs help."

Blair hung her head and bit her lip, uncomfortable in her silence. Once again, her mother shut her down before she had a chance to speak.

"Mrs. Bottom, I would like to hear from Blair. You have a habit of speaking for your children when I ask them questions." He turned to Blair and looked at her over the top of his glasses. "Are you aware of how thin you are, Blair?"

"No, doctor."

"Do you diet?"

"I eat good food. I just don't want to get fat like my sister." She knew the dig hurt Bethany, but she didn't care.

"Please smile for me."

"Pardon?"

"Please smile, Blair."

She smiled, baring her teeth like a mongrel protecting her territory. She didn't want to smile too broadly or the doctor would see her yellowed teeth. She knew that throwing up dissolved the enamel, discolored her teeth, and a few of them had decayed. Dentists scared her since she hadn't been to one in ten years. She was too terrified of going because of the pain she knew would be involved. In her emaciated state, she was far more sensitive to pain than she used to be. The slightest bump bruised her and hurt for hours. Sometimes days.

Fitzhugh sighed again. Blair didn't like that sound, like air sucking through a wound. Dead leaves rustling over a grave. She knew she was a bit too thin but at least she wasn't a lardass like her sister. Why did the doctor have to notice her? She, Mother, and Kyle were here for Bethany. Blair didn't want any attention.

"Blair, do you sometimes vomit after you eat?" the doctor asked.

"Why would I do that?" she snapped. *Don't get angry or he'll pay more attention to you.* She didn't want the doctor to notice her. She wanted Mother's attention, but Mother was so focused on Bethany that, as usual, Blair fell between the cracks.

"It's a way of getting attention," the doctor said.

"I don't do anything like that." Why did he keep repeating her thoughts? He must know her secret. She thought she hid enough, but apparently she hadn't. The doctor knew what she had done to herself. He knew she wanted to cease to exist, to fade away, to die. Her vanishing body would help her to reach her goal. Her heart raced as the conversation progressed. She didn't know what to do or say. More than anything she wanted to flee the examination room. It would be a huge mistake if she did.

"Are your periods regular?"

How did he know her periods had stopped? She was glad they did. Her breasts stopped growing, too, which was even better since the boys in school snapped her bra strap. The teasing humiliated her. She wanted to shrink into herself, to disappear, to go somewhere where no one would notice her.

No one except Mother. She couldn't even stand to be hugged because the feel of arms around her ached. Too much weight on her hurt her bones. At the same time, she craved companionship, the love and attention of someone who cared about her.

"If you're willing to come in I'd be happy to talk to you, Blair. I think I can help you."

"Really, doctor. Blair is fine," Mother said. "It's Bethany who needs your help, not Blair. Blair is here to support her sister."

I'm here because if I didn't come, you'd never let me hear the end of it. Blair clenched her jaw, driving a railroad spike of a migraine into her skull.

He handed a card to Blair, who stuffed it into her back pants pocket. "If you ever want to talk, feel free to call me. You may email me, too. My phone number and email address are on the card."

"She don't need no help." Blair heard the exasperation in Mother's voice and wished she could shrink into the chair until she faded into the upholstery. At least Mother didn't take the card away from her. By the time they left the doctor's office, Mother had forgotten about the card, leaving Blair in peace.

After visiting the doctor, to celebrate Bethany's new way of life, the family downed three large grease-laden meat and double-cheese pizzas Mother ordered as takeout. The smell of tangy tomato sauce and steaming sausage turned Blair's stomach. She hated pizza, but she ate one slice to shut everyone up. Swallowing hard to prevent herself from throwing up in the car, she leaned back, rolled down the window, and closed her eyes.

"Blair, roll up that window," Mother said.

"I can't. I feel sick."

"Oh, stop it. You're just begging for attention. This is a cause to celebrate your sister's new diet and losing weight."

"By buying her a meal with enough grease to fatten up a football team?"

"Blair, watch your mouth. I'll ground you if you don't mind your manners."

Blair turned her head and stared out the window so Mother couldn't see the sting of tears that couldn't fall from her eyes, she was so dehydrated. Her chest tightened with anxiety, and the pain around her heart recurred, flowing to her left shoulder. She was having another anxiety attack. She suffered in silence, heart thumping so hard it hurt, breathing so shallow stars exploded before her eyes. As familiar street signs whizzed past, she gripped the car seat as if to brace herself for some impending horror. But she couldn't put her finger on exactly what.

Walking from the car to the trailer left Blair so exhausted she crawled into bed. She'd been napping a lot lately. The slightest exertion drained her of all energy. She'd skipped school three days last week because she had some kind of flu that wouldn't let go. What little appetite she had completely disappeared. Despite her run-down condition, she somehow found the strength to bathe Bethany ever day as Mother's ordered. Rage drove adrenaline into her system. If only she could put that energy to good use.

Alone in her room, she removed the doctor's card from her pocket and stared at the phone number. Maybe she should call. She wanted to talk to someone, anyone who would listen. She felt so alone—unwanted and hopeless. The only thing she seemed to be good for was scrubbing her sister's fat folds and helping her stuff her face with ice cream.

As bile roiled in her esophagus, she raced to the bathroom, slammed the toilet seat into the upward position, and projectile vomited into the bowl. Undigested chunks of pizza flew past her teeth and splashed on her face. The sound of vomit smacking the water sickened her so much she vomited more. Blinking, she stared at the puke and was not surprised to see blood.

"Blair, don't you mess up that bathroom. Clean up after yourself," Mother called.

"I will." At the sink, she splashed water on her face and brushed her teeth gently so her gums wouldn't bleed again.

"Are you okay?" Mother asked.

"I'm fine." She spat into the sink. Despite her careful brushing, she had loosened a tooth. She spat more blood on the porcelain, then washed it away with running water.

"Good, then come out here and help me dress your sister," Mother said.

Fuck that sea pig. "I can't, Mother. I want to lie down. I feel sick."

"Well, go lie down then," Mother said, exasperation in her voice.

Once in her room, Blair opened her closet door and stared at herself in her full-length mirror. Jeans and a t-shirt hung on her weak frame as if she didn't exist beneath it. Her body held no shape so the clothing had little to cling to. It took most of her energy to undress down to her underwear. She tossed her clothing on the floor, not caring where it fell. Her backbone jutted beneath her skin. She ran one finger down her ribs, which curved like corrugated cardboard. The plates of her hipbones protruded and her stick-thin legs and arms gave her a scarecrow look she didn't have last week. Her skin had taken on a dull sallow tone, flaking on her waist where her belt had rubbed and irritated. The skin on her face felt dry and tight, as if pulled taut over a drum. Jutting cheekbones, lantern jaw, and hollowed-out eyes defined her face.

She pulled the scale out from beneath her bed—the one Mother forbade her to have since scales made Bethany feel ashamed and guilty. She managed to sneak it back in the house after Kyle tossed it in the dumpster. Blair stood on it and held her breath. Seventy-eight pounds. She lost four pounds since last week. Her head spun and her chest hurt. It hurt to breathe. Must have been that stubborn flu going around. She felt so sick, she crawled into bed and didn't get up when Mother called her for dinner.

Over the next two weeks as Bethany grew, Blair faded further away. Despite the doctor's orders, Bethany begged for burgers and fries, claiming chicken and broccoli didn't taste as good. Mother bargained—if Bethany would eat a few bites of chicken and broccoli she could have only one burger and small fries. The doctor couldn't possibly have a problem with that. Her little girl was hungry and Mother felt badly about how miserable Bethany felt over her new diet. Maybe breaking her into it gently would work better than cold turkey.

Blair in the meantime had become so irritable and jealous of the attention Mother gave Bethany, she stayed in her bed day and night. She refused to move even when Mother ordered her to bathe her sister. She even stopped talking. Blair's flu had become so bad Mother left her alone in bed and forced Kyle to help tend to Bethany. Mother couldn't understand why Blair was so angry with her sister. After all, Bethany needed their help. She couldn't clean herself. She couldn't even turn over in bed to get more comfortable. Blair was mobile, went to school, and was perfectly capable of helping around the trailer. All Bethany could do was eat. And eat she did.

In the doctor's office, Bethany hoisted herself from her wheelchair and waddled over to the industrial-sized scale. Blair had seen similar scales in veterinarian's offices. This scale made her think of her sister as a prized heifer, being weighed before judgment at the county fair.

The doctor pursed his lips. He didn't look pleased. "Bethany, you've gained four pounds in the past two weeks. You need to lose forty before I'll even consider going ahead with surgery. What have you been eating?"

"She's had her chicken and green veggies, doctor," Mother said. "But she is so miserable because the food just don't taste good. So I let her have a couple of burgers sometimes. I know I shouldn't have done that."

"Mrs. Bottom, if Bethany is serious about surgery, she needs to lose the weight. Maybe being more mobile will help her."

"But she can't walk," Mother said.

"I'd like to hear from Bethany. You're still answering for her."

"I can't walk too good," Bethany said. "But I do want the surgery. I won't eat any more burgers or pizza. Or fries. I've been drinking lots of water but I like my Coke."

"Here's what I'll do, Bethany. Walking may help you. I can remove your lymphedema, which will help you get around better. I would like to schedule you for surgery next week. I have an opening on the twelfth. One of my patients cancelled. Can you make that date? I'd need you here at seven that morning. It requires hospitalization for several days. Your insurance covers the surgery. My assistant already checked."

"I can be here," Bethany said.

"Good. Please stick with the diet and don't eat fast-food or junk food. Drink water. You may have flavored seltzer water but I'd prefer plain water. Either bottled or tap."

"I can drink tap water."

"Now, would all of you excuse me? I would like to talk to Blair alone."

"Blair? Why?" Mother asked.

The doctor smiled at Blair. "If she is going to help your sister get better, she needs to be well herself. She seems to have a touch of the flu."

"I can buy her medicine. She'll be fine," Mother said.

"Yes, that's good, but I would still like to talk to Blair alone."

"Okay. We'll wait in the waiting room," Mother said.

After they left, Blair curled into her chair, wishing she could vanish. She could fool Mother, Bethany, and Kyle, but she couldn't get anything past Dr. Fitzhugh.

"So, Blair. I'm concerned about your weight. Your sister is getting all the attention but I think your condition is more serious than hers. You vomit after you eat, don't you?"

How'd he know that? Blair said nothing. She stared through the doctor, wide-eyed, and swallowed her fear.

"How are you doing in school?"

Her bony fingers coiled in her lap. She had chewed her nails, making them scream an angry red. The slightest bump hurt them. A bandage covered one that she gnawed down to the quick. "I'm doing okay."

"Do you get along with the kids at school?"

She clenched her jaw, fighting back the words that begged to spill forth. She trusted no one, but Dr. Fitzhugh was the first person to notice her in months. "No, they don't like me."

"How do they treat you?"

The words burst through like water pouring through a broken dam. Her rage gushed so quickly she couldn't hold it back. "They hate me. They call me names and laugh at me. No one will sit with me at lunch. I don't even like lunch."

"You throw it up."

"Yes." The word was out before she could stop it. There, her secret was out. What would she do about it?

"You have every right to be angry, Blair. How do you feel about taking care of your sister?"

Years of fury spilled out, and Blair was unwilling and unable to stop it. "I hate her. She's a sea pig. I will never be that fat. It's all her fault, you know. She sits on the couch all day watching TV and stuffing her face with burgers and fries. I don't know why I have to wash her and turn her over all the time. I wish she were dead. I wish all of them were dead. I'm going to be stuck taking care of her for the rest of my life. I can't even bring friends over, not that I have any."

"Blair, I think you're taking your anger out on yourself by becoming so thin. Your life is out of control, and the only thing you can control is your weight. You want attention from your mother but she's not giving it to you. I'm concerned about your health. I'd like to hospitalize you and help you get better. I also know of a good therapist with experience in eating disorders you can talk to. How do you feel about that?"

At the sound of the word *hospitalize*, Blair stiffened. "I hate hospitals."

"It's the best way to get the help you need."

"I can't afford it."

"We can take a look at your insurance."

"But Bethany is the one who needs help. She matters."

"So you do."

Did she? No one cared she'd been so angry over dinner three nights ago—she'd clenched her teeth until a molar cracked. Her cuticles hurt from tearing the skin off with her fingers and teeth. She held her rage in until her chest hurt. What good would a hospital stay do? She'd only return to the double-wide and her life of tending to her sister's every need.

"Blair, do you want me to help you?"

She stared into her lap. "No one can help me. I'm trapped. Even if I start to get better, I'll only go back to the same old thing. Day in and day out."

"Do you wish your life were better?"

"Yes."

He held out a business card. "I gave you one of these the last time you were here, but here's one again in case you threw it out. Please think about what I said. Call me. Even if you just want to talk. I'm here for you."

She took the card and pocketed it. Biting her lip, she stared at his knees. She couldn't look him in the eye because she was afraid he'd see into her soul. He'd guess more of her secrets and she'd be vulnerable. Instead, she nodded, stood, and walked out the door.

Bethany missed her scheduled appointment, but at least her mother rescheduled. Dr. Fitzhugh wasn't worried about her. He had not heard from Blair since their chat a week earlier, despite her seeming interest. Was her mother preventing her from contacting him? After all, Bethany was her pet and she catered to the girl's every whim. With her mother enabling her behavior, Bethany would never lose weight. But Fitzhugh couldn't stop thinking about the stick-thin girl who sat in his office. She was a mere shadow—a reflection of her family's sickness. Shadows weren't noticed, and neither was Blair. Fitzhugh took notice, however, and he knew that scared her. He had hoped he'd hear from her.

Worried and curious, he dialed the phone number and waited.

"Hello?"

"Mrs. Bottom, this is Dr. Fitzhugh."

"Oh, doctor, I'm so sorry we missed your appointment. Bethany is doing real good. She ate fruit for breakfast and I'm making her some chicken and peas right now."

"Actually, I'm not calling to talk to you about Bethany. I would like to speak to Blair."

"She's sleeping, doctor. Blair has the flu."

"How long has she had it?"

"Over a week. She's been sleeping a lot for the past two days."

"Would you please tell her that I called? She may reach me at my work number." He left his cell number with Mrs. Bottom as well. When he rang off, he wondered if he should have insisted on talking to Blair.

Blair overheard her mother on the phone with Dr. Fitzhugh. She wanted to answer but she felt too sick to get up. Instead, she rolled over, bunching the blankets between her legs. She buried her head in her pillow as she fought off a pounding headache. No, she couldn't just lie here all day. She needed to talk to the doctor.

The bedroom door opened and Mother stepped into the room.

"You need anything from the store?"

"No, I'm fine."

"Watch your sister. If she needs anything take care of it."

Of course, she was her sister's lackey. "Will do, Mother."

When Blair heard the door close and the car drive away, she crawled out of bed and walked to the living room to get the phone receiver.

"I'm hungry," Bethany said. "How about you sneak me some cookies?"

"You're not supposed to have sweets."

"C'mon, just a few? Who are you calling?"

"None of your business."

"I'm telling mom you called someone."

"Go ahead."

"You're gonna get in a heap of trouble. I'll see to it."

Blair ignored her sister and returned to her room. She dialed the number as Bethany muttered threats from the other side of the door.

"James Fitzhugh."

"Dr. Fitzhugh, it's Blair."

"I'm glad you called. How are you feeling?"

She spoke in a low, conspiratorial whisper. "I can't stand it anymore. If I have to wash Bethany one more time I'll scream."

"What about your flu?"

"It's not too bad. It beats wiping her ass."

"Have you been to school?"

"Not this week. Too sick. And too fed up. I can't stand it there. I have nowhere to go. I don't feel safe or secure anywhere."

"I think a stay in the hospital will do you a world of good. Your insurance covers in-patient treatment. How do you feel about coming out in three days?"

"I'd love to but Mother will never allow it. I know she has to give consent. I'm only fifteen. Mother won't even let me rest. She makes me get up every few hours to care for Bethany. I even have to cook for her now."

"I'll come for you in three days early in the morning. Be packed for a weeklong stay."

"I don't think I can get away with it, but I'll try. I can't take much more of this. I'm ready to snap."

Dr. Fitzhugh couldn't stop thinking about Blair. She sounded so frantic on the phone, he wished he'd picked her up then. Now, three days later, he was ready for her. He had already prepared what he'd say to her mother once he confronted her with Blair's serious condition.

He pulled into the driveway and heard the TV blaring from the trailer. The lights were off. Was no one at home? Yes, they were. A rusty Ford Pinto was parked near the shuttered windows. Concerned and wary, Fitzhugh got out of his Mercedes, walked to the front door, and knocked.

The door opened and the stench hit him square in the face, an odor like meat festering in the sun. With great fear, he pushed the door open.

Mother sat in her overstuffed armchair dressed in a white muumuu that had turned crimson with her blood. The slit below her chin gaped like a second mouth. Fitzhugh pressed his hand over his own mouth in horror. A tissue holding several bloodied teeth and a pair of pliers sat on the table next to her. The teeth couldn't have been pulled while the woman was alive. Her screaming would have been horrendous.

Bethany lay in her bed, commanding attention even in death. A pillow covered her face, presumably used to smother her. Fitzhugh removed the pillow and was aghast to see a double cheeseburger stuffed in her mouth. Her dead eyes, wide with terror, stared ahead, looking nowhere.

There was no sign of the brother, but he didn't live with the family. That left one other person.

Oh, dear God, Blair! Fearing the worst, Fitzhugh rushed down the narrow hall, opening doors until he found one that was blocked. He turned the doorknob but something obstructed the door. He shoved hard. Blair's bedroom dresser had been pushed up against the door.

The stink of urine, feces, and filthy clothing slammed him in the face. At first it was hard to see into the room because the windows had been covered in black plastic. The doctor flicked on a lamp and light flooded the room.

Trash-filled bags lay in a pile on the floor. Blair had tried to clean her room but her effort was futile. Boxes of laxatives and a half-empty glass of water sat on a battered wooden bedroom dresser. Open dresser drawers overflowed with soiled underwear, mussed t-shirts, and jeans far too large to fit Blair. Throw pillows and dolls sat in a pile on the floor near a window, as discarded as Blair had been in her own life.

Wrapped in her bed sheets in a mummified fashion, Blair lay face-up on the bed, her hollowed-out eyes staring wide, seeing nothing. Her translucent pale skin was pulled taut over her skull. Her face wore fear and dejection like a caul. Head thrown back, cracked lips—whatever words they'd wished to express forever left unsaid. There was no muscle beneath her skin. Only sinew and bone. Fitzhugh could count her ribs. Her arched back had curved as her body fought for its life in her final moments. He couldn't determine for certain, but judging from the lividity and decomposition of her body, Blair had been dead for at least two days.

Her right hand had clenched in death, and her fist held something. Fitzhugh pried open her fingers, breaking her index and middle fingers in the process. He found his business card in her palm.

Scrawled on the back were the words FREE AT LAST.

AND THE SKY WAS FULL OF ANGELS

BY L.L. SOARES

When his time in the war had ended, Cyril returned to a home he didn't recognize. It wasn't that the town had changed that much, but that *he* had. He had been away much longer than he thought, and was still disoriented. He had sustained some pretty serious injuries, and wasn't sure if he would ever heal enough to be his former self again.

Mama and his brother Donny were waiting at the station when he got off the train—the same train station he'd left three years before. The place seemed frozen in time, but Mama looked older, and Donny was a few inches taller. The way they looked at him made it obvious he had changed a lot since they had last seen one another—but then again, he knew that already.

Clearly, from their reactions, he had not changed for the better.

Mama hugged him and Donny took his duffle bag. They walked out to the parking lot and the pickup truck, which looked a little more beaten-up than before. There were patches of rust, and a smattering of dents and scratches. They asked him to get inside the cab, between them, but Cyril hopped in the back and stretched out in the truck bed. No one asked him twice. Instead, Donny started the engine and they drove away from the lot.

Cyril watched the train that had brought him speed away to its next destination. He wished he was still inside, moving forward forever and never stopping.

His father didn't bother to get up when they got home. He sat on the couch, and remained there as they went inside, looking Cyril up and down, but making no effort to stand.

"Your son's home," Mama said. "Don't you have anything to say to him?"

His father kept staring, almost glaring. Then he reached out his arms and Cyril went over and hugged him.

"So how was the war?" his father asked.

"How do you think it was?"

"Well, you're back in one piece. Could be worse."

Mama asked Cyril if he wanted something to eat, but he had eaten on the train. He said he just wanted a lie down, and Mama told Donny to take him upstairs. So, the two of them went up the staircase and Donny showed him to his old room. It was exactly the way he had left it, except now his duffle bag was on the bed where Donny had put it.

"I guess you don't need any help taking a nap," Donny said. "I'm sure you know how to do that."

Cyril nodded, forced a laugh, and clapped his brother on the shoulder. He told him it was good to see him again. But Cyril didn't go so far as to say it was good to be home. Because he didn't believe that. He hadn't wanted to come back here, but he had nowhere else to go.

A whistling in the middle of the night woke him, and he got up and went over to the window. A missile shot into the sky from a nearby military base, but he never remembered the base launching missiles before. Cyril could almost read the lettering on its side. He wondered where it was going. There were many possible destinations, but it was probably just a test. He just had never seen one so close to a civilian population before.

He could hear the whistling in his head long after the missile was gone. In fact, the sound got louder in his mind, the whistling of a hundred other missiles he had seen, combining into one long screech threatening to deafen him.

He waited. Like everything else, the sound eventually dissipated.

He tried to go back to sleep, but it was useless.

"How long have you been home?" Chan asked. "It's so good to see you!"

When Cyril had seen her in the back of the deli, sitting at a table with a friend, he was sure she would pretend not to notice him. But she got up from her seat and rushed over to him.

"You have to come sit with us," she said, leading him and the tray he was carrying back to her table. "You know Anna." Cyril looked at Chan's friend and nodded.

"I just got back," he said. "Yesterday. I felt so exhausted that I took a nap and slept like twenty-four hours."

"You must have been very tired."

It still hurt to see her. Even after all he had been through, the memory was still fresh in his mind of her breaking up with him, the incident that made him decide to join the military. Back then, she had seemed so cruel the way she had told him she found someone else and that she was leaving him. He was just a kid and it felt like his world was ending.

"So, how's Harry?" he asked.

"I wouldn't know," she said. "We broke up a long time ago. Maybe six months after you left. He graduated and went abroad. We haven't talked in over a year. Good riddance, I say."

He was glad to know his rival was out of the picture, but he couldn't help feeling a sense of loss. He could have tried to get her back after they split, but he was an ocean away, tempting death. He had missed the opportunity.

"I missed you, Cyril," she said. "I didn't know if you were ever coming back. If you'd *want* to come back, after the way I treated you."

"Did you treat me badly?" he asked. "I don't remember."

She smiled, seemingly happy he'd forgotten. Too bad he couldn't forget.

"So, are you with someone else now?" he asked, just blurting it out. The girls laughed at the awkwardness of the question.

"No, not right now," Chan said. "Do you want to get together sometime?"

"Sure."

He ate, noticing that the girls were done, and just stayed around to talk to him. He told them a few war stories. Nothing too graphic or scary. Weird customs he'd come across. A few close calls. Then Chan and Anna stood and Chan asked for his phone. She punched in her number. "Call me."

He watched them go. He finished his lunch and then walked around town, going in some stores, killing time until Donny came to drive him home.

***

"Cyril?"

"It's no use. It didn't work."

"Cyril, can you hear me?"

"No, no, don't wake him. Here, let me give him another sedative."

"But I want to know how he's feeling."

"It doesn't matter now. This one was a failure."

"Maybe we can salvage it somehow."

"No time. We were told to just move on to the next one if something doesn't work. We've got a schedule to follow."

"But all that time hooking it up. All that expense."

"They'll just write it off as a loss. It really doesn't matter."

"I heard a grunt. Cyril? Can you hear me?"

"He can't hear anything. He's not conscious."

***

"So how long are you planning on staying here, freeloading on your parents?"

Cyril turned his attention from the television to his father.

"Cyril can stay here as long as he wants," Mama said.

"No, he needs to get a job. He needs to pay rent if he stays here."

"Dad, he just got back home," Donny said.

"Well?" his father asked. "Do you have plans?"

"I won't be here too long," Cyril said. "I just wanted to get my bearings. I'll be out of your hair soon."

"Make sure of it. I can't afford to be feeding all kinds of extra mouths."

Cyril had money put aside—it accumulated while he was in the army. He didn't spend much, just put it in the bank. He was sure it was enough to hold him over until he got a regular job. But he wasn't going to give it to his father. He was going to find a place of his own in town.

"I heard you were talking to that Andrews girl," his mother said. "Did you see her in town?"

"Yes, it was unexpected."

"Stay away from her," his father said. "You know how much grief you got the last time. Her folks don't want anything to do with people like us."

"All I did was talk to her," Cyril said. "It was nothing."

"Don't even do that."

He had let his buddy Andy talk him into going to a party at the beach. Many of his old friends were there. People he had gone to high school with. There was a bonfire crackling on the sand.

Chan was there with her friends. She watched him from the other side of the fire, and then came over to him when she noticed him looking back.

"Good to see you again," she said.

"Yeah, it's good to see you, too."

"I'm going to get some wings," she told him.

"What?"

"Wings," she said. "My father arranged it all. It will happen this weekend. I'm so excited."

"That must cost a fortune."

"Well, my daddy's got it," she said. "What else is he going to spend it on? I've wanted wings my whole life."

"They've made a lot of progress," he said. "I saw a doctor talking about it on television. He said they perfected it now. You can get all kinds of amazing things these days."

"They call them accessories," she said. "I already picked out what they'll look like and everything."

"You do seem pretty excited."

"I am. I really am. This is the most exciting thing I've done in years. And there won't be time when I get a real job and settle down and have kids and all. No time to do something like this."

He nodded.

"While you were gone, I went through a long depression," she said.

"Oh."

"Not because of you. Not anything you did. I just took it really bad when Harry and I broke up. And I guess I felt some guilt about how I treated you, too. Things got pretty awful there for a while. I wasn't eating or anything. Finally, we found a medication that helped. I don't get so sad anymore."

"I'm sorry to hear you went through that."

"I'm sorry for the way I treated you," she said. "Sometimes I think about how we ended things, how *I* ended things. I feel really bad about how I did that. You didn't deserve it."

"I got over it," he said.

"You almost got killed getting over it," she said, "I know you joined the army because of me."

"No, I just needed to get away, to see the world outside of this stupid town. I would have left anyway."

"If we'd stayed together," she said. "I'm sure you would have stayed here."

"I don't know."

"Did you think about me while you were over there?" she asked.

"Sure. Lots of times. You're not someone who's easy to forget."

She looked like there were tears welling up in her eyes. She had always been an emotional girl. He found it attractive. "I'm sorry, Cyril. Honest I am."

"I believe you."

"And I'm so glad you didn't die in the war. I'm glad you came back, even if you hate it here."

"I'm glad I'm not dead, too," he said, and laughed, trying to lighten the mood.

Andy came over to where they were talking. "Cyril, let's go. There are other parties to go to."

He didn't want to go, but Chan said goodbye to him and went back to her friends. There was no reason to stay.

He awoke with pains in his chest and a strange heat in his spine. Cyril sat up in bed and tried to get past it, tried to wait it out, but the pain wouldn't leave. He called for his mother, and she got upset and went for his father, who took charge of the situation. His father demanded he get it checked out, helped Cyril go out to the truck, and they drove to see the family doctor.

Dr. Hammond admitted him to the hospital in town and they did some tests. When the last test was over, the doctor called Cyril into his office. Cyril was feeling better by then. There were X-rays hanging on a lighted panel on the wall.

"I have to admit, I've never seen anything like this before," Dr. Hammond said. "It's awful strange."

He showed Cyril on the X-rays—there was a black box inside his chest.

"Can't make heads or tails of it. Looks like it's hardwired directly into your nervous system. I don't think I could remove it, even if I wanted to. It would be much too dangerous."

Looking at the X-rays, Cyril realized he had made a mistake, that he should have suffered in silence, no matter how long it took. There was no reason to involve anyone else in this.

"So, you said that you were badly injured in the war. That you were in a coma?"

"Yes," Cyril said. "For five months, they said. There were times when I went in and out of consciousness, but what I remember about it doesn't make sense."

"Well, someone obviously surgically implanted this device," the doctor said. "I don't have a clue what it is, or what it does, and I'd be terrified to touch it. Like I said, it's connected to *everything*."

"Let's just drop it, doc," Cyril said. "I'm okay now, and it's obviously something they put in me when they saved my life. A military thing."

He looked at the X-rays again. He knew that they put something inside him. He could feel it. He should not have let his father bring him here. But he admitted to himself that he had wanted to *see* it for himself. Seeing the thing made it more real.

"I could ask some colleagues of mine about it, if you want."

"No," Cyril said. "Don't bother. I'm pretty sure I remember now, something about a new kind of pacemaker. My memory's just blurry sometimes."

"Well, you've been through a lot," Dr. Hammond said. "I guess that's what it could be. And you seem to be okay now. Aside from this, you appear to be in pretty good shape, considering all that's happened. But I can at least give you some medication, in case the pain comes back."

"No, I don't need any drugs," he said. "You haven't told my parents about this, have you?"

"You're a grown man, Cyril," Dr. Hammond said. "I've only told you. It's not my place to tell anyone else."

"Well, please don't," he said. "Let's just forget about this for now."

Cyril promised himself that he would never make another sound if it happened again.

They had begun texting each other throughout the week. He started it, since she had put her number in his phone. He reached out to her, not expecting to hear a reply. She told him to meet her at the beach where the party had been. It had gotten colder, and they were alone.

"I'm glad you came," she said. "I'm going for my wings tomorrow. I'm not sure how long I'll be away."

They kissed on the secluded beach as the tide came in. It happened so naturally.

"Remember when I said I was so sad when Harry broke up with me?" she asked.

"Yes."

"That wasn't true. I never really loved Harry. And I broke it off with him. My parents wanted me to marry him so badly, but I couldn't go through with it."

"Then why the depression?" he asked.

"I always regretted breaking up with you," she said. "My parents kept pressuring me. Telling me it could never work out. They threatened to cut me off financially."

"They pressured my parents as well. They won't talk about it, but I think they threatened them somehow. In a way, I was glad when you found Harry. You deserved better."

"But I didn't really. Don't you get it? I always wanted you. But everyone conspired against us."

He didn't know what to say to that. But she did not wait for his reply. Instead, she kissed him again. It was like all those years they lost hadn't happened. It didn't take long for her to begin removing his clothes, then her own. He did not resist, and they made love on the sand.

When they were done, she said. "You're the last person I'll ever have sex with without wings," she said. "Tomorrow I'm leaving, but I'll be back as soon as I can. And we'll go far away from here."

"I'll plan on it," he said.

She kissed him again and slipped away into the night.

"You're always moping around the house," his father said, watching him from the couch. "I thought you were going to find a job."

Cyril was waiting for Chan to get back, and worried about her. She said she probably wouldn't contact him for most of her convalescence, but that didn't make him worry any less. She was having major surgery, after all.

And he certainly couldn't call her family to see how she was doing.

Meanwhile, he just bided his time. Why find a job now, when they were going to leave town once Chan healed up?

"I thought you said you were going to find your own place," his father said.

"Why do you want me out of here so much? I'm paying rent now."

"Barely. You're just taking a long time getting back on your feet," his father said. "And I'm afraid you'll stay here forever. I have a lot of friends whose kids came back home after a divorce or whatever, and then they never leave."

"You don't have to worry about that," he said. "I'll be out of here soon enough."

"Not soon enough for me. Donny's going away to college in the fall. I thought we were done raising kids."

Cyril's mother entered the room then and looked from Cyril to his father. "Are you two fighting again?"

"Of course not," his father said.

"Why do you have such a problem with me?" Cyril said. "You've been hostile ever since I got back."

"Hostile? I have no idea what you're talking about."

"Of course you do. You used to talk about your time in the army all the time. I thought you'd be proud of me for going, too."

"Sounds like you spent most of the time in the hospital instead of the battlefield."

"That's not true," Cyril said. "I got injured, sure, and it was pretty bad. But I saw a lot of fighting before that happened."

"Your son was a hero," his mother said, intervening. "He got hurt saving his friends."

"Some hero," his father said. "I like soldiers who don't spend most of the time in a hospital bed."

"You guys didn't even try to contact me, see if I was okay."

"We didn't find out until much later," his mother said.

"I knew they'd take care of you," his father said. "They have the best doctors money can buy. Hardly anybody dies in war anymore."

"Mama, I thought you'd at least write."

"He wouldn't let me," she said, her eyes welling up with tears. She excused herself and left the room.

"Now look what you've done," his father said. "She'll be blubbering for hours now."

"I'll never understand you," Cyril said.

"Of course you won't. That's why we never bonded, you and I. Ever since you were a teenager, it's like I had a space alien living in the house. Your brother Donny is so normal. I don't know what happened to you. I raised you both the same way."

Cyril thought about things Donny had confided in him over the years. He was tempted to bring them up, to throw them in his father's face, but he couldn't bring himself to do it. His brother had trusted him, had said those things in confidence.

"I'm going to my room," Cyril said.

"Of course you are. That's what freeloaders do."

Upstairs, Cyril texted Chan again, but didn't hear anything back.

"So you're leaving town again when she comes back?" Andy asked. They sat on the beach, passing a joint back and forth.

"Yeah, and I can't wait to get out of here. My father's driving me insane."

"He's always been a real hard-ass," Andy said. "For as long as I've known you."

"He hasn't changed."

"You mean your running away to join the army didn't win him over?"

"Not even close."

"My father used to be a prick, too. I'm glad he took off on us. All he did was argue with my mom all the time."

Cyril nodded his head and took the joint back, took a long drag. There wasn't much left of it.

"She's getting wings," Andy said.

"Yup," Cyril said.

"I bet they'll look amazing."

Twenty-eight days passed before he finally heard from her. He had almost given up, thinking she had changed her mind, so the text message surprised him.

Meet me @the beach at midnight

She probably wanted to make a big deal about the unveiling of her wings. He didn't blame her. As he responded, telling her he'd be there, he couldn't help getting goose bumps. This was going to make the long wait worthwhile.

Back when he had left the military hospital, no one said a word to him. Doctor Fresno, who had always been hovering somewhere nearby, who always seemed so interested in his case, was nowhere to be seen that day. Cyril asked about him and a nurse told him it was his day off.

After the IED took him out, Cyril drifted in and out of consciousness for a long time. The voice he heard whenever he regained consciousness was almost always Dr. Fresno's. As he got dressed that last day, he looked at himself in the mirror and was amazed how *whole* he looked. How normal. If they had replaced anything, he couldn't tell. He could feel some differences, some strange aches and pains, but it was nothing he could put his finger on. He was physically heavier, although he didn't look it. The lean face looking back at him was the thinnest he had ever been. But when the nurse had him step on the scale earlier in the day, he was astonished at how much he weighed.

He had wondered if there was something new inside him. The X-rays that Dr. Hammond had shown him confirmed it now, even if he had no idea what it was. A black box. Cyril knew he wouldn't get any answers, and had no desire to pursue it.

He remembered looking at his medical chart the day he left the military. It was written in handwriting he couldn't read. But there was a word that was clear at the bottom. *Failure*. It was circled several times, with enough force to almost tear the back of the page. When the nurse saw him looking at it, she quickly snatched it away, and claimed to know nothing when he asked her questions.

Dr. Fresno had never answered questions. He always changed the subject.

Cyril didn't like Dr. Fresno. One of the few reasons he wanted to go home was to get away from the man.

Looking in the mirror that day, at his thin, nude body, he couldn't help but wonder why they didn't send him back to the battlefield. Why they were discharging him and letting him go home. It didn't make sense. He could have gotten back in shape and they needed men on the battlefield. The war was getting bad again.

And then he'd remember that word. Failure. *Circled.*

It was a little before dusk when Cyril got the beach. Chan was there with some of her friends. When she saw him, she ran over.

"You came," she said.

"Of course I did."

"I was worried," she said.

"It's good to see you back," he said.

"I thought about you all the time. I'm sorry I didn't text you more. Most of the time, they wouldn't let me have my phone. My father kept saying I had to rest."

"So, you have the wings now?" He looked her over. "I don't see anything."

She was wearing shorts and a bikini top, and she turned around so he could see her back. There were the tiniest of scars on her shoulder blades, but that was it.

"You'll see," she said. "They're beautiful."

Looking at her back, he couldn't figure out how anything could be there, but he decided to wait and see.

"Who are your friends?" he asked.

"Girls I met in the hospital," she said. "We became friends. There wasn't much else to do there. They agreed to come here today. We're going to put on a show for you."

"Just for me?" he asked, looking up and down the beach.

"Yeah."

It was starting to get dark and she said that it was almost time, so she ran back to her friends and he squatted down, sat on the sand, and waited. He couldn't take his eyes off her, even though he could just see her outlined in the moonlight as it got darker.

And then the wings sprouted from her back. It happened so quickly, so unexpectedly, that it almost knocked him off balance. They telescoped out of her. They didn't look like birds' wings, with feathers. They looked like they were made of glass, fiberglass maybe, and they glowed bright white. Like the light people say they see sometimes when they have near-death experiences. A beautiful white light. A *heavenly* light.

The other girls started to release their wings, too, and they were other colors. All glowing brightly like neon lights.

And then they each started to fly.

Their wings flapped like birds' wings and they were up in the sky, holding hands, like a chorus line of angels.

He stared up at them, amazed. They were so beautiful.

And this is the girl I'm running away with, he thought. *I'm going to get a second chance with her.*

The girls let go of each other's hands and made a series of geometric shapes in the sky, like an airborne Busby Berkeley movie with glowing, multicolored lights.

Cyril started to feel dizzy. He thought it was the lights, but there was a rumbling in his stomach, and a high-pitched keening in his ears that was getting louder. He felt like he was going to throw up. He tried to fall over on his side, but instead his legs forced him to stand. He felt like he was overheating and tore at the fabric of his shirt, ripping it away.

His spine was on fire.

In his mind, he could hear Dr. Fresno's voice. Something unintelligible. Then something that sounded like "drones."

Like the beautiful, functioning wings that had magically sprouted from Chan's shoulders—the wonderful products of miraculous technology—something emerged from his chest. Something that looked like a cannon or a bizarre gun.

And the keening in his ears got louder still, blocking out all other sounds. He heard something like radio chatter and static.

The weapon in his chest aimed into the sky and fired something like lightning. One of the girls screamed and then fell back to earth, with wings weakly beating, trying to save her, until she crashed into the ocean below.

There was a whirring and more chatter and another of the girls was hit and falling. And then another. And then Chan.

The angels were gone from the sky. The thing in his chest revolved frantically, and then it folded back inside him, and he felt a sharp ache inside.

Cyril looked out over the water, in the moon's light, trying to see if anyone made it to the surface. Then a wing emerged, because he saw a faint green light. He forced himself forward, despite the pain, and ran into the water, and broke into a swim, forcing himself toward where they fell. It was so awkward at first, because he was much heavier than he realized and started to sink, but then he adjusted himself. He had always been a strong swimmer.

Another wing broke the surface, and then another, and he swam toward them. He saw one that was glowing white, but not as bright as before.

He found himself in the middle of a ring of floating bodies, and broken, dimly lit wings, none of them moving.

Cyril stared up at the moon.

And the keening began again.

SHOPPING SPREE

BY MEGHAN ARCURI

I slice off a bit of her right thigh.

I mirror the cut on the left.

Is it symmetrical?

Of course it is. I'm good at my job. Damn good.

I move her right ear up to match her left. Apparently God—or whoever—isn't as good at his job as I am.

I plump her lips and erase her freckles. It pains me to do the latter—I love that girl-next-door look. But this isn't about what I want. It's about what the magazine wants. Sometimes I agree with their specs, sometimes I don't.

Like this next one—spread her eyes apart.

Ridiculous. But warranted, according to them. Same with increasing the size of her breasts. They are divine to me, a perfect handful. But everyone always wants more. As a chronic ass man, though, I ultimately don't care.

The last few items on my list are to straighten her bangs, lighten her skin tone, remove her blemishes, and brighten her eyes.

I execute the specifications flawlessly, make a few subtle tweaks of my own, and sit back in my chair.

The woman on the screen before me is, by industry standards, beautiful—young, tanned-but-not-too-dark skin, large breasts, small thighs, and thick, dick-sucking lips.

I'd definitely fuck her. If she were real, that is. But this person does not exist in the real world. Everyone will just think she does. A moral quandary, to be sure, but I like to think of it as art. Art I'm damn good at.

I work for a small, online fashion magazine. As such, I wear many hats, two of which are taking and touching up photographs. The money's not great, but I have a fair amount of independence, answering only to my boss ... and her specs.

I make some small adjustments to the photograph and save the changes. I have about an hour before I need to leave. The coffee house down the street is playing one of my favorite foreign films. At this time of night, the office is empty and quiet—perfect for finishing a few projects.

My phone buzzes. I sigh at the interruption, but the clock on my computer tells me I should be getting ready to leave.

As I shut down the computer, the phone buzzes again. The number is not attached to a name in my contacts. Usually I wouldn't answer, but this number has an air of familiarity to it.

"Hello?"

"Is this Dewey Melville?" The gruff, male voice on the other end is clipped, angry.

"Yes."

"What the hell is going on?"

"I have no idea what you're talking about."

"I'm talking about my girlfriend."

The last time I had sex, I paid for it, so I'm fairly certain I didn't sleep with her.

"Does she have a name?"

"Mila."

Mila. The woman in the photograph I worked on earlier this evening.

"What's the matter with Mila?"

"I think you should see for yourself. Are you at your office?"

"I was just about to leave."

Muffled sounds come through the phone—a high-pitched voice, the man's voice, a sigh.

"Dewey?" The woman's voice is shaky, panicked.

"Mila?"

"Something messed up is going on. I need to see you."

"Can't you tell me over the phone?"

I really want to see that foreign film.

"No! I need to show you in person." Her tone is hysterical, desperate.

I sigh. "I'm at the office. I'll be here for another twenty minutes or so."

"We'll be right over."

She hangs up.

What could she possibly want with me?

My stomach rumbles. I haven't eaten since lunch, so I head to the conference room-slash-kitchen, hoping beyond hope someone left something decent in there from today. As I pull open the door to the fridge, the smell of decay—sweet and rotten—assaults my nose. My money's on the clear plastic bag of black slop that was once a cucumber. Or maybe it's Billy the HR guy's moo goo gai pan. He's been grazing on that epicurean delight every day for the past two weeks.

I grab a bottle of water, miraculously unopened, and exit the conference room. The office, although small and dumpy, has two floor-to-ceiling windows. They have no blinds or curtains, so at this time of night, they act as a mirror. I look awesome. My skinny jeans and button down just tight enough to reveal all the hours I spend at the gym.

As I lean closer to the window to smooth out my mustache and beard, a man and woman walk through the main doors behind me.

His stance is aggressive—shoulders hunched, arms forward, hands tight. She looks meek—drooping frame, hood up, face down.

"Mila?" I ask.

The hooded woman nods her head.

"You're lucky you're still here," the guy says.

Good to know he's still an asshole. He insisted on being there for Mila's photo shoot, claiming to be her agent, in addition to being her boyfriend. He spent the whole time telling her what to do, telling me what do to. Or trying to, anyway. I ignored him, yessing him to death but doing what I wanted. I'm the one who went to art school, after all. He's just some money-grubbing cretin.

"I'm always here," I say, leading them to my cubicle. "What seems to be the problem?"

Mila puts her hands on her hood but hesitates.

"Show him," the cretin says.

Mila pulls back her hood.

Tears stain her cheeks, but they're not what make my heart race.

"What the hell?" I say, leaning closer to her.

Her lips are thick, her eyes are bright, her freckles are gone.

"Are you wearing any makeup?" I ask.

"No." She pulls a wipe from her bag and runs it across her cheek. It comes back clean.

Holy shit.

I hustle to my desk and turn on my computer. I open Adobe® Photoshop® and call up the image of Mila I worked on an hour ago.

I flop into my chair.

She looks exactly like the photograph—after I manipulated it.

How can that be?

I run a hand through my hair, sweat forms at my neck.

Mila and her boyfriend hover behind me.

"So this is your fault," the guy says.

"What the hell, Dewey?!" Mila says at the same time.

"How is this possibly my fault?" I ask, rising to face the guy. He is at least four inches taller than I am and a lot wider, but I've learned not to let my smaller frame be a disadvantage. It's all about tone, eye contact, and posture. And confidence. I've got confidence in spades.

The guy blinks, clearly confused by his impotent intimidation tactics. He takes a step back.

He fishes a headshot of her from his coat pocket. "Because she used to look like this," he says, holding up the photo, "but now she looks like that." He points at my computer screen.

"And you think I did it? Like I'm a wizard or something?"

Idiots. I don't know what's going on, but these people are crazy to think I had anything to do with it.

Then Mila gets in my face. "Something majorly fucked up happened. I'm different. I'm completely fucking different. I don't know how it happened, I don't know why it happened, but it fucking happened. And I look just like the picture on your computer, so you have to tell me how this fucking happened!"

She is hysterical, trembling and crying. Her pointed finger pushes into my chest. She's so close to me, her spittle sprays my cheek. I hope she doesn't have any diseases.

I place my hands on her shoulders. "You're right. Something majorly fucked up did happen. But I have no idea what." I grab a chair from the next cubicle. "Why don't you sit down, and we'll try to figure this out."

Mila complies.

My screensaver is on. It's a picture of me at the gym doing a dead lift. I love that shot.

I move the mouse to wake the computer.

"Let's try a few things, so we can rule them out."

I open the original image, the one of Mila's previous look. The sheer act of opening the image didn't change her back.

"When did this happen?" I ask.

"About an hour ago."

"That was right about the time I was working on this. So there's definitely a correlation. Did you feel anything?"

"We were watching TV in my apartment when I started to feel funny. Tingly. First my legs, then my face, then my chest, then my face again. And when I went to the mirror to check it out, it was me, but it wasn't really me, you know what I mean?"

I nod. "What if we tried changing something right now?"

I have doubts about the success of the attempt, as I don't believe in magic, but curiosity tugs at me.

"No." The boyfriend. Mr. Control Freak.

"She's already different as it is," I say. "And it could help to figure out the root of the issue."

"No."

Who is he, the U.S. Congress? Why is he being so difficult?

"Luke," Mila says, putting a hand on his arm. "He's right. I want to know what's going on with my body. I need to."

He grunts and paces in and out of the cubicle.

Eventually he says, "Okay."

Thank God we have his blessing.

"I'll do something subtle, like change your eye from brown to green. How does that sound?"

"Fine," Luke says, as Mila nods.

I use my mouse to manipulate the tools and make her left eye green.

"It's ... tingling," Mila says, rubbing her eye.

Her eye—the one in real life—is now green.

My breathing speeds up.

I'll be damned.

Mila pulls a mirror from her purse. "Oh, my God."

Luke squats in front of her and tilts her chin.

"What the hell?" He turns to look at me. "What the actual hell?"

I shake my head, the only response I'm able to muster. This is some Twilight Zone shit right here.

"Let me try something," I say. I hit *Ctrl-Z* to undo. As she rubs her eye, it changes back to brown.

"This is messed up! Really goddamned messed up," Luke says. More pacing. "What do you think it is? The computer? The mouse?"

I can't stop staring at her. It's unbelievable.

"Dewey?" Mila says. "What's going on?"

Her pallid face and moist upper lip—not to mention her panicked tone—snap me from my trance.

"As much as I hate to say it, I have no idea."

"Is it me? Is there something wrong with me?"

"I doubt that ... but ..." I grab the mouse again. "... you've just given me a great idea."

I open my screensaver—the image of me at the gym—in Photoshop. I select one of my irises and use the tools to change the color from brown to green.

"Well?" I ask, facing the couple.

"They're both still brown," Luke says.

Damn.

I didn't feel any tingling, either.

"Why did it work with her photo but not yours?"

"I'm not sure. But we can conclude that the computer and mouse are not the culprits," I say.

"Then maybe it is me," Mila says.

"Are you a witch?" I ask.

"No!"

"Then it's not you." Although her freckleless face still perplexes me.

She sighs and looks at the computer screen. "When did you take that photo of you?"

"About a month ago." I follow her gaze. Something other than the screen captures my attention.

"Maybe the timing has something to do with it. Or where you took it," she says.

"Maybe the when or where are not important, but maybe the what is." I pick up the camera sitting next to my keyboard. It's the one I used for Mila's photo shoot. It is small and sleek and silver. We recently moved into this office space, dumpy as it is, and the former tenants had left the camera in the storage closet. I tried to contact them, but was never able to. I checked with our lovely neighboring tenants—the law offices of Rena, Butler, and Mann—but they knew little about them and had no contact information. Said they were here one minute, gone the next. So, my boss and I went with the "finders keepers" rule. I used it for the first time with Mila. It's a great camera.

I turn it on, point it at myself, and take a picture. Then I upload the image into Photoshop. Even for a quick selfie, the photo is fantastic. I managed to use the lighting to capture my near-perfect bone structure, as well as the multiple hues of brown—dark chocolate, milk chocolate, and mocha—in my eyes.

Putting the cursor over my right eye, I click on some of the tools again.

My eye tingles, becoming warm and itchy.

I leap out of my seat. I blink and blink, squeezing my eye shut until the tingling stops.

Mila's eyes widen, and she hands me her mirror.

Holy hell!

One of my eyes is brown, but the other is green. I rub my hand over the green eye. It stays green.

"What the ..." I drop the mirror, and fumble with the keyboard, hitting *Ctrl-Z* to undo.

More tingling, more itching.

"Is it back? Is it back to normal?" I ask, turning my face toward Mila.

"Yes."

I pick up the mirror with a quivering hand. My shaking reflection confirms Mila's words—both my eyes are back to brown. My heart pounds, the blood rushing through my ears. I wipe away the sweat that's formed on my neck. Twilight. Zone. Shit.

"It's the camera, then?" Mila asks.

I rub my eye again and take my seat, as my breathing slows.

"It sure as hell seems like it," I say. "If someone had told me a camera could do something like this, I wouldn't have believed them. I'm still having trouble believing."

"Where did you get that thing?" Luke asks.

I explain how it came into my possession.

"So what you're saying is, you don't know anything about it," Luke says.

Condescending ass.

"I know that it altered your girlfriend. And for that I am truly sorry, Mila."

"It's all right." She takes a deep breath. Her shoulders relax. "I mean, it's totally freaky, but I'm glad to have an answer. I thought I was hallucinating or something. I'm sorry about my outburst before."

"Don't give it a second thought," I say. "Now that we understand the root of the problem, we can take action. If you'd like, we can try to change you back to your former self. Unfortunately, I think the best we can do is try to match you back to the original photo. It won't be exactly the same, which will cause me an existential crisis if I think about it for too long, but since I'm skilled at what I do, it'll be damn close."

Mila and her guy stare at each other, she looking at him questioningly.

"You know how I feel," he says. "But now is the time to decide."

Interesting. Perhaps Prince Charming likes the new look better than the old one?

"Well ..." Mila says.

"Well, what?" I ask.

"This may sound crazy, but I don't think I want to go back to what I was."

The boyfriend gives a hefty sigh and shakes his head.

Interesting. I had that one backward.

"Why not?" I ask.

"Don't get me wrong. As it was happening, and immediately afterward, I was totally freaked out. But after we hung up with you, I had a chance to take in all the changes. I mean, I've never liked my freckles. And my eyes are so much brighter and prettier now."

Never liked the freckles? Pity.

"But he shifted your ear, babe. He spread your goddamned eyes apart. It's not you!"

"It is now, I guess." Mila shrugs. "I kind of like it."

Luke storms out of the cubicle. Mila follows him and puts a gentle hand on his shoulder.

"You know I've always hated my dull skin. And I've always talked about getting a boob job." She runs her hands over her ample breasts. "Don't even get me started about how awesome these are."

Luke faces her.

"You know you kind of love them, too," Mila says, her full lips forming a sly smile.

"But that camera." Luke points to my desk. "It's totally messed up. We don't know what's really happening with it."

"True ..."

"May I make a suggestion?" I ask.

Luke rolls his eyes, as Mila says, "Sure!"

"Why don't we give it a few days? I'll experiment with the camera—on inanimate objects this time—and you see if your changes are really something you want to live with forever. Give me a call at the end of the week, and we'll see where we're at."

Mila looks up at Luke. He shrugs his shoulders.

"Sounds great!" Mila says, and she hugs him.

"Terrific."

I begin experimenting after they leave, foreign film be damned.

I start with my stapler. It's not sexy, but I should know if this works on objects other than people.

Using the sleek camera, I take a photo of the stapler, upload it into Photoshop, and play around. Any changes I make on the computer become a reality. I change its color from black to red. I change its size. I even give it Mickey Mouse ears. Then I play around with photos of my coffee mug and chair. All behave as the stapler did, as Mila did.

I then open the photograph of myself, the one I took earlier. I am not inclined to make any changes, as I tend to like the way I look. And I'm still not quite over the green eye bit. Only one thing bothers me about my face at the moment—a zit has been forming under my nose. One of those insidious fuckers that hurts to touch and hasn't broken the surface yet, but when it does, it'll look like a second head.

Using the *Healing Brush tool*, I copy a clear patch of skin from my cheek and color over the horrendous zit. The spot under my nose tingles and warms. I pull a mirror from my desk drawer and, miracle of miracles, the zit is gone. The spot doesn't even hurt to touch anymore.

The camera has tremendous possibilities, both practical and artistic. I hope Mila sticks with the changes. If she likes what I've done, she may have other friends who would like it, too.

A few days later, as I shut down my computer for the evening, my phone rings.

It's the same number as the other night.

"Dewey? It's Mila."

"Hello, Mila. How are you? Is everything all right?"

"Everything is great. Did you get a chance to play around with the camera? Does everything seem okay with it?"

"You mean other than the magical changes it makes?"

She laughs. "Yes."

"All things considered, it seems okay."

"Good. I was wondering ... are you free tonight?"

Propositioned by a model. This job does have its perks.

"For you, certainly. What did you have in mind?"

"Well ... I ran into one of my girlfriends today. She's a model, too. And she wanted to know all about my new look. I couldn't help myself, so I told her about you and the camera. And she totally wants in. Do you think you could do to her what you did to me? We're both free tonight, if you are."

Propositioned by two models? Even better.

"I take it you're going to keep the changes," I say.

"Definitely."

"Luke's okay with that?"

Not that I care, but I'm just covering all the bases.

"Once I reminded him that I wanted plastic surgery anyway, and he'd have to help me pay for it and recover from it, he was totally fine with it," Mila says. "Oh and Isabella— my friend—she's willing to pay you."

One would have to be foolish to pass up two beautiful models and extra cash. Not to mention a chance to apply my art in such a unique way.

"That sounds wonderful. The office is clearing out now, so why don't you come by in an hour or so."

"Awesome!"

"See you then."

The models arrive exactly an hour later.

Mila is still her radiant—although freckleless—self.

"The changes definitely suit you, Mila," I say, as I kiss her hand.

She giggles and blushes. "Thanks."

"Do you feel all right? That is, have you noticed any negative effects from the changes?"

"I feel great! I've gotten more looks and compliments in the past few days than I have in the last month. This is amazing. And when Isabella saw me"—she pulls her friend into the cubicle with us—"she had to try."

Isabella puts out her hand. I give her the same treatment I did Mila.

At first glance, I cannot imagine what this beautiful creature wants to change. Her wavy, raven-colored hair shines all the way down to her waist. Lush lashes surround her large, dark eyes, and her full lips give me less-than-Christian ideas.

But at second glance, her eyes are spaced a little too far apart, her eyebrows are uneven, and her nose and chin are angled and sharp.

I lead them to the open space back by the storage closet. This is the spot where I photograph the models for the magazine. The conditions are not exactly ideal, but it's mostly irrelevant to me. My artistic strength lies in Photoshop. I can make anything look good.

I have her strip down to as little as possible without making her feel exposed. For her, that means yoga pants and a tank top. She doesn't appear to be wearing a bra, which makes many different parts of my body react, but I try to keep my focus on the task at hand. I take multiple photographs from multiple angles. When I have enough, we return to my cubicle. I grab two chairs for them before downloading the photos.

After everyone is settled, I ask, "What did you have in mind?"

"Well ... there's my eyebrows, of course. They're so thick and awkward. And my skin could be smoother and clearer. And I'd love to lighten my eyes, the way you did with Mila's. My thighs are too fat, and I hate this flab right here"—she pinches the flesh between her tank top strap and upper arm—"and then, of course ..." She giggles and places her hand on her pert breasts. "... I'd love for these to be bigger ..."

Always with the breasts.

"... and a little more meat here might be okay, too." Another giggle, as she smoothes a hand over her ass.

Finally. The ass. Hers is full and round and firm. But a little more "meat," as it were, would be just fine.

"Although I feel you are quite right as you are"—she blushes—"you are here to deal with things that, I presume, have been troubling you for some time."

"Yes."

"And although I feel making your desired changes would certainly enhance your look, might I suggest a few others? Others that might get to the core of the issues you feel you have?"

"Sure."

I discuss symmetry and bone structure and body part ratios. My art background, hard at work. I make suggestions based on these concepts. Isabella soaks it all up, like an eager student with her professor. She agrees to everything. Naturally.

Then we get to work. The whole process takes about twenty minutes.

"Well?" I say, before saving the image.

Isabella can't stop looking in the mirror. Can't stop smiling. Can't stop caressing her face or her breasts or her fine ass. I need a cold shower.

"I think her expression says it all," Mila says, also smiling.

"I freakin' love it!" Isabella says. She jumps out of her chair and pulls me into a hug, her new, plump breasts pushing into my chest.

Yes. A cold shower.

"Wonderful," I say, pulling away. I save the changes.

"Here." Isabella reaches into her bag and pulls out a bunch of cash. It is more than I expected, but not as much as I'm worth. "Is this okay?"

"For you? Absolutely," I say. "But I was wondering something."

"What's that?" Isabella asks.

"Do you two have other model friends who might enjoy something like this?"

"Hell, yes," Mila says, as Isabella nods. "And not just our model friends."

"Would you be able to put a list of names together? If you wouldn't mind, they could come with one of you, and I can help them realize their full potential."

"Definitely," Mila says. "What should we tell them in terms of cost? I mean, I didn't give you anything."

"You owe me nothing, Mila, as it was a complete accident with you. I might charge a bit more than this," I say, holding up the cash. "Especially depending on what they want done."

I give them a range of figures that might work. "Would they be able to afford that?"

"They can definitely scrounge up that kind of cash for something like this," Isabella says. "I can get you more if you want."

"Not necessary. Are you happy with what we've done tonight?"

"Yes. Very much."

"Then we are all set," I say. "Just work on those names for me, and we can get started."

This is a much better use of my art degree than complying with the specs of some online fashion rag. All the decisions are mine. And the extra money doesn't hurt either.

Over the next few weeks, Mila and Isabella bring me several clients—all women, which is just fine by me. Each comes in with her own ideas, some of which are decent, some of which are terrible. Using examples from the Internet, I show them what is possible, and why my ideas work so well. They love everything I suggest, but they especially love the results. Not to mention the ease and simplicity—no gym—and no plastic surgery, and at less than half the cost.

Many tip me. Some with cash. Some with other treats. The cash goes right into my savings account. I should be living in a nicer apartment, in a better neighborhood.

And don't think I didn't eventually experiment with myself. Just a bit ... you know ... down below. After nothing crazy happened with Mila, I figured, why not? Why should the models have all the fun? Mila's last few friends seemed to have enjoyed that change quite a bit.

The money ... the sex ... both immensely pleasurable. But to create. To enhance these women and make them the most perfect versions of themselves they can be. That's what gets me off the most.

In my day to day, I start looking at every woman differently—my favorite barista, the mail carrier, my boss, even some of the actresses from my beloved foreign films. The ones I once thought were the ideals of beauty. All could benefit from my work, my vision.

The possibilities seem endless.

A few nights later, Isabella arrives with another model, Kim. I set up the camera. We take the shots, then go to my cubicle and download the photos.

"I need to use the ladies' room. Want me to fill your water bottle while I'm up?" Isabella says to Kim.

"No, thanks."

"I'll be right back."

As she leaves, Kim scoots her chair behind mine.

Sometimes I like to start with the body, but today I begin with the face. I zoom in on it.

"What did you have in mind here?"

"Can you remove the crow's-feet?"

As she points at the screen, she knocks over her open water bottle onto the keyboard.

"Shit!" I scramble to clean it up, grabbing some napkins from my desk drawer. I blot the desk, the mouse, and the keyboard.

As I throw aside the napkins, a loud thud sounds behind me.

Kim lies on the floor.

"Oh my God!" I say, kneeling next to her. "Are you okay?"

But she is not okay.

Her head is missing.

Her goddamned head is missing.

I run my hand over the space where her head should be. Nothing is there. No blood, no bones. Nothing. Her neck is still there, but it's covered with a flap of skin.

No head remains on the image on my computer screen, either. She must've deleted it when she spilled her drink.

Holy hell!

Heat rushes throughout my body. I stumble back to the keyboard and hit *Ctrl-Z*. Her head reappears on the screen and in real life.

But she's not moving.

I run back to her. Her jaw is slack, her eyes are open, staring at nothing. The odors of shit and piss fill my nose.

"Kim?" I tap her shoulder. She doesn't respond. "Kim! Wake up!" I shake her. Her head lolls to the side.

I put my hand over her nose and mouth. She's not fucking breathing.

I try giving her mouth-to-mouth, pumping her chest, but nothing happens. I don't know CPR.

My whole body trembles, sweat forms everywhere. I lean back on the wall of my cubicle, my breaths shallow and erratic.

I don't know what's taking Isabella so goddamned long in the bathroom, but I need to figure something out before she comes back.

This wasn't supposed to happen. All the women I've worked on, all the beautiful work I've done. I was creating happiness. I was creating beautiful art. The camera, Photoshop, both my instruments and my inspirations. And this stupid bitch had to have an open water bottle near my computer.

I inhale slowly to help calm myself.

The camera.

Photoshop.

I rush to my chair and zoom out to see her full body on the screen. Using the *lasso tool*, I outline her entire body.

I hesitate for a minute, but I see no other way. This is entirely her fault, but I would be the one to go down for it. I would go to prison, lose my job, lose my art. This would ruin me forever. All because of some ridiculous water bottle.

No. Way.

I delete the body on the screen.

Kim's body disappears from my cubicle.

I move to where the body was. It's gone. Nothing remains.

I return to the computer and save the image.

Then I spend the next few minutes throwing up in the garbage can.

"Are you okay?"

Isabella has returned.

I nod.

"Where's Kim?" she asks.

I wipe my mouth with a napkin. My hands still tremble.

"Dewey, what's going on?"

I shrug. "Don't really know. This stomach bug came out of nowhere. Fortunately, Kim had already left before I became violently ill. She'd received a phone call and said she had to leave immediately. She said to say sorry to you, but she'd be in contact with you later."

"That sucks. I'm so sorry. Do you need anything?"

"Just my bed, thanks."

"You sure?"

I nod.

"I guess we'll reschedule later. Kim or I will shoot you a text."

"Sounds good."

"I hope you feel better soon," Isabella says as she leaves the office.

I hope so, too.

Two nights later, Mila comes by with another friend. I am uncharacteristically nervous—shaky hands, shallow breathing. I step away, taking a second to calm myself.

The incident with Kim was entirely her fault. I had nothing to do with it. I repeat this to myself a few times. As I inhale, my body relaxes.

When I return to my chair, I ask Mila and her friend to remove all food- and drink-related items from my desk. Regardless of fault, I have no desire to repeat what happened with Kim.

With the desk clear, I sit and begin my work. It is just me, the camera, and Photoshop. And after a few minutes, I am right back in it. The beauty of it, the art of it. I am myself again. I am at home.

About an hour after Mila and her friend leave, my phone rings.

Recognizing the number, I hesitate before answering.

"Hello, Isabella."

"Hey, Dewey. How are you feeling?"

"Much better, thank you. To what do I owe the late-night call?"

"Have you heard from Kim at all?" she asks.

My heart stutters. "No. Have you?"

"No. That's not like her. We talk all the time."

Shit.

"I'm getting worried," she says. "Did she say what that phone call was about before she left the other night?"

"I'm afraid not. She gave a few, short responses to whomever she was speaking, hung up, made some quick apologies, then left."

"Dammit." Isabella pauses. "I think I'm going to call the cops."

My heart thunders. "Why would you do that?"

"Because no one's heard from her. Not me, not her boyfriend, not her parents. And Kim's not the type to just disappear. I'm really scared."

I am about to protest, but that would be ill-advised.

"Can I help you somehow? Do you need me to come over?"

"No. My boyfriend's working late tonight, but he'll be home in about an hour. So I won't have to deal with this by myself for too much longer. But thanks, Dewey."

"Let me know if I can help in any way."

"I don't know how this works, but the cops may want to talk to you. I know that totally sucks, but it'll help Kim."

I squeeze the phone. "Not a problem at all."

"Thanks, Dewey."

"You're welcome."

We disconnect. I slam the phone on the desk.

That can't happen. The police cannot come here to question me. I cannot be blamed for something that wasn't my fault. I can't stop the work I've been doing. I've come too far. I have more I wanted to accomplish. And the money is too damned good.

I wake my computer and click on Photoshop.

I open the photo of Isabella, the one from a few weeks ago.

She really is a beautiful woman, made even more so by my insights. By my work. Work that could benefit hordes of others.

One phone call to the police and that will never happen.

I use the *Healing Brush tool* and put the cursor over Isabella's nose. I click the mouse.

Her nose disappears.

I move the cursor over her mouth. More typing, more clicking, and her mouth vanishes.

I minimize her photo, then open the photo of myself—the one I took with the camera. I am loath to do what I am about to do, but this seems to be the only way.

Using the tools, I work on my hair, eyes, nose, and chin. My whole face tingles.

I pull a mirror from my drawer. New color for my hair and eyes, different bone structure for my nose and chin. It's a shame to ruin my perfection, but the new look is amazing. I am unrecognizable. Almost even to myself.

I save the image.

When fifteen minutes pass, I maximize Isabella's photo. I hit *Ctrl-Z* a couple of times. Her mouth and nose reappear.

After burning all my files onto a thumb drive, I clear my computer, removing any evidence of my extracurricular work.

I grab the camera and turn out the office lights.

It's time to move on.

Another town needs my art.

CLOSER

BY CHARLES COLYOTT

A single, flawless snowflake lights on her lashes, fading into an improbable tear with a single blink of her wide, wondrous eye. She draws close, the wool of her gloves scratchy but welcome on his freshly shaven cheeks. Gazing up at him, she smiles with lips longing to be kissed.

In this moment, she is everything, encompassing his every sense, intoxicating. It is New Year's Eve again. But here at the top of the world, away from the crowds and the noise, there is only a boy and a girl and a future that stretches before them impossibly long. The night air is bracingly cold, but she is pressed tight against him. He is conscious only of the warmth and softness of her small body, the heat of her breath against his ear.

She whispers just three little words.

He kisses her, and her lips are soft as a sigh against his.

Opening his eyes with a gasp, Josh saw the shrink smiling a knowing smile and felt an overwhelming sense of disorientation. "Jesus Christ," he said.

"Are you alright, Mr. Bell?"

Josh leaned forward, pressing his palms hard against his eyes and taking several deep breaths.

"Mr. Bell ...?"

"Yeah. Yeah, I'm okay. I just ... fuck ... that was intense. It was really real." His heart began to pound against his ribcage. His stomach dropped.

"Yes, it can be incredibly realistic. Are you feeling any physical discomfort?"

"No. I just ... okay, yes. Yes, but I think it's just seeing her. Again, I mean. I just ..."

"Do you need some time before we continue?"

"No. No, I'm okay. I'm fine." He took several deep breaths and reached for the bottle of water on the generic table before him. Everything in the office was generic. It was the best of all possible doctor's offices, everything simultaneously warm yet detached, comforting yet sterile.

Josh Bell sat up, let out his breath in a shuddering sigh, and nodded. At this reassurance, the shrink, Dr. Goddard, smiled broadly. He pulled a penlight from his shirt pocket and shined its surprisingly bright beam into Josh's eyes. "I have to tell you, Mr. Bell, I'm excited for you. I am so thrilled to be involved with this project. We've already seen some amazing breakthroughs from patients who've spent a lot of time in conventional therapy. People who've had no relief until ReminEssence."

Leaning back, the shrink rolled his chair to the nearby computer workstation and studied the display. "The diagnostics look good. Any disorientation while using the app should pass ... usually within a few days. You're going to want to clean the surgical site two to three times per day for the first week, but don't baby it. For all the amazing stuff your implant does, we're talking about a minimally invasive procedure, physically. I have you down for counseling every day this coming week, and that's important. Generally that first week, you're going to have a lot of ... stuff that gets kicked up. It can be a lot to deal with. We're here to help. Next week, we're going to try for three sessions. That can be adjusted up or down as needed. But for now, I want you to just take a minute at the end of each day to initiate the implant and start getting the network primed."

Josh frowned and looked down at the printout of care instructions from the nurse. "I don't understand. What does that mean?"

"Well," Goddard began, "right now we're trying to build as accurate a picture as we can. So your job is to just remember your loved one as vividly as possible. Every little bit helps. Sights, sounds, smells ... every detail, however small, helps to build the sim. The good news is that it's much less work than it sounds. Patients generally appreciate the process. With the implant initiated, you will re-experience those memories, much like you just did for our calibration test. Your subconscious mind may start to feed in details that your conscious mind doesn't even realize it remembered. I can't stress this enough, though: Only spend about a minute each night. It's easy, as I'm sure you can already imagine, to get overwhelmed if you do too much."

Josh unconsciously rubbed the small incision behind his ear and gave a half smile as he said, "Should I set an egg timer or something?"

Goddard, serious, said, "It wouldn't hurt. The time distortion can mess with your head, especially in the beginning."

"Nobody said anything about any ... distortion ..."

"It's nothing you need to worry about. You'll only experience it while the implant is engaged. Have you ever fallen asleep and experienced what felt like a lengthy, vivid dream ... only to wake and find that you'd only been asleep for a minute or two? That's the sort of thing I'm talking about."

"So a minute could seem like, what, an hour?"

"Sure ... it's different for everyone. The takeaway here is don't overdo it, especially at first. And try not to get too caught up in any unpleasant stuff. Don't obsess over arguments or that sort of thing. While that data is important, you don't want to get so stuck in it that it starts to affect your life."

Josh looked down at his hands.

"Okay?" the doctor said.

He nodded.

"And keep in mind that this is just the preliminary work. The next stages are going to blow your mind."

Josh left the office and stopped at a grocery for a bottle of aspirin and a microwave dinner. He wanted to pick up a six-pack, but Doctor Goddard had strictly prohibited alcohol during the trial.

Back at his apartment, Josh dug out his keys and crouched to pet the local stray tabby who hung around his building. He let himself into his apartment, set his things on the island, got his dinner in the microwave, and checked his messages.

There was already one from the clinic confirming his follow-up appointment. He went into the bathroom, switched on the light, and turned to see the quarter-sized hairless patch just above and slightly behind his left ear. The incision concealed beneath a neon-green bandage was semicircular and puckered, and it had begun to throb in time with his heartbeat.

Thumbing the new bottle of aspirin open, he swallowed the pills with a handful of water from the tap and looked up to meet his own bloodshot eyes in the mirror.

One minute.

Hell, he could do a minute while waiting for his food to cook.

He turned off the lights in the living room, pulled the drapes shut, and settled into his chair. With a timer set on his cell phone, he switched over to his new ReminEssence app, still in beta, smirked at the load screen with its pictures of happy, laughing people—the sort who graced picture-frame and wallet inserts everywhere—and felt a twinge of gnawing anxiety in his gut.

This is what you've always wanted, he thought, even though that wasn't exactly true.

What he wanted was a do-over, another chance, and that was something he could never have.

This would have to do.

The app loaded with a cheerful harp-strum sound effect, and Josh opened the tab marked "Initiate!" His finger hovered over the button for the briefest of moments, hesitating. Then, as he pressed the oversized green button on his phone screen, he felt something shifting, moving inside himself. He was only vaguely aware of the numbers counting down from five to zero on his screen.

Then the room was gone.

He was gone, too, that sad-eyed bastard he'd seen in the bathroom mirror. He could feel it.

Here, in the cheesy club down the street from his first apartment, he was a young, reasonably decent-looking man with everything ahead of him. All around him were familiar faces, people from the neighborhood. Their hair, those clothes ... had they ever really looked this way?

He remembered the timer and panicked at the thought of wasting his time. On that night, he knew, he'd spotted

Theresa Kaufmann. He'd seen her, and he'd meant to say hello.

Across the club from him, she was there. Theresa Kaufmann, his old next-door neighbor. They'd gone out a few times in, what, sophomore year? They'd even drunkenly fooled around one night after a senior party. If Josh was completely honest with himself, which he almost never was, he would admit that on that night, the night when his entire life changed, he had originally sought her out hoping to take her home.

But then he saw Katy.

He felt it all again, so sharp, so raw, the same old feelings. The club—hell, the world—softened at the edges and faded into the background. The My Bloody Valentine record playing on the jukebox became a dull drone, the voices of friends and strangers receding to white noise. In his vision, the room seemed to distort, everything shifting, bending to be nearer to her, and he was no exception. He'd forgotten that her hair, that first night, had been black instead of the warm auburn she usually wore—part of her Goth phase, she joked later. It was shorter than he'd remembered, exposing the elegant line of her neck. She wore a shabby cardigan and jeans, though her outfit looked like something she'd pulled from Goodwill (she had). He thought she was the most beautiful girl he'd ever seen. More than twenty years later, he still felt the same.

He walked over, noticing that he could feel the scuffed carpet beneath his feet, and banged his shin on a low table. He cursed, and not just because it was part of the memory— it hurt, and he could feel it.

He was still walking, psyching himself up to talk to this beautiful girl, when her eyes met his. Any confidence he had, any sense of worth, anything he thought he knew, fled beneath her gaze.

"Can I get you a drink?" he said.

"Why, are you a waiter or something?" she replied.

He shook his head. The corner of her mouth twitched into a half smile and she said, "Are you trying to pick me up?"

He felt a rush of heat in his cheeks and started to back away, attempting to make a quick, painless exit before he made an even bigger fool of himself.

But then she was there, her arm casually around his, and telling her friends she was leaving for a bit.

And they walked, arm in arm, away from the club and Teresa Kaufman and a dull, mediocre life. To a gas station, where she bought an orange soda, which they shared. To a park, where they sat on the swings and talked about how much they hated clubs. How neither of them would have even gone if not for their respective friends, the kind of friends who always seemed determined to drag a miserable introvert along just to make the night that much more awkward.

They talked through the night. About everything, and, to Josh, it was all fascinating.

Under a cold November moon, with steaming breath, they kissed for the first time. She tasted like cherry lip balm and cigarettes and it was, up to that point, the greatest night of his life.

Josh wanted to grab that kid and shake him. That kid had no idea what he was in for. The highs, the lows.

He disconnected from ReminEssence, feeling the pure, concentrated bliss of youth fade into the drab monotony of middle age. Weight and time bowed his frame, and tears fell unbidden from his eyes.

Forty-five seconds later, his timer went off.

Josh didn't hear it. He never heard the microwave, either.

He wept in his chair until sleep took him.

By the end of the first week, his incision had nearly healed. He had also worked his way, steadily, arduously, to a minute each night. Before his surgery, he had believed he would cheat the system. He imagined spending all of his spare time immersed in the past, in her. He'd dreamed about it. The truth was, the experience was better than he could have dared to hope, but also infinitely more painful.

He lived through their entire courtship in all of its odd, unlikely, passionate glory. He slow-danced with her in the rain at the zoo as an array of exotic birds screeched, watching with perplexed, cocked heads.

They shared a Thanksgiving dinner of vending-machine chips and candy after her car broke down on their way to her family gathering.

He relived their first clumsy attempt at sex, with each of them far more eager than skilled.

He spent a day nursing her through a bout of stomach flu.

Countless times he relived his twenty-first birthday, a day spent almost entirely in bed, with their skills improved and their eagerness undiminished.

He saw her awkwardness as he introduced her to his family at Christmas, and he held her as she watched her grandmother succumb to pancreatic cancer.

They loved and fought with equal ferocity, just as they always had. And, more than he had consciously remembered, they just were. In quiet, boring times they lay, her leg casually draped over his, her hand on his chest. Watching TV. Reading. Listening to music in dark, smoky rooms, skin to skin.

He relived the morning, early in their relationship, when he brought her coffee in bed, prepared with just the right amount of cream. "God, I love you," she'd said automatically. Her wide eyes found his, and brimmed with tears. He realized that she meant it.

Nights out with friends and shows, dinner-and-a-movie dates and family functions. Quiet, languid days. Long, passionate nights.

He lived and relived them all, and the whole of his life with her, back in the real world, amounted to what? An insignificant scattering of moments.

His therapy sessions helped to sort through it all, to put things into perspective. But still he couldn't help but feel as though ReminEssence had done nothing more than tear the scab from a wound that had not, and would never, heal.

"You've expressed a reluctance in returning to the initial memory you used during calibration. During your orientation, you were told to pick your best memory of your chosen loved one. So, I'm curious. Why the reluctance?"

"Because that was the end."

"I don't follow."

"We had that last perfect night. And it *was* perfect. But I never saw her again."

He couldn't say the words, couldn't explain that it wasn't just their love that had died. There were no words to explain that a part of him died that night, too, and that nothing had worked or made sense since that New Year's Day. That the words he'd written to her on their first anniversary as an ironic, cheesy, but simultaneously heartfelt statement had been an unwitting prophecy: "I fell for you ... and I'm still falling."

He'd been falling for years, for decades it seemed, and never hit the bottom, though he was always sure he had. He had always managed to sink somehow lower.

No career, no family left, no relationships that ever worked. A shitty, dumpy apartment with blank walls and thrift shop furniture, that's all he had.

The ad in the newspaper had promised a paid clinical trial of a new form of therapy. He leaped at it because he didn't know what else to do anymore, and the alternatives were starting to scare him.

He had never truly expected to see her—to touch her face, to smell her hair, to hold her—after all this time. But those stolen moments, those beautiful dreams, were such a small portion of his day. They only magnified his misery and tedium.

The cruelest joke was that, with repeated use, he found the time distortion becoming greater, not less. He could now relive a single time Katy smiled at him forty times in less than a minute, becoming intimately familiar with the way the breeze caught her hair, and the way the fading sunlight illuminated her eyes just so. But to what end?

He had that much more time to appreciate how much color had leached out of the world with her absence.

"It will be important to confront that memory, Mr. Bell. It may be key to moving on to the next phase of our program," Goddard said.

When he arrived home that night, that's what he did.

New Year's Eve again. But here at the top of the world, away from the crowds and the noise, there is only a boy and a girl and a future that stretches before them impossibly long.

He is conscious only of the warmth and softness of her small body, the heat of her breath against his ear.

She whispers three little words.

He kisses her, and her lips are soft as a sigh against his.

He woke to the sound of a harp coming from his phone. A notification was listed, but the icon accompanying it was unfamiliar. When he opened it, the harp sang out again. The message read simply, "Congratulations."

When he looked closer, the icon featured the logo of ReminEssence App, superimposed with a giant number two.

Not knowing what to expect, he quickly thumbed open the app and hit the initiation button. As it counted down, he felt the familiar sensation in his head and waited for the world to fall away.

This time, however, the landscape was different. He'd planned to revisit a day in late December, a day he had thought was critical, a day he later convinced himself she'd been acting oddly. But he found himself in a courtyard. Snow had collected in the fountain and in the corners, but the cobblestones themselves were only slick with a thin, dirty slush. Looking past the courtyard, he recognized the tall, sleek building and he muttered a curse.

"We don't have to be here."

He turned and saw Katy sitting on the edge of the fountain. Though he had every curve and angle of her memorized now, he almost didn't know the woman before him.

This wasn't twenty-three-year-old Katy. She'd aged, at last, though as beautiful and vital as ever.

"Why are you staring at me?" she said.

This wasn't a memory, couldn't be.

"Is it really you?" he said.

She laughed. "Well ... of course not. You know better than that. Welcome to the mysterious phase two."

He frowned.

"Okay. So ... you made me. Out of your memories."

"What?" He felt an odd panic in his chest, a sense of some fundamental wrongness. A blasphemy. "Why?"

"Because, as I'm sure you've noticed, it's not satisfying to just dredge up old shit all the time. Now," she gestured at herself, "we can interact. Blank slate. Just like two people. We can talk, hang out, whatever you want."

Seeing what must have been disappointment on his face, she said, "I'm sorry, that was blunt and rude." She looked at the gray sky before saying, "Look, the shrinks put this safety program in your implant, okay, and it makes sure that you know that none of this is real." She took his hand. Her hand, so small in his own, was freezing. Without thinking of the absurdity of it, he brought her hands to his mouth and warmed them with his breath. She smiled, leaned in, and rubbed the cold tip of her nose against his.

"Just between us, though?" she said. "There was a girl you once knew. However well you knew her—and I'm not making any judgments here—*that* concept of *that* girl, formed from all your experiences with her, is what you fell in love with. *I'm made from those experiences, too.* And with all the super-duper, advanced analytics and heuristics and all that fancy A.I. stuff ... I mean, I'm as much her as she was. Just don't tell them I said that, please."

He must've looked like an idiot, just standing there, staring, but she only smiled.

God, that smile.

When the reality—if he could even use that word—of his situation struck him, he asked her the question. It had kept him up at nights, and ruined relationships. It had eaten his life.

"Why? Why did you go? How could you?"

Her smile faded. His chest was tight and a lump rose in his throat. But once he started he found it difficult to stop. Before long, he was a blubbering, incoherent mess.

She watched him, her face oddly cold. Once he regained control over himself, she said, "Goddamn it, Josh. We can do anything, go anywhere you want, and you immediately go right for the worst? You haven't seen me, really seen me, in decades, and *that's* the first thing you bring up? Jesus. How about a 'Hello' or an 'I missed you, Katy'? I mean, I get it. I fucked up, okay? I hurt you and I'm sorry ... but can't we start over? Can't we just be us and leave the past behind for a while?"

"I want it out."

Goddard looked up, surprised. "Mr. Bell, I'm sure we can work this out. Why don't you have a seat?"

"No. I'm done. I can't do it anymore. Just take it out."

"I can certainly schedule an extraction, but I have to say I'm surprised. Of all our participants, you seemed to be seeing great progress."

"This isn't therapy. This is hell. You can't do this to people. You think anyone wants this? To have what they've lost just shoved into their faces? I've lived through this over and over and over and I still can't stop it. There's nothing I can do to stop it."

The texts came in on his way home. The first was a confirmation of his extraction appointment. Three days. He had to wait three days for the neurosurgeon to return from presenting ReminEssence before the F.D.A.

Three fucking days. And already the craving was there. To see her. He needed it more than he'd ever needed alcohol, more than any junkie ever needed smack. Regardless of what she said, he needed to know.

The second text had no phone number attached, just the company logo. It read:

Coming tonight? I miss you.

-K <3

"This is too painful for me. I thought it would help, but it's just too much."

"Can I help?" she said.

He laughed bitterly. "What could you possibly do?"

He felt her gaze, but couldn't bring himself to look at her.

"You could tell me why. That's what you could do," he said. "But you won't."

She didn't respond. After several minutes of chilly silence, he turned to face her. He was surprised to see that she was crying. Her eyes showed genuine hurt, and her lip quivered the way it always had when she was not only upset but angry.

"I'm sorry," he said reflexively.

"Why do you do this?" she said. "I said I was sorry and I said I wanted to get past this. Why do you have to keep bringing it up? I fucked up. Message received loud and clear, okay? I don't know how to break it to you but not every goddamn thing is about you, Josh. You came here tonight to tell me that you're running away. Why? Because *you* can't deal with the fact that *I* ran away. Do you even hear yourself? Your righteous indignation? Yes, Josh, you're the only one hurting." She laughed derisively and got up to walk away. He grabbed her arm and said, "Don't. Don't you dare. I spent twenty years of my life wondering what the hell I could've done differently, wishing I could go back, wishing I wasn't such a piece of shit."

"Oh, twenty years? Twenty *whole* years? You poor little baby. Do you have any idea how long I've waited for you? You know time moves differently here. You know that I'm alone. What you maybe don't know is that, while you've had twenty years to get over me, the only thing I know—the only thing I'm made of—is love for you. You want to know why I did what I did? Well, so the fuck do I."

She sobbed, and he found himself comforting her. Intellectually, he knew she wasn't real. He knew she was just a construct. But he could smell her perfume and her hair, he could feel her tears on his skin, and none of it mattered. If this wasn't real, what was it? If this wasn't real, what was?

The extraction was canceled.

He couldn't do that to her.

And in the days and weeks that followed, how many lifetimes had they spent together, more than making up for lost time? How many more was she forced to spend alone? How much time inside could he physically take, and what would happen if he kept pushing the boundaries?

It was a drab New Year's Eve in the outside world and, though he wanted to spend it with Katy, the migraines he'd started having got worse.

Still, it was an anniversary of sorts.

He hadn't been in years—it had always been too painful—so he didn't know about the bar. Back on their last day together, the rooftop of the Belmont had been a private garden accessible only to the guests in the top suites. They'd dressed to the nines, drunk champagne, and danced in the ballroom. But it was here, on the roof, looking out on the city, that they'd shared their kisses at midnight.

That it was all gone, replaced by a trendy open-air bar with overpriced drinks and hipster bartenders, felt so tragic, so wrong.

He ordered champagne, found a bench near the spot where they once stood, so long ago, and he drank until the pain ebbed away.

She whispers three little words.

He kisses her, and her lips are soft as a sigh on his.

"I've missed you," she said.

He leaned down and kissed her.

"I'm here now," he said, sitting across from her.

They had stopped meeting in the courtyard and often met, instead, at the Italian place where he'd proposed to her on her birthday. No matter how many times they came— thousands, maybe—she always ordered the same thing and he always made a joke about it. After dinner, they would go for a walk down by the river and past the zoo. They would wind up back at her place and make love in the flickering blue light of the television. He would wake sometimes and find her sitting beside the window, watching fat, fluffy snowflakes become gray sleet, and he would see that she was crying.

"I'm just happy," she'd say and offer an apologetic smile.

Time being what it was, he did his best to keep track of his time inside with their calendars and, each year, plan something extravagant for their anniversary.

Although they could technically go anywhere—the implant could draw on satellite data to recreate nearly any location—Katy was usually content to stay close to home. On this occasion, though, she chose a beach in Sardinia. As they walked along the sand, she said, "I don't know if you remember, but I used to say that I wanted to come here if we ever got married."

"Of course I remember. Does it live up to your expectations?"

"It definitely doesn't suck," she said with a grin.

"Well, hey, maybe we can come back for our honeymoon."

Nothing changed outwardly, but he knew her well enough to feel that he'd said something wrong.

"You okay?" he said.

She hugged herself. "The wind off the water is just a little chilly, that's all. Can we go back to the room?"

and her lips are soft as a sigh on his.

"I know. I get it. But you have to understand why I ask, right?"

"No, I don't. Because everything is perfect and you have to ruin it every goddamn time."

When she stands, she bumps the table, knocking over the wine. She doesn't notice as she pushes past the waiter on her way out.

Fried rice and pot stickers on Thanksgiving, because neither of them felt much like cooking. Old movies in bed on Christmas because at some point, with just the two of them, all the trappings of the holidays just felt silly. As the year drew to its end, he couldn't help but feel a sickness forming deep in his gut. She was pulling away again, growing distant. Never in any obvious way, exactly, but he *knew* her. What had once been comfortable silences became a vacuum of dread.

It couldn't happen again. Not again. He would never survive it.

If he was such a piece of shit that he couldn't even hold on to an imaginary girl, maybe he didn't deserve to.

He was out of breath, they both were, as they emerged from the stairwell on the roof of the Belmont.

"Christ, I don't remember there being so many stairs!" She giggled, her heels in one hand and half a glass of champagne in the other.

He almost told her then that the garden didn't exist anymore, back in the "real" world. That their secret oasis had been erased and now served as a hookup spot for frat boys. The words nearly escaped his mouth, but he knew it would only bring her down, and they'd been having such a good night. It must've been the champagne making him maudlin, but this night and this place were irreparably tainted for him. He didn't know why she'd insisted they go, but he wished now that they'd just stayed home.

She drew him to the stone bench near the east edge of the building, where they could see the skyline and where the fireworks would begin just after midnight.

She sat and cuddled close for warmth. Looking up at him, she said, "Are you okay?"

He looked at her, so beautiful in the moonlight, and he answered truthfully.

"No."

She put her hand on his and squeezed gently.

"Katy, I don't think I can do this again."

All those years ago it had been perfect, everything so dizzyingly perfect. Champagne kisses in the virgin snow before carrying her across the threshold into their room. She helped him peel her cold, wet dress from her shivering skin and they warmed each other beneath a blanket in front of the fireplace.

And in the morning, he found her note.

He hadn't heard the sirens.

When he emerged, dumb and bleary-eyed, into the cold light of New Year's Day, the crowds had more or less dispersed, the official vehicles had gone. All that remained of the most unforgettable woman in his world was a rust-colored stain along the side of the fountain in the courtyard.

"I'll never understand why. I'll never accept it."

"If I had answers to give you, you know I would. All I can say is I love you. *I* have always loved you, Josh."

"God, it just never ends. I go through everything in my head and I think of everything I said and did and I think of a hundred what ifs. And then I think of everything you ... she ... did, and I get so angry. But then it all just begins again and it's just waves and they're beating me down and I can't let it go. I want to, God I want to, but I don't know how. I don't want to be this anymore. None of this is fair to you."

She studied him, her eyes shining in the strange light of the evening. "It's okay."

"No, it isn't." He stood and looked out at the city. He took a step toward the edge and could see the courtyard far below. Katy slipped her arms around him from behind, her small hands on his chest.

The air was bracingly cold, but she was pressed against him and he could feel the warmth and softness of her small body and the heat of her breath against his ear.

"There were days, many days, when I used to think about coming up here and just ending it. I wanted to feel what you felt. And then to just not feel anything anymore."

She said, "I know."

"I think ... Katy, I think when I go back to the outside ... I think I'm going to do it."

He expected her to fight him, to argue, but she just brought her mouth to the side of his neck and kissed him softly as a sigh.

She whispers three little words.

"You already have."

He feels the dull thrum of the implant begin to blur his vision, but her hands ball into fists, grabbing handfuls of his shirt.

"No," she says firmly. "Stay with me. Look at me."

He turns slowly, the disorienting buzz of the implant beginning to recede.

"Listen to me, Josh. You have to stop. All the obsessing, reliving every bit of our old life over and over? What has it gotten you? We can't change the past. I can't take back what I did. And you can't take back what you did. What we have to do now is face reality."

He wanted to say, *And what did I do?* But he knew. Without that godawful thrum, he could think clearly. He remembered the champagne, the bar. He'd been just about where they were right now. Amid the surprised cries of the patrons, he'd taken determined steps to the edge, vaulted the protective fencing, and launched himself into the frigid blackness of space.

And he'd keyed the initiation sequence, intending only to say goodbye.

"I can't tell you how many times we've been through this ... you never want to accept it, always so sure that you'll figure out all the answers if you can just see it all again. Always wanting one more time. But it's never worked and it never will. There's no great mystery. I was fucked up and sick inside, and there was nothing you could do about it. I'm so sorry, but that's all there is to it. I would take all of it back if I could, believe me."

"Am I dead then? And is this ... what," he laughed, "Heaven?"

"I can't see the outside like you can, but I know you're falling. That much you told me."

"When?"

"When you first came. But the way time moves ..."

"How long has it been? How long do I have?"

Her eyes, luminous and serious, met his. "Seconds? Minutes? Days? A hundred thousand years? I don't know, Josh."

He slumped to the bench, the strength in his legs gone.

The implant began to hum again, fitfully. Katy grabbed him again. "No. No, you have to listen. What you think you're looking for doesn't exist. It's not back there and it never was and whatever you do it is not going to be there. It's not somewhere out there, either. It's right here, right now, and the only thing I can tell you for sure is that I'm not going anywhere."

She took his face in her hands and kissed him.

"But we don't know how long we have," he said.

"Nobody ever does," she said. "But do you know what we have that everyone else doesn't?"

He shook his head.

She grinned, though her eyes welled with tears. "We know that we'll be together until the end of the world."

They went to a new Greek place for dinner the next evening, and each of them ordered dishes they'd never tried before. A carriage ride took them through the park, and Katy laid her head on his shoulder as the horses' hooves clattered on the cobblestones. When spring arrived, they celebrated by spending a week in Venice before traveling on to Rome and

Naples. Nights were spent with the television off, learning each other's bodies anew.

He gave up on calendars and clocks and ceased putting much faith in the natural cycles of an unnatural place. However long it had been, and it had been a great long while by any standard of measurement, they came to see their lives only as an eternal now, and they were happier for it.

They were on a beach in Fiji, watching the waves roll in, when Katy turned to him and said, "What are you thinkin' about?"

"Just that it's hard to believe."

"That sky? I know. It's righteous."

"No. That I'm dying."

She shifted onto her side, her lithe, tan body contrasting starkly against the pale sand.

"Oh, I see," she said, grinning as she glanced around at their surroundings. "Is that what you're doing?"

He smiled and leaned in for a kiss.

Her lips were soft as a sigh against his.

The ocean held its breath, the waves pixelating, and all became still.

DOG DAYS

BY GRAHAM MASTERTON

Okay, Jack was much better-looking than me, but I was funnier than he was, and women love to laugh. That was how I picked up a girl as stunning as Kylie, when Jack was still dating Melanie Wolpert.

Melanie Wolpert might have been a judge's daughter and she might have screamed like Maria Callas whenever she and Jack did the wild thing together, but she had masses of wiry black curls and millions of moles and she thought that *The Matrix* was an art movie. Apart from that, she was a Scientologist and she smelled of vanilla pods.

I met Kylie in the commissary at Cedars-Sinai. We were standing in line with our brown melamine trays, and both of us reached for the last Cobb salad at the same time.

"Go ahead," I said. "You have it. Please. I shouldn't eat Cobbs anyhow, I'm allergic."

She peered into the salad bowl. "I don't even know what a Cobb is."

"You're having a Cobb salad for lunch and you don't even know what a Cobb is?"

She shook her head. "I'm Australian. I've only been here for two weeks."

Yowza, yowza, yowza, she was amazing. She was tall, nearly as tall as me, with very short blonde hair, sun-bleached and feathery. She had strong cheekbones and a strong jaw and wide brown eyes the color of Hershey's chocolate. Her lips were full and cushiony, and when she smiled her teeth were dazzling, so that you wanted to lick them with the tip of your tongue, just to feel how clean they were.

She had an amazing figure, too—beach ball-breasted, with wide surfer's shoulders, and long, long legs, and those wedge-heeled Greek sandals that tie up with all those complicated strings. I realized almost instantaneously that I was in love.

"Don't worry," I told her. "I'll have the Five-Bean Surprise."

"Okay ..." she said. "What's the surprise?"

"Well, it's not really a surprise, if you eat that many beans."

We sat down together in the far corner of the commissary, and I pointed out John G. Dyrbus, MD, the proctologist, and Randolph Feinstein, MD, who specialized in aggressive kidney tumors, and Jacob Halperin, MD, who could take out your prostate gland while he was playing *Nobody Loves You When You're Down and Out* on the harmonica.

"I'm a physiotherapist, myself," said Kylie. "Children, mostly, with muscular disorders."

"Kylie, that's an interesting name."

"It's aboriginal. It means 'boomerang.'"

"You know something?" I told her. "I don't believe in boomerangs. All that ever happens is, one Aborigine throws a stick, and it hits this other Aborigine right on the bean, so this other Aborigine gets really pissed and throws it back. So the first Aborigine thinks, 'that's amazing ... I throw this stick and five minutes later it comes flying back.'"

Kylie laughed. "You're crazy, you know that?"

And that was how we started going out together. I took her to The Sidewalk Café at Venice Beach and bought her a Georgia O'Keeffe omelet (avocado, bacon, mushrooms, and cheese.) I took her to Disneyland, and she adored it. She met Minnie, for Christ's sake, and I still have the picture, although it's wrinkled with tears. I took her bopping at The Vanguard and I bought her five kinds of foie gras at Spago. We drove up to see my cousin Sibyl in San Luis Obispo in my '75 Toronado, with the warm wind fluffing our hair. Sibyl served us chargrilled tuna and showed Kylie how to throw a terra-cotta pot.

Idyllic days. Especially when we went back to my apartment on Franklin Avenue, cramped and messy as it was, and fell into my bed together, slow-motion, with a full moon shining through the open window, and Beethoven's 5th Piano Concerto tinkling in the background, and Juanita next door clattering saucepans in the sink like a Tijuana percussion band.

For a beautiful girl, Kylie was a strangely clumsy and inexperienced lover, but what she lacked in experience she made up for in strength and energy and appetite. I'll tell you the truth. There were some nights when I almost wished that she'd leave me alone, and give me a couple of hours to get some sleep. Just as my eyelids were dropping, her hand would come crawling across my thigh and start tugging at me, like I was some kind of bell rope, and much as I liked it, I used to wake up in the morning feeling as if I had been expertly beaten up.

I should have counted my blessings. We had been together only eight-and-a-half weeks when the inevitable happened and we ran into Jack.

We were strolling along the beach eating ice-cream cones when I saw him in the near-distance coming toward us, with that monstrous mutt of his bounding all around him. Even if you hated his guts, which I didn't, you had to admit that he was a great-looking guy. Tall, with dark brushed-back hair, a straight Elvis Presley nose, and intensely blue eyes. He was wearing a black linen shirt, unbuttoned to reveal his gym-toned torso, and knee-length khaki pants.

While he was still out of earshot, I turned to Kylie and said, "Why don't we go for a latte? There's a great little coffeehouse right on the boardwalk here."

"Oh, do we have to?" she pleaded. "I just love the ocean so much."

"I know. The ocean's great, isn't it? So big, so wet. But I'm really jonesing for a latte and the ocean will still be here when we get back."

"How can you feel like a coffee when you're eating an ice-cream cone?"

"It's the contrast. Cold, hot—hot, cold. I like to surprise my mouth, that's all. I believe in surprising at least one of my organs every single day. Yesterday I surprised my nose."

"How did you do that?"

"I tried to walk through the balcony door without opening it. But—come on, how about that latte?"

I glanced quickly toward Jack, trying not to make it obvious that I was looking in his direction. I was growing a little panicky now. Apart from Brad Pitt, Jack was the only person in the world I didn't want Kylie to meet.

"Well ..." she said reluctantly, "if you're really dying for one ..."

But then Jack's dog ran into the surf, barking at a trio of seagulls, and Kylie turned and saw it, and said, "Look! Look at that gorgeous Great Dane! My parents used to have one just like it! Oh, it's so *cute*, don't you think?"

"That dog is bigger than I am. How can you call it *cute*?"

"Oh, it just is. Great Danes are so lovable. They're intelligent, they're obedient, and they're so *noble*. I adore them."

"Listen," I said, "I could really use that latte."

But I don't think that Kylie was even listening to me. She clapped her hands and called out, "Here, girl! Here, girl!" and the stupid Great Dane came galloping across the beach toward her, wagging its stupid tail, and then of course Jack recognized me and shouted out, "Bob!" and ze game was up.

"Bob! How's it going?"

"You two *know* each other?" asked Kylie, kneeling down in the sand and tugging at the Great Dane's ears with as much enthusiasm as she tugged at my bell rope. "Oh, you're a beautiful, beautiful young woman, aren't you? Oh, yes you are! Oh, yes you are!" God, it was enough to make me bring up my Cap'n Crunch.

"Sure, we know each other," said Jack, hunkering down beside Kylie and patting the Great Dane's flanks. His grin was ridiculously dazzling and his knees were mahogany brown and he even had perfect *toenails*.

"Jack and I were at med school together," I explained.

"We were the Two Musketeers," said Jack. I was beginning to wish that he would stop grinning like that. "Both for one and one for both, that's what Bob always used to say."

"But—we went our separate ways," I told her. I chose oncology because I wanted to alleviate human suffering and Jack chose cosmetic surgery because he wanted to elevate women's breasts."

"You're a cosmetic surgeon?" Kylie asked him, and I could tell by the way she tilted her head on one side that Jack had half-won her over already. A dishy cosmetic surgeon with a beautiful dog and mahogany knees. What did it matter if he didn't know any one-liners?

"How's Melanie?" I asked him. "Still as voluptuous as ever?" I gave him a sassy wiggle and winked. Come on—I was fighting for my very existence here.

"Oh, Melanie and I broke up months ago. She met a divorce lawyer. A very rich divorce lawyer."

"Sorry to hear it." Jesus—Kylie was even *kissing* that goddamned dog. "You—ah—who are you dating now?"

"Nobody, right now. It's just me and Sheba, all on our ownsome."

Kylie stood up. "Listen," she said, "Bob and I were just going for a latte. Why don't you and Sheba join us?"

"I thought you didn't want to go for a latte," I told her. "I thought you wanted to stay on the beach."

Kylie didn't take her eyes off Jack. "No ... I think I could fancy a latte. And maybe one of those cinnamon donuts."

The three of them walked up the beach ahead of me— Jack, Kylie, and Sheba—and all I could do was trail along behind them feeling pale and badly dressed and excluded. *Thank you, God*, I said, looking up to the sky—*Ye who giveth with one hand and snatcheth away with the other.* Kyle turned around and smiled at me and just as she did so a seagull pooped on my shoulder.

The café was called Better Latte Than Never, which I thought was bitterly appropriate. I sat at the table with Jack and Kylie and tried to be witty but I knew that it was no use. They couldn't take their eyes off each other. When I came out of the bathroom after rinsing the seagull splatter from my shirt, I saw that Jack's hand was resting on top of hers, as naturally as if they had been friends all their lives.

"What a great *guy*," said Kylie, as we drove back along Sunset. "He's so interesting. You know, not like most of the men you meet."

"He's multifaceted, I'll give you that. Did he tell you that he knits?"

"No, he didn't! Maybe he could knit me a sweater!"

"I don't think so. He only knits blanket squares. They're not very square, either. I think it's some perceptual weakness he inherited from his mother. Did he tell you that his mother played the glockenspiel? She only knew one tune but it could reduce strong men to tears."

"You're jealous," said Kylie. Her eyes were hidden behind large Chanel sunglasses—the same large Chanel sunglasses that *I* had bought for her on Rodeo Drive.

"Jealous? What are you talking about?"

"I can tell when you're jealous because you belittle people. You always make it sound like a joke but it's not."

"Hey, Jack and I go way back."

"And you're jealous of him, aren't you? I'll bet you always have been."

"Me? I'm an oncologist. You think I'm jealous of some tit doctor? Besides, his breath smells of cheese. That was one thing I always noticed about him, but I never liked to tell him. His girlfriends always used to call him Monterey Jack, but he never figured out why."

"You're jealous."

I looked at her acutely, but all I could see was two of my own reflection in her sunglasses, in my crumpled lime-green T-shirt with the damp patch on the shoulder.

"Do I have anything to be jealous *of*, do you think?" I asked her.

At that moment, I almost rear-ended a dry-cleaning van and her answer was blotted out by the screaming of tires, so I never heard it.

Of course, I knew what it was. I took her out to 25 Degrees on Thursday evening for hamburgers. We sat in one of the black leather-upholstered booths, which I thought would be romantic. It's incredible what a reasonably supple person can get up to, in a black leather-upholstered booth. But she was unusually preoccupied, and she kept fiddling with her fork, around and around, and when our orders eventually arrived, she said, "I've been thinking, Bob."

"You've been thinking that you should have ordered the three-cheese sandwich instead of the turkey burger?"

"No, not that."

"Let me see. You've been thinking that you hate this loose-weave sport coat I'm wearing? No, I don't believe that's it. Aha! *I* know what it is. You've been thinking that you and I should stop seeing each other because Jack has called you and asked you out on a date. A threesome. Him and you and the houndess from hell."

She looked at me sideways and there was genuine remorse in her eyes. "I'm sorry."

"You're sorry because Jack has called you and asked you out on a date, or you're sorry you waited until our food arrived before you told me about it? Because I can't possibly eat a twelve-ounce cheeseburger while my throat is all choked up."

"I'm just sorry. I didn't mean to hurt you."

"Nobody ever does, Kylie. Nobody ever does. But I shall have my revenge. Jack may be good-looking and he may be able to charm the turkey-buzzards out of the trees, but you will very soon discover that Jack suffers from premature ejaculation. And, because of that, your lovemaking will last for no more than nanoseconds. Don't ever sneeze when Jack's making love to you, because you might miss it."

Kylie looked away. "As a matter of fact, Bob, he's very good. He's tender, and he's creative, and he can keep it up for hours."

I sat up straight with my chin tilted upward and I didn't know what to say. I don't know what upset me the most— the fact that she had already gone to bed with him, and that he was obviously better in bed than I was, or the Australian way she said "tinder" instead of "tender."

Eventually, I shuffled my butt sideways out of the booth and stood up. The waiter came up to me and said, "Something wrong, sir?"

"Yes. This isn't what I wanted, none of it."

He frowned and flipped back his notepad. "I think you will find that you have everything you asked for, sir."

I shook my head. It isn't easy to argue when you're trying to stop yourself from crying.

"You're going, sir? Who's going to pay?"

"The lady will pay," I told him. "She—ah—"

"Bob," said Kylie. "Don't let's end it like this. Please."

"How else do you want to end it? You want violins? You let me take you out for hamburgers and you'd already gone to bed with him?"

She shook her head.

"Good," I told her. "Have a nice life. Jack and you and that bitch of his. Hope he can tell the difference between you."

I shouldn't have said that, but I had fallen for Kylie in a way that I had never fallen for any girl before. It wasn't only her fabulous looks, and the way that other men swiveled around and stared at her whenever we walked past together, although of course that was part of it. It was her utter simplicity, the way she trusted the world to take care of her, and her genuine surprise when it didn't. It was the way she propped herself up on one elbow when we were lying in bed and stroked my hair, as if she couldn't believe I was real.

She was magical, in every sense of the word. And that evening, after she had told me that she and I were through, all I could do was creep back to my apartment like a wounded animal and lie with my face buried in her pillow, smelling her perfume.

The phone rang. After a long while, I heaved myself off the bed and answered it.

"Bob? It's Jack."

"Jack? Not my best friend Jack? Not my old med school buddy? Both for one and one for both?"

"Bob ... I don't know what to say to you."

"I have a good idea. You could say, 'Bob, I'm going to go to the top story of Century Park East and I'm going to jump off.'"

"Please, Bob. Don't joke."

"Who the fuck is joking? You think I'm joking? I put a curse on you, Jack! I swear to God! You and your fucking Great Dane! I curse you!"

There was a lengthy pause. Eventually, Jack said, "Can't say I blame you, buddy. Stay well. Don't be a stranger forever."

I hung up. There was so much I could have said, but most of it would have been obscene, and what was the point?

Six weeks and three days later my curse worked.

It was a Saturday morning and I was driving east on Olympic, on my way to see my friend Dick Paulzner for a game of squash. I pulled up at the intersection of Western Avenue and who should be waiting at the traffic signal right ahead of me but Jack, in his fancy-schmancy Porsche Cayenne SUV. Sitting much too close to him, with her fingers buried in his hair, was Kylie, in a pink baseball cap, and hunched up in the backseat like somebody's Hungarian grandma was Sheba.

My Jeep was burbling away like it always did, because of a sizable hole in its muffler, and it wasn't long before Jack checked his rearview mirror and saw that it was me. He said something to Kylie and Kylie turned around and gave me a little finger wave.

I ignored her. But then she took off her baseball cap and waved it wildly from side to side, and I could see that she was laughing.

I could go to confession three times a day for the rest of my life and still not to be forgiven for what I did next. I saw scarlet. All the hurt and all the rejection and all the anger, they all boiled up inside of me, and I went temporarily mad. That was supposed to have been *my* life, sitting in that SUV in front of me. That was supposed to have been *my* happiness. Instead of that, I was sitting alone in the vehicle behind, being laughed at by the girl of my dreams.

I pressed my foot down on the gas, and rear-ended the Cayenne with a satisfying *bosh!*

I could see that Jack and Kylie were both jolted, and Sheba was knocked right off her seat and onto the floor.

Jack and Kylie turned around and shouted at me, although I couldn't hear what they were saying. I shrugged, as if I didn't understand what they were shouting for, and then I pressed my foot down on the gas again. There was another *bosh!* and the Cayenne was shoved forward three or four feet.

Now Jack was really mad. He climbed out of the driver's seat and came storming toward me swinging Sheba's metal-studded leash. Just to annoy him one more time, I slammed my foot down and rear-ended the Cayenne again.

This time, though, there was no loud impact. Jack's foot was no longer on the brake pedal and he must have left the Cayenne in neutral. My Jeep barely nudged its rear fender, but it rolled forward another ten or twelve feet, well past the traffic signal.

Without any warning, a huge red Peterbilt semi came bellowing across the intersection and struck the passenger side of the Cayenne. The collision was so devastating that the SUV was pushed all the way across Olympic and onto the sidewalk on the opposite side of the street, demolishing a mailbox.

Even today, I can't recall the noise of that crash. It must have been deafening, but the way I remember it, there was no noise at all, only the silent crumpling of metal and the glittering explosion of glass.

When my hearing suddenly returned, however, I heard the screaming of twenty-two tires on the blacktop, and Jack screaming, too, as if he were trying to drown them out.

I jumped down from my Jeep and ran across the road, dodging around the traffic. The truck driver was climbing down from his cab, too—a heavily built Mexican in a red T-shirt and baggy green shorts, and a Dodgers cap screwed on sideways. He stared at me with bulging brown eyes, and said, "There wasn't a damn thing I could do, man. I stood on everything, but there wasn't a damn thing I could do."

The passenger door of Jack's Cayenne had been crushed in so far that it had bent the steering wheel. The tangle of metal and plastic was almost incomprehensible. But I could see blonde hair and blood and one of Kylie's hands reaching out from a gap in between the door and the front wheel-arch—unmarked, perfect, with silver rings on every finger—as if she were reaching out for help.

"Kylie!" Jack was begging her. "Kylie, tell me that you're okay! *Kylie!*"

He climbed up onto the side of the SUV and tried to wrench open the passenger door with his bare hands, but it was wedged in far too tight.

"Somebody call an ambulance!" he screamed. *"For Christ's sake, somebody call an ambulance!"*

Of course, somebody already had, and it was only a few minutes before we heard the whooping and scribbling of a distant siren. Jack stayed where he was, leaning against the smashed-in door, pleading with Kylie to still be alive.

"I stood on everything," the truck driver repeated. "There wasn't a damn thing I could do."

"I know," I said, and gave him a reassuring pat on his big, sweat-soaked shoulder.

Two squad cars arrived, and then an ambulance, and then a fire truck, and the police made all of us spectators shuffle across to the other side of the street. The fire crew started work with cutters and hydraulic spreaders, trying to extricate Kylie from the wreckage. I could see sparks flying and hear the arthritic groaning of metal being bent.

Jack was sitting on the back step of the ambulance with a shiny metallic blanket around him. A paramedic was standing beside him, with one hand raised, as if he were giving him the benediction.

"I can't afford to lose my license, man," said the truck driver. "I got all new carpets to pay for."

But I wasn't listening. Instead, I was frowning off to my left, farther along Olympic. About fifty yards away, I could see Sheba, Jack's Great Dane. She was standing by the side of the road, quite still, more like a statue of a dog than a real dog.

Looking back at the smashed-up Cayenne, I could see then that the rear offside door had burst open in the collision, and that Sheba must have either been thrown out or jumped out. I was just about to tell one of the police officers that she was loose when Jack turned around and saw her, too, and sent the paramedic off to bring her back.

Two police officers came over to us. One of them shouted out, "Anybody here witness this accident? If you did, I want to hear from you."

I was interviewed twice by two highly disinterested detectives from the Highway Patrol, one of whom should have had a master's degree in nose-picking. But after the second visit, I received a phone call from my attorney telling me that there was insufficient evidence for a prosecution. Nobody had clearly witnessed what had happened, not even Jack, and the truck driver had been estimated to have been traveling at nearly forty miles an hour in his attempt to beat the traffic signals.

I wrote Jack a letter of condolence, but I think I did it more for my benefit than for his, and I never sent it. Kylie's casket was flown back to Australia, to be interred at the church in Upper Kedron, near Brisbane, where she had been confirmed at the age of thirteen.

Occasionally, friends of mine would tell me that they had run across Jack at medical conventions, or in bars. They all seemed to give me a similar story, that he was "more distant than he used to be, quieter, like he has his mind on something, but he's pretty much okay."

Then—in the first week of October—I saw Jack for myself. I was driving home late in the evening down Coldwater Canyon Drive, after attending a bar mitzvah at my friend Jacob Perlman's house in Sherman Oaks. As I came around that wide right-hand bend just before Hidden Valley Road, I saw a jogger running along the road in front of me. My headlights caught the reflectors on his shoes, first of all, and it was just as well that he was wearing them, because his track suit was totally black.

I give him a double-*bip* on my horn to warn him that I was behind him, and I gave him a very wide berth as I drove around him. I wasn't drunk, but I was drunk-ish, and I didn't want to end up with a jogger as a hood ornament.

As I passed him, however, I saw that he wasn't running alone. Six or seven yards ahead of him was a Great Dane, loping at an easy, relaxed pace. I suddenly realized that the Great Dane had to be Sheba, and that the jogger had to be Jack. He lived only about a half-mile away, after all, on Gloaming Drive.

I pulled into the side of the road and slid to a stop. Maybe I would have kept on going, if I had been sober. But Jack and I had been the Two Musketeers, once upon a time, both for one and one for both, and don't think I hadn't been eaten up by guilt for what I had done to Kylie.

I climbed down from the Jeep and lifted both arms in the air.

"Jack!" I shouted. "Is that you, Jack? It's me, Bob!"

The jogger immediately ran forward a little way and seized the Great Dane's collar. I still wasn't entirely sure that it *was* Jack, because he and the dog were illuminated only by my nearside taillight, the offside taillight having been busted earlier that evening by some overenthusiastic backing-up maneuvers.

"Jack—all I want to do is *talk* to you, man! I need to tell you how sorry I am! *Jack!*"

But Jack (if it was Jack) didn't say a word. Instead, he scrambled down the side of the road, his shoes sliding in the dust, and the Great Dane scrambled after him. They pushed their way through some bushes, and then they were gone.

I could hear them crashing through the undergrowth for a while, but then there was nothing but me and the soft evening wind fluffing in my ears.

"That had to be Jack," I told myself, as I walked back to my Jeep. "That had to be Jack and I have to make amends."

I didn't really care about making amends, to tell you the truth, but I did care about absolution. Like Oscar Wilde said, each man kills the thing he loves, and I may not have done it with a bitter look or a kiss or a flattering word. But I had done it out of jealousy, and maybe that was worse. I needed somebody to forgive me. I needed Jack to forgive me. Most of all, I needed *me* to forgive me.

I took the next left into Gloaming Drive and drove slowly down it until I came to Jack's house. It was a single-story building, but it was built on several different levels, with glass walls and a wide verandah at the back, with a view over the city. At the front, it was partially shielded from the road by a large yew hedge, and I parked on the opposite side of the street at such an angle that—when he returned from his jog—Jack wouldn't easily be able to see me.

I waited over twenty minutes. Two or three times, I nearly dozed off, and I was beginning to sober up and think that this was a very bad idea, when Jack suddenly appeared in his black tracksuit, jogging down the road toward me. Sheba was close behind him, running very close to heel.

Jack ran up the front steps of his house, and still jogging on the spot, took out his keys and opened the front door. He and Sheba disappeared inside.

There was a short pause, and then the lights went on.

Okay, I thought. What do I do now? Ring the doorbell and say that I want to apologize for killing Kylie? Ring the doorbell and say, here I am, you know you want to hit me, so hit me? Ring the doorbell and burst into tears?

I thought the best thing to do would be to let Jack wind down from his run, give him time to take a shower and pour himself a drink. Maybe he'd be more receptive when he was relaxed. So I waited another fifteen minutes, even though my muscles were beginning to creak.

Eventually, I eased myself out of the Jeep and closed the door as quietly as I could. I crossed the street until I reached the yew hedge. Looking through the branches, I could see Jack standing in his living room, wearing a tobacco-brown bathrobe, with a cream towel wound around his neck. He was holding what looked like a tumbler of whiskey and he was talking to somebody.

No, this wasn't the right time to ask him for forgiveness, not if he had company. I waited for a while longer and then I skirted my way around to the other side of the yew hedge, to see if I could make out who he was talking to, but I couldn't.

I looked around, to make sure that no nosy neighbors were watching me, and then I quickly crossed the lawn in front of the house and went down the side passage, where the trash bins were stored. It was completely dark here, and I could climb up on top of one of the bins, and heave myself over the wooden fence into the backyard.

There were cedarwood steps leading down from the verandah into the yard. I mounted them cautiously, keeping my head low, until I could peer over the decking into the softly lit living room.

Jack was pacing up and down in front of a large brown leather couch. A woman was sitting in the couch, a blonde, although I couldn't see her face. Her hair was feathery, rather like Kylie's, but it was longer than Kylie's used to be.

The sliding door to the verandah was a few inches ajar. I couldn't distinctly hear what Jack and the blonde were saying to each other, but I stayed on those steps for almost twenty minutes, watching Jack talking and drinking and stalking up and down. He appeared to be angry about something, and frustrated. Maybe he was angry because he had seen me, and frustrated that the law had never punished me for causing Kylie's death.

At one point, however, the blonde woman said something to him, and he stopped, and lowered his head, and nodded, as if he accepted that she was right. He approached the couch and kissed her, and tenderly stroked her hair with the back of his knuckles. If the look in his eyes wasn't the look of love, it was certainly the look of like-you-very-much.

He was halfway through pouring himself a second whiskey when his phone warbled. He picked it up and paced out of sight, but when he came back he said something to the blonde woman and screwed the top back on the whiskey bottle. Then he disappeared.

I waited, and waited. After about ten minutes Jack reappeared, and now he was dressed in a pale blue shirt and black chinos. He gave the blonde woman another kiss, and then he walked out again. I heard an SUV start up, around the front of the house, and back out of the driveway, and turn northward up Gloaming Drive.

I didn't really know what to do next. The only sensible alternative was to go back home and try to talk to Jack some other time, although I seriously doubted that he would ever agree to it. I crept crabwise back down the steps and groped my way back along the side of the house, in the shadows.

But then I thought, *what I need here is an intermediary, a go-between, somebody who can speak to Jack on my behalf, and explain how remorseful I feel.* And who better to do that than somebody he's obviously very fond of? Who better, in fact, than the blonde woman on the couch?

Women understand about guilt, I reasoned. Women understand about remorse. If I could convince this woman that I was genuinely sorry for what I had done to Kylie, maybe she could persuade Jack to forgive me.

I climbed quietly back up the steps again. I didn't want to startle her, especially since she might well have had a gun, and I was technically trespassing. I didn't know how fierce Sheba could be, either, if she thought that I was an unwelcome intruder (which, to be honest, I was.)

The living room was already in darkness, although the hallway and several other rooms were still lit. I could hear samba music, and water running.

I crossed the verandah and went up to the sliding door. I hesitated, and then I called out, "Excuse me! Is anybody home?"

This is crazy, I thought. I *know* there's somebody home.

"Excuse me!" I called out, much louder this time. "This is Bob, I'm an old friend of Jack's!"

Still no answer. I waited and waited, and below me the lights of Los Angeles sparkled and shimmered like the campfires of a vast barbarian army.

I should have gone back down those steps and gone home and forgotten that I had ever seen Jack again. Sometimes we do things for which there is no possible forgiveness, and all we can do is go on living the best way we can.

But I slid the verandah door a little wider and stepped inside the living room. It was chilly in there, severely air-conditioned, and it smelled of dried spices, cinnamon and cloves. I crossed to the center of the room. On the wall, there was a strange painting of a pale blue lake, with ritual figures all around it.

I heard the woman singing in one of the bedrooms. "*She walks with a sway when she walks ... she talks like a witch-lady talks.*" She sounded throaty, to say the least.

"Hallo?" I called, although I was aware that my voice was still too weak for her to hear me. "This is Bob, I'm a friend of Jack's!"

I heard the clickety-clacking of Sheba's claws on the hardwood floor. I prayed that the next thing I heard wouldn't be "*Kill!*"

I glanced down at the brown leather couch where the blonde woman had been sitting. Six or seven scatter-cushions were strewn across it, with bright red-and-yellow covers, and fringes. On one of the cushions lay a ski mask, in a brindled mixture of black and brown wool. I picked it up and stared into its empty eye sockets. There was something about it which really gave me the willies, as if it was a voodoo mask.

"*Put it down,*" said a harsh woman's voice.

"Hey—I'm sorry," I said, lowering the ski mask, and turning toward the hallway. "I was just—" It was then that I literally sank to my knees in shock.

It was Sheba, the Great Dane. But Sheba didn't have Sheba's head any more. Sheba had Kylie's head.

She walked toward me and stood in front of me. There was no question about it, it was Kylie. Her face was haggard, with puffed-up lips, and her jaw looked lumpy, as if it had been smashed and rebuilt. But those Hershey-brown eyes were still the same.

"Jesus," I said. "Jesus, I'm having a nightmare."

"You think *you're* having a nightmare?" she croaked.

I struggled to my feet and sat on the couch. Kylie/Sheba stayed where she was, staring at me.

"Christ, Kylie. This is unreal."

"I wish it was, Bob. But it isn't. How did you get in here?"

"I—just climbed over the fence. What *happened* to you, for Christ's sake?"

"I died, Bob. But I was brought back to life."

"Like this? This is insane! Was it Jack? Did Jack do this to you?"

Kylie closed her eyes to indicate "yes."

"But how could he do it? I mean, *why?*"

Her voice was very strained, but she hadn't lost her Australian accent. "Jack says that he was so much in love with me, he couldn't bear to lose me. That crash—my entire body was crushed. Legs, pelvis, rib cage, spine. I wouldn't have survived for more than two or three days. So that was when Jack decided to sacrifice Sheba, to save me."

"But how did he get away with it? Doing an operation like that—it must be totally illegal."

278

"Jack has his own clinic, remember, and three highly qualified surgeons. He persuaded them that they would be making medical history. And he paid them all a great deal of money."

"But how about you? Didn't *you* have any say?"

"I was unconscious, Bob. I didn't know anything about it until I woke up."

I have never fainted, ever—not even when my cousin Freddie ripped off three of his fingers with a circular saw. But right then I could feel the blood emptying out of my brain and I was pretty darn close to it. The whole world turned black and white, like a photographic negative, and I felt like I was perspiring ice water.

"What do you feel about it now?" I asked her. "How can you manage to *live* like this?"

She gave me a sad, bruised smile. "I try to treat myself with respect, and I try to treat Sheba with respect. That's why I go out running, to give her body the exercise she needs. We always go out at night, and I always wear that ski mask, so that nobody can see my face and my hair."

"But you can *talk*. Dogs can't talk."

"Jack transplanted my vocal chords. I still get breathless, but I don't find talking too difficult."

She came up closer. I didn't know if I could touch her or not. And if I did, what was I supposed to do? Kiss her? Put my arm around her? Or stroke her? I still couldn't believe that I was looking at a huge brindled dog with a human woman's head.

"Most of all," she said, "I try to be Kylie. I try to forget what's happened to me and live the best life I can."

I looked her straight in her Hershey-brown eyes. "You can't bear it, can you?"

"Bob—I *have* to bear it. What else can I do? How does a dog commit suicide? I can't shoot myself. I can't hang myself. I can't open bottles of pills. I can't even get out of the house and run out onto the freeway. I can't turn the door-handle and I can't jump over the fences at the sides."

"But how can Jack say that he loves you when you're suffering like this?"

"He's in total denial. He says he loves me, but he's obsessed. He's always bringing me flowers and perfume. He bought me that painting by Sidney Nolan. It must have cost nearly a quarter of a million dollars."

I sat on that couch staring at her, but I simply didn't know what to say. The worst thing was that I was just as responsible for this monstrous thing that had happened to her as Jack was. I had killed her. Jack had given her life. But what a life. It made me question everything I had ever felt about the chronically sick, and the paraplegic, and the catastrophically injured. At what point is a life not worth living anymore? And who's to say that it isn't?

For the first time ever, I couldn't think of any wisecracks. I could only think that tears were sliding down my cheeks and there was nothing I could do to stop them.

Kylie said, "My grandma had a dog she really loved. He was a little fox terrier and his name was Rip. After my grandpa died, Rip was the only companion she had. She used to talk to him like he was human.

She coughed, and took a deep breath.

"Rip got sick. Cancer, I think. As soon as he was diagnosed, my grandma asked the vet to put him down. She held my hand on the day we buried him, and she said that if you truly love someone, whether it's a person or a pet, you never allow them to suffer."

"What are you saying to me, Kylie?"

She came even closer. I reached out and touched her cheek. She was very cold, but her skin felt just as soft as it had before, when we were lovers.

"Help me, Bob. I'm sure that it was fate that brought you here tonight."

"Help you?" I knew exactly what she was saying but I had to hear it from her.

"Let me out of here. That's all you have to do. Open the door and let me run away."

"Oh, great. So that you can throw yourself in front of a truck?"

"You won't ever have to know. Please, Bob. I can't bear living like this any longer."

I stroked her hair. "You're asking me to kill you for a second time. I'm not so sure I can do that."

"Please, Bob."

I stood up and walked across to the Sidney Nolan painting over the fireplace. "What does this mean?" I asked her. "These figures ... they look kind of aboriginal."

"They are. The painting's called *Ritual Lake*. It represents the mystical bond between men and animals."

I looked down at her. She looked exhausted. "All right," I said. "I'll help you. But I'm damned if I'm going to let you get yourself flattened on the freeway."

"I don't care what you do. I just want this to be over."

I led her through the hallway to the front door, and opened it. Just as I did so, Jack's Audi SUV swerved into the drive, its headlights glaring, and stopped.

"*Hurry!*" I said, and began to run down the steps, with Kylie close behind me.

But Jack must have seen that the front door was open and he was quicker than both of us. As we reached the bottom step, he opened the door of his SUV and jumped down in front of us.

"Bob! Bob, my man! What a surprise!"

"Hi, Jack."

Kylie and I stopped where we were. Jack came up to me and stood only inches in front of me, his eyes unnaturally widened, like those mad people you see in slasher movies. He was holding Kylie's metal-studded leash in his right hand and slapping it into the palm of his left.

"Taking Kylie for a walk, were you, Bob? I'm amazed she trusts you, after what you did to her."

"As a matter of fact, Jack, I came round to talk to you."

"You came round to talk to *me*? What could you possibly have to say to me, Bob, that I would ever want to listen to?"

"Well—maybe the word 'remorse' means something to you."

"'Remorse'? You're feeling remorse? For *what*, Bob? For mutilating the woman I love so severely that *this* was her only chance of survival? Ruining her life, and *my* life, and ending Sheba's life, too?"

"Jack," said Kylie, in that high, harsh whisper. "Nothing can change what's happened. All the rage in the world isn't going to bring me back the way I was. I forgive Bob. And if *I* can forgive him, can't you?"

"Get back in the house, Kylie."

"No, Jack. It's over. I'm going and I'm not coming back."

"Get back in the house, Kylie! Do as you're damn well told!"

Kylie turned on him. "I'm not a dog, Jack! I'm not your bitch! I'm a woman, and I'll do whatever I want!"

Jack swung back his arm and lashed her across the face with her leash. She cried out and cowered back, just like a beaten dog. I grabbed hold of the leash and swung Jack around, trying to pull him off balance, but he punched me hard on my cheekbone and I fell backward into the bushes.

"Now, get inside!" Jack snapped at Kylie, and lashed her again.

This time, however, Kylie didn't cringe. She leaped up on her hind legs and pushed Jack with her forepaws. Even though she was a female, she must have weighed at least one-hundred-thrity pounds. He collided with the door of his SUV, and then dropped onto the driveway.

"You bitch!" Jack yelled at her, trying to climb to his feet. But she pushed him down again, and then she ducked her head sideways and bit him—first his nose and then his cheek. I saw blood flying all across the front of his pale blue shirt.

"*Get off me!*" Jack screamed. "*Get off me!*"

But now Kylie bit into the side of his neck, viciously hard. He bellowed and snorted, and the heels of his shiny black shoes kicked against the bricks, but she refused to open her jaws.

"Kylie!" I shouted at her. "For Christ's sake, let him go!"

I clambered to my feet and tried to pull her away from him, but Sheba's body was so smooth-haired and muscular that I couldn't even get a proper grip. I took a handful of Kylie's blonde hair, and pulled that instead, even though I was irrationally worried that I might pull her head off. But she kept her teeth buried in Jack's neck until his blood was flooding dark across the driveway, and his shoes gave a last shuddering kick.

Eventually, panting, she raised her head. The lower half of her face was smothered in blood, but her eyes looked triumphant.

"You've killed him," I said, flatly.

"Yes," she said. "That was his punishment for keeping me alive."

I checked my watch. It was almost a quarter of midnight.

"We'd better get going," I told her.

We drove west on Sunset, not speaking to each other. There was a full moon right above us, and its white light turned everything to cardboard, so that I felt as if we were driving through a movie set.

We looped around the Will Rogers State Park and then we arrived at the seashore. I parked and opened the passenger door so Kylie could jump out.

I walked out onto the sand, dimpled by a million feet. Kylie followed me, panting. We reached the shoreline and stood together at the water's edge, while the surf tiredly splashed at our feet.

There was a warm breeze blowing from the south-west. I looked down at Kylie and said, "Here we are, then. Back at the ocean."

"Thank you," she said.

"Jesus Christ. I don't know what for."

"For helping me to end it, that's all."

She trotted a little way into the water and then she turned around. "You're right about boomerangs," she said. "They don't really come back. Ever."

With that, she began to swim away from the seashore. Looking at her then, you would never have known what had happened to her, because all you could see was a blonde girl's head, dipping up and down between the waves.

I stood and watched her swimming away until she was out of sight. Then I threw her leash after her, as hard and as far as I could.

SWITCH

BY JASPER BARK

For months, Krasinki's life had been going slowly down the pan. Then his phone rang and it began to race down it.

Krasinki's head throbbed in time to the ring tone. The double whammy of Jack Daniels and a stinking cold took turns kicking his head. He'd passed out on the couch the night before and did not want to be conscious.

He'd had precious little sleep for days now. He kept waking in the middle of the night choking on thick wads of phlegm, his mouth and throat full of it. Phlegm he'd usually swallowed by the time he staggered to the john to spit it out. Thick, white, and ropy, it made him retch just seeing it in the bowl. And the smell. Aw, brother, don't get him started.

Sitting up hurt, but not as much as turning his head to look for his phone. His niece and nephew had chosen the ring tone and he had no idea how to change it. The little shitheads thought it was cute to choose a blaring siren, because he was a cop.

Krasinski would have smacked them both if he'd caught them. Never mind his faggot brother-in-law and his liberal view of parenting. Kids need to be kept in line and, if the parents weren't willing, Kraskinski was happy to step up. Lucky for the brats they were on their way back to New Jersey when he found out.

The phone blared from beneath a pile of takeaway boxes on the coffee table, Krasinski swept them aside and grabbed it. He forgot to press accept before he put it to his ear and the ring tone sent an ice pick of pain into his temples. Krasinski coughed, his mouth was lined with phlegm, most of which he'd swallowed.

He stabbed at the screen and croaked, "Krasinski."

"Finally. The fuck you been shithead? I rung you at least four times in a row." It was Captain O'Hannagan. The motherfucker was always on his ass. Guy couldn't have wished for a worse boss.

"I'm sick," said Krasinski. "Called in yesterday."

"Like I give a shit. Suck it up and get your ass into the precinct. We got a perp in here who's been asking for you specifically."

"So, tell him to go fuck himself."

"It's a she and, given what she's been up to the last few nights, I ain't gonna tell her to fuck anything. She's one of your old collars, that's why she's asking for you. This is your shit and you gotta clean it up. No one else in the precinct wants to touch it and I don't blame 'em."

"Can't it wait?"

"No, it can't fucking wait. If you don't get here in the next hour, then the next I time I see you will be to take your badge and gun and put my boot up your ass!"

He sighed and hung up. There was nothing more to say. His boss was an asshole. The mole on Krasinski's top lip was itching like a motherfucker. That was never a good sign. Last time it itched this bad, Arleen left him for that insurance salesman. The little prick had been slipping her the salami for nearly a year while Krasinski pulled double shifts so they didn't lose their house. Then Krasinski lost the house to Arleen in the divorce settlement.

He tried to put it from his mind as much as possible these days. If he didn't, he'd lose himself to blind, violent rages that ended in self-destruction and regret. His philosophy was that some truths are too bitter to dwell on, even when you can't help but swallow them.

Krasinski hadn't seen the divorce coming. In fact, the only warning he'd gotten was his itching mole. It was like a weather vane for every ill wind that blew into his life. The fat, black growth sat on his upper lip like a quivering turd. He'd had it his whole life. In fifth grade, he'd knocked Richey Mullins's front teeth out for teasing him about it. His mother said the only reason he became a cop was so he could grow a mustache to cover it.

Krasinski scratched at it as he searched through the piles of dirty laundry on his bedroom floor, looking for a shirt and underwear with the least amount of stains. For breakfast, he knocked back a couple of DayQuil and then chewed some Tylenol, hoping that would be enough to get him through the next few hours.

As he unlocked his apartment door, Krasinksi found a lump under the welcome mat. He felt it under his foot and it crunched as he stood on it. He pulled back the mat and saw a strange black object beneath.

He picked up the object and looked at it. What the fuck was it doing under his welcome mat? He'd never seen the thing before. Where did it come from? It was made of black feathers and hair, wound together with wire and thread. The hair looked familiar, but he couldn't think why. The object looked like some weird fetish, such as a voodoo doll or something.

It was in the shape of a face, but nothing Krasinski had ever seen. Its eyes and a nose were made from tiny shells, it had no mouth. The lower half of the face seemed to be a pair of round buttocks. How did this get in his apartment? Did someone break in and leave it? The whole thing seemed screwy.

Some of the black hookers he busted carried similar things around with them. Same with the Latino drug dealers, some crazy voodoo or Santeria, or whatever these people were into. They often thought it gave them power or protection. Lot of fucking good it did them when they got pinched. Was that what this was, some ex-con out to get revenge on him with some black magic bullshit?

Krasinksi got a sick, nauseous feeling just looking at the weird face. Something about it was wrong, very wrong, at a basic level. Like the flesh-crawling feeling you got when busting a pedophile. His mole started itching so bad it was almost vibrating.

Krasinksi crushed the face in his fist. He was about to throw it in the trash when something stopped him. He didn't want to leave it in his home. It wasn't that he was superstitious, it just didn't look hygienic. He dropped it in his front jacket pocket, to dispose of outside.

When he reached the dumpster in back of his complex, he reached into his pocket for the fetish, but it was gone. Krasinski searched his other jacket pockets and still couldn't find it. Damn thing must have fallen out on the way down. Good riddance to it.

He climbed into his car and heard a crunch when he sat down. There was an uncomfortable lump pressing into his buttock. He reached around and pulled something out of his back trouser pocket. It was the face. How in hell did it get in his back pocket?

Krasinski distinctly remembered putting it in his front jacket pocket. Could he have moved it to his back trouser pocket without realizing? Surely not—the meds he'd taken weren't that strong.

What's more, he'd stepped on the face, crushed it in his fist and then sat on it, but it didn't look harmed at all. It kept its shape, despite being made of feathers and hair. Krasinski didn't want to think about it. He wound down his window and tossed the thing out as he pulled away from the curb.

Krasinski clicked on the radio. Tom Grant, one of his favorite shock jocks, was interrogating some egghead.

"So, let me get this straight, Professor," Grant was saying. "The best way to travel between galaxies is via a wormhole."

"That's right," said some pencil-neck.

"So that's how aliens have been traveling to Earth for centuries?"

"Well, there's no conclusive proof that extraterrestrials have ever visited Earth ..."

"Oh, there is, Prof. Believe me, there is, as our regular listeners will be able to tell you."

Kraskinski snorted and shook his head.

"But the problem with these wormholes," Grant continued, "is that you can go in one end and come out the other in a completely different universe, like a parallel universe. Am I right?"

"You are indeed. In fact, it's even stranger than that."

"How so?"

"Well, due to the nature of quantum mechanics and the unstable behavior of exotic matter, you might not only come out in a different universe, but also out of a different wormhole altogether."

"Sounds like my paycheck," Krasinski muttered. "Goes into my bank account and comes right out my ex-wife's."

He clicked off the radio. Grant was a good man, but he was given to some kooky ideas, conspiracy theories and the like. Krasinski liked him better when he was baiting liberals and winding up pinkos.

Liberalism was all well and good for the bleeding hearts, with their college degrees and their smug sense of entitlement. But they should try working vice for a couple years and then see how they feel. No one can see the things a cop sees, deal with the scum a cop has to, and remain a liberal for long.

Krasinski pulled onto the exit ramp and took a different route downtown. He avoided the main route because the underpasses were all snarled up. Someone on the city council had a brother-in-law in construction, because the roads were always under repair somewhere.

Traffic was a nightmare. You could drive into one tunnel and find yourself coming out of a completely different one in the wrong part of town. Just like a wormhole, Krasinski mused. In fact, you probably came out of a different tunnel into a totally different universe. Krasinksi grimaced. Grant's show had him thinking like a fucking geek.

Krasinski's detour took him through one of the rougher parts of town. Every other building he passed was burnt out or boarded up. Junkies and gang bangers lounged on stoops, old people shuffled along the sidewalk like they were begging to be put out of their misery, and young children flipped him the bird as he drove past.

The whole neighborhood smelled like shit, so bad he could taste the shit on his tongue. Krasinski gagged, he was gonna vomit. He left the neighborhood and pulled off the road by an overpass. He opened the door and leaned out the side of his car.

The ground was strewn with broken glass and torn candy wrappers. Here and there he saw a syringe and even a disposable diaper. Krasinski's cheeks bulged, he bent forward and a torrent of brown puke spilled from his mouth. It looked and tasted like shit, like he was spitting out mouthfuls of diarrhea. What the fuck had he eaten last night?

Another wave hit his mouth and he leaned farther out so he didn't spatter the car. It tasted worse than the last batch, burning his tongue and lips. Did he order takeout chili last night? Was he that out of it? He didn't recall. The weird thing was, he didn't feel his stomach heave. Didn't feel the puke rising in his throat. It was just there in his mouth, forcing its way out.

A couple of bums watched him from a piss-stained couch. They passed a bottle back and forth, but stopped when the smell of Krasinski's puke wafted toward them.

"Aww, man, that's nasty," said one of the bums, his face covered with a matted, graying beard.

"Hey muthafucka," said the other, who wore a fraying beanie. "Take that shit elsewhere."

Krasinski gave 'em both the finger. He spat out the last of the puke and wiped his mouth. Man, it really did taste like diarrhea, smelled even worse. Maybe he should call the precinct, tell 'em he was sicker than he realized. He didn't want to give O'Hannagan the satisfaction of kicking his ass, though.

Krasinski searched under the passenger seat for the fifth of rye he kept there. It was nearly empty, but there were a couple of good swallows left. He unscrewed the cap and used it to rinse away the taste from his mouth. The burn of the whiskey took away the hot sting of the puke. Of course, now he'd go into work stinking of alcohol, but who gave a shit. It was medicinal and it was supposed to be his day off.

The station smelled as foul as it always did. A mixture of stale sweat and floor polish, tinged with gun oil and spite. O'Hannagan caught Krasinski at his desk, on the second floor, before he'd even had a chance to sit down.

"Fuck's sake, Krasinski. You look like shit and smell worse," O'Hannagan said.

"Told ya I was ill."

"My heart bleeds. Try growing a pair." O'Hannagan was a tall man with broad shoulders and giant mitts for hands. He looked like the sort of mick cop who should be pounding the beat in some old movie. Yet he was always immaculately dressed, in clothes way too expensive for a Captain's salary.

O'Hannagan held up a slim manila folder. "Got the details of the case right here. Perp was picked up for giving mercy fucks to a bunch of hospice patients, can you believe that? They're fucking dying and she's going round like Florence Fucking Nightingale with her legs open. Except—and here's the sick thing—she's taking them all up the ass, strictly anal for these stiffs."

"So what are we holding her on? Attempted rape, necrophilia, assault with a deadly asshole?"

"Nope, none of the patients want to press charges, won't even testify. We've only got one witness, an orderly from the ward. All the same, the hospice wants to press charges. They want her on trespassing, assault, and exploiting a vulnerable person."

Krasinski sat down heavily, with a grunt, his bulky frame sinking into the chair. He massaged his temples and flicked through the arresting officer's report as O'Hannagan droned on. Krasinski had learned to tune his Captain out whenever he started talking about a case.

O'Hannagan always wanted to put his own particular spin on an investigation and force you to see things his way, making sure you only followed the leads he thought were pertinent. If you let him, O'Hannagan would have you going into one case and then coming out investigating another case altogether. A bit like a fucking wormhole, Krasinski thought, and then scolded himself for thinking like some limp-wristed science gimp.

The Captain liked to jump on Krasinski's cases because he'd worked vice, too. But he had one of the worst records for closing cases in the department. Only reason he was promoted was because his family was influential in the department ranks and had friends at City Hall. It sucked, but, like most things to do with his job, Krasinski tried not to think about it too much. Like he always said, some truths are too bitter to dwell on, even when you can't help but swallow them.

Finally, the Captain left him alone and went off to scream at some other poor schlub. Krasinski's head throbbed and he couldn't take in much of the report, his eyes glazed over as he turned the pages. His cheeks bulged again and he let out a silent belch that stank worse than his puke, like the kinda fart that would clear a locker room.

The fuck was the matter with his guts? He rubbed his sizable stomach. Where was all this gas coming from? It didn't matter, he was only delaying going down to the see the perp.

His heart sank the minute he saw the name on the arrest sheet—Rosalita Gonzalez. One previous arrest for soliciting and it had caused Krasinski a shitload of trouble. Just had to be her, didn't it. No wonder his mole was itching.

Krasinski poured himself a cup coffee. It tasted and smelled almost as bad as the puke he'd brought up earlier. But it would take the taste out of his mouth and cover the smell on his breath. Finally, he made his way down to the interrogation room in the basement.

"Miss me?" Rosalita said the minute he entered.

"Yeah, like a genital wart."

Krasinski's mole started to itch like crazy, but he ignored it. He pulled back the empty chair and sat opposite Rosalita. She was short and buxom, with a big rack and an ass to match, but her waist was tiny. She was wearing tight blue jeans and a low-cut black top that put her cleavage on display. She would have been hot, even for a thirty-year-old, if it wasn't for her shit-eating grin and her superior attitude. That was the thing Krasinski hated about college graduates, the way they always thought they were smarter, and more entitled, than working stiffs like himself.

"So, Ms. Gonzalez ..."

"Call me Rosalita."

"I don't think so. I got one question for you."

"I'm all ears."

"What the fuck do you think you're playing at?"

"Isn't it obvious?"

"No, to be perfectly fucking honest with you, it isn't obvious. It's probably the least obvious behavior I've come across and, given my line of work, that's saying something. So, I ask you again, what the fuck do you think you're playing at?"

"Maybe I'm just trying to get your attention."

"Is that why you had the Captain drag me in here off my sickbed?"

"Oh, you poor baby."

"Suck my dick."

"Do I have a choice this time?"

"Depends how much I'm paying you, I guess."

"I'm not a hooker."

"One previous count of soliciting says different." Krasinski held up her rap sheet. "Plus there's your recent escapade in the hospice. Bit of an entrepreneur are we, looking for a new market to corner? Where'd you hide the money they were paying you? Or did you have someone on the inside collect it for you? Some half-dead pimp."

"I told you, I'm not hooker, I never have been. That's what I told you last time, or have you forgotten?"

"I've worked a ton of cases in my time. Why the fuck should I recall yours?"

"Spare me, Krasinski. I'm not that dumb and neither are you."

"That's Detective Krasinski to you. And yes, I do remember you, okay. Big deal."

"Then you'll also remember I told you I wasn't guilty."

"Funny thing, just about everyone I arrest tells me they're not guilty. A jury doesn't always see it that way, though."

"Except I *was* innocent ... that time. I wasn't a hooker. I worked for social services. I was also studying for my MA in social work, specializing in the plight of sex workers and streetwalkers. That's what I was doing when I was picked up with the other girls downtown. I was interviewing them."

"So why didn't you tell that to the arresting officers?"

"I did tell them, I even showed them my credentials. They didn't care, they just bundled me into the van with the rest of the girls. I also told the processing officer and he asked to see my credentials, but the arresting officers had them and wouldn't give them back. So they sent me to the holding cells. I told the officer at the door of the cells and he said I had to speak to the detective in charge of the case. That was you. When I did finally get to speak to you, five hours later, do you remember what you did?"

"Enlighten me."

"You laughed in my face, told me to 'tell it to the judge.' Then you walked away."

"And you started busting my balls."

"Oh, so you do remember?"

"Maybe it's coming back to me."

Rosalita flushed, took a deep a breath, and clenched then unclenched her fists. Krasinski smiled to himself. He was getting to her. Good. Maybe he could catch her off guard, get her to give up what she was doing in the hospice and why she'd dragged him down here.

"So you came back to the cell, didn't you?" said Rosalita. "You came back to the cell and took me out for interrogation. At least that's where you told me you were taking me. But instead, you dragged me into a darkened room and proceeded to rape me, anally rape me."

"All I did was put you back in your place."

"Oh, that's what you call it?"

"You loved it, and you know it."

Rosalita took another deep breath. Was that a tear he saw in the corner of her eye? She blinked it away quickly. He really was getting to her.

"I filed a complaint of course," she continued. "Had to undergo a full medical examination. I didn't love that, I can tell you. They took swabs and I had to give a stool sample. But you knew how to cover your ass, didn't you?"

"Don't know what you're talking about."

"There was a woman who rode in the van with me, Yolanda was her name. An unfortunate soul with a serious addiction who kept giving me death stares. Told me she was going to fuck me up, first chance she got. Well she got her chance. She was a three-time loser and this was her third strike, until you offered her a way out. I had to shit your cum into a bucket in a room full of strangers, but what came out on the test report came from a totally different ass altogether. It wasn't even my sample. They didn't find any semen, but they did find evidence of long-term drug use in the tox screen. That's because it was Yolanda's sample, not mine. You pulled a switch on me."

"Prove it."

Rosalita covered her nose and mouth with her hands, palms together like she was praying, trying to cover her expression. She closed her eyes but he definitely saw tears this time. She was starting to break. Wouldn't be long before he had her right where he wanted her.

"I did three months in county because of you."

"Count yourself lucky it wasn't longer, even for a first-time offense."

"I lost my job and I got thrown off my college course. I can never work in social care again. Ten years in the profession straight down the pan, because I'm an ex-con and a proven drug user. None of it true, none of it fair, all because you pulled that switch."

"Boo fucking hoo. Is that what this is all about? Are you acting up because life just isn't fair and things didn't go your way this one time? Are you pulling this stunt so they'll re-open your case? Cos let me tell you right now, that ain't gonna happen."

"No, that's not what this is all about."

"Then what is it then? Just what the fuck are you playing at?"

Rosalita looked up at the ceiling and blinked several times. She didn't bother to hide her tears now. They ran freely down her cheeks. She sighed.

"Oh God, are you really going to make me say this?"

"It's an interrogation, lady. Of course I fucking am."

"Okay," Rosalita dropped her head and stared at the table. "Maybe I want it again."

"Come again?"

"What happened in that room, maybe I want it again. Maybe I haven't thought about much else since it happened. Maybe I really did do all this just to get your attention."

"Get the fuck outta here."

"Is that so hard to believe?"

"You've changed your tune all of a sudden."

Rosalita lifted her eyes from the table to meet his. "So, how about it."

Krasinski shook his head. "If you think you can make all this go away by putting out, you got another think coming.

I'm not about to let you walk just because you spread your legs for me."

"I'm not asking you to let me walk, I'm asking you to put your big Polish dick back up my ass. Is that too much for a girl to hope for?"

Rosalita slipped her foot out of her shoe and ran her toes up the inside of Krasinksi's leg. She smiled at Krasinski as her foot reached his crotch and found his cock. Krasinski knocked her foot away.

"You're some piece of work, y'know that?"

"That's ripe coming from you."

"What's that supposed to mean?"

The smile was gone from Rosalita's face, replaced with a mocking sneer. "You swagger around like you're this big macho cop, who doesn't take shit from anyone. But the minute a woman asks you to put out, hands it to you on a plate, you run away with your tail between your legs. What's the matter, can't you handle a real woman?"

"Now just a minute."

"That's it, isn't it? That's the reason you put it up my ass in the first place, because you don't want a woman, do you? What you really want is another little boy, like you."

Krasinksi stood bolt up, knocking his chair over, and raised his hand. Rosalita stood too, leaning across the table to offer him her cheek.

"Go ahead," she taunted. "It'll only make this so much easier."

Krasinski dropped his hand. He turned away from her and paced toward the door. "Puta!" she shouted after him. Krasinski turned on his heel and stomped back. He grabbed Rosalita by the arm and yanked her toward the door.

"Is this what you want, is it?" he said, pushing her out of the room.

"So you finally grew a pair."

"I'll show you what I grew."

Kraskinski dragged Rosalita down the dimly lit corridor and pulled her through a door at the end. The room beyond was dark. Krasinski reached for the light switch but Rosalita found his hand first.

"No," she said. "Leave it off."

He dropped his hand and Rosalita ran her fingers up his arm, over his chest and down toward his belt. He felt himself stiffen as her fingers undid his fly and reached inside. Despite how shitty he'd felt earlier, his cock strained at the front of his trousers like a rabid Doberman on a short leash.

Rosalita teased his underwear down and her fingers found him. He let out a deep guttural groan as she grasped his shaft with one hand and slid back his foreskin with the other. Her palm lightly brushed the swollen and exposed end of his cock as her thumb and forefinger encircled the sensitive girth, just below his helmet. He began to throb as she built up a slow rhythm and he grunted his appreciation. She was good at this. It was a damn shame she wasn't a hooker. All that talent going to waste.

"You like that?" she said, as his breaths came fast and shallow.

He didn't answer. He put his hands on her shoulders and he pushed her backward. He heard her rump hit the side of a table and he advanced on her like a beast of prey. His hands found her waist and gripped it. Before she could respond, he spun her round and fumbled with the front of her jeans. He undid them and tugged at the waistband, pulling her jeans, then her panties, down to her knees.

She reached around to touch him and he swatted her hand away. He put his hand between her shoulder blades and pushed her forward until her face was pressed down on the surface of the table. She wanted it rough, she was going to get it rough.

He freed his cock from the front of his trousers and pushed it between her buttocks, prodding at the shallow curve between them until he found her hole. She reached around to help him, but he grabbed her wrist and twisted her arm against her back.

He leaned over her and the end of his cock found her rectum. He thrust hard and pushed his way in. She was a lot less tight than he remembered. Guess that was all the anal Olympics she'd indulged in since then. He probably should have worn a rubber, but it was too late for that now.

He pushed in farther and something scraped against his cock. It felt, for all the world, like teeth. What the hell did she have up there? He worried, for a moment, about losing his erection, but took one last stab at her butthole, pushing himself farther in.

He got about halfway in and started to choke. There was a sour taste in his mouth, like stale sweat and urine. He went a little deeper and found he couldn't breathe. There was something in his mouth, something blocking his windpipe. It was long and fleshy and shaped like a truncheon.

In his panic, he clenched his jaw muscles and felt a sharp, stabbing pain in his cock. Something was biting him down there and he still couldn't breathe. His throat was blocked by whatever was in his mouth, but where in hell had it come from?

He threw his head back and reached to his mouth to try to get it out. His fingers couldn't find anything in his mouth, but he could still feel it pressing on his tongue and gagging his throat. His erection began to wilt. He retched once, a gag reflex. Then his throat suddenly relaxed and he finally drew breath.

Krasinki pushed himself away from Rosalita. His cock left her and he stumbled backward, falling on his butt. The hard floor sent jolts of pain through his ass. His cock shriveled into his nut sack and the overhead light flickered on.

Rosalita was standing next to the light switch over by the door. Her jeans and panties were around her ankles.

Krasinksi was gripped with the sudden fear that one of his colleagues would walk in and catch them.

Rosalita smiled, a ball-breaking, superior smile, as though the tables had just turned in her favor. She had the sudden swagger and confidence of someone who has just played a long game and is about to make good on it. Fear began to creep through Kraskinski's guts, like frostbite.

"That all you got?" said Rosalita. "What's the matter, didn't get to put me in my place this time?"

She laughed and Krasinski shuddered. He fumbled with his fly and tried to stand. Rosalita took short steps toward him and put her foot on his hand, trapping it against his shrunken cock. He froze.

"I told you I wanted it again, didn't I? I just didn't tell you the terms. You see I really haven't thought about much else since it happened. All those weeks in prison and queuing up for my social security check afterward, it's rarely left my mind. That's a lot of time to think about one single thing. A perfect amount of time to plot and plan."

Krasinsky couldn't work out how Rosalita had gotten so ballsy and sure of herself. Nor why it filled him with a stone-cold sense of foreboding.

"Did you know they can do incredible things with body modification these days?" she told him. "If you know the right people, you can get the most amazing things done. Luckily, I know people who know the right people. Thanks to them, I've had some unique work done on my asshole. I think you realized that as soon as you were in there. To get the full effect though, you have to see it. You won't understand its genius until you do, and trust me, it really is a breathtaking piece of work."

Rosalita took her foot of his crotch and turned around to present him with her butt. Krasinski got the sense that something wasn't right with it. It didn't look like a normal ass, but he couldn't tell quite how.

Then Rosalita bent and pulled back her butt cheeks to show him her sphincter. It was not the puckered hole he was expecting. It didn't look like any asshole he had ever seen. It did look incredibly familiar though. In fact it was a sight he'd seen in the mirror just about every day of his life.

Rosalita's asshole had been modified into a perfect replica of Krasinski's mouth.

The lips, wet and bulbous, were exact facsimiles of his own, only they ran vertically, not horizontally, between Rosalita's buttocks. Above the lip that perfectly resembled his top lip, a mustache sprouted, running along one side of the crack between her cheeks. Pushing its way out of the mustache was the all-too-familiar mole, a quivering growth on the underside of her buttock.

It wasn't possible. It must be a trick of some sort. It was too real, too lifelike. No one could do that sort of work on an asshole, could they? As if in answer, Krasinki's mole started itching.

"I can see you're impressed," said Rosalita. "To be honest, so was I the first time I saw it. It took every last penny of my savings, but it was worth it. So were the hours I spent camped outside your house, snapping photos of your mouth whenever you came out."

Krasinski felt his sense of foreboding escalate into full blown panic. He knew, suddenly and irrevocably that the cause of all his ills lay between Rosalita's butt cheeks.

"It had to be accurate for my surgeon you see. She's amazing, wouldn't you agree? Some people's talent is so great they can even change the way the world behaves. Especially if their talents lie in more than one area. Do you know how rare it is to find an underground surgeon who also knows the ways of the old country? Can you believe how lucky I am to have stumbled on someone who's not only an artist with the scalpel, but a beloved servant of the Orichás? That's right, a high priestess of Santeria. It's almost too much to hope for."

Krasinski remembered the face he'd found under his door mat. Its misshapen form, with a pair of buttocks for a mouth, crafted from feathers and hair. He knew now why the hair had looked so familiar, it was from his mustache. He'd wondered how it had gotten from his front jacket pocket to his back pocket, but right now he'd give anything not to know the answer.

Rosalita pulled apart the lips of her butthole and Krasinski felt something press against his mouth. She plunged her middle finger into her asshole and Krasinski felt it between his lips. He gagged as the finger slid across his tongue and down his throat. How was this happening?

"The work they did on my sphincter wasn't just a piece of cosmetic surgery. It was a magical working. Everything that goes into my asshole comes out in a different place altogether, without ever touching me. Everything that comes out of my asshole goes into a different place altogether. Have you guessed where that is yet?"

"Bullshit," Krasinski stammered. He hated how high his voice was, how scared it sounded. "I don't believe a word of this, you're full of shit."

Rosalita smiled. "You have no idea how right you are. Before they hauled me in I took an emetic. It went right through me. I've been holding it in, especially for you, ever since. I only had one little accident. But you know about that already, don't you?"

"I don't know what you're talking about."

"I think you do. But that's okay, I've been dying to give you a little demonstration."

Rosalita bent her knees and squatted over him, like she was about to take a shit. Krasinski scooted backward, trying to get away from her butthole. He was backed against a wall, though.

Rosalita huffed, as though she was pushing something out of her butt. The lips quivered and the mole above them twitched. Krasinski felt his own lips quiver, and his mole twitch in perfect synchronization.

He smelled shit again. It was so strong he could almost taste it. Then he did taste it. Rosalita sighed and Krasinski's mouth filled with liquid shit. His cheeks bulged as it spilled over his chin and slipped down his throat. How was this possible? What had she done to him?

The diarrhea dripped from his chin onto his least-stained shirt. He tried to stand and fell forward onto his hands and knees. Rosalita squatted down and tensed again. Another torrent of steaming crap poured from his mouth onto the tiled floor in front of him. His mouth was enflamed. His lips and tongue burned and throbbed.

"How'd you like those ghost chilies I ate?" Rosalita chuckled. "Hot, aren't they?"

Krasinski reached out a hand and pushed Rosalita. She fell forward and laughed as he got to his feet. Krasinski walked to the door. His legs shook and his foot skidded on a puddle of excrement. The whole room stank like a sewer.

He opened the door and rested his hand on the jamb, spitting the last of the crap from his mouth. Roslita laughed again, she was enjoying this. It was what she'd schemed and waited so long for. Krasinski's heart was pounding against his ribs. Sweat drenched his back and soaked into his shirt.

A wave of nausea came over him. He bent forward and actually puked this time. The stomach bile burned the back of his throat. Rosalita got to her feet behind him.

"It seems you're not the only one who can pull a switch," she said. "But you don't seem impressed. What's the matter, don't you like the switch I pulled? I thought it would amuse you."

Krasinski felt tears in his own eyes now. He felt like a little boy again, scolded by his mom for stealing cookies. What Rosalita had done to him, what she'd done to herself, it wasn't ... she wasn't human.

"The thing is," Rosalita continued. "You haven't put it all together yet have you? Even with what I've just revealed, you still haven't worked out what I was doing in the hospice. What I've done to you."

Panic began to grow in Krasinski, like the sound of a distant police siren approaching. There was something he was missing, something important.

He staggered down the corridor and out of the basement, his speed mounting with his alarm. When he reached the central stairwell he was almost sprinting. He took the stairs two at a time.

He moved through the office, as quickly as he could, ignoring the other cops who wrinkled their noses and looked at him with disgust. He got to his desk and opened the file, rifling through the papers without even sitting down.

There was one detail he had to find. O'Hannagan had mentioned it but Krasinski hadn't been listening. His eye had glanced over it on one of the pages but he hadn't taken it in.

"Jesus, Krasinksi, the fuck happened in the interrogation room?" said O'Hannagan, looming over his desk. "You try to suck the evidence out of her ass?"

Krasinski didn't reply. He just stared at a single page of the report. Then he burst into tears. Huge wracking sobs shook him as he bawled like a tiny brat who's just seen his dog run over. Tears and snot ran down his face, mingling with the shit caked to his chin.

O'Hannagan and the other cops were appalled. Krasinski could feel the revulsion radiating off them. He didn't care. He remembered what Rosalita had told him: *Everything that goes into my ass comes out in a different place altogether, without ever touching me.*

He knew everything now. He knew what the thick, white, phlegm that choked him every morning was. He knew what Rosalita had done to him.

He realized all this the moment he saw the description of the hospice on the report. *St. Dunstan's House, Palliative care for patients with advanced illnesses arising from HIV and AIDS.*

He just couldn't take it all in yet. Because some truths are too bitter to dwell on, even when you can't help but swallow them.

HYPOCHONDRIA

BY MARTIN ZEIGLER

After taking his blood pressure (which was normal), his pulse (which was normal), and his temperature (which was normal), I stood at the terminal and typed in Collier's reason for seeing us today—which, as usual, was alarming.

What I wanted to do—what I always wanted to do at this point—was go over to Collier, hold him in my arms, and whisper in his ear not to worry. But I couldn't do that. It just wasn't something a certified physician's assistant did to a patient.

So, instead, I smiled in as professional a manner as possible and informed Collier that the doctor would be in to see him shortly. I then left the examining room and quietly closed the door behind me, all the while thinking how nice, how wonderfully nice, it was to see him again.

What wasn't so nice was seeing Dr. Grumboldt at the nurses' station with his arms crossed, glaring at me. He didn't look at all pleased at the prospect of seeing Collier Williams shortly or at any other time.

"Tell me, Katie," he said at his usual volume, plenty loud for me but not so loud as to penetrate examining room doors, "what's he dying of this month? Type 2 Hangnail?"

"He does seem concerned, Felix."

"That's what you always say."

"That's because he's always concerned."

"About what this time? In fifteen words or less."

"Doctor," I said, "you have a computer, too, you know."

I flashed a brief smile, still professionally, but not in the same professional way as I did a few minutes earlier.

Dr. G, on the other hand, merely rolled his eyes and expelled a huff of exasperated air before disappearing into the examining room.

I knew, of course, what was troubling Collier. I'd keyed in his words as he spoke them. He was experiencing pain in his left leg, which he feared might be a blood clot that would soon break loose and wind its way up his vein and into his heart, killing him instantly. And, yes, he knew what it was called—*deep-vein thrombosis.*

Simply based on the symptoms he had described and on recent tests, of which he'd had several, I doubted that DVT was the problem. But I was certainly no MD.

Dr. Grumboldt was, though, and he more than willingly shared his prognosis with me after he'd emerged from the examining room and shut the door.

"Blood clot, my gluteus," he said.

He then stormed into his private office and shut *that* door.

The good doctor, you see, was put on this Earth to work miracles. To cure the incurable. To revive the dying. To make the blind to see and the lame to walk. Certainly not to waste his time, his talents, and his expensive education listening to the heart, peeking into the ears, and depressing the tongue of a patient who, every month, lumbered through our clinic's front door believing he was at death's door.

The door now swung open. Not death's door, but the examining room door again. And with a decided spring in his step, Collier approached my desk and said, quite cheerfully, "Will you please thank the doctor for me?"

"I'll be glad to, Collier."

"Calf muscle," he said, with a shrug and a grin. "Doctor said I should stretch it more. And that's what I'll do as soon as I get home."

This was a much different Collier from the nervous, fretful one whose pulse I had taken a half-hour earlier. A striking change, to be sure, but not a surprising one. I witnessed this metamorphosis every time he visited. As to which stage of Collier I preferred, I would have gladly wrapped my arms around either one—the frightened Collier to assure him, or the assured Collier to maybe ruffle him up a little.

I did neither, of course. Being a physician's assistant with a code of ethics, I merely suggested that stretching both legs might be a better way to go.

"That's a great idea, Katie," Collier said. "Have a good night."

If I wished him a good night in return, I don't recall. All I remember was staring after him as he left the clinic and realizing that this was the first time he had ever called me by name. Whether he'd known it already or had simply read it off my ID badge didn't matter. He called me by name.

But that reverie was cut short by the sound of yet another door opening and Dr. Grumboldt calling me by name.

"Yes, doctor?"

"Is he gone?"

"Is who gone?"

"You know who."

"If you mean Collier, he just left."

Dr. G looked both ways before crossing the narrow, carpeted hallway to my workstation. "Lousy calf muscle is all it was," he said.

"Yes, I heard. Collier wished to thank you."

Dr. G shrugged it off. He clearly had more important things on his mind than accepting gratitude. "What was it last month?" he said.

"Pardon me?"

"Oh, now I remember. He came in here thinking he had diabetes because he was thirsty. And a month before that, it was testicular cancer. Only it wasn't TC. It was a minor groin pull. And before that, he thought he'd come down with a flesh-eating disease, when it was just dried skin."

"Everything turned out for the best," I said.

"And then there was the colon cancer because of green stool. And the colon cancer because he had the runs earlier that morning. And the colon cancer because he hadn't taken a crap all day."

"But he didn't have colon cancer, and he didn't have colon cancer, and he didn't have colon cancer. What a relief that must have been for you."

"The bloodshot eyes. Remember the bloodshot eyes?"

No other appointments were scheduled for the day, and I so much wanted to go home, rest my tired feet, maybe take a hot bath. But the examining room still needed cleaning, and there were many minor chores to attend to, mostly having to do with the delicate care and feeding of the insurance companies. I had neither the time nor the desire to stand around and listen to Dr. Grumboldt ripping into Collier. And yet there I was, looking at the doctor and asking, "What about the bloodshot eyes?"

"I'm surprised you don't remember. Williams wasn't able to sleep because he was convinced he had liver cancer. All night long he was in his bathroom examining himself in the mirror. Next morning he comes in here shaking in his boots over liver cancer and pinkeye."

"Yes," I said, "I do remember. And he ended up having neither. He left here feeling much better than when he came in. Just as he did today. Just as he's done a dozen times. And isn't that why we're here?"

"It's been more than a dozen times. It's been thousands."

"Oh, Felix, it has not."

"Well, hundreds, then."

"Look, I admit Collier sometimes obsesses a little over a perceived illness of some sort, but ..."

"What do you mean *sometimes?* What do you mean a *little?* It's *always* and *a lot.* And you need to put a stop to it."

"A stop to what? And what do mean *me?*"

"I'll show you exactly what I mean."

He ducked back into his office and re-emerged a second later carrying a thick manila envelope in both hands like a stone tablet.

Plunking it down on the countertop, he said, "Here. Sweet talk him into getting this done. Pronto."

Collier and I had the office all to ourselves. Dr. Grumboldt had ever so graciously allowed us to use it just so long as I worked my magic within thirty minutes.

Thirty minutes? It had taken me all night and most of the morning to get through that *War and Peace* of a medical journal he'd slammed on my desk. And only near the last few pages did I finally come around to admit that this procedure might just be the way to go.

Yes, as hard as it is to believe, Dr. Grumboldt and I agreed, although for different reasons. While I saw the procedure as a way to forever free Collier of undue stress and anxiety, Dr. G undoubtedly saw it as a way to forever free *himself* of an undue pain in the ass.

"Thanks for coming in on such short notice," I said.

Collier nodded politely and sat in the red leather chair. I took the blue one right next to it, wondering if it was mere coincidence that these colors matched the ones you're likely to find in diagrams of the circulatory system.

"Give it to me straight," Collier said. "I can take it."

That caught me by surprise. "What do you mean?"

"The doctor found something, didn't he? Something horrible."

At first, I couldn't fathom why Collier would think this. But then, glancing around the office, I immediately understood. To me, this was just a self-important doctor's self-important room with a self-important mahogany desk that was twice as big as it needed to be. To Collier, it was something else—a set of four walls cluttered with framed diplomas and certificates, every one of them in a specialty dealing with deadly and incurable afflictions.

In other words, Collier thought we were here to discuss getting his affairs in order.

"Oh, no, no, no!" I insisted. "It's nothing like that."

I reached out and touched his arm—to set his mind at ease, of course, but also to simply touch him, if only briefly.

"You're the picture of health, Collier. You're forty-two years old—my age, in fact—and you're fit as a fiddle. And if I could come up with any other cliché for being in perfect shape, I—ah, I know. Healthy as a horse. There's one. You are definitely healthy as a horse."

Before he could dwell on whether fiddles were fit or horses healthy, I quickly added, "And it's because of your terrific health that Dr. Grumboldt wanted me to see you."

"I get it. He doesn't want healthy people coming into the clinic."

I almost had to laugh. If only Collier knew how close he came to describing G to a T.

"Oh, Collier. By all means, if you're ever worried about something, you should come in and see us. Right away. Without hesitation."

He nodded, a little skeptically, perhaps.

"But it's the worrying part that has us worried. You seem to do a bit of it. And we were wondering if maybe you'd be willing ..."

"To seek counseling."

"Oh, goodness, no."

He held out a hand. "No, Katie. Maybe I should see a psychiatrist."

Heavens, he did remember my name. My ID tag was tucked underneath my sweater.

He leaned forward in his chair, rubbing his hands, clutching them, seeking the right words. Finally, he looked at me and said, "I bicycle a lot."

Now, this came out of the blue, and part of me, the professional part, immediately wanted to get back to our reason for being here. After all, we were on Dr. Grumboldt's clock. But the other part of me, the part that really liked the man sitting here beside me, butted right in and took over. "Oh, I love biking. And I ride into work whenever I can."

"Nice. Ever do any racing?"

"Goodness, no. Trails are about my speed."

"Nothing wrong with that," he said. "How about swimming?"

"Oh, yes. Again, I'm not very fast. But there are times when I feel I could do laps forever."

Collier laughed. "When it's too rainy out to go bicycling, I head to the nearest indoor pool and get wet inside instead."

I laughed as well. "Somehow, it's not so bad. Getting wet inside."

Collier blushed suddenly and I realized what I'd just said. And now both parts of me wanted to get back on track right this instant.

Fortunately, Collier must have felt the same. "What I'm getting at," he said, after clearing his throat, "is that when I do this stuff—the biking, the swimming—I never worry about a thing. I've taken ugly spills, crashed into other racers, dropped the front wheel into storm drains pedaling full bore down the street. And, afterward, I've just brushed myself off and kept going. Swimming? Same story. I've slammed my head against the edge of pools. Swallowed gallons of whatever they use in place of chlorine these days. And it's no big deal.

"But put me in my apartment at the end of the day ..."

He drew in a deep breath and let it out slowly. "And I begin to notice every itch, scratch, sore, ache, and pain. Every little anomaly that isn't bicycle-related. I focus on these things and I can't let go. And the next thing I know, I'm on the Internet scrolling through all these gross-looking images of the worst kinds of infections and cancers. And from that point on, it's all over. If I see it, I have it."

Collier certainly returned to the topic, and I admired him for how he did it. "If it's any comfort," I said, "you're not alone."

"Oh, I'm alone, all right."

My professional part was about to explain what I meant, when my other part just had to ask, "No special someone to confide in?"

"Nope. When it's not me on my bicycle or in a pool, it's just me in a chair in the middle of my living room dwelling on me in a chair in the middle of my living room. Which makes me think it should be me on a couch in the middle of a shrink's room."

Collier smiled, if only slightly. And I had to, as well, even though I knew he was being serious. "Collier, you're not crazy, okay? You just think about your inner workings too much. And that's why I called you here. To see if you'd be willing to let something do all that thinking for you."

"Something? Not someone?"

"Yes. It's a device. It's called a Diagnotron."

"A what?"

I repeated the name. He laughed and I repeated his laugh. "It does sound a bit silly, doesn't it?"

"Just a little bit," he said. "And what's it do, exactly?"

"Think of it as your personal early warning system. It keeps watch over your body, night and day, always on the lookout for anything troublesome. On the off chance it finds something, it alerts you by sending a text message to your cell phone. At which point you can seek treatment very early on. Otherwise, you're free and in the clear."

I thought I'd worded that pretty well. It had the hopeful, positive sound I was aiming for, and I eagerly looked to Collier's watchable face for an equally hopeful and positive reaction.

Bless him, it didn't come. "By 'anything troublesome,'"

he said, "do you mean a really horrible disease?"

"Well, yes, but ..."

"Which ones?" he said. "The fatal ones? The chronic ones? The debilitating ones? The ones ..."

"All of them," I said. "Every serious disease known to man."

His mouth dropped. "Every single one? There are thousands! Maybe tens of thousands! The list goes on forever! Why, in one medical encyclopedia I read, the S entries alone take up over eighty pages!"

"Yes, but Collier, isn't that the way you'd want it? If the Diagnotron gives you a clean bill of health, isn't it good to know that all the bases have been covered? That nothing's been left out?"

He was in near panic. "But what if I don't get a clean bill of health? What if, when the Diagno thing alerts me, my brain will already be half-eaten away by some dread disease? What if ..."

"Collier, Collier. The Diagnotron will detect whatever it is long before the first sign or symptom shows up. It will also detect the nastier things that seldom, if ever, show *any* signs or symptoms."

"Oh, I know all about those," he said, with a marked spike in confidence. "Silent diseases, they're called. I recently read up on them. And now, I not only worry when I have a pain, I worry when I don't."

I was beginning to realize that Collier had this charming ability to be serious and amusing at the same time.

"You needn't worry in either case, "I said. "You just look at your cell phone. If there's no alert, you don't have anything. If there is an alert, you'll have caught the culprit early enough to get it treated successfully."

"Even if it's liver cancer?"

"Yes. Even liver cancer. Or any cancer for that matter.

But ..."

"What about pinkeye?"

"That, too."

"And if I do get an alert, what do I do? Go to a doctor and show him my phone?"

"Yup."

"Or her?"

Even in his state of panic, Collier was being a darling. "That's right. And he or she will review the text alert and know exactly what to do. But what I'm trying to say, Collier, is that it'll never come to this. You won't be seeing any text alerts. That's because you have the fiddle thing going on. The horse thing. Plus, you don't smoke, you don't drink, and you keep in good shape."

Really good shape, I wanted to add. But a quick reflection told me that a little flab at his edges wouldn't bother me a bit.

Collier nodded and slowly started to breathe more evenly. "My God, listen to me. I'm getting carried away, aren't I?"

I wanted to reach out and touch him again, this time letting my hand linger. Instead, I said, "It's perfectly natural, Collier. This is strange, new territory we're covering, and you have every right to be concerned. But it's also wonderful, hopeful territory. And all I can suggest is that you give this a try. Let the Diagnotron do your worrying for you. That's what it's paid to do."

He slowly eased back into his artery-colored chair. "I have to admit—this is starting to sound better and better."

"Speaking of being paid, did I tell you that this won't cost you a cent?"

"The Diagno thing, you mean?"

"The Diagnotron, the procedure, any of it."

"Procedure? There's a procedure?"

"Well ..."

"What is this thing anyway?" he asked. "Is it something I wear on my head like a football helmet? Is it a gadget I stick in my pocket? Is it like a wristwatch? A cell phone app? And how's it able to look at me and tell what's going on?"

I hesitated. This was the moment I had been dreading since this morning, but I knew we would need to get here at some point. "Uh, it doesn't actually sit outside and look in, Collier."

"Oh?"

"It's a surgical implant."

I nervously awaited his reaction. The poor thing was already wrapped in knots over bodily invasions by every deadly form of bacteria and virus in the known universe. God only knew how he'd take to the idea of deliberately being invaded by a surgeon with a scalpel.

As it turned out, he responded fairly calmly. Either that, or he was in a state of shock I didn't recognize, despite my training and experience.

"Please, go on," he said. Not in a fearful or suspicious way, but in a way that seemed genuinely curious.

And so I began to run through, in as human a way as possible, the pertinent information I had gleaned from my dusk-to-dawn reading. I explained that the surgery would be more of a minor procedure taking no longer than an hour. That the Diagnotron, roughly the diameter of a quarter and about as thin, would be implanted just beneath the skin at the right-hand side of his chest.

I paused frequently and asked if he had questions. I encouraged him to interrupt. At any time, Collier could have called a halt and given me a "thanks, but no thanks." After all, this was his future we were talking about.

But at each of my bullet points, so to speak, Collier kept nodding his head in understanding and insisting with his eyes to keep going.

So I talked about the implant's amazing circuitry and how it would never rust or corrode, how the strategic placement of its electrodes would manage all the diagnostic analysis we had been discussing, and how it's equally amazing battery would last a good ninety years before it needed replacing.

All the while, I kept hoping for more pushback on his part. Some sign of doubt. A frantic question or two about liver cancer. Because, as much as I believed in this procedure, I was beginning to feel that the more and more I went on, the more and more I sounded like one of those hearing-aid pitchmen you encounter at the state fair.

Only at the end, after I'd exhausted everything I knew or thought I knew of the Diagnotron, did Collier finally raise his hand into the air and begin waving it like an anxious grade-school student. And for an instant, I thought, this is it. He's heard enough. This is where he asks permission to go to the restroom and never comes back.

Instead, when I called on him, he said, "Katie? When's the soonest I can get this done?"

Two weeks later, after work, I drove out to City General to visit him. It was the least I could do, considering that I had talked him into this. Dr. Grumboldt, who had started the ball rolling, felt no similar compunction. He likely figured his time was better spent elsewhere—meaning anywhere but City General.

For a second time, I found myself in total agreement.

Collier seemed delighted to see me as I knocked on the open door to his private room. "Katie," he said. "Look!"

Sitting up in his hospital bed, he pulled aside the top of his gown to reveal the thinnest of scars. It was covered with a row of equally spaced steri-strips that looked almost like the white stripes on a slightly bumpy crosswalk.

"Surgeon said the procedure went perfectly. He tested the Diagno thing and said it works like a top. He said I should be able to drive home by this evening."

I looked the scar over. Collier probably thought I was giving it a medical assessment. What I was doing was wondering which steri-strip to kiss first.

"The racing scar on my left knee looks a lot worse," Collier said with a smile. "But this isn't what I really wanted to show you."

He reached over to the bedside table and grabbed his cell phone. "See?" he said.

All I saw was a blank message screen.

"They did the implant last night," he said. "I've been here ever since. And look. Not one alert. Not a single one."

"That's terrific, Collier."

"You know," he said, "I think I'm going to be okay."

He was a changed man. With the Diagnotron now a permanent part of him, he was ready to face life anew, no longer under the control of his fears.

At first I wanted to hang around, talk about biking and swimming and everything his new life had to offer. But something told me that this was as good a time as any to wish him a good night. There would be plenty of time for more than idle chat during his monthly visits to the clinic.

It was only later, as I was driving home, that the truth suddenly hit me. Because he was a changed man, there would no longer be any monthly visits.

Or any visits for the matter.

Meaning that, in all likelihood, I would never see Collier again.

The next morning, at work, I wondered if should give him a call, maybe do the unthinkable and ask him to dinner. But no, this still would have been frowned on. Even if his visits were a thing of the past, Collier was still registered as a patient at the clinic.

So I set about my morning collating lab reports, scanning the day's appointments, updating patient records. Doing anything to keep my mind occupied. And when I happened to look up, there he was, silently standing in the hallway, his face completely ashen.

"Collier?"

If his name had been on the appointment roster, I would have spotted it like a lighthouse beacon in the fog. So he somehow must have slipped by the receptionist. But it didn't matter how he got here. The point was, he was here—and with the most fearful look on his face I had ever seen. He was almost as pale as the walls, whose color had been chosen by experts for its soothing quality.

Without uttering a word, he held out his cell phone to me. I leaned over the counter for a closer look. Just then, Dr. Grumboldt swung around the corner. He was whistling, of all things. But when he spotted Collier the whistling stopped.

"Hey there, Mr. Williams," he mumbled, obviously caught off guard. "Glad you dropped by to tell us the good news. About your operation. But we already know about it. So have a great life."

Dr. G patted him once or twice on the shoulder and tried to squeeze past, but Collier quietly stepped in his way. "DAD," he said.

"I'm, uh, afraid you have me mixed up with someone

else there, Mr. Williams."

"DAD," Collier repeated, more insistently.

"Your father? He's in town? Glad you came in to tell us. Hope both of you have great life."

"No," Collier said. From his cell phone, he read aloud the same words I had just seen. "'Alert. Your Diagnotron has detected chemical indicators of DAD.'"

The doctor's smug look took on an almost fascinated cast, as if Collier's cell phone had suddenly turned into a rare bacterium. "Let me see that."

Dr. G's eyes grew more and more animated as they scanned the details of the alert. "By golly, it *is* DAD," he said. "Katie, find out who has a machine and order a DAD scan. No rush."

"Wait a minute," Collier said, obviously shaken. "I thought all I had to do was show you the alert and you'd know how to treat it."

"Not much anyone can do about DAD except order a second opinion and hope it's different."

"And what exactly is DAD? The alert doesn't say."

To be honest, I had never heard of it either. Which was scary, considering I was a certified physician's assistant. But the fact that Collier knew nothing about it was scarier yet.

Dr. Grumboldt gave him a look as if the poor man had just asked an utterly inane question, like what acne was, or a sunburn.

"It's DAD," the doctor said. "You know? DAD? D,A,D? Disintegrating Artery Disease?"

So that's how it began. Every week, on the dot, Collier would trudge into the clinic, his face whiter with fear than the week before, his hands trembling, desperately trying to hold steady his cell phone with its latest Diagnotron alert.

I'd then pass the word onto Dr. Grumboldt, who could do little else but order yet another test that would confirm or deny the diagnosis. Yes, the diseases were that awful—all different, all rare, all untreatable even in their very early stages, and all virtually guaranteeing a life, however long or short, filled with unbearable misery.

And, yes, they were all diseases I knew nothing about. I could barely stand to read up on them. The introductory paragraphs alone would send chills down my spine and a rush of pity through my heart for dear, sweet Collier.

There was Schenkblatt's Syndrome.

There was Fetid Liver Disease.

There was Acute Incendiary Blinkoma, which causes the eye sockets to spontaneously combust.

There was Potemkin Step Disorder.

There was Fecal Throat Paralysis.

There was Pretzelic Spinal Percosis, Proctolic Cotangenitis, Malignant Hyperantarctic Macrocomplasia.

One week he came in with three Diagnotron alerts in a row, all marked, strangely enough, extremely urgent, even though there was absolutely nothing that could be done: Verdant Stool Carcinoma, Aqueous Stool Carcinoma, Immovable Stool Carcinoma.

And while Collier was sweating bullets over test results that hadn't come back yet and dreading appointments for upcoming tests, he would arrive at the clinic once every seven days with yet another alert that required yet another test.

He was a nervous wreck. I was a nervous wreck. Dr. Grumboldt was around the corner, whistling, ecstatic over no longer having to deal with Type 2 Hangnail.

There were times I wanted to comfort Collier by doing more than just holding him in my arms. But at the same time,

I didn't want to feel as if I might somehow be the cause of his next alert.

So I offered advice, all of it feeble and ineffectual. No matter what unrecognizable affliction flashed on his message screen, I found myself delivering useless, feel-good platitudes like, "You have to stay positive, Collier," and "Collier, at least you caught this early enough."

He would simply look at me as if I were speaking a language he had no hope of understanding. He would then slog out of the clinic, hunched over and miserable, looking nothing like the Collier I once knew—the Collier who, every month, practically danced out of the examining room with his usual thumbs up.

But gradually I saw a light at the end of the narrow, carpeted hallway. The test results started coming back and one by one they proved to be negative. Negative! Negative, in medicine, is a good thing, and that's what I kept telling Collier as the encouraging news kept pouring in.

But it was hard for him to breathe a sigh of relief over escaping one disease when a new and different disease kept arriving at his body's doorstep like the Sunday paper. I imagined, for him, it was like a cycle of best news, worst news, best news, worst news—a cycle that would never end.

And then, early one afternoon, while Collier was in the examining room putting on his shirt after being stethoscoped for something called Hindenburg Lung, Dr. Grumboldt was at my station drumming his fingers on the countertop and looking extremely irritated.

"Schedule a Hindenburg Lung scan?" I asked. "No rush?"

"Forget it, Katie. No more tests. And cancel all pending ones. Williams's Diagnotron is a joke."

"Oh, goodness. Do you think it needs replacing?"

"Hell, no. The next one and the next one after that will do the same damn thing. His is working, all right. Too well, in fact. It's not only hooked into his body, it's hooked into his soul, whatever the hell that is. It's taken on his personality. It's become just as bad as he is. Even worse. It can dredge up the names of diseases all on its own, without Williams having to move a finger to look them up. And not just any diseases, mind you, but the rarest and goddamn worst of the bunch."

"Why, Felix, I've never heard you refer to diseases so disparagingly before."

"That's because he doesn't have them! If there were honest-to-goodness killers floating around in his guts, that would be one thing. But the tests are coming back negative. Meaning, we're back to the same bullshit as before, except now it's the Diagno-damn-tron that's suffering delusions instead of Williams."

"Poor Collier."

"Poor Collier? What about me? I can't take it anymore. Whatever you do, get him to ditch that annoying piece of crap. Pronto."

It turned out, I needed to do no such thing. As soon as Collier was out of the room (and the doctor back in his), he was angrily and repeatedly slapping the right side of his chest and demanding, "Rip it out. Now. This Diagno con is like a parasite. I'll take whatever life hands me. Lung disease, liver disease, brain cancer. Anything but these alerts. I'd rather have something horrible than be told every week I have something worse. And even if I do have something worse, I don't care anymore, because I don't plan on seeing a doctor ever again as long as I live."

"But Collier, everyone needs to see a doctor on occasion—"

"Weren't you the one who said I'd *never* need to see a doctor? Never, ever, ever, because I'm a horse with a fiddle?"

"Please, Collier," I said, giving it one last try, "if you want the device removed, let me drive you to City General right now. I'll sit with you. And I'll be more than glad to take you home afterward."

"Thanks for asking. But no."

And without the slightest smile or a last goodbye or a Katie, he was gone.

A year went by. Collier had made good on his word. During all that time, he had not shown up once at the clinic. And except for a message from City General early on that his Diagnotron had been removed successfully, no mention was made of his visiting any doctor anywhere at any time.

I did not want to forget him. But I did need to get on with my life. And so, by and by, I let his memory settle into that area of the brain reserved for those special moments when we want to feel sad.

And then one day in the break room, as I poured myself some coffee, Dr. Grumboldt came behind me and slipped a sheet of paper alongside my cup. I began to read it while sipping, expecting some bureaucratic imposition from on high, but three sentences into it I stopped. I set my cup down with more force than I should have.

"No, no, no," I said, my voice quavering. "Please tell me this isn't Collier."

Dr. G shrugged as if this weren't any big thing. So I continued reading, expecting the news to improve.

It didn't.

About a month before, you see, Collier was admitted into City General. Apparently, the removal of his Diagnotron ten months earlier had not been so successful after all. A post-operative infection resulting from the surgery had slowly worked its way into his system. Although a loaded dose of industrial-strength antibiotics quickly cleared the infection, the damage inflicted on his internal organs during those ten months had proved to be irreversible.

I wanted to cry, but I somehow managed to rub a professional palm over my eyes and ask, "What does this mean?"

Dr. Grumboldt's expression was hard to decipher. It wavered somewhere between dead seriousness and unbridled glee. "I'll tell you what it means, Katie. It means honest-to-goodness, real-life problems, not fake, imaginary ones. It means fact, not fantasy. It means sci, not fi. And I can't wait to get started."

"Get started on what? And how does this involve you? It's City General's problem. They caused it."

"*Au contraire*, Katie. I dashed off an email to them. I let CG know in no uncertain terms that, as Collier's Primary Care Physician, I'll manage his treatment from this point on."

"You? A year ago, you wanted nothing to do with him."

"I certainly do now. As medical care professionals, we must remain flexible. And I'm absolutely willing and able to attend to Mr. Williams's daily care."

"Daily care?" I fluttered the sheet of paper he'd handed me. "There's nothing in here about daily care."

"Oh, yeah. That's in another email I got. I'll let you read it later if you want. The bottom line is that his internal organs are shot. I mean seriously shot. If they don't receive constant attention, they'll break down and fail. Just like that."

I was nearly speechless. "But every day?"

"Every day for at least five hours. Except for holidays, but we can work around that."

"But ... but what will we do?"

"Every day, when Williams comes in, we'll first determine which of his organs requires the most attention. We'll then administer the appropriate procedure on that organ. Is that clear enough?"

"What ... what kinds of procedures are we talking about?"

"Katie, Katie, Katie. The obvious ones, of course."

I stood there stunned as he counted them off on his fingers—demacritation of the kidneys ... incremental laparoscopic resection of the spleen ... reverse colon flushes by way of the esophagus ... topological inversions of the stomach and gall bladder ... intensive hydrogen ignition within the respiratory system ... direct hypodermic injections into the pancreas or liver, depending on which one secretes the most pus.

I hadn't heard of any of these but nodded as if I had, inwardly grateful that at least Collier's heart had been blessedly spared any damage.

"Oh, one more thing," he said. "If his heart turns out to be the lucky organ of the day, it will need to be stopped for a full thirty seconds and then resuscitated, like doing a system reboot."

I was beginning to feel ill. I had to support myself on the counter before getting the next question out. "How—how will we even know which organ to work on?"

"By doing a daily blood draw, of course. Not through his arm but through his jugular. Using a quarter-inch-thick McGunning's needle."

"Every day?"

"Are you even listening, Katie? Yes, every single day, including weekends. Except, of course, for major holidays. Some days we'll have to double up on organs. That ought to make Williams happy, getting those three or four days of reprieve every year."

"This is ... this is so unbelievably horrible."

"No, it's all unbelievably good. It means keeping meticulous notes, which I hope someday to turn into a medical paper. I already have a title. 'A Daily Regimen of Multi-Organ Care Following Sepsis-Induced Damage Resulting From Faulty Diagnotron Extraction.'"

"No, I'm referring to Collier. Your patient. You do know

what a patient is, right?"

Dr. Grumboldt glanced at his watch. "Good point. We have a few patients waiting, don't we? Dump your coffee and let's get a move on."

As he turned to leave, I felt the sudden urge to hurl my porcelain cup at him in the hopes it would shatter against his skull. Instead, I quickly came to my senses. I caught up with him in the hallway and asked, "Doctor, I'll be assisting you, won't I? With Collier, I mean?"

"It depends. You seemed a little shaky back there on some key points. How are you with a quarter-inch-thick McGunning's needle?"

Until a few minutes ago, I had never heard of a McGunning's needle, quarter-inch-thick or otherwise. But I did a quick estimate in my head. "I'm more accustomed to the six-millimeter McGunning's, but being that I'm a medical care professional, I'm flexible."

He looked impressed. "Good. Get started with the appointment and treatment protocols."

"Pronto?" I asked.

"You got it."

To me, Dr. Grumboldt was never meant to be a physician. He was better suited to do insignificant research deep in a basement lab, as far away from humanity as humanly possible. For him, the botched Diagnotron removal promised a future of seeing his name in published medical journals.

For me, it promised something else entirely. It promised how nice, how wonderfully nice, it was going to be to see Collier Williams—my Collier Williams—not once a month, not once a week, but just about every single day for the rest of his life.

GEHENNA DIVISION, CASE #609

BY SANDRA R. CAMPBELL

For the last two days, the body of his sister had dangled beside the bed. Gently swaying, her toe-tag hung inches above the threadbare carpet. Long tendrils of ghastly hair swirled around her head and reached down to tickle his bare arm.

Zared Wayward stared past her at the paint-chipped wall. He couldn't bring himself to turn off the bedside lamp. After days of sleep deprivation, his dreams were playing out in the furnished space of his bedroom. Zared couldn't switch-off his visions any longer—Madeline's death was no suicide.

Swinging his legs to the floor, Zared pushed the imaginary body of his sister aside and grabbed the manila folder he'd left on the nightstand. The file labeled Gehenna Division, Case #609, shook in his hands. Three years of his life was a small price to pay for the sanctity of a loved one's soul.

So, why was he still holding the file? Why hadn't he signed the contract?

Gehenna was a last resort, the only option Zared had left. He would go deep undercover with the new division under the charge of Ezra Knight, the scariest and most intimidating person Zared had ever met. Ezra was twice the size of the average man and his rust-colored horns, etched with bright-blue markings, towered over an oblong crown of black hair. His pasty skin stretched tightly over each sharp feature. Almost every visible inch of him had some sort of piercing or elaborate tattoo. But the most disturbing thing about Ezra's demonic look was his black pupils rimmed in fire. Eye tattoos weren't uncommon, but Zared had never seen one with a living, moving flame.

No one in the division knew what Ezra had looked like before the body modifications. Then again, Ezra was a lifer. Zared, however, could come back. He'd be normal again. *What're a few extra surgeries? Whatever they change, they will change back.*

A slim, cold hand rested on his shoulder and the smell of Madeline's perfume wafted across his nose as Zared opened the folder. The contract's details sprawled over twenty pages. He glanced over at his sister, the rope still tight around her neck. The scent of her perfume grew rancid. Sulfur assaulted his senses as her gray lips twisted and opened in a silent scream. Her soul was being tortured in Hell and here he was preparing to ponder the fine print. The pen practically flew out of the nightstand drawer. As soon as he scrawled his signature across the dotted line, Madeline's ghost vanished.

I'm going to Hell.

Zared leaned across the stainless-steel sink only to rear back in disgust. The reflection in the mirror wasn't a face he recognized—or wanted—but it was the visage he needed for the job. *Vanity be damned!* Madeline meant more to him than his college-boy good looks. The only identifying mark that remained was the small tattoo on his left shoulder, a dedication to their parents after the accident—Madeline had the same one. Zared prayed it would be enough.

"How's it going in there?" The voice on the other side of the door was like a cracking iceberg and held an otherworldly edge. "You're not crying, are you?"

"No, Sir," Zared shouted over his shoulder, still unable to take his eyes off the atrocity before him. His trembling hand flittered over the subdermal implants that ran along the center of his bare skull. Two weeks ago the head that now had three protruding shark fins was bump-free and covered with silky brown hair. His square, masculine jaw had been extended and given a sharp point, his tongue split, and his skin decorated in graphic tattoos and oddly placed piercings. Anger curled his fingers into a tight ball, knuckles turning white from the strain as he slammed his fist into the mirror. The cracks that splintered across the glass only accentuated the monstrosity he'd become, that he had agreed to become to save Madeline's soul.

A gnarled hand opened the bathroom door and tossed a bundle on the floor behind him. "Put these on." Jagged nails scratched the wood as the grisly hand slid the door closed again.

Zared stared at the pile of clothes at his feet. Once the uniform was on, there was no going back. But then, he reminded himself, there was no going back after the hours of painful surgery and recovery he'd undergone. He was a demon now, at least on the outside, one of the Gehenna, an elite law enforcement team transformed and trained to survive the rigors of Hell.

Now, with just over a month of special ops training, he was going into the field. Zared had one arm in the heavy fire-retardant jacket when the bathroom door flew open.

"What's taking so damn long?" Ezra fumed as he stalked to the toilet. He shot Zared a burning glare as he reached for his fly, and then paused. "What did you do?"

Zared looked down at his clothes, the jacket drooping off one shoulder as he lifted his arms to inspect the uniform. "What?"

The floorboards groaned under Ezra's steel-tipped boots as if he'd suddenly gained a hundred pounds. "Where's Uvall's brand? I clearly stated upper *right* shoulder."

Unable to handle Ezra's heated stare, Zared slid the rest of the way into the jacket. He mumbled. "It's on my left shoulder."

The geyser of piss that battered the shallow porcelain bowl was almost as threatening as Ezra's raised fist. "Left shoulder! Shit for brains, are you trying to get yourself killed?"

"I couldn't cover my tattoo. Madeline won't believe me without it." Zared bowed his head. He'd purposely broken protocol for the sake of getting Madeline out of Hell as fast as possible. With the tattoo, he wouldn't have to waste time convincing her of his identity. One look and she'd know without a doubt, but it was a high-stakes gamble to shift the brand. At the time he thought it would pay off. Now he wasn't so sure.

"So, you're willing to risk her soul, your life, and possibly mine, all for the sake of a crappy memorial honoring a couple of belligerent drunks? Z, I thought you were sharper than that."

The Waywards might have been deadbeats and their family dysfunctional, but they were all Zared and Madeline had, though not for long. Zared drilled his superior with a hard look that would have been terrifying had he been a real demon. But for someone like Ezra, Zared's weakness was disgustingly transparent.

Zared took a deep breath and unclenched his fists. He was already on thin ice, and he knew that at no point could he risk losing his cool with Ezra. "I'll keep my arms covered."

"Yeah." Ezra zipped his pants and stabbed the flusher with a single knuckle. "What happens if you screw up down there and someone demands to see your credentials? You can't show them your *left* shoulder. Even the lowest demon is smarter than that."

The Gates of Hell stretched beyond the misty clouds that hovered far above Zared's head. There was no visible end to the thick, towering poles made of shimmering maroon and black scales—the skin of the beast. Lucifer's scales were said to be tougher than iron, impervious to fire, and impenetrable to all weaponry. The Gates were a fortress that only an idiot would enter willingly, Zared told himself, even as he stepped closer and placed his hand on the rough, scaled post. He immediately pulled away as small yellowish blisters sprouted painfully along his palm.

"Put your gloves on," Ezra barked with a shake of his head, and then he turned to dismiss the SWAT team.

Peering inside the gates, Zared noted the narrow stone path lined by high oak trees. A rather peaceful looking trail led down a steep slope his human eyes could not follow.

"Where's the staircase?" Zared asked as he pulled on a pair of leather gloves, still keeping a watchful eye on the picturesque scenery of the netherworld. "I heard it was here, too."

Ezra, gazing through the Gates, drew up beside him. The flames surrounding his black irises flickered. "Heaven's entrance is directly behind you."

Zared whipped around. Surely Ezra was playing some joke on him. After all, the staircase to Heaven was supposed to be absolute perfection, single floating steps of pristine marble winding brilliantly into a clear, blue Heaven. Such a sight could not be missed, but when Zared turned around the only thing he saw was a pile of crumbled stones in front of a suspended wall of dead vines.

"They deactivated the staircase a year ago."

Zared walked over and brushed his gloved hand over the brittle vines. He watched the small particles float to the ground. "How is that possible?"

"Heaven's an elitist club now. Unless you're one of the few who has dedicated your life to the church or has become disgustingly wealthy to buy a get-out-of-jail-free card, there's no admission."

Zared considered Ezra's words. If what he said was true, Madeline would never get into Heaven. She was innocent of the suicide that landed her soul in Hell, but she'd never been *pristine*. She had a rough time after their parents' car accident and might have slept around a little and developed a few addictive vices, but none of that made her horrible or evil.

Zared rolled his shoulders and spoke through gritted teeth. "Why didn't you tell me ... before?"

A slow grin lifted the edges of Ezra's black-tinged lips. "Why, Z? Would you have chosen differently if I had?"

"Of course!" Zared said, biting down on the right side of his newly forked tongue "I can't get her out."

"You can move her from the Seventh Circle and into Limbo," Ezra growled. "Madeline doesn't have to suffer for eternity. Instead, she can reside in a pleasant time and place. That's the best any soul can ask for nowadays, to end up in the First Circle of Hell."

"Why haven't people been informed?" Zared asked, turning around to face his superior. Madeline deserved better than Limbo.

Ezra gave a shrug of his massive shoulders, then tipped his horns in Hell's direction. "You ready to go?"

The crack of the duo's boot heels echoed on the stone path that led through a forest, down a steep hill, and into a quaint town. The buildings, streets, and outlying area looked like any small town in rural America. The people milling about the streets, in various periods of dress marking their time of death, greeted them with quickened steps and downcast eyes as they went about their daily business.

This is where Madeline will end up.

Zared took a hard look around. He heard no screams of torture, witnessed no flesh being torn from bone, and he decided it would be enough.

"Over there. That's where we have to go," Ezra said, pointing to the solitary house at the end of Main Street. The red painted sign hanging out front read "Mayor's Office."

The double doors to the mayor's office swung open before the pair reached the front steps. A rich voice bellowed from the dark interior. "Come in, Mr. Knight."

A rolling shiver traveled down Zared's spine as he climbed the wooden stairs and stepped into an empty foyer. The plush carpet beneath his feet swallowed the sound of his entrance. He followed Ezra across the room to a single door, a knocker in the shape of a fist its only adornment. It should have taken six or seven steps to reach the door on the other side of the room, but after five minutes they remained several steps away, not having moved an inch closer.

Ezra stopped and threw his hand up, signaling Zared to halt. "What's with the games, Neville?"

"Who's that with you?" the disembodied voice rang out. Zared felt the heat of scrutiny even though no one else was in the room. "I've not seen *this* one before."

"He's moving up the ranks. Meet Z."

The fist-shaped knocker on the door moved, a bony finger unfolding to point at Zared. "What's your name, demon?"

Zared stifled his immediate response with a grunt. Lower-caste demons did not reveal their true identities. In Hell, names had meaning. Names held great power. If Zared had slipped up, he would have blown his cover and squandered his chance to save Madeline.

"Everyone calls me Z. You should do the same."

The door-knocker's middle finger shot upward and, to ensure the intended insult was seen, stilled for a moment and then curled repeatedly, beckoning the pair to enter.

Ezra reached the door first, but he moved aside for Zared. Steeling his nerves with a deep breath, Zared opened the door and stepped into a great hall that far exceeded the size of the house they had entered. A floral pattern with blooms the color of coal covered each blood-red wall. The floor under his feet shone like a floating oil spill, fluid liquid movement. Above him, a glass roof displayed a night sky even though they had arrived in the middle of the day.

In the center of the vast open space sat a simply constructed wooden desk. Behind it a plump figure with horns and cloven feet waited. He wore royal garb, an elaborate coat decorated with gemmed cuffs. Atop the desk, to the plump figure's right, was a bloodstained dagger. As Zared and Ezra approached, the demon slipped a hand beneath his jeweled collar and fingered a red-and-black beaded necklace.

"Why do I have the pleasure of a visit from the Gehenna?" Zared noted the demon, Neville, spoke without a single inflection in his voice.

"There's been an infraction in the Seventh," Ezra answered.

Neville pulled the beaded necklace over his bottom lip and slid it back and forth through his partially open mouth. "You don't say. And what would that be, *exactly*?"

A moment of silence passed. Ezra nudged Zared's elbow, but he couldn't find the words to answer while his gaze was transfixed on the demon's necklace. Drops of milky saliva had stuck to the red beads, but not to the black ones.

"The Harpies pilfered a soul into perdition before the case could be brought before the Council," Ezra said with a growl that resounded through the great hall.

"You have proof that this soul was unjustly sentenced?" Boredom oozed from Neville's pores, but he sat straighter in his chair.

"I do," Zared said, finally coming to his senses. He pulled case file #609 from inside his jacket, opened the file to the autopsy report, and tossed it on the demon's desk.

Zared knew the report by heart. The autopsy had proven that Madeline's first vertebra was not dislocated, which usually happened in a suicide by hanging. It also stated that postmortem lividity was found in the buttocks of the body and not in the lower limbs, which indicated Madeline was not dangling. She also had several bruises and scratches—common defense wounds—on her hands, arms, and legs.

"Whoever did this to Madeline Wayward did it against her will. And those damn Harpies know it," Zared said through clenched teeth.

Neville glanced up from the report, a single brow raised in doubt. "Says here she was a heroin addict. In fact, Ms. Madeline Wayward has many infractions on her record."

Ezra marched to the desk, the tips of his boots thumping against the wood. "I never said her soul was clean, but her fate is not in the Seventh. We're moving her here."

A groan sounded as Neville leaned back in his chair. "Fine. You have my permission to enter. Travel swiftly and don't get caught. I will not suffer Lucifer's wrath for a weak soul and a *pair* of meddling humans."

Zared ground his teeth to keep from shouting. Ezra had failed to mention that Neville, or anyone, was aware of the undercover work they were doing. Their fate was in the hands of a *demon!* Red sparks impeded his vision, and Zared stumbled as he turned to leave, drawing a sideways glance from Ezra.

The fantasy of Zared ramming his fist through the center of Ezra's repulsive face kept repeating and quickly spiraled until Zared could hold his tongue no longer. "What the fuck was that?"

Ezra stilled and then slowly turned like a Halloween mannequin on a display wheel. "What?"

"They know!" Zared spat. "Hell knows about the Gehenna Division." The bigger question on Zared's frantically spinning brain was, if Hell knew humans were moving about, impersonating demons to reclaim souls, why did they allow it?

Bending forward, Ezra flared his nostrils and looked like a bull ready to charge. "Of course, it's *Hell*. Do we have a problem here?"

Instinctually Zared moved a step back. "Jesus, man! What else haven't you told me?"

Each vertebra of Ezra's spine snapped as he straightened into his seven-foot frame.

A hush settled over them for a long moment. Finally, Zared said, "You failed to mention the closure of Heaven's staircase."

"And?" Ezra said, moving on.

Watching Ezra march toward the door with little regard for his distress only made Zared panic more. He grabbed hold of Ezra's bicep and growled under his breath. "*And* now I find out that we're not really undercover, that Hell has full knowledge of our work. This is seriously messed up."

"Yes, this is *seriously* messed up." The clack of cloven hooves echoed through the hall as Neville moved around his desk and approached the men. "Mr. Knight, your shark-finned rookie isn't going to make it."

Before Zared turned around, his hands fluttered over his head. He'd forgotten the implants were there.

"That's right, Z. You're a demon, a behemoth without emotion, and yet the stench of your virtue is tantalizing. One whiff and the wild imps will fly from their tunnels and caves. They will descend on you from every portal in Hell and devour your flesh before you reach the Fifth." Neville swiped the line of drool from his mouth.

A heavy weight landed on Zared's shoulder. "Don't worry. I can handle whatever comes at us. We're good," Ezra said, but his words fell on deaf ears.

Shoving Ezra's hand aside, Zared fought against an overwhelming tide of doubt. He paced aimlessly, rubbing the implant that elongated his chin to a sharp point, and wondered how he'd gotten himself into this. *Ezra told me demons were smart. He warned me. So what am I doing here?*

Zared realized he had never truly suffered the pangs of heartbreak until that moment. The pain of his sister's death wasn't nearly as horrific as realizing her flesh would forever remain between the putrid lips of an insatiable beast because he'd failed. Worse, if he couldn't survive past the Fifth Circle, Madeline wouldn't even know he had tried.

A foul odor crawled up Zared's nostrils, interrupting his thoughts. Neville was next to Ezra, both of them staring keenly. Then Neville's round cheeks rose with a smile, almost burying his tiny pig eyes. "Grant me a small taste and I'll transport you to the Seventh and spare you the agony of failure."

"A taste of what?" Zared asked, even though he already knew the answer.

Between Neville's stumpy fingers was the dagger. He pointed the rust-stained handle at Zared. "For a piece of your flesh, I will place you in the Seventh. And with that leap from here to there, you gain a small chance to rescue Ms. Wayward."

Zared knew he couldn't think about what he was doing. He took the dagger. Removing his left glove, he rotated his bare hand, searching for the best place to start. The hangnail on his thumb, he decided. He slid the thin blade under the cuticle and moved it down, cutting through meat. He sliced the knife to the first knuckle and around, all the way to the bone, like he was peeling an apple. The pain was excruciating, but the only sound Zared made was a single grunt when he finally ripped the flesh away and handed it over to Neville.

The demon slipped the bloody meat between his lips and chewed. Sighing with obvious delight, Neville swallowed and stamped his hoof seven times.

The air was dryer and hotter in the Seventh, and a thick coat of white dust covered the barren landscape. In the distance, a lopsided hill rose out of the desolate plain. As Zared moved closer, he realized the small mountain wasn't made of rock and dirt but human remains. Near the bottom, the brittle bones had been reduced to a baby-fine powder, slowly crushed under the ever-increasing weight piled on top. The bones in the middle of the pile were fragmented, broken and shattered, but at the peak, the bones were solid skeletons glistening with moisture. Zared knew those bones were fresh.

Ezra, unaffected by the increased temperature and suffocating humidity, walked ahead of Zared. Reaching the base of the hill, he plunged his fist into the crumbling bones.

Zared cradled his injured hand and gasped for air. Realizing he was on the verge of heatstroke, he staggered to catch up to Ezra only to collapse near his feet.

"Ah, this is the good stuff," Ezra said.

Zared closed his eyes and wiped the sweat from his brow. When he opened them again, he could hardly believe what he saw.

Ezra had his hand jammed under his nose and was eagerly snorting the calcium dust from his skin. Tilting his head back, he stretched his arms wide. "Best high in Hell, Z."

"What's wrong with you?" Zared scrambled to his feet.

Ezra is a complete lunatic.

"Take me to my sister!" Zared said, cringing as he shoved his injured hand back into the leather glove.

Ezra rubbed a larger bit of bone from his upper lip and walked toward the backside of the hill, waving for Zared to follow. "This way, rookie."

Soon a circle of tall pillars came into view. The columns surrounded a large rectangular table. Perched atop each pillar was a long-toothed Harpy. Lying on the stone table, wearing nothing but a sheer drape, was his sister. Her sleek brown hair was splayed over the rough end of the slab. She looked almost peaceful with her arms crossed neatly over her chest. As Zared and Ezra approached, a single Harpy screeched and Madeline opened her eyes.

Zared ran for the table, but he didn't make it there in time. He could only watch as the bird-like beasts swooped down on his sister and dug their sharp claws into her flesh. She was awake and screaming when they tore through her midsection and carved out her insides.

Within minutes, they'd reduced his lovely sister to a slick bloodstain and a moist pile of bones. Zared reached the stone table and fell to his knees, a vociferous roar exploding in his ears. All his anguish and hate released in a single cry. The pain was suffocating him, but whoever had done this to Madeline was going to suffer more.

Zared's deafening bellow had scattered the Harpies back to their perches, where they sat patting their bloated bellies and picking leftover strips of meat from between their teeth. He cursed them and went about gathering his sister's bones, but a gnarled hand stopped him.

"This isn't behavior becoming of a demon, screaming and crying over the body of a pathetic sinner." A smirk tugged at the corner of Ezra's black lips.

"She's my sister. She doesn't deserve this!" Zared glared and then charged his superior.

Ezra's chuckle was cut short when Zared plowed his shoulder into the giant's gut, throwing all his weight into him. Zared pushed Ezra off his feet and slammed the bigger man's body to the ground with enough force to rattle the bones on the table. He followed the assault with a fast right hook. Then Zared smashed the palm of hand into the bridge of Ezra's sharp nose, which only re-kindled Ezra's devilish laughter. *Sick son of a bitch.* Zared cocked his fist to deliver a blow to the bobbing Adam's apple at the top of Ezra's throat.

"Stop!" The familiar voice stilled his arm mid-swing.

A blast to the center of Zared's chest knocked the air from his lungs and left him gasping on his side. Ezra sat up and cracked his knuckles. "Nice job, Fight Club. You just sealed your fate."

Rolling onto his back, Zared coughed to regain his breath. "Madeline?"

A delicate pair of ivory feet moved past his limited line of sight. Zared lifted his head from the dirt. A few feet from him stood his sister, fully intact with not a speck of gore on her, despite having been devoured by four Harpies.

Madeline tilted her head to the right. "Who are you?" Then she turned her questioning gaze to Ezra. "Is this another one of your tricks?"

Zared climbed to his feet and unzipped his jacket. "It's me. Zared. I'm here to help you."

Madeline raised an eyebrow and huffed, "You are *not* my brother."

"Oh, but he is. Your wish has been granted," Ezra said as he got to his feet, and then took a dramatic bow.

Zared thought that, besides being insane, Ezra was hammered. But he didn't give a rat's ass about Ezra's sick addiction to the dust of the dead. His sister was all that mattered, and he had to get her out of there. He'd taken a step toward Madeline when she began to retreat. Zared bared his left shoulder.

Madeline gasped and then seized his arm to inspect the tattoo. Running her fingers over the initials of her dead parents, she cried, "What did you do?"

Zared grabbed her in an embrace. Kissing the top of her head, he whispered, "It's what I had to do to save you. I can't break your soul out of Hell, but I can take you to a better place."

Madeline pulled away. Fat tears trickled down her face. "You shouldn't have come," she said, shaking her head. "Now that you're here, I can't say no."

Missing her touch, Zared reached out. "Say no to what? Come on. Take my hand. We're moving you to Limbo."

Madeline's entire body vibrated. "No!" she screamed. Turning her back on him, she yelled again and pulled clumps of hair from her scalp. "You have to take my place!"

Even through the extreme heat, Zared felt a chill building at the base of his spine. "What?"

"Every sinner is given the option of exchange, the opportunity to trade places with a soul that's cleaner than their own," Ezra said. He slammed his hand down on Zared's shoulder.

Comprehension hit him like an avalanche. Frozen in place, unable to move or speak, he finally understood. *They tricked* me.

Smoothing the tangles from her hair, Madeline returned to Zared. Her hands were in front of her, fingers intertwined and wringing like a ball of pink worms. "I'm sorry. You're the only decent person I know. I love you, brother, but I can't do this. You survived Mom and Dad's accident. You're stronger than I am. You'll survive this, too." An unsettling smile lifted the corners of Madeline's mouth.

Anger burned in Zared, melting his ice prison. "Have you gone mad?" The question needed no response. Of course she was crazy. She'd just been eaten by Harpies, he thought, and for the umpteenth time. "We're in Hell, Madeline! No one survives *Hell*."

Ezra stretched his massive arms out wide. "Z, the Gehenna is a sham. It's not real—but I am."

All the pieces quickly fell into place. Ezra's unnatural appearance and odd behavior had nothing to do with his sanity and everything to do with him being a true demon. The folder arriving at his office shortly after Madeline's death, the offer inside to join the Gehenna Division, the training and physical transformation that followed hadn't been so he could move around in Hell unnoticed. It was to keep him from ever being able to leave.

Ezra repositioned himself in front of Madeline, his flaming eyes steady on Zared. "One month into your sister's sentence, I came to her with an out, as I do with every new soul. Four weeks is a good breaking point. Long story short, she offered you as a replacement. And now that you're here, we can make a fair trade."

"A fair trade?" Zared scoffed. "What makes you think I'll go along with any of this?"

A toothy smirk transformed Ezra's grim face. "If you refuse the exchange, your sister goes back on the slab and you're still stuck here."

"Maybe she deserves her fate," Zared snapped.

A feminine gasp sounded behind Ezra. Zared couldn't see Madeline, but that didn't stop her grief-stricken face from invading his vision.

Rocking back on his heels, Ezra shook his head. "We both know that's not true."

"I shared information on the Gehenna. People know I'm here." Zared was grasping for a lifeline that wasn't there.

"You kept your tattoo. Put the demon brand on the wrong arm. You screwed yourself, Z. Besides, you signed."

The weakness in Zared's knees forced him to the ground. He hadn't read past the second page of the contract.

"You're not the first. Nobody reads the whole thing," Ezra said, now crouching beside him.

The most important decision of Zared's life was the one to save his sister's soul. The second most calculated choice he ever made was to keep the tattoo that would identify him as her brother. He never thought those small, valiant acts would be rewarded with an eternity of torture.

Ezra jabbed a thumb over his shoulder. "Now, will it be you or her on that table?"

Zared leaned forward and eyed the stone slab. A sudden wave of sadness crashed over him, washing away any lingering regrets. Madeline was his sister. He could still save her. "If I take her place, what happens to Madeline?"

Ezra stood and extended his arm to offer Zared a hand up. "I escort her to Limbo, as per the terms of our contract."

It only took a minute for Zared to say goodbye to his sister. Madeline couldn't voice much in return. She'd clung to him, shaking and blubbering sentiments of sorrow and admiration, two emotions he knew she was incapable of feeling. But that was okay. He'd loved her enough for the both of them. Despite the fear and ongoing agony he was about to face, saving her soul from eternal suffering had been the right thing to do.

Zared looked up into a gray, dust-filled sky. Other than the profiles of the fanged Harpies in the four corners of his vision, there was nothing to see, and so he waited. He knew it was only a matter of time before the beasts descended on his body and took their fill. The only thing worse than anticipating the first feast were the last words Ezra spoke before leaving.

"See you in thirty days, Z."

GOLDEN AGE

BY JAMES DORR

Whenever she was sick or troubled or feared for her family, my grandmother's grandmother always "made do." That was the saying she used in the diary that passed on to me. Which, in turn, I will pass on to my granddaughter. The memory sphere I'm recording this on will go with it, as my own diary. What, in my grandmother's grandmother's time, was called a bequeathing.

Why this one granddaughter? Call it a custom—because she's the youngest of my descendants, female to female, just as I was my grandmother's youngest. I've been married five times in the two-hundred-ninety-eight years I've lived. Most of the children I've borne have been sons and, of the exceptions, after the stars were opened for settlers, the daughters *they* raised joined so many others of their generation and left the planet.

The only one who stayed was my granddaughter, Angela, named after me and, like me, the youngest—at least that I know of. A homebody, just like me, Angel Carnovan.

Neither of us, in an obvious sense, would be thought much like my grandmother's grandmother. Her name was Jessica and her *one* husband, who took her West, was named Thomas Haskell. That was a time when the West was a frontier—technically, all that meant even then was the western part of the American continent. But that was more than a hundred years before even the start of what now is the City, its crystalline domes and ruby-tinged spires spanning thousands of miles over both land and ocean. She and her husband were pioneers.

She tells about her life in her diary, sometimes in terms that even I who have lived so long cannot understand. She says, for instance, that their house was built out of sod—dirt with plants still growing in it.

The only "house" I've ever lived in was made of prestressed concrete and steel. Although, when I was young, I remember some buildings still built from wood.

And that's one reason I've started this diary—to set down some of the facts *I* remember. But mostly because, as the years have gone on—the nearly three centuries in which I've "made do" in my own way—I've run out of new things to accomplish.

I do not intend to use dates in this diary. Jessica never did in hers, except to note when something took place as part of a holiday like Christmas. I can remember Christmas myself—it took place in winter, a season that I can remember, too, even though, nowadays, city life has eliminated the weather changes we used to call seasons. And that's the point of the custom I mentioned and that, I hope, Angela will see fit to follow when she feels it's time for her own bequeathing. As the youngest granddaughter of, in turn, a youngest granddaughter, I form the longest bridge between Jessica and the present.

And even though I am a homebody, I was, in my own way, a pioneer just like my grandmother's grandmother.

Jessica lived in a hut made of sod, while I grew up and continue to live in an apartment of concrete and steel. When I was young, though, streets separated the buildings—passageways open to the sky.

It was when I was thirty-two, and already married to my first husband, that I lost my right leg in one of these passages. Rather than using conveyor tubes, people went about their errands in wheeled machines. One of these struck me.

I woke in darkness—that I remember. Later I was in a bed in a hospital—back then they weren't called Renewal Centers—and one of the doctors told me they had cut off my leg. That was not uncommon, even then, for an accident that severe. What was new, however, was the technique they used to fix me.

The doctor said my leg could be replaced.

And this is why I was a pioneer, too. I did not realize it at the time I signed the papers. They had dead things called artificial limbs in those days—ugly, clunky appurtenances made of metal and plastic. I thought all the doctor was talking about was providing a leg like that for me.

However, I woke to darkness again. Darkness and pain. I started to scream. A light went on. The doctor stood next to me, holding my hand.

"Angel," he said. "Do you know what you are?"

That was when *he* said that, if I could learn to use my new leg—if my body did not reject it—I could call myself a pioneer, too.

The weather report says it should be raining outside the City. Jessica suffered from rheumatism, a disease affecting the joints, and she says in her diary that as she grew older the pain would get worse whenever it rained.

Why do I think of that?

I suffered pain, too, when I was young. The doctor warned me that learning to use my new leg would be hard. It was agonizing—not so much the learning, but the tests they had to perform on me as I did so. The needles. Electrodes. The metal in flesh. Because, if either they or I did anything wrong, the flesh might not knit to its semi-living biograft frame. My new leg would die.

It is hard to remember now that there was once pain. Biografts nowadays, of course, are completely painless and over within a matter of hours. But mine took six months before they were sure of it—six months of agony. Then another twelve months of checkups.

After all, mine was the first.

It's raining again. They told me at the Renewal Center that this sphere is not a real diary, since I don't necessarily add to it every day. It doesn't matter. When one is nearly three-hundred years old, one is willing to wait for a few days, or even a few weeks, between recordings. To just put in highlights.

Jessica only wrote highlights, too. She told of her marriage in decades, not days. But my first husband, after having tried his best to help me through the worst of the pain, divorced me within four months of the time I left the hospital.

My second husband was the doctor. After what we had been through together—still went through with the biweekly checkups—somehow it seemed natural that we should be married. And so it was not surprising that, when my hand was crushed severely in an accident sometime later, we both thought immediately about biografting instead of just trying to fix the damage.

This time, while I still had to take tests, the pain was much less. My experience from before had not only been the first successful whole-limb replacement, but it had also pointed to problems with anesthesia that since had been met. In years to come, even minor, painless tests would often no longer be needed either, but this was back then. And while it was only my left hand that was to be biografted, this would be the first time the technique had been used to replace a manipulative organ.

Again, the biograft was a success. In fact, as we found out, my new hand worked better than the old one. When my second husband died, I had had my left kneecap, my right arm and shoulder, and even a section of my spine replaced by grafting. By then, I was no longer always the first. Ironically, though, my husband died young of a ruptured spleen. Soft-tissue biografting wasn't to be perfected until shortly after I'd married my fourth.

I started out last time by pointing out that it was raining. Jessica often talked about weather in her diary, of snow in the winter and dryness in fall. This is the season—once called spring—when the predominant weather outside the part of the City I live in is rain. However, I knew it was raining then, not from the calendar or from the external weather report, but because, when I woke that morning, I realized I felt a dull pain in my leg. I thought of Jessica, when she was older and had rheumatism—pain of any sort, of course, is unusual now. That's the reason I went to the Center.

They were surprised when they looked up my medical record and found out how long it had been since my leg was replaced. I asked them if it might be wearing out, and they said it was doubtful. They told me that even the earliest biografts, including mine, had been designed to be self-replicating, the same as human cells only much better—barring some hideous accident, made to last forever. However, they also said they had never heard of a biograft causing pain.

I told them the pain was scarcely annoying. And it wasn't. Even now, although in an absolute sense it has worsened, it's more an *interesting* thing. Like everyone else, I've had virtually every part of my body, inside and out, biografted by now. I'm used to being free from all but the most carefully monitored bodily feelings—and, to be honest with myself, I found that I was enjoying the difference.

Nevertheless, the doctors asked me if I thought I'd be able to wait for up to two weeks before I came back in. They said they wanted to run tests first on some other early biograft tissue.

I told them I'd make do.

I remembered my third husband—the one I lost to the Mars expedition. He, like Jessica's Thomas, was a pioneer. But unlike her husband, he went it alone. He went out in a ship of explorers, intending to construct his bubble and get settled first, and then to send for me. He never came back.

His ship was torn open in some kind of accident—so the government agency said. The bodies of its crew and passengers, thrust into space by escaping oxygen, were never found.

I almost didn't marry again, but, of course, I did. My fourth—Angela's mother's father—was also a pioneer, but neither he nor I found this out until they perfected the

Bateman Drive, fifteen years later, and the first ships went out to the stars. He wanted to go, too, not right then, but eight years after that, with the first large-scale emigration. That was when Earth was so overcrowded that even the Reactive Party agreed the initial planets should be opened to civilians.

I absolutely refused to go with him and, when he became more and more insistent, *I* initiated divorce proceedings.

I waited thirty-eight years before I married my fifth—but right now my thoughts are still back on my third. The one that was most like Jessica's Thomas.

I won't describe him. Oddly enough, the memory of what he looked like has faded, although there are pictures. That may be why—I can look those things up. The memories that stay, of him and the others, are memories of how a hand felt on a thigh. The sound of a voice when it whispered so low I could hardly hear it. The spark in the innermost depths of an eye.

What remains also are memories of an age, a decade, a year together. And memories of what the world outside was doing.

After my third husband died, more ships went out—I always read the last entry I've made before I record more. That's how I remember what I had been thinking. In any event, after he died, they learned from what they had managed to find of my husband's ship, just like the doctors learned more about biografting from all the tests they performed on me. The new ships were safer and the times became exciting, even without my husband to share them. Back then, after my third husband's death, they referred to the time as a "golden age of exploration."

The reason I thought of my husband before—when I started to make my last entry—is that the Center had called me that morning. They had no news for me yet, they said, but they needed still more tests. They asked me to come in.

I did so, let them take tissue samples, and asked them again if my leg wasn't simply wearing out. Again they smiled and assured me that they didn't believe that could happen, but one did let out that what they wanted to test this time involved techniques they might use to remove a biograft.

In other words, since this apparently would be the first time, they needed to learn how to replace what was itself a replacement.

And so it's been more than a week since then and they still haven't called back, but I'm not surprised. I still remember how much went into my leg in the first place for checking and rechecking. Making absolutely sure that everything was done correctly. That's the problem with pioneering—the "golden age" doesn't come until after. After *you've* done it, successful or not, so others can follow.

It occurred to me, just now, that golden ages don't always have to be exciting. In fact, if I stop to think about it, we're living in a golden age now. This is not an age for pioneers anymore, however. Ours is an age of beauty and art, as well as of caution—of absence of death, at least here on Earth, other than through the rarest of accidents. An age of no pain.

And yet, *I* have pain. My hand hurts now, and my leg— the pain in my leg has become familiar enough to no longer be noticed, but the leg itself is so stiff that it's hard to walk without assistance.

When I first felt the pain in my hand, I called the Center, despite their saying that I should wait until they were ready. They told me now that they had hit unexpected problems with their testing, but, if the feeling I was complaining about became too intense to tolerate, I could come in. I thought about it. The doctor I talked to implied that they *could*, with what they thought they had learned by now, replace a biograft if that were all there would be to it. The problem, however, was that they did not know how long such a second-generation replacement would last before it, in turn, began to go bad. They thought it would not be a long time, with what they knew thus far.

Still, I thought, even a temporary replacement would be better than being in pain. Except, as before, the pain was at worst just a minor annoyance compared to the *interest* that I was feeling it at all.

Today the Replacement Center called me. I had finally decided not to go in—at least not yet—and they wanted to know why they hadn't seen me. This time they said they had all but resigned themselves to the idea that any biograft would end up being temporary over the long run, even for first-timers. Nevertheless, with that came acceptance that people could simply replace replacements as often as needed, even if the periods between these replacements might become progressively shorter.

I knew the procedure would be without pain—that wasn't the problem—and yet I told them I wanted some time to think about it. I didn't tell them the pain was spreading, or that, as I found myself getting used to it, it was getting progressively easier just to make do.

After we talked, I did think about it. I thought about how, since my fifth husband and I decided to separate, I had rarely left my apartment. Everything I needed was brought to me if I asked for it—sent by robotube to my apartment, just as Jessica's needs were taken care of by her children as she grew older. So, if I was slower in my movements, or even if my right leg stopped working altogether, it wouldn't matter. I thought of my last husband, how he and I had been married nearly forty-five years before we realized how bored we had become with each other. How, when our children had grown up and left us, we knew each other's every move, every mannerism, what each would say. We tried to separate temporarily, to report on the new things we'd see in hopes of bringing new life to our marriage. We found that everything there *was* to be seen or done that might have held our interest together had been done already.

We left on good terms, each knowing neither would marry again. We left with dignity knowing the problem was not in ourselves but in our surroundings. What we needed— *all* that we needed—was something new, but our world was exhausted.

The Center called again—several times—but I told them I would still wait. That I would still make do. I did not tell them the pain—it had reached my chest by now—was the one difference that, far from hurting me, brought life back to me. I read my grandmother's grandmother's diary again and again, especially the final pages. I read about death. I read about how she helped to ease her husband's passing. I read about how, after that, she made do.

I started to think in the terms she thought in. About how she accepted that she couldn't move as well as she used to— her legs had given out just as mine have. She thought of the various aches in her body as nothing more than the pain of aging, and she accepted the pain on those terms.

She thought of it as the pain of changing.

She thought that, without change—even if the change implied death—she would not be living.

And thinking of her, I think of my own life—a life that, by and large, has been a good one. The life of a pioneer, too, in its own way.

But one that has, for just one person, ultimately been too long.

THE WRITERS

MEGHAN ARCURI

Meghan Arcuri writes fiction and poetry. Her short stories can be found in various anthologies, including *Chiral Mad* and *Miseria's Chorale*. She lives with her family in New York's Hudson Valley. Please visit her at meghanarcuri.com or facebook.com/meg.arcuri.

JASPER BARK

Jasper Bark is infectious—and there's no known cure. If you're reading this then you're already at risk of contamination. The symptoms will begin to manifest any moment now. There's nothing you can do about it. There's no itching or unfortunate rashes. But you'll become obsessed with his books, from the award-winning collections *Dead Air* and *Stuck on You and Other Prime Cuts*, to cult novels like *The Final Cut* and acclaimed graphic novels such as *Bloodfellas* and *Beyond Lovecraft*.

Soon you'll want to tweet, post, and blog about his work until thousands of others fall under its viral spell. We're afraid there's no way to avoid this—these words contain a power you are hopeless to resist. You're already in their thrall and have from the moment you read this bio. Even now you find yourself itching to read the rest of his work. Don't fight it, embrace the urge, and wear your obsession with pride!

E.A. BLACK

E. A. Black's dark fantasy and horror fiction has been appeared in *Wicked Tales: The Journal of The New England Horror Writers Vol. 3, Stupefying Stories*, and *Teeming Terrors*. She has also written *Roughing It*, a sci-fi medical thriller inspired by *The X Files, The Andromeda Strain*, and *Outbreak*. She writes erotic fiction with the pen name Elizabeth Black.

An accomplished essayist, her articles about sex, erotica, and relationships have appeared in *Good Vibrations Magazine, Alternet, CarnalNation*, the *Ms. Magazine* blog, *Sexis Magazine*, Clarion blog, Erotic Readers and Writers Association blog, *On the Issues, Sexy Mama Magazine*, and Circlet blog. She also writes sex toys reviews for several sex toys companies.

Born and bred in Baltimore, she grew up under the influence of Edgar Allan Poe. She lives in Lovecraft country on the Massachusetts coast with her husband, son, and three delightful cats. She has never been under the knife. Visit her website at http://eablack-writer.blogspot.com/. Friend E.A. on Facebook at https://www.facebook.com/elizabethablack.

JASON V. BROCK

Jason V. Brock is an award-winning writer, editor, scholar, filmmaker, and artist whose work has been widely published in a variety of media (*Weird Fiction Review* print edition, S.T. Joshi's *Black Wings* series, *Fangoria,* and others). He describes his work as Dark Magical Realism. He is also the founder of a website and digest called *[NameL3ss]*. His books include *A Darke Phantastique, Disorders of Magnitude,* and *Simulacrum and Other Possible Realities*. His filmic efforts are *Charles Beaumont: The Life of Twilight Zone's Magic Man, The AckerMonster Chronicles!,* and *Image, Reflection, Shadow: Artists of the Fantastic*. Popular as a speaker and panelist, he has been a special guest at numerous film fests, conventions, and educational events, and was the 2015 Editor Guest of Honor for *Orycon 37*. A health nut/gadget freak, he lives in the Vancouver, WA area, and loves his wife Sunni, their family of herptiles, running their technology consulting business, and practicing vegan/vegetarianism.

SANDRA R. CAMPBELL

Sandra has published several paranormal novels: *Butterfly Harvest, Dark Migration* and *The Dead Days Journal* with more titles on the way. Her short stories have appeared in Suspense Magazine and various anthologies, with two horror shorts currently in production with Chilling Entertainment. Sandra is a member of the Horror Writers Association, Maryland Writers Association (M.W.A.) and the director of a M.W.A. critique group. Check out her website/blog at sandraRcampbell.com.

CHARLES COLYOTT

Charles Colyott lives on a farm in the middle of nowhere (Southern Illinois) with his wife, daughters, cats, and a herd of llamas and alpacas. He is surrounded by so much cuteness it's very difficult for him to develop any street cred as a dark and gritty writer. Nevertheless, he has written the Randall Lee mysteries, Black-Canto I of the Nephilim Codex, and appeared in several anthologies, including *Read by Dawn II*, Dark Recesses Press, *Withersin* magazine, *Terrible Beauty Fearful Symmetry*, and *Horror Library* Volumes III, IV, and V. You can contact him on Facebook, and, unlike his llamas, he does not spit.

JAMES DORR

Indiana writer James Dorr's *The Tears of Isis* was a 2014 Bram Stoker Award® nominee for Superior Achievement in a Fiction Collection. Other books include *Strange Mistresses:*

Tales of Wonder and Romance, Darker Loves: Tales of Mystery and Regret, and his all-poetry *VAMPS (A Retrospective)*. His latest, out in June 2017 from Elder Signs Press, is a novel-in-stories, *Tombs: A Chronicle of Latter-Day Times of Earth*.

An Active Member of HWA and SFWA with more than five-hundred individual appearances from *Alfred Hitchcock's Mystery Magazine* to *Xenophilia*, Dorr invites readers to visit his blog at http://jamesdorrwriter.wordpress.com.

JACK KETCHUM

No stranger to controversy, Jack Ketchum's first novel, *Off Season*, published in 1980, was a turning point in the field of horror fiction. Stephen King said of him, "Jack Ketchum is an archetype, no writer who has read him can help being influenced by him and no general reader that runs across his work can easily forget him, he has a dark streak of American genius."

Jack has received four Bram Stoker awards and three nominations. His novels have been adapted for film, including *The Lost, The Girl Next Door, Red, Offspring*, and *The Woman*. Visit his website at http://www.thejackketchum.com for more about his latest releases, movie adaptations of his work, and other information.

ADRIAN LUDENS

Adrian Ludens is a dark fiction author and radio announcer living in Rapid City, South Dakota. His collection, Ant Farm Necropolis, is available in multiple formats from various online book vendors. Also available are previous collections: Bedtime Stories for Carrion Beetles and When Bedbugs Bite. Adrian enjoys watching hockey, reading, listening to all kinds of music, and exploring abandoned buildings. For news and updates, visit adrianludens.com.

GRAHAM MASTERTON

Graham Masterton made his horror debut in 1975 with *The Manitou*, the story of a three-hundred-year-old Native American shaman who is reborn in the present day to take his revenge on the white man. A huge bestseller, it was made into a classic movie starring Tony Curtis.

Since then, Graham has written over a hundred novels—horror, thrillers, and historical romances—as well as numerous short stories. Before he took up writing novels, he was editor of *Penthouse* magazine. It was there that he met his late wife Wiescka, who became his agent and sold *The Manitou* in her native Poland even before the collapse of Communism—the first Western horror novel to be published in Poland since the war.

Apart from five *Manitou* novels, Graham has also published the *Rook* series, about a remedial English teacher who recruits his slacker class to fight ill-intentioned ghosts and demons; the *Night Warriors* series, about ordinary people who battle against apocalyptic terrors in their dreams; as well as many other supernatural thrillers, including *Family Portrait*, *The Pariah*, and *Mirror*.

Graham's website is www.grahammasterton.co.uk.

SHAUN MEEKS

Shaun Meeks lives in Toronto, Ontario with his partner, Mina LaFleur. Shaun's work has appeared in *Haunted Path*, *Dark Eclipse*, *Zombies Gone Wild*, and *A Feast of Frights* from the Horror Zine, as well as his own collection, *At the Gates of Madness*. He will also be featured in the anthologies *A Six Pack of Stories*, *The Horror Zine 4*, and *Fresh Grounds Volume 3*, and will be releasing a new collection with his brother called *Brother's Ilk* in late 2012 and his new novel, *Shutdown*, in early 2013. To find out more, visit him at www.shaunmeeks.com.

Shaun's story "Taut" appeared in *Zippered Flesh 2: More Tales of Body Enhancements Gone Bad*, and his story "Despair" was included in *Someone Wicked: A Written Remains Anthology*.

JEFF MENAPACE

A native of the Philadelphia area, Jeff has published multiple works in both fiction and nonfiction. In 2011, he was the recipient of the Red Adept Reviews Indie Award for Horror. Jeff's debut novel, *Bad Games* became a #1 Kindle bestseller that spawned two acclaimed sequels, and now all three books in the trilogy have been optioned for feature films and translated for foreign audiences. His other novels, along with his award-winning short works, have also received international acclaim and are eagerly waiting to give you plenty of sleepless nights.

Free time for Jeff is spent watching horror movies, The Three Stooges, and mixed martial arts. He loves steak and more steak, thinks the original 1974 *Texas Chainsaw Massacre* is the greatest movie ever, wants to pet a lion someday, and hates spiders. He currently lives in Pennsylvania with his wife Kelly and their cats Sammy and Bear. Be sure to visit his website at www.jeffmenapace.com or his Facebook page at www.facebook.com/JeffMenapace.writer.

CHRISTINE MORGAN

Christine Morgan grew up in the high deserts of California but headed for water and trees as soon as she was able. A resident of the Pacific Northwest ever since, she's recently moved to the Portland area and settled in amongst the bizarro and weirdo-creatives community.

Her stories span many eras and genres, with a particular focus on combining horror and dark fantasy with ancient or medieval cultures. She's best known for her Viking-themed tales, a collection of which—*The Raven's Table*—came out in 2017 from Word Horde.

As a reader, she's a regular contributor to *The Horror Fiction Review*. As an editor, she's responsible for the Fossil Lake anthologies as well as a few other projects. She also enjoys baking, and modifying Barbie dolls into custom strange creations.

Christine's most recent projects include the modern thriller *Murder Girls*, the pioneer blizzard horror novel *White Death*, and her extra-gooshy Deadite Press debut, *Spermjackers from Hell*. She's had short stories in many anthologies and is currently at work on a book called *Lakehouse Infernal*, with the kind permission of Edward Lee.

BILLIE SUE MOSIMAN

Billie Sue Mosiman's *Night Cruise* was nominated for the Edgar Award and her novel, *Widow*, was nominated for the Bram Stoker Award for Superior Novel. She's the author of fourteen novels and has published more than one-hundred-sixty short stories in various magazines and anthologies. A suspense thriller novelist, she often writes horror short stories. Her latest works include *Frankenstein: Return from the Wastelands*, continuing the saga of Robert Morton from Mary Shelley's classic, and *Prison Planet*, a near-future dystopian novella. She's been a columnist, reviewer, and writing instructor. She lives in Texas where the sun is too hot for humankind. All of her available works are at Amazon.com. Check out her blog, "The Life of a Peculiar Writer," at www.peculiarwriter.blogspot.com.

Her story, "Second Amendment Solution," was published in *Uncommon Assassins*. Billie's story, "The Flenser," appears in *Someone Wicked: A Written Remains Anthology*.

WILLIAM F. NOLAN

William F. Nolan writes mostly in the science fiction, fantasy, and horror genres. Though best known for co-authoring the classic dystopian science fiction novel *Logan's Run* with George Clayton Johnson, Nolan is the author of more than 2000 pieces (fiction, nonfiction, articles, and books). An artist, Nolan was born in Kansas City, MO, and was an integral part of the writing ensemble known as "The Group," which included Ray Bradbury, Charles Beaumont, John Tomerlin, Richard Matheson, Johnson and others, many of whom wrote for Rod Serling's *The Twilight Zone*.

Of his numerous awards, there are a few of which he is most proud: being voted a Living Legend in Dark Fantasy by the International Horror Guild in 2002; twice winning the Edgar Allan Poe Award from the Mystery Writers of America; the honorary title of Author Emeritus from the Science Fiction and Fantasy Writers of America, Inc.; the Lifetime Achievement Award from the Horror Writers Association in 2010; recipient of the 2013 World Fantasy Convention Award along with Brian W. Aldiss. He was also named a Grand Master by the World Horror Society in 2015. A vegetarian, Nolan resides in Vancouver, WA.

DANIEL I. RUSSELL

Daniel I. Russell has been writing horror since 2004 with many short stories published in publications such as *Andromeda Spaceways Inflight Magazine*, *Pseudopod*, and *The Zombie Feed* from Apex. His debut novel *Samhane* and short story "By the Banks of the Nabarra" were both nominated for Western Australia Tin Duck awards in 2011, as was the story "Broken Bough" in 2012. He is the author of *Come into Darkness*, *Critique* and *The Collector Book 1: Mana Leak*. His novel *Mother's Boys* is due for release in 2013 from Blood Bound Books and his work will also be appearing in Brett McBean's final novel in his *Urban Jungle* trilogy. Daniel is currently the Vice President of the Australian Horror Writer's Association and was a special guest editor of *Midnight Echo*.

L.L. SOARES

L.L. Soares is the Bram Stoker Award-winning author of the novel *Life Rage*, which was published by Nightscape Books in the fall of 2012. His other books include the short story collection *In Sickness* (with Laura Cooney), published by Skullvines Press in 2010, and the novels *Rock 'N' Roll* (Gallows Press, early 2013), *Hard* (Novello-Blue, fall 2013), and *Buried in Blue Clay* (Post Mortem Press, May 2017).

His short fiction has appeared in such magazines as *Cemetery Dance, Horror Garage, Bare Bone, Shroud,* and *Gothic.Net*, as well as the anthologies *The Best of Horrorfind 2, Traps*, and *The Forsaken: Stories of Abandoned Places*. He also co-writes the Bram Stoker-nominated horror movie review column *Cinema Knife Fight*, which has a whole site built around it at cinemaknifefight.com. No matter how many times he forces radioactive arachnids to bite him, he just can't seem to get the amazing abilities of a spider. To keep up on his endeavors, go to www.llsoares.com.

JEZZY WOLFE

Jezzy Wolfe is an author of dark fiction, with a predilection for absurdity. A lifelong native of Virginia Beach, Jezzy lives with her family and quite a few ferrets. Her poems and stories have appeared in such ezines and magazines as *The World of Myth, The Odd Mind, Twisted Tongue, Support the Little Guy*, and *Morpheus Tales*. She has also been published in a variety of anthologies, such as Graveside Tales' *Harvest Hill, The Best of the World of Myth: Vol. II*, Library of the Dead's *Baconology*, Western Legends' *Unnatural Tales of the Jackalope*, and the Choate Road fun book, *Knock, Knock ... Who's There? Death!*

She was a founding member of Choate Road.com and at one time cohosted the blogtalk radio shows "The Funky Werepig" and "Pairanormal." In addition to her brand of humor and horror fiction, she maintains both a blog and storefront for ferret owners and lovers, known as FuzzyFriskyFierce. **You can visit Jezzy on her author's blog at jezzywolfe.wordpress.com, on her ferret blog at FuzzyFriskyFierce.wordpress.com, or at her storefront site at www.cafepress.com/fuzzyfriskyfierce.**

MARTIN ZEIGLER

A retired software developer, Martin (Marty) Zeigler spends a good deal of his time writing fiction—primarily mystery, science fiction, and horror. His stories can be found in small-press anthologies and journals as well as online. In addition to writing, he enjoys reading, watching movies, dabbling on the piano, and taking long walks around his hometown of Portland, Oregon.

THE COVER ILLUSTRATOR

SHELLEY EVERITT BERGEN

The magnificent book cover graphic was created by Shelley Everitt Bergen, who was born in Canada where she still lives with her husband Gord of nearly thirty-five years. They have one grown son, Aaron.

Having something to do with art and books is certainly nothing new to Shelley. She has created the artwork for many book covers over the years, including the *Zippered Flesh* and *Zippered Flesh 2* anthologies.

She is a founding member Groundfrost Illustration & Design (2004) along with fellow artist Antti Isosomppi, where she functions as both artist and administrator. Together they created the artwork for the graphic comic *Lobster Girl*, written by John Morvay, which went on to become the best-selling independent comic of 2008. In more recent years, they added artist Matt Shealy into the fold. Groundfrost has created artwork for clients such as The Black Eyed Peas, Kanye West, John London, The Killers, God Forbid, Dead Eyed Sleeper, and Fragments of Unbecoming, to name but a few. Find Groundfrost at https://www.facebook.com/GroundFrost-Illustration-Design-117966144892596/.

Though not a writer of horror, Shelley's first novel, *Siren's Song*, co-written with J.M. Henrickson, was released in August of 2014 and was well received. She is currently working on her second novel, *The Lord of Winter Keep*, this time as an independent author.

If interested in commissioned artwork, Shelley can be reached at gbergen3@shaw.ca or https://www.facebook.com/shelley.everittbergen.

SPECIAL THANKS

We'd like to thank all the wonderful supporters of Smart Rhino Publications. We'd especially like to thank those kind folks who supported us during our Indiegogo campaign for the book, including (in alphabetical order):

Jasper Bark
Mark L. Barnes
Chris Basler
David Benton
Tim Curran
Kevin Davis
Missy Hodges
Frank E. Hopkins
Dana King
Wendy Kirk
Dee Lawrence
Dennis Lawson
Kirsten & Ovidio Lopez
Adrian Ludens
Rena Mason
Quintin Peterson
Lynn Reynolds
Eve Stylianides
Lillian White
Lorraine A. Winsey
Shannon Winward

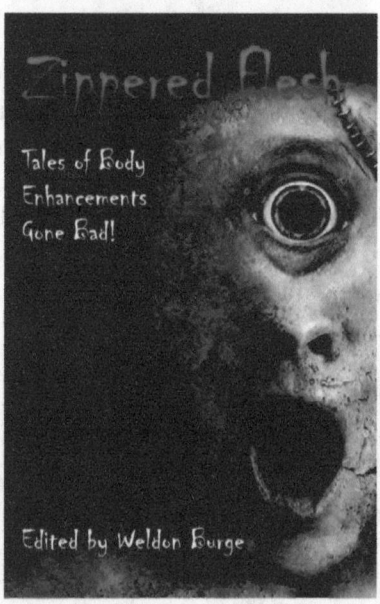

ZIPPERED FLESH:
Tales of Body Enhancements Gone Bad!

In this dark anthology of demented stories, bizarre body enhancements play pivotal roles in the plots—and things are never pretty or pain-free. The twenty stories in this collection are not for those who are faint of heart or squeamish, or who are easily offended by disturbing imagery, bloody violence, and freakish body augmentations. Love chilling tales? You'll savor this anthology!

Michael Bailey * Michael Laimo * Adrienne Jones
Charles Colyott * Christopher Nadeau * Scott Nicholson
J. Gregory Smith * John Shirley * L.L. Soares * Aaron J. French
Graham Masterton * Michael Louis Calvillo * Jezzy Wolfe
Elliott Capon * Armand Rosamilia * Lisa Mannetti
P.I. Barrington * Jonathan Templar * Rob M. Miller
Weldon Burge

ZIPPERED FLESH 2:
More Tales of Body Enhancements Gone Bad!

So, you loved the first **Zippered Flesh** anthology? Well, here are yet more tales of body enhancements that have gone horribly wrong! Chilling tales by some of the best horror writers today, determined to keep you fearful all night (and maybe even a little skittish during the day).

**Bryan Hall * Shaun Meeks * Lisa Mannetti
Carson Buckingham * Christine Morgan
Kate Monroe * Daniel I. Russell * M.L. Roos
Rick Hudson * J.M. Reinbold * E.A. Black
L.L. Soares * Doug Blakeslee * Kealan Patrick Burke
A.P. Sessler * David Benton & W.D. Gagliani
Jonathan Templar * Christian A. Larsen
Shaun Jeffrey * Jezzy Wolfe * Charles Colyott
Michael Bailey**

UNCOMMON ASSASSINS

Hired killers. Vigilantes. Executioners. Paid killers or assassins working from a moral or political motivation. You'll find them all in this thrilling anthology. But these are not ordinary killers, not your run-of-the-mill hit men. The emphasis is on the "uncommon" here—unusual characters, unusual situations, and especially unusual means of killing. Here are twenty-three tales by some of the best suspense/thriller writers today.

Stephen England * J. Gregory Smith * Lisa Mannetti
Ken Goldman * Christine Morgan * Matt Hilton
Billie Sue Mosiman * Ken Bruen * Rob M. Miller
Monica J. O'Rourke * F. Paul Wilson * Joseph Badal
Doug Blakeslee * Elliott Capon * Laura DiSilverio
Michael Bailey * Jame S. Dorr * Jonathan Templar
J. Carson Black * Weldon Burge * Al Boudreau
Charles Coyott * Lynn Mann

INSIDIOUS ASSASSINS

There is a peculiar allure of insidious characters—and especially assassins, hit men, and their ilk. With this fascination with evil characters in mind, Smart Rhino Publications decided to publish this anthology, **Insidious Assassins**, a sequel to **Uncommon Assassins**.

Jack Ketchum * Joe Lansdale * Lisa Mannetti
Carson Buckingham * Christine Morgan *DB Corey
Billie Sue Mosiman * Meghan Arcuri
Austin S. Camacho * J.M. Reinbold
Ernestus Jiminy Chald * L.L. Soares * Doug Blakeslee
Shaun Meeks * Martin Zeigler * James S. Dorr
Adrian Ludens * Joseph Badal * J. Gregory Smith
Patrick Derrickson * Jezzy Wolfe * Doug Rinaldi
Martin Rose * Dennis Lawson

SOMEONE WICKED:
A Written Remains Anthology

Avaricious, cruel, depraved, envious, mean-spirited, vengeful—the wicked have been with us since the beginnings of humankind. You might recognize them and you might not. But make no mistake. When the wicked cross your path, your life will never be the same. Do you know someone wicked? **You will.** The twenty-one stories in the Someone Wicked anthology were written by the members of the Written Remains Writers Guild and its friends, and was edited by JM Reinbold and Weldon Burge.

Gail Husch * Billie Sue Mosiman * Mike Dunne
Christine Morgan * Ramona DeFelice Long * Russell Reece
* Carson Buckingham * Chantal Noordeloos
Patrick Derrickson * Barbara Ross * JM Reinbold
Shaun Meeks * Liz DeJesus * Doug Blakeslee
Justynn Tyme * Ernestus Jiminy Chald * Weldon Burge
Joseph Badal * Maria Masington * L.L. Soares
Shannon Connor Winward